Redheart

REDHEART

BOOK ONE OF THE LELAND DRAGONS SERIES

BY JACKIE GAMBER

THIRD EDITION

Published by Big Imagine 2022

ISBN: 978-1-7360238-1-5

Library of Congress Control Number: 2008908545

First edition published 2008. Second edition published 2011.

Cover Art by
Interior Design by
Ellen Kjiersten Gamber

Written by
Jackie Gamber

For Autumn

Blade and I thank you

Your enthusiasm reminds me why I love stories

REDHEART

CHAPTER ONE

Kallon soared. He thrust his crimson wings to chase the clouds, tethered to the earth by only his massive shadow. He flew faster, but his shadow could not be outrun. He felt it below him, dragging across the dusty field like an anchor, pulling him downward. With a defiant twist of his wings, he veered straight up into the cobalt sky.

The sky was where dragons were meant to thrive, and it was the place they returned to when they died. At least, according to his father. Kallon had believed it once. He had believed the stories of dragon valor in a world where humans and dragons worked together toward a common future. But that was long ago. Kallon didn't believe in anything anymore.

It became harder to breathe, and Kallon's eyes burned and watered. His wings resisted moving. He'd gone as high as he could go. He paused.

As far as he could see, the sky was the same unlimited blue. There was no rail, no net. There seemed nothing to keep him from going forward—yet, there he was forced to stop, as every dragon before him stopped. With a groan of regret, Kallon hung his head and descended.

He followed his shadow across a field of withered meadow grass. The field gave way to sand, and the sand to stones. Mammoth fists of bulging granite welcomed him home to the foothills of the Leland Mountains.

Then he heard something. Instead of disappearing into his cave, he swooped above a high cliff and circled back. He dropped down to his feet, curled in his wings, and stood still as the mountains to listen.

A scream. From somewhere beyond the next peak came a human scream. He snorted. Too bad it wasn't something more interesting. His ears had long since grown deaf to the cries of humans.

Then the scream came again. It was the sound of terror. The kind he used to hear from children as his shadow passed over the ground near them. He shuddered, and found himself turning toward the sound. He hadn't wanted to go home yet, anyway. He supposed it wouldn't hurt just to look.

He flew low over the meadow until he caught the human scent. No, not one human—several. He landed quietly, and loped toward a grove of ancient firs, some of which were taller than his head. Careful not to rustle any branches, he poked his face through the trees. There he saw the humans and discovered the source of the scream.

Three men stood around a female, who crouched in

the center of them. There was a leader, it seemed, who cackled an evil laugh and was goading the two younger men toward her. His voice was louder than the others, and his stringy hair was the color of dung. "Go on," he said, and shoved his friend toward her.

The woman shrieked and lunged, stabbing a knife at the air.

The man jumped away, but the leader darted behind the woman and grabbed her wrist, then wedged the inside of his elbow against her throat. "Give me that little toy," he snarled.

The woman struggled. The leader yanked away the knife and pushed her to the ground. He slapped her face. Kallon could see her shoulders heave as she whispered in a hoarse voice, "Please. Don't do this."

Kallon was still considering what he ought to do, when there was a sudden shout.

"Dragon!" cried one of the men.

"Bloody 'ell!" yelped another.

The leader just stood gaping as wetness dribbled down his pant leg and puddled around his foot.

"Run!" The man near the female jumped to his feet, and hollered again, "Run!"

The leader snapped to awareness. He flung up the knife, which tumbled through the air to bump Kallon harmlessly on the nose. Kallon growled, anyway. The leader stumbled back. Kallon sucked in a deep breath and bellowed like thunder. The man wailed, and finally bolted after the others.

The men collided with trees and smacked into each

other in their panic. Kallon stopped bellowing to smile. Cowards. Then he swung his face to the woman. He found her gaze locked on him, and his smile dissolved, taken aback by the look in her eyes.

He had grown accustomed to screams, shouts of fear, and the look of terror in the eyes of humans. But this woman reacted to him with none of these. Her face seemed to register… relief. Then her eyes closed and she fell backward onto the ground.

Kallon inched forward through the trees. He bumped her shoulder with his snout. She didn't respond. "You dead?" he asked. He nudged her again.

Her chest rose and fell with breath. Blood trickled from her nose and mouth. She smelled more pleasant than he thought a human could smell, like the musky forest path drenched in sunshine. He sniffed her again.

He knew he should leave her right where she laid. She was no business of his, and he didn't know the first thing about tending to her anyway. But she'd looked at him differently than most humans, and it stirred something within him he couldn't explain. He lifted a claw to his cheek and rubbed, unsure of what to do. Then he mumbled, "Going to regret this."

He grasped her with his forelegs and soared off toward home.

§

Riza slowly opened her eyes. Or did she? It was so dark, she wasn't certain. Pain stabbed at her temples.

Her mouth felt stuffed with wool. She tried to sit up, but wobbled too much, and had to try again.

Where was she? And what was that smell? She wrinkled her nose. Even through her pain and dulled senses the odor was intense enough to water her eyes. The farmers must be fertilizing the fields again. With a groan, she laid back her head and let her eyes fall closed.

But what was she lying against? Something poked down her spine, and she felt the ground beneath her slithering. Her eyes snapped open again. As they slowly adjusted to the dark, she looked at her shoulder, and then to what rested beneath it.

Dragon scales. Her breath stopped. Surely she was still dreaming, they couldn't be real. She reached a fingertip to see. Those dark scales were rising and falling, rising and falling, as though attached to something breathing.

"Sleep well?" There came a voice like the crackle of shifting gravel.

Riza shrieked. She darted away, crawling in panic, her body numb and unable to stand. She veered, expecting any moment to feel her skin erupt with a blast of fiery dragon breath.

"Not the way out," the dragon said. She could hear the groan of its bones as it shifted its immense weight. Even the ground quivered, and in her mind the dragon grew to enormous proportions, fueling her terror. She crawled on.

"Not the way out!" The thundering voice became more insistent. A clawed foot thrust out to stop her.

"Going to bump your…."

Her head cracked against something hard. She jarred her spine and rocked with a fresh wave of pain. Tiny lights like fairy dust danced around her eyes before she collapsed against the outstretched foot. She clung to the dragon's scaly paw as she leaned across it to retch.

"…head," it finished. She felt its rumbling sigh as much as heard it. It nudged her to the dusty floor of the dark place. She couldn't move. She couldn't think.

The dragon muttered as it heaved to its feet, and then lumbered off toward a splash of pink light. She strained to focus. The pink light pulled into the arched shape of an open doorway. It was large enough for the passing of a dragon. It was the way out.

The dragon smothered the light as it passed. She felt the tip of its tail slither past her foot, and she recoiled inside, though she couldn't move enough to even twitch. Then the pink light returned as the dragon moved on. It was leaving.

Outside, the dragon arched its back, and then gave a shake that started with its mighty head and rippled down its spine to its pointed tail. Wings burst from its back. She gulped in surprise. Before she could release her next breath, the dragon was gone.

The dragon was gone, giving her a chance to escape! It hadn't burned her alive, hadn't crunched her bones. It had only left, giving her a chance to get away. But why? Why bring her to this place at all if the dragon wasn't even going to—?

Then she remembered. The men in the forest.

The dragon head in the trees. It had saved her, maybe intentionally. Maybe it brought her back as some sort of pet. Pet Riza. She burst into a giggle as she romped on all fours in her mind, chasing a stick thrown by a great, curled dragon paw. The ground beneath her began to sway. Fairy dust tickled her eyes again. Then everything went dark.

Moments later, Riza felt a nudge against her cheek. Or was it hours? Endless darkness and staggering pain made it impossible to know. Her head was throbbing so that she felt her eyes might burst if she opened them. So she didn't.

"Must drink," spoke an oddly familiar voice that floated somewhere near her ear. Something pressed to her mouth, and cool liquid splashed against her lips and dribbled down her chin. She groaned, not wanting to open her mouth for fear she might retch again. "Drink," the rumbling voice urged.

She finally did, and the bitter drink splashed fire down her throat. She tried to turn her head, but a sharp jab against her cheek turned it back, and more liquid filled her mouth before she could resist. She spluttered, and slapped at the helping hands. "Enough!"

Her fingers felt the curve of a sharp claw, and a scaly foot. Her bleary eyes flew open and met the hovering stare of the dragon. She didn't even know she had a voice to scream with, but out it came in a shriek. The dragon winced. The wooden mug he'd been holding skittered across the floor, and he gave a shout of his own.

"Human!" He slapped his paws over his ears, and

reared back into a wash of sunlight streaming through the cave opening. The light exploded across the scales of his massive shoulders, his head, his wide open jaws, and burst with sparks that lit more glittering sparks, until his face seemed swallowed by a wall of flame.

"Quiet!" he shouted.

Riza couldn't help but go quiet. She stared up at him, her breath leeching from her lungs.

He released his paws from his ears, and slapped them to the ground. "I'm not going to eat you. Maybe I ought to, just because you're stupid." Out of the direct sun, his blinding radiance sputtered out. He turned his back and stomped to a far wall. There he plopped, dropped his chin against the floor, and sulked.

She stared for a long time before she gathered the courage to speak. When she finally did, she was surprised that her voice didn't tremble. "You're not going to eat me?"

"Could have already. Lots of times." A trail of moisture leaked from the dragon's snout, and the pink tip of his tongue snaked out to flick it away. "Brought you some food." He turned his head further away.

For the first time, she noticed a small woven basket near her feet overflowing with bright raspberries. Balancing atop the berries was a round loaf of bread. Wetness sprang to the back of her throat. She was devouring handfuls before she even realized. She reached for the bread. The crust was stale, but when she broke it, the inside was soft and melted on her tongue like warmed snowflakes.

As she chewed, her eyes wandered over the cave. In the frail daylight, she could see layered shelves of granite imbedded in smooth walls of rock. The ceiling was so high it disappeared into shadows. Pale, broken sticks littered the sand floor. An insistent drip-drip of water echoed from a far place beyond the dragon where the light couldn't penetrate.

The dragon. He was staring at her, his head cocked, one eye narrowed. She was frightened again, and gulped down the last mouthful of bread, which stuck in her throat. She lowered her chin, and tried to become very small.

"Stop looking at me like that," the dragon said. Unsure of how she was supposed to look at him, she simply remained silent, and lowered her gaze. But her mind raced. Should she run? Where would she run? She didn't even know where she was, or how far the nearest village was.

"Looked at me different before," it said.

"I did?" She dared to peek up at him, but he was no longer watching her. He'd begun to walk toward the cave entrance. Each of his footfalls sent a ripple through the sand. Muscles clenched beneath his thick hide. His serpentine tail wavered toward her, and, this time, she nearly darted out a hand to touch it. Startling herself, she resisted the impulse.

He stepped out and was bathed in brilliant sun. Now she could see that he was the rich, red color of mulled wine. Each of his scales caught the sun with a dazzle, and, when she squinted, she saw they sparkled from a delicate dusting of gold.

He wasn't as large as she'd imagined. His basic shape was similar to a horse, and maybe the length of three of them. Atop his skull rose a dignified crown of bony ridges, crimson at the base, and then fading into varying degrees of reddish-brown toward the tips. Leathery wings relaxed against his back.

Magnificent, really. A majestic, flying horse.

"When did I look at you differently?" she asked. He didn't respond.

She crawled forward. Her back was stiff from the hard ground, and her muscles resisted painfully, but when she reached outside, she lifted her chin with a smile.

Friendly sun kissed her cheeks. A breeze tenderly stroked her hair. She stared up at the translucent blue sky, and at the tips of wispy elms that danced for ivory clouds. She tried to find the top of the cliff above the cave, but it was too high, and flowering vines coiled across the granite, camouflaging it with the mauves and oranges of wild roses.

She inhaled the peaceful beauty, and it coursed through her to her numbed fingers and toes, reviving them. So she pushed up from her hands and knees, trying to stand, and she spoke again. "When did I look at you differently?"

"Before," the dragon said, his face toward the elms.

"Before, when?"

"In the trees." He swung his gaze toward her. His brown eyes fastened onto her face. They were filled with such depth, such expression, that surprise knocked her like a hand to the ground. She fell back, staring at his sadness.

"Weren't afraid of me then." His wings snapped at the air. "Go if you want. You're not my prisoner."

Before she could reply, he was high above her, wings pumping straight up toward the sun, and she was engulfed by his shadow.

CHAPTER TWO

Jastin Armitage shifted in his saddle as the black leather creaked in protest. It had already been a long journey, and there was still no sign of the small village for which he was bound. But it was there. He sensed it as surely as he felt the relentless sun against his back and the dry wind breathing hot into his eyes.

He'd been to Leland Province before. It had been many years ago, but he already recognized the land's haphazard tilt that quivered the knees of Blade, his chestnut mount. What he didn't remember was the scorched landscape that spread out before him like a rutted desert.

"Ho," he called to Blade, and tugged at the reins to swerve past a bear-sized boulder that marked a sharp turn. To his memory, a bend in Chirp's Creek lay just ahead. He reached for his water bladder, intent on refilling it, his wind-parched lips already tasting the cool splash of creek water.

Blade tamped a hoof against the bank of the creek.

But, no. Not a creek.

Peering over the edge of the road, Jastin found only a crusty path of dried mud littered with fish bones and pebbles. Cursed, forsaken place. He dragged his palm against the back of his clammy neck.

Blade whinnied softly, head swaying as if to mourn the dry bed, as well.

"Come on. We'll drink in town."

The horse obeyed, and Jastin thrust the empty bladder back into his saddlebag.

Blade's hooves struck a hollow rhythm. Perspiration beaded on Jastin's brow, but disappeared instantly, gulped up by the dry, greedy air. To pass the time, as he often did, he mentally inventoried his weapons hanging in precise order against Blade's flanks; a crossbow with a full quiver of arsenic-tipped bolts, a curved mace, a leather pouch with vials of liquid scents. His polished sword was kept at his side at all times. He rested his gloved hand against its sheath.

The afternoon dragged mercilessly on until, finally, trembling like a phantom through the haze of brutal heat, a village appeared. He squinted to make out the details of the place, and as he grew closer, he grunted in disappointment.

Ragged dirt paths were beaten into the earth by accident. Here and there as paths crossed, thatched buildings of wood and stone hunkered, war-weary, against a losing battle. The stench of despair leaked from its streets and oozed toward him like a perfume of horse manure and day-old fish. In the far distance, farmlands barely endured between thickets of withered trees, as though daring the miserable earth to deny them their right to exist.

Jastin drew up Blade to another halt. He shielded his eyes and stared past the village and its doomed farmlands to the sight beyond it. The Leland Mountains. Great spires of gray and marbled brown broke through the blanket of emaciated treetops and stretched from east to west, with a dramatic crescendo just beyond the village.

These were the mountains that had first called him years ago. These were the mountains to which he returned. He set his jaw, eyes searching them for dark secrets.

Blade whinnied.

"Very well," Jastin said. He prodded his mount, and they loped into town. There, he slowed to read a wooden sign that was carved simply, "Welcome to Durance." Below the carved letters, a painted footnote read, "No dragons." Maybe there was extra money to be made here after all.

He spied the livery, and threaded Blade through the deserted street. Where was everyone? Somewhere, a bored goat bleated. At the stables, he swung a thick leg from his mount's back and hit the ground with both feet. Several minutes later, a young boy peeked around a door.

Jastin tossed him the reins. "Plenty of water for him."

The stable boy nodded.

"Got a tavern?" Jastin asked.

The boy pointed across the street to a square building with a wooden roof. The signpost beside the door had cracked and hung upside down, lazily flapping with each gust of dusty wind. The Brown Barrel Inn. Jastin strode toward it.

There were more men at the bar than townsfolk in the village square. He slapped down a coin, and gave the tender a nod. "Ale."

A tankard slid toward him. He eagerly drank, but nearly choked. The ale was warm and stale, and just a day or two from vinegar. He managed to swallow the mouthful, and raised his drink in a salute. "Best ale I've had in days," he said. "Now, how about some good food for a weary traveler?"

The tender paused in drying a goblet. "Food we have. Good?" He glanced at the men near him and exchanged smiles.

"Well, it will fill your belly!" said one customer.

The room broke into laughter. The tender tossed his rag over his shoulder. "We lost our cook," he said with a wink.

"Didn't pay her enough?" Jastin asked.

The barkeep smacked the dried goblet onto the bar. "Pay her? You mean we were supposed to pay her?" He threw back his head and guffawed.

"Heard tell she died of her own food," came a puny voice from across the room.

"You remember the time I found that pig's ear in my stew, Temin?" A man seated at the bar smacked his drinking buddy on the arm, startling the other so that he nearly toppled his mug.

Temin clutched the mug protectively and glared. "Whole town remembers, Berl. You won't let it rest." He looked around his friend's shoulder at Jastin. "Besides, it wasn't a pig's ear."

Berl stuck a finger toward Jastin's nose. "Was too. Seen enough pig ears to know."

"Eaten enough, you mean," said Temin into his mug. "Don't see how one more in a bowl of stew should make a difference." The man sucked at his drink.

Berl hunkered over his own tankard with a scowl. "Principal. A man ought to be able to order a simple bowl of stew in a public place and not have to worry about seeing a wrinkled old pig's ear sticking out like a flag on a banner wagon."

"I gave you a new bowl free of charge, didn't I?" came the growling voice of an enormous man who emerged from a door behind the bar. He planted fat hands on the wood, his belly squeezed against its edge. His nose was wide. Rust-colored hair clung in fuzzy patches to his head. "And it wasn't just her cooking losing my customers. The sight of her," he said, and shuddered.

"Kept the rats away, though!" said the barkeep. More laughter hit the roof. The men clanked their tankards together and drank to that.

Jastin couldn't help but chuckle. For such a desolate town, spirits were high in the Brown Barrel Inn. Now was the time to strike. He set his tankard on the bar.

"Rats, maybe, but what about dragons?"

The laughter silenced. Men at the bar exchanged looks. "It's just a word," Jastin said, and rested his elbows on the bar, eyeing the men. "No dragon trouble in this town? Is that what your sign meant?"

The silence continued for some minutes, until the barkeep set his hand on the bar. "You got an interesting way of making conversation, stranger, but you're right about our sign. No dragons around here, not for a long time." He poured a fresh mug of ale, and pushed it toward Jastin with a pointed look.

"Just curious, my friends," said Jastin. "I've had run-ins with a dragon or two, myself, and I like swapping stories while I drink." He tugged his coin pouch from his waist, and let the heaviness of it thud to bar.

A wrinkled old man stared at Jastin's full pouch, and then lifted his chin. "Dragons ate my goats last summer. Ever' last one, they did." He looked into his empty mug and sighed. "Spent ever' last copper I had on a new herd."

Dark frowns settled onto the old man. Jastin only smiled, and clapped him on the back. "Barkeep," he said. "A filled tankard for my friend!"

After another short lull, a mousy and toothless man rose from his stool. "I seen a dragon." He offered his empty tankard with grimy hands.

"Is that so?" Jastin caught the barkeep's eye and nodded to the man's empty mug. It was filled, too.

Another man spoke out, then another. Voices ran over top of voices as Jastin settled comfortably onto his barstool. The men clamored for ale as their stories of dragons spilled from their mouths like sap from the willow trees. Each man's gory details bested the one before him.

Then a young man stood up in a darkened corner of the room. His hair was long and stringy, and the color of dung. "Hey!" He called out over the others. "I seen a dragon. Day before yesterday. Right outside the village."

All eyes in the tavern turned. Jastin raised his eyebrows. "You don't say." He carried a fresh, foamy mug of warm ale to the man and held it out. "Tell me about it."

§

"My fellow dragons," Fordon Blackclaw announced in his carefully practiced bellow. His ebony claws gripped the carved podium at the center of the dragon council arena. "As leader of your honorable council, it is my oath-bound duty to remind you that this conflict is not in the best of interest of the Dragon-Human Relations Pact."

"We have a right to speak our minds," called a Green, whom Blackclaw didn't recognize.

Leaning aside, he whispered to Fane Whitetail, his advisor. "Who speaks?"

Fane squinted across the stadium. "He is too young to be Min Greenscale, though he bears the same snout. Perhaps a son?"

Blackclaw looked out across the arena that was

writhing with scaly dragon heads and spines. He hadn't seen so many tribes gathered in one place, even here on Mount Gore, in a great number of years.

He was heartened, and sucked in a deep breath of pride. His ideas were working. His ending would come to pass. Anticipation raised wetness at the back of his throat, and he had to swallow to keep from spraying spittle when he next spoke. "It is true, honorable Kind, that you have the right to speak your minds. With this I will not interfere. But you must remember that words, once spoken, cannot be disclaimed. This is my official stance. Mark it for the record." He nodded toward the wispy half-breed Blue standing in as recorder, who dipped his claw into red ink and scrawled across a parchment.

Blackclaw retreated from the platform and sank onto the bench reserved for council members. Hale Brownwing rose to speak in turn, but he wasn't listening. Blackclaw's eyes lingered on the recorder as the arguing among the dragons continued. "Whitetail." He crooked a claw at his advisor, who scrambled to his side. "Remind me who the half-breed is, and why he is considered qualified as recorder."

"His training was impeccable, and came highly recommended. There is no basis for judgment of qualifications according to color alone, or a mix of color, as it were."

Blackclaw narrowed his eyes on the advisor's nervous expression. "Did you read that straight from the by-laws?"

"No, sir, although I could do so if you wish it." Blackclaw could almost hear the gulp from Whitetail's throat. It humored him.

"Not necessary, but thank you." His gaze found the half-breed again.

"Humans have broken nearly every pact vow themselves! Why should we be held to a standard that has long since been destroyed?" came a growled shout from the crowd.

"What do you call it, do you suppose?" Blackclaw said. He leaned toward Whitetail, though his eyes remained on the recorder. "Blue with Green. Is that Teal?"

"Do you wish to establish a new line? A teal line would be unusual, but completely possible."

"Are you daft, Whitetail?" Blackclaw rapped a fist on his advisor's bony skull. Hard. "Teal line? What would be next? Puce?" He glared. "Can I dismiss you yet?"

"Y-yes. Through the proper channels, of course. It could take months, however." Again with the gulp.

Blackclaw couldn't help but smile, just a little. The scrawny rat of an advisor had come to be an asset, really. He'd already proven that he had no scruples, and would protect his position on the council at whatever cost. Plus, the White had no pride. What better quality could there be in a right-hand dragon?

Blackclaw waved his paw. "Well, make yourself useful then, and draw the council to a close. I have grown bored with the bickering." His eyes found the crowd again. So many dragons. So many angry dragons. He tried not to grin.

Whitetail waved Brownwing from the platform and cleared his throat as he took his own place. "Council Leader Blackclaw wishes to thank all dragons for today's valuable meeting. Your voices have been heard, and your righteous anger has been marked."

"What about the pact? What is he going to do about the humans and their mining?" asked someone.

"We are tired of waiting for our promises of land!" said another.

Whitetail raised a glistening paw. "These matters are being discussed." He glanced over his shoulder, and Blackclaw gave him his cue with the nod of a head. Whitetail looked back out across the gathering, and continued. "Such concerns are valid, and will be addressed. But the situation requires diplomacy. Council Leader Blackclaw does not wish to draw the humans into…" Dramatic pause. "…war."

Murmurs broke out. Dragon feet pawed the ground. Blackclaw drank in the sweet turbulence from his place on the bench. It had been said. Finally, after all these months and years of careful planning and waiting, the word had been said. War. Deep within Blackclaw's belly, a rumbling hunger reawakened.

"With this in mind, return safely to your lands. All of you are welcome again next month, when the council will give voice to their decisions." Whitetail descended the platform.

Blackclaw watched the mass fracture and slowly

scatter. Jaws of Greens and Browns snapped in discontent. Pale wings of Whites and Grays billowed, but didn't fly. In the open-air stadium of Mount Gore, dragons were hesitant to leave.

"They are disappointed," said Whitetail, drawing near. "They are restless."

"Yes. Just as I had hoped." Blackclaw hefted himself from his bench, waved off the council members crowding to speak, and retreated. He rapped Whitetail on the spine with the tip of his tail. "Get me dinner. I will be in the Great Hall."

Blackclaw squeezed through a side exit of the stadium, and circled around to descend carved steps toward the manor. There, he paused. He again admired the dragon statues bracing the entryway arch. Reproductions of past council leaders glared up at the sky, with granite spouts of fire exploding from their jaws.

Soon, his own image would join those on this mountain who had gone before, and he would be immortalized. He would be the greatest hero. It was his destiny.

He chafed at the thought of sharing the arch with Bren Redheart, his incompetent predecessor. He glared at this stone dragon, whose claws reached for an unseen enemy. What a worthless competitor, really. It was almost a shame the way the Red had died, with barely a struggle, as though the attack came as no surprise. As though he was expecting it. Welcoming it. How disappointing.

"He was not fit to lead as you have done," said

Whitetail from behind him.

"Redheart strangled our tribes with talk of honor, and made them weak and pitiful." He spun to face Whitetail, and pointed a sharpened claw toward the Redheart statue. "Can you explain to me how it is that his likeness shares the arch with the truly great leaders of our time?"

"The council commissioned the work before you took power. It would have reflected poorly on you to deny them."

"Yes, yes, you idiot, I remember that part. What I mean to ask is what he ever did to deserve the honor in the first place! Pathetic coward. He died the same way he led." Blackclaw turned his eyes once more to the statue. "I had underestimated the impact of his mate's death on his confidence."

"But some of his greatest accomplishments came after Sera's death. His signing of the Mount Chaste agreement, the Battle of the Vast Plain—"

Blackclaw's fist was around Whitetail's throat like the crack of a whip. He squeezed scaly flesh, pulled Whitetail's head toward his own, and met Whitetail's frightened gaze. "He was a worthless, broken creature that deserved to die."

"Of course," Whitetail wheezed. "He deserved to die."

Blackclaw held his grip, struggling with the impulse to shake the pasty dragon and throw him over the mountainside. When Whitetail's eyes clouded red and lolled in their sockets, Blackclaw released him. "He deserved to die." He whirled around. "What do you hear of the human dragon hunter? It seems time he should be contacting us." No reply. Blackclaw glanced back at Whitetail, who was moving his jaw, trying to talk, and rubbing his welted throat.

"Speak up, Whitetail. And where is my food?"

"No word from the human," Whitetail rasped. "Your meal awaits you in the Great Hall."

Blackclaw growled. "Bring it to my chambers instead. I have work to do with the circlet."

CHAPTER THREE

Kallon swerved for a landing in the fading light of late afternoon. He'd flown far and fast, only slowing when his wings began to ache as though they might drop off. He'd pushed himself until he was weary and empty, as he always did. Even still, rest evaded him as it always did. He lingered, swooping and circling over his foothills, aimless.

Perhaps it would be a nice night for sleeping near the mountain lake. The pines were crisp and fresh in the cool air, so different from the arid wind near the human village. The thought made him wonder how much longer he had to enjoy the lake before it, too, disappeared into dust, as so much Leland water had already done. And not just the water, but the land as well. All around him, brown death crept on silent feet, slowly overtaking. Even his cave, hidden deep in the mountains, was beginning to feel different. Unfamiliar.

He considered the lake again, and paused to stare off in that direction. He scowled. It was too far. He was too tired.

He supposed he would just go home. He should have been satisfied at the thought. The human had no doubt moved on, and he would again, finally, know a long, blessed night of solitude, without her jabbering in her sleep at all hours. So what if the emptiness of his cave somehow felt lonelier? He was always lonely, and he liked it that way. It would be good to have his home back to himself. He was relieved, no, overjoyed to be alone again.

He thumped to the ground. Then his nostrils widened. Faintly, he detected the human's scent. He poked his head into his cave, blotting out the dusk behind him. "Still here?"

There was a sniff, and a shuffling. "Yes," came the soft reply.

He snatched back his head in surprise, and blinked. She'd stayed after all? In went his head again. "Why?"

"Well," whispered the human so quietly, that if Kallon's ears weren't so sensitive, her voice might not be heard at all. "At first I waited so I could thank you."

He didn't know what to make of it. He hadn't expected her to stay, and hadn't expected his heart to skip when he heard her speak. He dropped his flanks to the ground, and sat, bewildered.

"Do you want me to go?" she asked, her voice a bit stronger.

He didn't know the answer to the question.

"I'll go if you want."

"Dark is near," he finally said, pushing to his feet

to lope inside. He lowered his snout to peer at the tiny creature where she sat against the wall, hugging her knees. There was still fear in her eyes, but she met his gaze. "Do you want to go?" he asked.

"No," she said. "Not in the dark."

"Then stay if you want." He scooped up the wooden mug where it lay on its side, and plunged it into a small bucket of liquid. "Should drink more." He offered her the mug.

The girl nodded, but didn't reach for it.

"You need to drink," Kallon said.

"I know," she said. "But I just want to sleep."

"First drink." He stuck out the mug that dangled from his claw like a child's toy. She sat up, and stared at it as though she'd never seen one before.

"You don't drink out of mugs. You don't have tableware or cupboards or a pantry." She blinked up at him. "Where did you get that one?"

"Fine, don't drink." He set the mug on the ground.

"Do you have human friends somewhere?"

He snorted. "No friends. Anywhere."

"Then where did you find this mug? And where did you get that loaf of bread for me to eat?"

He watched her through narrowed eyes, as she curled pale fingers around the mug. "Thought you said you wanted to sleep."

"How can you speak my language?" She gave a sharp look, and he thought he caught of a glitter of emerald in her eyes. "And why did you help me? Why didn't you just eat me or something?"

Kallon sighed, and curled his chin to his chest, eyes squeezing closed against her ceaseless questions. "I don't eat humans." Then his eyes popped open, and he thrust his snout near her face. "Could start though. You're noisy."

She fell silent, and lifted the mug to her mouth. She stared up at him for several minutes before blurting, "Do you have a name?"

He rolled his eyes. "Of course."

"Well, aren't you going to tell me what it is?"

He tipped his head, and eyed her for a long time. He hadn't planned on sharing his name with her, though now as he considered, it seemed safe enough. He himself hadn't said it in so long he thought it might come bumbling off his tongue in a knot. "Kallon," he finally said.

"Kallon?"

He winced. In her voice, his name sounded small and soft, and not at all flattering.

"Just Kallon?" she asked.

More questions. Every time he answered one, she bubbled out another like the mountain stream that gurgled incessant droplets, drip, drip, drip, into the darkest parts of his cave's most secret place. He turned his gaze to the fading sun, and sighed again. "Just Kallon."

§

In the night, Riza watched faces dance and jeer.

Men's hands tugged at her clothes. She tried to scream but had no voice, tried to fight them off but had no strength. She was blind and defenseless.

Near her ear came a rumbled whisper. "What is wrong?" The voice jolted her with panic, but it snatched her from the grip of that place between waking and sleeping, where she'd been trapped.

She sat up. "Kallon?"

"Me," he answered.

She opened her eyes to see his jowls smack into a wide yawn. His lips peeled back from incisors as long as her fingers. His tongue flopped out. He gave a satisfied shudder, clamped his mouth shut, and threw his weight to roll onto his back. "Who'd you think?"

She tried to breathe normally. Her heart was still racing from the dream she'd just had, and it didn't help that she'd awoken to a mental image of being impaled on one of his teeth. She scooted away from him a few inches. "I had a dream," she said. "I couldn't wake up from it. That place is frightening." She began breathing easier, and her wits were finally coming around. "I'm still in your cave, right?"

Kallon answered a sleepy, "You are."

She nodded, remembering now. She rested back against the wall. She could feel the dragon's body heat, and could hear the rumble of his breath in his chest. She felt oddly better for his company. "What time do you think it is?" she asked.

Kallon slumped from his back to his side, legs thumping against the ground. "Don't know," he mumbled. He covered his eyes with his foreleg.

"Midnight? Later? Earlier?"

Kallon groaned. "Don't know. Somewhere between high moon and dawn, perhaps."

She looked out through the cave but she couldn't tell. Her headache had dulled to a throb, and she felt stronger. Her muscles were sore, but had stopped trembling. She lifted her arms in a tall stretch, testing them. "Because if it's near dawn, I may just as well get up."

Kallon's paw dropped from his eyes, and he raised his head. "Then get up. Or go back to sleep."

"Except that if dawn isn't for a few hours, I'm not going out there in the dark. Not at least until dawn."

He peered down his snout at her. "Whatever your plans, do they require talking?"

Riza winced, and drew her shoulders up to her ears. "Sorry."

He watched her for a moment, his eyes narrowed. Then he lay back down and let out a long breath against the dusty ground. His wings relaxed toward the floor.

"It's just that sometimes I wake up at night and can't get back to sleep," she explained.

Kallon pulled his head up with a start and glared at the ceiling of the cave. Then he growled. "Going to keep talking, then?"

"Well. I can stop," she said, and held up a hand. "If it's bothering you."

He sighed. He shifted his weight and crawled forward, and she watched his bulk bear down on her.

"Talk," he said, his nose inches from her own.

She glanced away. "Oh. I—I suppose that was all I had to say." She swallowed hard before looking back up at his face. To her surprise, he was smiling.

"Do this a lot?"

"Sometimes." More often than she'd like to admit. Most times it happened, she would work on an unfinished rug she'd been braiding, or she'd sneak out to stroll along a tiny brook behind her father's house. She liked to try to count the stars. "But I don't want to go out there tonight," she said.

Kallon tipped his head. "Go where? To the frightening place?"

"What do you mean?"

"What do *you* mean?" he asked. "Said before that you had a dream and couldn't wake up. That it was a frightening place."

"Oh." She nodded, remembering. "Yes, the place between waking and sleeping. Doesn't that ever happen to you?"

"Don't think so. Don't remember dreaming."

"It feels like a real place at the time. Like while I slept, my soul went wandering without me, and can't get back. But that makes me sound crazy, doesn't it?"

Kallon's brown eyes were warm on her face. "Not crazy."

She smiled. "Well, lots of people think I'm mad. You wouldn't be the first." She suddenly couldn't help but laugh. "I can just imagine what they'd be saying if they saw me now, sitting in a cave in the middle of the night having a conversation with a dragon as though it was the most normal thing in the world."

He didn't respond to that. His eyes probed, searching right through her to the wall behind. She shifted her weight.

"Who thinks you're mad?" he asked.

"My father, for one." That came out more quickly than she meant.

"Why?"

"Why does he think I'm mad?" When Kallon nodded, she shrugged. "Well, I suppose, because I didn't want to marry a farmer and have a thousand babies, and live in the same village I'd always lived in."

"Didn't know humans could have a thousand babies."

She smiled a little. "We can't, really. I just mean that he wants me to have a lot of them, and be like everyone else, and think like everyone else."

"You don't think like everyone else?"

She considered that a moment. Her father had told her often enough that she didn't think like a girl was supposed to think. She'd always wanted to ask him how a girl was supposed to think, but she'd already known what he'd say. What she really wanted to know was if other people had the same, rigid beliefs as her father.

She'd shared an idea once with Isaak Hoag, the man her father wanted her to marry. As they'd walked beneath a dark sky that flickered with lights like tiny torches, she'd gazed up, and had forgotten her father's warnings to keep her mouth shut. She'd wondered out loud.

What if the sky isn't the end of our world, but just the beginning? she'd asked. *What if someone on one of those far-away torches is looking back at us, wondering the same thing?*

Isaak had tugged her to a stop, and he'd stared down with hard eyes to say, *Talk like that around here will you get you a burnin' platform to stand on.*

It hadn't been the first time she'd heard that threat, but she'd vowed it would it be the last. That had been the very night she'd begun plans to leave and never go back.

"You don't think like everyone else?" the dragon asked again.

"I don't think like my father, or like Isaak Hoag," she said. "Sometimes I wonder about my mother. She died before I ever had a chance to know her, but somehow, I think she used to feel crazy, like me." She almost added something, but changed her mind.

"What?" The dragon nudged her shoulder with his snout.

"Well." Very quietly, hesitantly, she said, "I think sometimes that my mother wanted to leave, too, but just couldn't bring herself to do it. I think, maybe, she did the next bravest thing she could manage. She just closed her eyes, and died."

Riza could feel the heavy weight of his gaze now as it pressed her back against the wall, slowly crushing her. He was quiet for a long time, until he finally said, "That is a lot of thinking."

More silence lingered between them, until his eyes shifted away, and the weight of them disappeared. She breathed in relief. "How long have you lived here alone?" she asked.

"Don't know. Since I was young."

"Why do you stay here?"

His head slung to the ground, and his breath stirred a tiny windstorm. "My territory."

"Don't you ever get lonely?"

His head jerked up and his eyes took on the look of Isaak Hoag. "My territory. It was my father's, and his father's. Don't see how it matters to you, human."

She silenced herself with her hand over her mouth. Then she poked her finger into the dirt floor, and doodled a lopsided circle. "So you'll pass on this territory to your son when you have one?"

His eyes turned downright cold. "Won't have a son. I'm the last Red."

She was instantly sorry she'd asked. She never meant to, but she always asked just one too many questions. She huddled against the cave wall and hugged her knees to her chest.

Kallon swung his head to stare out into the sky. Darkness was unraveling, sliced by horizontal, purple ribbons.She watched his eyes reflect this sparkle.

Then, without her even asking, he spoke. "Long ago, dragon territory was the whole earth. Used to be more lines than now." He blinked slowly, and turned to her. "Mine isn't the first to die out, and won't be the last. You humans will see to that."

"Why don't you fight back?"

"Fighting. All you humans know." He nodded his head toward her cheek, and she touched the tender place where she must have been bruised. "You prey on one another, use violence to feel powerful. It's beyond you to understand that not every creature thinks the way you do."

"You don't think like everyone else?" Riza asked, and smiled.

He only swung his gaze back to the mouth of the cave. Once more, his eyes reflected the sun that was now a glowing half-nugget of gold against the horizon. The wash of color filled the cave, and the songs of early birds filtered cheerfully into the dusty air around them. "Sun is up. Safe for you to go," he said, his voice flat.

She didn't know what she'd said that made him want to send her away, but she affected a lot of people that way. She slowly pushed to her feet. "I'm sorry," she said, and she meant it.

When her dizziness passed, she took a step toward the outside. "I think I will be fine now." She watched him, waited for him to respond. Or nod. Anything.

But he only stared into the sky.

"Riza," she whispered. "That's my name, in case you were wondering."

He must not have been wondering, because he didn't react. So she kept moving. Each step became stronger than the last. She reached the outside, and breathed deeply of the sweet morning light, drenched with dew. She gave a last glance over her shoulder to the dragon, who seemed no more than a statue. Then she lifted her chin, and faced the new day by walking directly into it.

§

Riza wasn't sure how long she'd walked before she finally stopped to rest. She leaned against the scratchy bark of a willow trunk and slid to her bottom. Where was she going, anyway? She looked up at the blistering morning sun. Rays stabbed like flames through the naked arms of pin oaks and knobby ash trees, and raised tears to her weary eyes. She was forced to look away.

Before she was taken to the dragon's cave, she'd been traveling south. With a few saved coins in her pouch, a sack of dried meat and bread, and her father's knife, she'd headed out before dawn woke the village. She'd offered no goodbye to her father, no note, no explanation. No explanation would have been good enough, anyway.

She'd spent several days walking and several eerie nights alone, surrounded by the sound of wildlife that seemed more ominous than she'd remembered it sounding when she was home, safe in her bed. But she had begun to grow accustomed, if only a little, to the sounds of nature all around her. It had helped remind her she wasn't completely alone.

She felt alone now, though. She was in far worse shape. She had no knife, no provisions, and no money at all. Perhaps she'd been hasty in leaving the dragon's cave, despite the overpowering stench. She hadn't even asked directions.

What she needed was a plan. She looked back from where she came, recognizing the gradual up-slope of the dry earth. Rubble and stone lay like a trail of crumbs for her to find her way back to the cave, if she needed. After all, the dragon had helped her once, and finding him again would be better than starving to death.

She looked forward. The earth continued downhill, until it flattened out around a patch of sapling pin oaks with branches too gnarled for trees so young. This forest was as thirsty and pitiful as the forest of her home village. But, growing saplings meant there was water somewhere. She pushed to her feet, determined to find the water before dark.

Her battered boots rubbed and pinched. Perspiration tickled like crawling spiders down her back. She tried to twist her matted hair around her head, and even speared it several times with twigs to hold it, but it sagged and clung to her neck anyway.

She searched on, and found herself circling paths she was sure she'd already seen. She veered toward promising low spots, but all she found were puddles of crunchy leaves. As the day wore on, her hungry stomach twisted angrily, and she felt as though she had a fat stick in her mouth where her tongue was supposed to be.

And there was no water. Hours of searching left her legs trembling. Finally, they refused to move. She wanted to collapse, or at least sit, but she was too afraid she might not get back up again. She hugged a gray oak, instead.

It was then that she realized the sun was fading. An unfamiliar fear slithered across her skull and crept, whispering, into her ears. It was almost dark.

She tried to think past the welling panic. She'd spent many a night in the forest before, and the darkness was a little unnerving sometimes, but nothing she'd ever been afraid of. There was nothing in the dark that wasn't there in the daylight.

Except now there was. Now the night held memories of monsters. Monsters with lecherous grins wet with saliva, and cold hands that gripped and pinched, and eyes, so many of them, that buzzed and hovered like black bees against a black wall and festered with death.

"Stop it!" Riza shouted, and slapped her hands over her face. She had to stop thinking like that, and get moving again. She would just have to find the pebble trail back toward the cave, and beg another night's stay with the dragon. It would be fine. Everything was going to be fine.

But when she began moving again, she realized she'd lost the direction of the pebbles. A few steps this way, and a few that way only led her back to the same gray oak. She followed an upward tilt of the land, but it leveled out again. She didn't know where she was. She didn't know where the dragon was.

Were the trees getting thicker as the light got smaller? She spun around, searching for an opening. She eased between two thick trunks, and, just as she was about to give in to her panic, a wide path rose up and parted the trees. She threw herself toward it and ran.

She came to a stop in a small field. She could see the dark outline of a lumpy house in the near distance, with windows ablaze with torchlight. The sight calmed her, and she took a minute to catch her breath.

Porkers grunted close by. She followed the sound. They were nosing the dirt of their sty, ignoring her, and weren't even using the box of straw in the corner. She considered climbing in. Compared to the dragon, the pigs smelled springtime fresh. Then she spotted a small, lopsided barn just a few feet away.

She ran for the stone wall of the house, and, pressing against it, she snuck toward a corner and peeked around. A rectangular patch of light streamed to the ground through a front window. She avoided it, and dashed for the barn.

The barn door was ajar. She moved to ease herself through it, but a water trough caught her eye. She dropped to her knees, and dipped a hand into the water. It tasted of dust. She was briefly glad for the dusk, so that she couldn't see the water as she cupped it again and again to her mouth, barely breathing between swallows.

It wasn't enough. She leaned over the side of trough, and with a splash, immersed her whole head. She shook her hair, and blew bubbles that tickled her nose. Then she withdrew with a gasp. She probably smelled like a pig, and looked like one, too, but she didn't care. She felt immensely better.

"What do you do there?" came a man's voice. She shrieked and dove through the barn door, tripping on her own feet. She sprawled on the dirt floor.

Near her hand, a stream of moonlight widened. The scrape of the opening door drowned out her second cry of fear. She scrambled to her feet, and whirled around to face the man realizing too late she'd just trapped herself in the barn with him.

"What are you doing?" he repeated.

She could think of no excuse fast enough. She could think of nothing at all. His dark, angry eyes consumed the last of her strength, and her legs gave out. She dropped onto a scratchy pile of straw.

Behind the man, a woman's voice called, "Mr. Armitage!"

The man turned to block the door, his gloved hand on the rusted latch. "Yes, Mrs. Fennipen?" Hurried footsteps halted, and Riza could see the wrinkled cheek of a woman just past the man's shoulder. Riza wished she could call out, but her body wouldn't respond. She could only stare from her place on the straw.

"Forgot your candle," said Mrs. Fennipen. "Can't get into town 'n back in the dark." A fat pillar candle lofted toward the man's face, and its flame deepened the creases of the hand that held it. "Mr. Fennipen is awful glad to have another man around the place. You're sure you don't know how long you'll stay?"

"No, I'm afraid not," he said, and took the candle. "But, Madame, if you keep feeding me like you did this eve, you might have to kick me out when you grow tired of me."

Mrs. Fennipen gave a girlish giggle. "You're the charm, Mr. Armitage." She pressed a strand of graying hair back into her low bun. "What brings you to the barn?"

"I chased something inside. A rat, I think. I was just going to go inside and finish it off."

At that, Riza jerked. Somehow, she had to find the strength to get out of there. Maybe she could pry a hole in the wall. She tried to pull herself toward a loose plank, but her arms wouldn't bend.

"Nasty things, rats," said Mrs. Fennipen. "Can't get used to 'em, no matter how many I see. You have the key to get back in?"

"I do. Good night to you, Mrs. Fennepin."

Riza managed to reach one arm toward the plank, and dug her nails around its edge. Just then, his rumbling voice came from behind her. "Are you going to tell me what you're doing here?"

Riza froze. She slowly turned her face toward him. She tried to speak, really she did, but no sound came out.

He took a step. He leaned in so close she could feel the warmth of the candle he held. "What happened to your face?" This time, his voice was gentle.

He kneeled. Her heart raced painfully and she closed her eyes, willing him to disappear. She felt his fingers under her chin, and she was pulled forward. "Did someone hit you?"

When she tried again to speak, her eyes opened.

She met his dark gaze, which hovered and buzzed like black bees against a black wall.

"So. You're wanting to borrow the place for the night." He rose to his feet and stepped back. She could breathe again. "Don't make off with anything that doesn't belong to you." He turned, closed the barn door, and slid the bolt home from the outside.

Riza wanted to weep with relief, but she was too drained for even tears. She collapsed to her side, half on the straw and half on the dirt floor. Before she could realize she was uncomfortable, she was asleep.

Chapter Four

When the time came for dawn, the sun was still hiding. It hung back behind a curtain of dreary clouds, failing to take its place on center stage. The trees stood as audience anyway, their naked arms embracing the heavy air.

Kallon left no shadow against the dusty earth this morning. His usual romp in the skies did nothing to lift his mood. He felt as bloated with darkness as the clouds he danced with, and the longer he lingered there, the heavier he felt himself become. Finally, he gave up, and swung low to the ground without landing.

Above the dank scent of promised rain, he smelled something else. He turned his head toward the rubble at the top of his mountain.

A familiar old man picked his way carefully, one arthritic hand curled around the crystal tip of his walking stick. The other hand he held out to his side, as though pretending to fly. His baggy trousers rustled and slapped against his bowed legs, and his beard danced in the rising wind like the wild, white hair of a gypsy girl.

Kallon swerved to pass over the man once. Then he angled his thick wings, and came to a landing behind him, so gentle that he stirred less stones than the noisy wind. The man turned, and pointed his staff toward the sky. "Smells like rain."

"Noticed," Kallon replied.

"Came to see the girl."

"Gone," he said, and swung his head toward the village.

"Already?" The man scowled, and stabbed his stick into the dirt. "Curses." He then turned his back to Kallon, and continued along his path down the mountain.

Kallon pushed off to hang in the air above the man, his wings beating lazily. "Orman, where are you going?"

"Didn't come all this way for nothing. If I can't see the girl, I'll see you instead." Orman tapped his stick against a boulder the size of Kallon's head, which was blocking the path. The boulder wobbled, and then politely rolled out of the way.

Kallon grumbled. "Don't want company."

"Noticed," said Orman.

By the time Orman Thistleby reached the base of the path, the wind was so fierce it snapped his wiry gray hair against his scalp. He didn't seem to mind, though, because he lingered outside the cave without going in. "Scared her away, didn't you?"

"No." Kallon landed again, and tucked his wings against his spine to saunter into the dark opening. "She wanted to leave." He heard Orman huff, and he glanced back to see the wizard cross his arms against his scrawny chest. "You're going to get wet out there," Kallon called.

"Won't rain." Orman grunted. "Smells like it. Feels like it. But it won't." He hobbled into the darkness, anyway. Inside the cave, he scraped the crystal of his staff across the ground as though striking a flint, and the foggy gem blazed with a glowing orange light. "Your father wouldn't want this for you, Kallon. You spend too much time alone." He waved his stick, and the cave crackled with warm torchlight.

Kallon leaned back against a wall, and drew up his feet beneath him. He rolled his eyes at Orman's comment, and gave a grunt of his own. "You're one to talk."

"That's different!" Orman shook his stick. "Have my books, have my duties, my magics. You have nothing but yourself. With your rotten attitude, you can't be much company."

Kallon's nostrils flared. "That's none of your business."

"Is too my business. Your father's wishes are my concern." The rumpled old man shambled closer. He pressed the tip of his staff between Kallon's eyes. "He was the most honorable creature I knew. Aside from your mother, of course. He lived up to his promise to protect me to the death, and didn't turn his back once. Not once, I tell you." And his stick went tap, tap, tap against Kallon's forehead.

Kallon shook his head to knock the irritating staff

away from his face. "That was the old way. I want no part of it."

At that, Orman withdrew, his brow bunching together. "Much to be done still. Your seat on the council as Herald of the Reds waits for you."

Kallon lowered his snout and met Orman's gaze. A gust of steam curled from his nostrils. "The Reds are dead."

Orman's neck grew several inches as he straightened his shoulders. He opened his mouth, but only the sound of his breath issued. Finally, he ground the heel of his boot into the cave floor and turned away. "Fordon Blackclaw leads the council in your stead. All of Leland reeks of his darkness." He peered over his shoulder at Kallon and clicked his tongue. "Dragons murmur of war with humans. Your father would have much to say."

Kallon blew a puff of breath between his teeth, which hit Orman full-force in the back. It sent the wizard stumbling several steps out into the howling wind, forcing him to plant his walking stick into the rocky sand to keep from falling.

Orman spun to glare at Kallon, the sharpened crystal of the staff glowing white. "Still got plenty of breath for a dead dragon."

Kallon just flopped his chin to the ground with a grumble, stirring up a cloud of dust that tempted his nostrils to sneeze. But he was too miserable to sneeze. He simply lay there, immersed in the darkness, and silently cursed it.

§

Riza awoke to a slap of wetness against her cheek. Drowsy, she swiped the back of her hand across it. She groaned and tried to settle again. Her brain felt like a fuzzy blanket, and she wasn't ready to get up yet. But she did wonder what time it was. She opened her eyes to see another drop of morning dew slip through a crack in the barn roof and splatter against her cheek. Remembering where she was, she sat up quickly.

Too quickly. She groaned again as her back and hips wrenched. Her legs felt heavy as timber logs, and her feet were swollen inside her worn boots. Would she ever feel like herself again?

She didn't have time, though, to feel sorry for herself. She could do that later. Right now, she had to pull herself together for another day of walking. She had to find some food and a job, and a better place to sleep than this rickety barn. It was time to put her plan into motion. As soon as she came up with one, anyway.

She hauled her weary self up out of the straw. Her joints didn't want to bend, and she wasn't even sure she was standing yet. Then she hobbled one tiny step forward. She had to grasp the low wall of a horse stall to keep from falling. She took a deep breath, blinked to wash the sleepy haze from her eyes, and tried again.

She considered it a small victory when she reached the barn door. It was already ajar, so she peeked out. The morning sky was thick with warning, and the wind whistled around her ears. Wonderful. Now a storm was coming, on top of everything else.

"Sleep well?" called a man's voice.

Riza's eyes darted to the man who sat on the bottom step of the farmhouse. The blade of his sword was stabbed into the ground between his boots, and his arms were crossed over the handle. His black beard was close-trimmed, making his hard features seem even darker. Staring at his eyes, her stomach clenched as though a clay brick had suddenly formed there. She was as afraid of him in the daylight as she'd been last night in the barn.

The man stood and took several steps toward her. "You've had some trouble."

She must be a mess to look at. She combed fingers through her hair, and smoothed the front of her bodice, but from the way his eyebrows quirked while he watched her, she guessed it didn't do much good.

"Someone in town got rough with you?" he asked.

"No. I haven't been to town yet," she said around her Adam's apple that got wedged too high in her throat.

His brows shot up. He moved a step closer. "Then you've come from the trees? The mountains?"

"Yes. Just now. Or, I mean, last night. But traveling before that. I mean—" Her own words weren't making sense even to her. She pressed her hand to her throbbing temple. "I'm sorry about the barn. I promise I'll pay you a night's rent as soon as I find work." She bowed her head, hoping this man would just politely let her be on her way. She moved to slip past him.

"What kind of work?" He swung out his sword, and the flat of the blade pressed against her belly. "I've been in this town only a few days, myself, but I know that employment is a rare find."

Riza backed up, guarded. His speech was refined, but his mannerisms just short of rude. If he'd planned on harming her, though, he'd had plenty of opportunity already. She couldn't figure him out. So she answered. "I'm willing to try anything. I'm…" She paused. "… eager."

"You're over-thin. Young, I'd wager." His lips pursed, and he slid his sword into its sheath against his hip. Then he crossed his arms, his dark eyes scrutinizing. "You might do well, though, in a job I heard available at the Brown Barrel."

"The Brown Barrel?"

He nodded. "Local tavern. Just down the road. I'll take you there." He turned, and began his way toward town.

"Now just a minute! When I said I'd do anything, I didn't mean that!" Her own town had a tavern, and she knew about those girls that entertained men there. No one was supposed to talk about it out loud, but it got talked about, just the same. She forgot the stiffness in her arms as she pressed both fists on her hips. "What do you take me for, Mister? I'm not a tavern girl!"

The man swung around on his heel, and glared. His eyes flashed. Then his face slowly shifted into an awkward smile. So awkward, in fact, that Riza wasn't sure if he might suddenly laugh, or possibly vomit. Neither happened. He bowed at the waist, and opened his arms. "Begging the lady's pardon," he crooned obnoxiously, "...the job opening is for a cook." He straightened again, and met her eyes.

Heat flushed over Riza's face. "Oh." She brushed an imaginary hair from her cheek. "Well, then. I appreciate your mentioning." She raised her chin, lifted her bedraggled skirt away from her mud-encrusted shoes, and prepared to follow him with all the attempted grace of a princess tiptoeing across a red carpet. All the while, she hoped a cliff would suddenly present itself so she could jump off of it.

Still holding that strange smile of uncomfortable amusement on his face, he took her hand. "I am Jastin Armitage, my indignant lady." He pressed a kiss to the inside of her wrist.

Riza was too shocked to snatch back her hand. "I'm Riza. Riza Diantus." His mouth lingered there on her skin, and she was appalled at the flutter down her spine. Then, his nose traveled another inch up her forearm. Was he sniffing her? She almost giggled out loud, but cleared her throat instead. She tugged her arm.

He didn't let go. Alarm prickled her neck just as a gust of dry wind threw dust into her eyes. She coughed, and blinked, and felt him release her hand. But he was suddenly closer, and he wrapped his thick fingers around her elbow. "Let's go, Riza Diantus," he said quietly. She couldn't decide if this shift in his voice made him seem friendlier, or more dangerous.

§

"Why are you doing this?" Riza asked the dark man as he dragged her through the village streets. There weren't many people around, maybe because of the brewing storm, but those who were stared hard at her. Most looks were downright hostile. She felt like a beggar.

"Why am I doing what?" he asked without looking at her. His eyes were focused ahead of them.

"Helping me." She watched his tight profile as she stumbled along to keep up. Deep creases surrounded his eyes, and frown lines curved around his mouth as though his face was used to scowling. Dust clung to his face everywhere, even the bottom edge of his dark beard. A thought struck her. "How long were you waiting on that step this morning? Were you waiting for me to wake up?"

"Here is the place." He tugged her through rugged doors and guided her toward the long, curving bar inside the Brown Barrel Tavern. "Sit here and don't speak."

"But I—"

He pressed a gloved finger to her mouth. "Do not speak. I'll be back shortly." He moved away.

The room was larger than any she'd been in before. The smoke from wall lanterns hazed the meager sunlight squeezing through high, tiny windows. She could barely make out the shapes of chairs and tables in the gloom. The stench of ale and sweaty male bodies made her breathe shallow so she wouldn't gag. It wasn't so different from the dragon's cave, really.

Her dark helper returned with another man. This man's bulbous nose was too large for his face. Deep pockmarks scarred his cheeks. His coppery eyebrows perched like woolly caterpillars over dark and tiny eyes. Riza shrank back.

"This is she," the dark man said. His finger rubbed at her cheek, too hard, to clear away some dust. "She's not much to look at, but a hot bath will scrape off the dirt, and her bruises will heal."

Riza stiffened. She wasn't a farm animal! Talking about her like she wasn't even there! She opened her mouth to protest, but his instant glare made her slap it shut again.

"Aye…but can she cook?" asked the new man. His face loomed closer, and his breath smelled of hot peppers. "Looks like she hasn't had a decent meal herself in weeks! I dun trust a skinny cook!"

"She can cook. Give her a day. If you do not want to continue her employment, no harm done."

"Aye, very well, Mr. Armitage," the new man said, nodding. He wrung his hands against his stained apron. "She can have a bath, but I'll take it out of her day's wages. It's in the back." He jerked his head. Then his fearsome look dissolved into the soft grin of a rumpled rag doll. "Rusic Landel, I am. Most call me Rust. I own the place, and if ye do right by me, I'll take good care of ye." His face scrunched into a long wink, and he lumbered away.

The dark man yanked her from the barstool to her feet. "Move."

"Stop hurting me." She glanced toward Rusic, whose back was turned as he wiped down the bar.

"Now you have employment. While you're bathing I'll get you some new clothes. Don't make me sorry for what I'm doing."

"I didn't ask you to do anything you're doing, so if you're sorry, don't blame me."

Again came his glare, and again she withered.

"But I am grateful, sir."

"Jastin." He released her arm as they reached the back of the room.

Before them was a curling staircase that led to inn rooms above. Set in the space beneath the stairs was a miniscule room with only a curtain for a door. Inside this, a half-barrel bathtub squatted in a corner.

"I'm taking a bath in there?" she asked, her hand holding aside the curtain. "I can't even see in there."

Jastin clenched his jaw, and leaned into the crawlspace to pull out a beeswax candle from a small table. "Light this. Then light that." He pointed at a large hole in the dirt floor that contained firewood covered with fist-sized rocks. "Heat the rocks, put the rocks in the water. I'll be back."

Riza spun to face him. "You're leaving right now?"

Jastin closed his eyes, and his thick fingers circled against his temples. He released a long sigh. "You need clothes. I'll get them and bring them back."

"But there's no door. Anybody could just walk in!"

Never mind that there were only a few men seated at the scattering of tables just beyond, most of whom were hung over and sprawled across those tables with their cheeks in puddles of their own drool. Her dark helper hadn't done much this morning to make her feel safe around him, but without him there she felt positively vulnerable.

He opened his eyes and narrowed them on her face. "Nobody is interested in looking in on a skinny beggar girl."

Her cheeks filled with stinging redness. The bruises on her face ached with the sudden rush of blood, and she touched her fingertips to them. Then she turned away. She couldn't decide whether his comment did more to offend her, or hurt her feelings. "I'm not taking a bath in a place with no door," she finally said.

His voice was softer when he replied. "Very well. You start the fire, and when I return, I'll post myself as guard outside the curtain. All right?"

She nodded without looking at him. When she heard his heavy boot steps move away, she turned to light the beeswax candle in the flame of a wall torch. Then she carried it carefully to the fire pit in the floor, and patiently waited for the wood to accept the flame.

Who was this man, anyway? The woman last night called him Mr. Armitage. Jastin Armitage. Why was he waiting for her outside the barn this morning, and why was he helping her? He obviously had nothing but contempt for her. Whether it was because he thought she was a beggar, or simply because she was a woman, she didn't know. And she disliked him right back. So why was she accepting his help? Frankly, she could think of no other choice.

She blew an encouraging breath across the flame that was beginning to overtake the firewood. The nagging hunger in her belly fed the nagging doubts in her mind over her decision to leave her father. So far in her journey she had been attacked, nearly eaten by a dragon, and now she was starving and forced to rely on a stranger for help. She'd underestimated how hard it was going to be, and the amount of resolve she was going to need. Maybe it was time to admit she'd been wrong. Not about hating the way her father treated her, but wrong about leaving. Perhaps her father had been right all along. She needed him, she needed their home. And she needed the comfortable, predictable life they'd led, despite how utterly miserable it made her.

She reached for heavy iron tongs beside the fire pit, and used them to retrieve the heated rocks. She carried them, one by one, to the bath water and listened to them sizzle as they sank to the bottom of the barrel.

Not just miserable, she reminded herself! She'd despised that village. Not the people, but the mindset. No one in that entire place gave a thought about what lay beyond the village gate. No one wondered if there were others who might act, and think, and live differently. They settled for the drudgery of rising from the same straw bed that they had woken from their entire lives.

Were they content? Some of them, she supposed. It

was evident in their happy smiles and cheerful whistling as they went about their daily chores. Her friend, Lilly, was like that. Lilly had married and already had a baby before Riza left, and Lilly's face shone like a buffed silver tray each time she spoke of her husband. Riza envied her friend sometimes for the bliss she knew from her simple life.

But Riza wanted more than simple. She wasn't certain what it was she wanted, but she was sure what she didn't want. If she had to take risks to learn, then that was what she would do. If she needed more resolve, she'd just dig down deep within herself and find some, somewhere. She wasn't going back. Ever.

It was a long time before she finally heard Jastin's voice though the curtain. "I have returned." A wooden chair scraped across the floor and stopped outside the closet.

"All right," Riza called out. She stood, and pinched the curtain close to the wall, making sure not a speck of space was left. "Don't come in. I'm going to get in the water."

There was no reply as she worked stiff fingers around her bodice, and then the loops of her tattered blouse. As she freed the collar, the entire thing pulled away in dirtied strips of cloth. She stared at it, amazed, finally realizing just how awful she must look. Next came her skirt, which had more dirt than material. The strings of her boots were broken in so many places she could just slip them from her feet.

She stepped over the edge of the barrel, and

lowered herself into the steaming water. She shifted her weight to settle within the circle of rocks at the bottom, and let out a long sigh of relief.

"Enjoying the bath?" Jastin asked through the curtain.

She closed her eyes, and leaned back. "I don't have a single place on my whole body that doesn't ache." The heat of the water seeped into her flesh, her muscles, and finally into her bones.

"How long has it been since you've eaten?"

"I don't remember." Her stomach twisted. She pressed a hand to it to quiet it. "But I'm not a beggar."

"No? Then tell me how you came to look like one." His chair groaned, and she could see his boots shift in the space beneath the curtain.

"By accident," she replied. Then she held her breath and submerged.

§

Jastin shifted in his chair, growing more impatient as he waited. What was the girl doing in there? Finally, she called, "All right, I'm coming out." When she emerged, she was wearing the new green dress he'd purchased. He could have afforded a more expensive dress, but hadn't he already done more than enough?

Her hair had turned dark cinnamon from the water, and was pulled back into a fat braid that dripped water down her back. Her eyes were the green of a placid lake within her pale, but freshly glowing, face. He hadn't noticed her eyes before. Her bruises stood out in splotches of purple from her temple to her ear. With no dust to mask them, they were as obvious as black clouds against an ivory sky.

"I've bathed my horse in half the time it took you to clean yourself," Jastin said.

Riza rolled her green eyes. Someday he might be inclined to teach her some manners. "It was your idea," she said. "But, thank you. I'll pay you back as soon as I've earned enough."

She took a step closer to him, and smoothed the rounded collar of her dress. It was a little roomy just below the waist where her hips would be if she'd had any. Likewise, the bodice gathered up across her chest, where she failed to fill that, too. But the sleeves and hem were the right length.

"Go speak with Rusic." He nodded toward the man in the apron.

As she took a step away from him, she looked over her shoulder. "How did you know my size?"

"I didn't. I told the clothier I needed a dress for a skinny little girl."

She frowned. Her round mouth opened as though she might speak, but she appeared to change her mind. Instead, she turned away and strode to the man who would be her boss. Perhaps she was learning manners already.

"Well, is this the same heathen of a beggar girl what asked me for a job this morn?" Rusic bleated, as a great smile broke out across his flushed face. "Wouldn't have known ye if I hadn't seen ye go into the little room with my own eyes!"

"I feel better," the girl said, smiling.

"I'll bet ye do! Now, if yer ready to get to work, I'll show ye the kitchen." He beckoned her around the bar with a wide hand.

When Riza disappeared into the kitchen, Jastin pushed off from the wall, and strode to a near table. It was dimly lit, the torch on the wall beside it purposely extinguished. A young man sat at this table. His hair was long and stringy, and the color of dung.

Jastin kept his eyes on the kitchen door as he pressed his palms to the tabletop. "Well?" he asked the young man.

"That's her," was the reply.

"You're certain? She's the one you saw in the woods a few days past?" He turned his gaze to the scrawny, grinning idiot.

"Sure enough." He stood, and his chair scratched against the floor. He extended his palm. Then his grin curled into an oily sneer, exposing stained teeth. "I recognize 'em finger marks on her face."

Jastin's teeth ground hard against each other, but he dropped a sack of coins onto the informant's palm.

"Pleasure doin' business," said the young man.

"Get out of my sight."

The young man did.

CHAPTER FIVE

A coo whispered near Kallon's ear. He peeped open one eye. An orange shaft of morning light punctured through the mouth of his cave and illuminated a gray pigeon. Round, black eyes stared up into his face, and it cooed again.

Kallon snorted, and a puff of cave dust enveloped the little messenger. "Tell Orman I'm not coming today. Not coming ever."

Pigeon wings fluttered. The dust settled like a heavy cloud onto its feathers. The bird leaped into the air and soared to Kallon's head, where it landed. Peckpeckpeck. It tapped with its dull beak.

Kallon snapped open both eyes, and tossed his head to send the annoying visitor flying. Feathers ruffled as the pigeon flailed and careened toward the cave wall.

Just in time, it managed to brake, and it dropped onto knobby feet. It cocked its head as it strode back toward Kallon, bobbling proudly.

It came closer and closer. Kallon lowered his snout.

A few more steps. Then Kallon snapped his maw like a lightning flash, and caught the thing against his tongue.

Orman's voice vibrated within Kallon's mouth. "If you eat another one of my birds, I'm going to turn you into a human!"

Kallon almost swallowed anyway. He rolled the tasty bird around in his mouth, contemplating, before he finally lowered his chin to spit the thing—Ptoo!—onto the ground. Wasn't worth it. Orman would never let him hear the end of it.

The slobber-covered pigeon rolled across the dust and became coated with sticky mud. Stiff feathers stuck out like porcupine quills. It gave a pitiful squeak, and sat dazed.

Then its little gray beak opened, and Orman's voice came from the pigeon's throat. "You're late! Were late last month and the month before."

"Not coming." Kallon gave the pigeon an irritable frown.

"Yes, you are."

"No."

"Yes!"

"Go away!"

There was a short silence as the bird's beak snapped closed. Its black eyes stared. Then came Orman's voice again. "I have the stone."

Kallon jerked up his head. He stared back at the bird, and felt his scales rise like hackles between his shoulders. His mother's stone? It couldn't be. Orman himself told him it was destroyed. "You're lying. You said it was gone."

"Thought it was. It isn't."

Kallon heaved himself to his feet. Orman wouldn't dare trick him in such a way. If the wizard thought it was the linking stone, it must be something near enough to fool the old man.

As Kallon moved, the muddy pigeon darted into the air, scattering clumps of dirt, and then ducked between dragon and stone to free itself into the waiting sky. It veered upward, toward the top of the mountain.

Kallon quickly followed.

He could have flown the path with his eyes closed, and sometimes did. He knew the way by sight, by smell, by instinct. Glancing below, he saw his shadow brush the limbs of a red oak that had been just a sapling on his first visit to Mount Krag, and to the home of Orman Thistleby.

He'd been excited then to learn humanspeak. He'd wanted to follow his father's example as a dragon knight, a respected vassal, honoring the Redheart name and the land earned by the mighty Reds through honorable service. His fledgling wings had beaten proudly beside his father's as they'd traveled, and he'd recognized the anticipation in his father's expression. It had been a day of great hope and promise.

Kallon's eyes grew hazy. Several feet short of Orman's dwelling he dropped, landed, and clenched his claws against the stone path. Memories brought feelings, and feelings brought pain. Gripping the mountain, he willed himself to forget.

"Changing your mind?" Orman's voice called out from where he stood several feet up the slope. His wrinkled hand wrapped the end of his stick as he peered down to Kallon.

"Maybe."

Orman nodded, and his watery eyes softened. "I miss them, too." He shuffled to turn. "Come on. Haven't got all day."

"You think you have the real stone?" Kallon asked as he followed the wizard up the path. Mountainside rubble shook and loosened beneath his heavy steps. Pebbles bounced and careened downward, slapping into leafless trees and cracked boulders.

"I know I do." Orman paused at the summit. "Felt it vibrate in my hand, heard your mother's whisper."

Kallon stopped again, just short of the plateau. "Heard her voice?"

"Come," said Orman. He shuffled away.

Kallon crested Mount Krag. Atop the plateau he circled slowly, admiring Leland's marbled mountaintops. But the nearest peaks were tattered and shabby, wearing their fissures as a threadbare cloak on a failing king. In the distance, mountains slanted like ancient gravestones. Had these peaks always been so feeble? Had he only just truly noticed?

Then his eyes found Mount Gore, Leland's tallest. This was the heart of the land, and the very center of the mountain chain. No fissures marred this bold crest. Blue-green firs blanketed its slopes, and wisps of cottony fog meandered lazily about its shoulders. It seemed the last bastion against the creeping death slowly overtaking Leland Province.

Mount Gore was also the chosen place for the meetings of the Dragon Council. At least, it once was. Kallon couldn't help but wonder if it were still true. Perhaps the leaders of each tribe were meeting there even now. Maybe they gathered, circled in the stone arena, discussing matters of dragons. Things with which Kallon no longer concerned himself.

"You should be leader, not Blackclaw," said Orman, near Kallon's shoulder. Kallon's eyes darted to the wizard's face. Orman made no movement; he only stared out past the gaunt mountains toward Gore.

"Stop doing that," Kallon said.

"What? Speaking?" Orman arched a single, bristled brow.

"Reading my thoughts."

"Stop thinking so loudly, then."

Show-off wizard. Kallon turned toward Orman's dilapidated hut. Thick slices of oak trunks were stacked vertically for its walls, and were held together with what smelled like red clay and willow sap. It seemed hardly big enough for the man to turn around in, and the thatch roof listed sideways, as though awaiting the help of a brisk wind to slide it to the ground. Orman's home had looked exactly the same for as long as Kallon could remember.

Outside, glass jars and clay pots and silver chalices lined a granite table, each filled with colorful shards of crystals. Below the table, in its shadow, other knobby crystals of red and brown were partially buried.

Kallon searched for a new scent, but didn't find one, so he moved to the blue and green cylinders bathing in a fragile current of water behind Orman's hut. "Where is your stream?"

"Nearly gone. Just as the rest of the water of Leland."

Kallon stabbed his tongue into the cool water. It still tasted sweet.

"Bah!" Orman batted at Kallon's tongue. "Dragon spit on my crystals! Now I'll have to clear them again." He mumbled fitfully as he spun the cylinders in the streambed to point them north. "Stop mucking about!"

"Where is my stone? I want to hear this voice you say is my mother's."

"*Your* stone?"

"If it was my mother's, it is mine. She would want it so."

"Yes. Well, I'm sure you're right about that. Wait here. And don't touch anything."

Kallon rested back on his haunches to wait. As he did, the back of his head collided into a dangling string of clear crystals hanging from the eaves of Orman's roof. They crashed and squawked like a flock of maybirds. He glanced to Orman.

Orman stopped in his tracks, and his shoulders tightened. But he didn't look back. He simply sighed, and continued into his tiny home.

"How did you find the stone after all this time?" Kallon called.

"Had a dream," Orman said, emerging from the hut with a deep purple crystal that dangled from a cord in his weathered hand. Kallon's breath caught. It was his mother's stone. It had to be. He remembered it.

"A dream?" Kallon asked. "After all these years you just had a dream?"

"Not any dream. I called for it." Orman sandwiched the crystal between his palms. He closed his eyes. "The wind has been rushing east to west, scaling down the mountainside with a message I can not hear. My human ears try, but they can not hear."

"But the stone—"

"The message is for you, Kallon Redheart. Made for your ears." Orman's eyes opened. "I called for a dream to help me understand, and I dreamed of your mother's linking stone. This stone."

Kallon poked a claw at the top of the crystal where it jutted up from Orman's hands. "Where did you find it?"

"In the boughs of a Dandria."

Kallon blinked. "A wishing tree? There have been no wishing trees in our woods since before I was born. Not since the Great Fire."

"There is one now." Orman narrowed one eye, and craned his wobbly neck toward Kallon's snout. "How long since you visited your parent's graves?"

His words were a fist to Kallon's gut. Kallon winced.

"If you had been recently, you would have found the tree for yourself. It grows wild and strong from your mother's grave."

The emotions he'd fought to control threatened once more. How could he visit when the very thought of doing so shuddered his scales and wrenched itself like a spear through his ribs?

He stared at the ground, unable to face Orman's heavy gaze.

"How it came to be in the boughs, I don't know," Orman continued. "Except to guess that it lay near the ground so long without being discovered that your mother took it upon herself to try to reclaim it. Only Dandrias grow so quickly, and so tall. The cord was wrapped around a fist of a branch, as though pushing it toward the sky for your mother to reach."

"Stop it!" Kallon snapped out his wings, unable to hear any more about his mother as though she were still alive, still thinking and feeling. "A tree grows where it will with no help from anyone. She is dead, Orman." He thrust out his claw to snatch the stone from the wizard. "Send no more birds to me. Unless you intend me to snack."

With that, he plunged off the side of the mountain, swerved up and away, and left Orman and the memories far below.

CHAPTER SIX

"Go take these mugs to Jaspar. He's been complaining for a month we've got too many leakin'." Rusic slid a basket of wooden cups into Riza's arms.

She bumped open the kitchen door with her backside, and carried the basket toward the bar. "Jaspar, I've got some new mugs."

Jaspar startled, and spun to face her. "Thanks. Just put 'em there."

She squinched up an eye at the bartender. "What's that behind your back?"

"This? Oh, I was just testing one of the leaky ones." He set a mug down hard, and ale sloshed onto his hand. "It seems fine after all."

"I don't know about that. Looks like some ale leaked onto your mouth. You've got a little foam, just there." She pointed toward his top lip.

He scowled, and batted his thumb at it. "A man gets thirsty, ye know!"

She grinned. "Well, now that you have new mugs,

you ought to stop going through so much more ale than usual. Unless, of course, the keg starts giving you trouble." She leaned toward the ale keg and poked at the spigot. "Looks sturdy, but you never can tell."

Jaspar snapped his bar rag at her.

She squealed, and hopped back, just missing a sting to her thigh.

"Haven't ye got some potatoes to peel, or something?" he asked, but he was smiling.

"Peeled and boiled," said Rusic, as he squeezed his girth through the kitchen door. "Soup's hot. And the whole kitchen's gleamin' like I haven't seen since I bought the place." He pointed at Riza. "How long ye been workin' here now?"

"A little over a week," she said.

"That so?" Rusic scratched his orange-red chin stubble. "Seems I haven't seen ye leave the place. Not that I'm complaining, mind ye. Ye've worked harder 'n I can afford to pay ye for."

"I like to stay busy. I don't mind."

"Still. If ye don't get out every now and again, the stale air poisons ye. Look at Jaspar. He used to have all his hair."

"Ha!" Jaspar scooped up his mug, and waved it toward Rusic's wide belly. "At least I don't have to sleep in my boots."

Rusic laughed, and slapped his hands against his gut. "That's just good food, and good lovin'. I store up for when famine strikes."

Jaspar guffawed, splashing ale down his apron.

"You been without a female longer than Lam Ferson's old ram!"

Riza snickered, and inched backward. "I'll just be in the kitchen."

"Oh, no, ye don't." Rusic caught her by the shoulders and led her around the end of the bar. "Yer goin' to gather me up some rosemary, and get some fresh air. There's a whole mess of it near Frog Boulder, past Jemiah Rode's pig farm."

"But that's in the woods."

"Aye. And yer not goin' to show up for work tomorrow morning. I can't pay ye for all yer extra work, but I can give ye a day off. Now scoot."

She resisted his pushing hands. "Why can't I get the rosemary tomorrow?"

"Yer missing the point of a day off."

"But I don't need a day off. There'll be more daylight left if I go tomorrow."

"Ye'll go now, cause yer boss is tellin' ye." Rusic patted her backside. "Off ye go."

"But—"

"And I don't want to see ye tomorrow."

She looked at Jaspar, pleading silently for his help. He shrugged, his blonde-white brows arching. Then she stared out the door into the afternoon. She tried to talk herself out of the apprehension creeping over the backs of her arms. She was a big girl. She could do this. She took a deep breath, and bolted out the door.

§

Kallon lay listlessly on the floor of his dusty cave, staring at the crystal in his paw. His chin hung to the ground, and each breath swirled tiny eddies in the powder near his nostrils. He felt empty, utterly alone and miserable.

Staring at the crystal only made things worse. He'd tried all afternoon to conjure a whisper from his mother, but the linking stone only sat on his palm like a withered twig, unmoving and lifeless. Why he'd bothered trying was beyond him. It seemed each time he finally accepted his loneliness, something came along to peel off a layer of scum from his murky heart, and stir up the shadowy depths. Though, this time, he reminded himself, he'd done the peeling all on his own. He'd dared to believe in the stone. He'd dared to try. Now he wallowed in the muddy heartache of disappointment.

Something scuffled outside. He lifted his chin. A limb rustled, and leaves scraped against stone. Someone was dragging vines away from the opening of his cave! His nostrils flared. A warning growl vibrated his muzzle.

"Hello?" A squeaking human voice jarred him to his feet. In all the years since his father's death, no human but Orman had ever tracked him to his cave. He was too surprised to think. Instinct lunged him toward the opening, and he bellowed. Heat sizzled from his jaws.

The human screamed, and in the dark distance at the back of his brain, he recognized the sound of it. He skidded to a halt.

"Kallon!" cried the voice.

He snapped his mouth shut. He scowled out into the hazy twilight. "Who knows my name?"

"It's me, Riza!"

He poked out his head to find the human female crouched near the ground, her arms over her head. He snorted, and she lifted her face.

"Don't be angry. I'm sorry to bother you, but please don't be angry." She blinked wide eyes at him. Tears welled, and then slipped silently down her cheeks.

Kallon thought suddenly of a delicately ruffled dayblossom shrinking into its stem for the night. He was seized with the impulse to dry the human's tears with his knuckle, and draw her inside to safety. But he didn't. He was so shocked by his own thoughts, he couldn't move. "You smell different."

"I do?"

"You snuck up on me."

"I did?"

Kallon nodded.

The human drew the back of her hand across her cheek, and a sprig of something dropped to the ground.

He realized her lap was full of greenery. "What's that?"

"Rosemary." She offered a fistful.

Kallon stretched his nose toward her hand. The rosemary smelled of the forest, only sweeter, and of the rain, only warmer. It was this that masked her scent.

"Why are you here?" he asked.

"I was too far from home when it started getting

dark."

"So?"

"I didn't want to be in the woods at night."

"Why not?"

"Because...well, because the dark frightens me."

"Don't I frighten you?"

She swallowed hard. She nibbled her bottom lip. Then she gave a tiny nod. "Yes. But not as much as the dark."

"Were you followed?"

"No. I don't think so. No one knows where I am."

"Good." He watched her wrap a sprig of rosemary around her finger. Then he pulled back into the cave. "Should have gone home. You can't stay."

"Wait!" Her scuffling feet followed him. "I won't make a sound. You won't even know I'm here."

"I already know you're here."

"Well, you'll forget I'm here, then."

"Was in the middle of something important." He was still in a sour mood, and eager to get back to feeling sorry for himself.

"Is it something I can help with?" she asked. "I can help you with what you were doing, and you can help me by letting me stay. Like friends do for each other."

Kallon swiveled his head, and frowned into her pale face. "I am not your friend."

She stiffened. Her emerald skirt, tucked up into a makeshift basket, slipped from her fingers, and rosemary sprigs dropped to the floor. She blinked at them, and sniffled. Then she sighed, and knelt to scoop them back up.

Something about her silence made him realize that his words had somehow hurt her. He shouldn't care about that, and didn't want to care. But inside his head, a voice nagged at him to apologize. Apologize for what? What had he done, except be honest? He wasn't her friend, and wouldn't be her friend, and didn't want her company!

So why did he feel as though he ought to say something nice? Maybe she was like Orman. Maybe she could read his thoughts and could tug at his feelings. "Stop doing that," he said, suddenly angry.

She paused in reaching for the last piece of rosemary. She withdrew her hand.

"Not that!" he said.

"What, then?" She stared up at him with frightened eyes.

Her expression sent him over the edge. "That!"

He snorted at her. Rosemary fronds shot from her lap as she scuffled backward in the dust like a shiny green beetle. He turned his back to her. "Just leave me alone. I want to be alone."

"Please, Kallon, I won't make a sound. I won't even breathe. Just don't send me out into the dark."

"...please."

The second plea came as a whisper. His scales bristled as he spun around to stare into the human's face.

That second sound was not her voice. It was someone else's. A voice he recognized.

"Why do you do this?"

The human hunched against the wall. "Kallon, you're scaring me!"

"...scaring me."

Again came the whisper of a second voice. From the girl's hand.

"Open your fist," he said, more anxious now than angry.

"What?"

"Open it!" He grasped her tiny hand and forced open her fingers. She held the linking stone. It had whispered, twice, in his mother's voice. "Wha-? How?" he tried to ask.

The girl stared down at the purple crystal as though seeing it for the first time. "What is that? What did I do?" She looked from his face back to the crystal. "It must have been on the floor. I don't remember picking it up."

Kallon suddenly felt too exhausted to hold himself up. He lumbered back a few steps, but the stone held his gaze. He was transfixed.

"Kallon? What is it? What's happening?" The girl tossed the crystal with all the disgust of tossing a squashed bug.

When the crystal hit the floor, Kallon's mind returned, along with his anger. He glared at her. "You do have magic. You're trying to make me help you."

"I don't know magic. I don't even know what just happened."

"Stop lying. You're using my mother's stone to trick me."

"I don't know what you're talking about! I didn't come here to trick you. I came here because I thought you would help me." She pushed to her feet, and batted at the dust on her skirt. "I was obviously wrong. Forgive me for thinking you had a kind bone in your body." She stomped toward the cave opening. And stopped.

"So go," he said.

She peered at him over her shoulder. Her voice trembled. "I can't."

"You can't walk two steps?"

"Maybe you could go with me."

"No. I don't go near the village anymore."

She turned, her hands twisting against her dress. Her eyes reminded him of the panicked stare of a doe as he swooped down for dinner.

He groaned.

"Just until dawn?" she asked.

"First tell me how you made the stone whisper."

"What stone?"

He narrowed his eyes. Then he pointed to the crystal near her feet.

"But I didn't hear anything," she said. "I didn't even know I was holding that thing."

"I think you are tricking me now. Again."

She walked toward him, and sighed so heavily he could taste her breath. "I only want to borrow a very small portion of the floor so I don't have to go out into the dark. Don't you see? If I have to go out there I'm afraid I'll…"

"Afraid you'll what?"

"I'm just afraid. Please don't make me go."

He wished he could reach inside her mind to find the truth. All he had was her word. And what good was the word of a human?

Then he felt her hand against his chest. Something passed between them. Hesitation. A shared breath. He pulled away, and moved toward the deepest part of the cave. "Not one sound. Not one."

He didn't even hear her settle. He strained to hear her breathe, but even that was lost to him. At first, he wondered if she finally did leave, except he sensed her there somewhere. She was a grain of sand stuck in his claw, and the more he shifted to get away from her, the more aware of her he became.

Finally, he resigned himself to her presence. He'd suffered through it before; he could do it again, just this once.

§

Fordon Blackclaw stared down from the alcove window of his personal quarters. Life carried on in the valley below. Torches flickered like orange stars. He could even hear the low rumble of dragon feet and the faint murmur of dragon voices from the distant village.

It was the oldest of all dragon communities; established eons ago, before grubby human hands began snatching land. The place had no formal name, all dragons knew of it simply as the "mountain village", though through the years, humans had come to call it

Wing Valley. It had a poetic sound that translated nicely in dragonspeak, and, considering the quality of human learning, the name was more complimentary than insulting.

The insults came later. Dragon history was full of them, beginning with the initial pact between dragon and human creatures to strive toward common goals. What dragon ever had anything in common with humans? How it ever came to pass that dragons allowed themselves into service beneath their puny overseers was mystifying.

He'd never understood how the position of vassal became one of respect. Where was the honor in fighting for humans during their childish conflicts? It only proved how feeble the creatures were, willing to risk life and limb of dragon, but not themselves. Even when humans weren't fighting, which was rare, highly skilled dragon warriors allowed themselves to become glorified bodyguards to venurs and wizards, and for what? For the ownership of tribal lands that belonged to dragons anyway!

It had only been a matter of time until humans abused the pact, perverting it to serve their own needs. More and more dragons became lost in battles, and fewer and fewer tribes received land payments. Blackclaw had seen it coming, even as a fledgling, though his warnings went unheeded. Recently, those dragons who had received long-overdue deeds had discovered too late they now owned territories emptied of prey and water, stripped of valuable crystals, and reduced to rubble.

Many dragons had been forced to abandon their territories. Tribes were beginning to band together into new, blended lines. So what had all the talk of honor gotten them? What had hundreds of years of loyal service rewarded them? A struggle to survive.

A knock broke through his ponderings. He smelled a fresh kill from the opposite side of the oak door, and knew it was Whitetail. "Enter," he said, and swung his gaze to the wispy dragon that shuffled in. "It will not be long, now, Whitetail. Dragonkind is finally sharing their anger aloud. Soon, they will come to realize what I have always known."

"Humans should serve dragons. You are not the first leader to suggest this."

"I am the first leader, however, who will make it come to pass."

Whitetail offered out a wooden tray that held a small bear carcass. "Humans will not easily comply."

Blackclaw snorted in amusement. "And what should this mean to me? Do you suppose this bear worried about the ants crawling across his dinner?" He wrested the tray from his advisor's grip, tossed the carcass to the stone floor, and pounced. The snap of bear bone echoed against the high granite ceiling.

"Shall I retrieve the circlet while you finish?" asked Whitetail.

Blackclaw grunted his response.

Whitetail shuffled toward the far end of the room. Beside Blackclaw's feather-stuffed sleeping roll stood a carved wooden table. A small but sturdy trunk squatted on top of the table. Whitetail opened the lid. Inside, golden headwear was drenched by torchlight, and a ruby crystal flashed. The Circlet of Aspira.

Blackclaw shoved away his meal, and lapped at his palms. "Give it to me."

Whitetail obeyed. Blackclaw delicately held the tiny crown. "If only I had mastered this years ago, Whitetail, all my dreams would already be history."

"What you lack in magic, you make up for in determination," said Whitetail.

Blackclaw swept his paw around the opulent chamber. "All things I have now came by my own power; things I have wished for since my earliest memories." He leaned toward Whitetail. "Have you ever wanted anything so deeply that the smell of your wish tickled your nostrils? Caused a rumble in your gut?"

"Yes, sir. Indeed."

Blackclaw nodded. "I will lead the dragons into a new era, Whitetail. Magic or no magic, it will come to pass." He held up the circlet. "Magic, however, would be quicker. I will not give up."

He pressed his thumb against his razor-sharp incisor. Then he smeared his blood across the face of the red crystal, and closed his eyes. He focused on his smoldering desire for control. He gritted his teeth, letting the wish consume him until he could feel it ignite in his heart. Vivid images welled up like smoke.

In his mind, shadows of angry dragons swept over farmlands, spitting flames and destroying. Humans fled, crying in anguish, begging for mercy. Those who did not submit were forced into chains and led away to suffer. They would die, in the end. All humans would die in the end, if necessary.

The circlet began to vibrate.

Stabbing pain shot through his wrists and sliced up into his shoulders. "I will not let go!" he shouted, as he always shouted, and held the circlet to his breast with all his strength.

A sudden blast of cold wind slammed into his spine and nearly sent him sprawling.

"The circlet will grant my desires!"

The wind redoubled, swirling into a tornado that tore his bedding from the floor, ripped scrolls from shelves in the room, and knocked Whitetail off his feet.

"Release the circlet!" cried Whitetail, clambering to brace on a wall torch.

"No! It is close! I can feel it working!" He heard a crack of bellowing thunder. Was it outside, or in the very room? He glanced toward the window.

Just then, the circlet was snatched by the howling wind.

"No!" He dove for it, but it dipped, bounced against his fist, and clattered to the floor. All went quiet.

He stood panting, and stared at the tiny crown of gold. Then he surged toward the window, eyes scanning the skies for dragon mobs demanding justice. No one. He searched the ground. Only the twinkling torchlight of the dragon village met his gaze. Echoes of dragon laughter found his ears.

Another failure!

He roared, and stomped toward the crown, scooping it onto a claw. "Imposter!" He spun to face his trembling advisor. "You have fooled me, Whitetail! This is only an imposter!"

Whitetail pressed his muzzle to the floor. "Forgive me, Your Eminence, but I assure you it is the circlet."

"Liar!" Blackclaw lobbed the circlet toward Whitetail's lowered head, and it careened against his bony skull with a crack. "The wizard tricked you. Redheart tricked you! It must be why he put up so little fight. He wanted us to take this one. The false one."

Suddenly it made sense. He smiled. That tricky Red. Blackclaw could almost admire the ruse. It had worked. He wasn't easily fooled, but Redheart and the wizard had managed it. "I am almost embarrassed that the truth has only come to me now. After all these years."

"Leader Blackclaw," said Whitetail, his voice muffled by the cold floor, which now had scrolls and feathers and ash scattered across it. "I must assure you yet again that the circlet in your possession is authentic." He lifted his chin. "It was tested by our own mage, and verified. I have witnessed its power."

Blackclaw seized Whitetail's puny horns and yanked him to his feet. "Of course it has power, you idiot. It is an excellent forgery." Then, with calm grace and majesty, he released the white dragon, bent to retrieve the circlet, and offered it out. "Now. You will find this wizard, extract the information concerning the authentic circlet, and kill him."

"And if he has no information?"

Blackclaw sighed. Why did he have to do all of the thinking? "If he claims he has no information, he is lying. If you cannot force it from him creatively, consider his fate to be your own. Understand?"

Whitetail nodded. He took the circlet, but did not meet Blackclaw's eyes.

Blackclaw poked him in the nose. "What is it, Whitetail?"

"Suppose the wizard has another vassal who comes to his defense?"

"I'm failing to see your concern."

"We barely managed to explain Bren Redheart's demise. How would we explain yet another dragon death?"

Blackclaw shook his head. "You did well in numbers in school, didn't you, Whitetail? Not too clever with creative thinking, though." He turned for the door. "The dragon slayer is already on his way here. Use him again. This time, though, do it without the mess." Then he pointed to the floor. "Speaking of mess, get this place in order. I will sleep across the hall tonight."

After a pause, Whitetail called from behind him. "The wizard's name was Thistleby, wasn't it?"

"It was," Blackclaw replied.

"Forgive me again, Your Eminence, but is this not an extreme measure? We both agree that your plan is working. I do not see how you even need the circlet anymore."

Blackclaw stopped. He turned to glare. "Whether the wizard leads us to the actual circlet is no longer the point. No one makes a fool of me, Whitetail. The old man will pay for the years of pain I have wasted."

"Of course," said Whitetail. "You are right, as always." He bowed his face so low to the floor that his breath created two pools of steam on the marble.

"Now get up," Blackclaw said. "Watching you grovel makes my back ache. Rouse me when you hear from the dragon hunter, but not a moment sooner." He slammed the door.

§

Sometime in the night, Kallon awoke, startled. Had he been dreaming? He could never remember his dreams, if he had them. But something had disturbed him. He sniffed and reached out, patting the ground, searching for the girl. He touched her leg.

She made a muffled little breathing sound.

Reassured, he settled comfortably again, and closed his eyes.

CHAPTER SEVEN

When Kallon awoke, the high morning sun had already baked the cave air. He wheezed, his thirsty tongue flopping. He wanted water. A lot of water. He shifted his weight to climb to his feet.

He felt movement. Only then did he remember the human, and he glanced back to find her lying against his rump. She was hugging his tail, which encircled her like a vine. He flicked his tail tip to budge her loose. She stirred, and then tightened her grip.

"Human," he said as gently as he could, so he wouldn't startle her. "Release me."

"Mm?" She opened an eye.

"Release me." He curled around to give her shoulder a light bump with his snout. "Going to drink some water. Do not want to drag you."

"Oh." She smiled and sat up, and rubbed her palms against her face. "What time is it?"

He unwound his tail from her legs. "The sun is high and very hot. Hotter than usual."

"I dreamed I was in the tavern kitchen, and the cooking fire caught my dress and was trying to eat me. Where are you going to get some water?"

"My lake."

She stood. "You have a whole lake all to yourself?"

"Not to myself. Anyone who wants to drink can drink, or swim."

"Can I?"

Kallon eyed her. "Any dragon." He left her there, and sleepily wandered toward the daylight. "The lake is high above my cave."

The human followed. She shielded her eyes as she gazed up and over the rock face. "A lake in the mountains? It must be beautiful."

"It is. It's my favorite sleeping place, besides the cave, of course." Kallon stretched his stiff wings. He didn't usually sleep so late in the morning, and his bones complained. But he felt more awake, and somehow more alive, than usual.

The girl gave an awkward smile. "I don't suppose I could climb up there."

"Unlikely," he said.

"If I had wings like you I could see it."

"Yes. But you have none."

"If I had wings like you I could fly just about anywhere I wanted." She jutted out her hands from her sides, and closed her eyes. "It must be wonderful to fly."

"Wonderful?" He hadn't thought of it that way. Natural, of course. Necessary. But wonderful? He pondered. "Feels right and good to taste the sun in my teeth and feel it bubble up like water beneath my scales."

The girl's eyes opened. She smiled. A strange look came over her face, and she seemed almost to glow. "I wish I could fly."

He lowered his snout, studying her. He gave her a quick sniff, searching for the source of her radiance. Apparently, only her face was affected. Did he look like that when he thought of flying? Maybe he used to, but not in a very long time. He probably didn't look like that when he thought about anything. But to never fly?

He couldn't imagine how it would feel to be stuck to the earth forever. "You'll never get any closer to the sky," he said.

"Unless I was a dragon. Or knew one."

"You know me. I'm a dragon."

She clasped her hands and squealed, "You would take me with you?"

He couldn't believe he didn't see that coming. "Now…I didn't say that. The lake is a long way up."

"I don't mind. I'm not afraid."

"It's just a lake. They're all the same."

"I haven't seen a lake in a long time." She reached for his side. "Do I climb? How do I…?"

He leaned away. "Human, I was only arguing that you do know a dragon. I didn't mean to invite you. Not now. Not today."

"But I'm here now, and I might not get another chance."

"I don't think it's a good idea."

She frowned, and her eyes drifted toward the

ground. "Oh. I see."

"So. You understand?"

"Yes." She nodded. "I understand."

"It's not that I don't want you with me," he tried to explain.

"Yes, it is."

Actually, she was right. That was exactly it. "But you understand. I like to be alone."

"Yes, I said I understand." She crossed her arms.

"Maybe another day—"

"You're not going to take me flying, ever." She moved toward the trees. "Thank you for letting me stay with you last night. I won't bother you any more."

She disappeared behind a gray elm trunk, and he watched her go. He wanted to fly, and tried to, but his feet were boulders. Even his wings sagged. Somehow, she'd sucked the enjoyment right out of it. He finally grunted. "Very well. Just a short trip."

Out popped her smiling face from behind the tree. "Really?"

"Hurry, before I change my mind." He offered his foreleg. "Climb here, then to my shoulders. Mind my scales, I don't like them pushed the wrong way." She came around to his leg, and stared at it as though afraid to touch it. "Change your mind?" he asked.

"No." She pressed one foot to his leg, then hopped up to bring the other beside it, and wobbled atop his knee. Her small hands scrambled for a hold against his neck, twisting his scales.

"Ouch! Human, take care!"

"Sorry." She pressed against his shoulder, and managed to swing one leg up and over his neck. She felt like a thousand ants across his back, crawling and nipping. His jaw tightened against the reflex to buck her off. Then she settled. Her arms gripped around his neck. "There. I'm ready."

"Hold tight."

"I am."

He fanned out his wings, then launched straight up. The girl gave no sound, but her arms squeezed tighter. He tilted, getting accustomed to her weight, and tried to stay as even as he could while still banking. Fat boulders and strewn rocks grew smaller beneath him. He leveled off and veered for the distant firs.

Of course the mountains looked different from this height, as they always did. From the ground, they were towering peaks. Impassable. But from up here, he could look down at them and soar right over. The rounded mountains were tamed, and only his shadow struggled across the crags.

"Kallon," came the girl's voice near his ear. "It's incredible."

He'd almost forgotten she was there. "Not afraid?"

"No. It's so beautiful." Her voice sounded strained, like she was trying to catch her breath.

He slowed. It wasn't so distracting, after all, having the girl along for the ride. He turned east, deciding to take the long way around.

"Look there!" she said as her weight shifted. "I see a tiny river. That must be why the trees here are so green.

So many other mountains are all rock and dead trees. Why is that?"

"No rain here for almost two years. Leland Province is turning into a desert."

"My home village has been dry, too, but it does rain. What happened to your rain?"

"Don't know. Orman says the magic here is as dry as the meadows. That something is killing the mountains."

"How sad. It's like a quilt, cut into squares of all browns and grays. Oh, except over there." She sucked in a breath. "Kallon, look. There are huge holes everywhere."

He tilted to look. Usually, he pretended he didn't see them. Looking now, his gut clenched. "That used to be some of the best hunting land around. My father taught me there how to swoop down onto a boar without making a sound."

"What happened to it?"

He sighed. "Let's get to the lake."

"Wait," she said. "I want to see. Can you go lower?"

He didn't want to. He didn't want to be reminded of how things used to be, but he dropped to go closer.

He slowed over the first gaping crater. It was a hole that could easily swallow him, and several more dragons, beside. The black dirt had been dredged and left for dead, and had decayed to a pale brown. The hole was so deep, he couldn't see the bottom.

"Who did this?" the girl asked.

"Humans."

"But why?"

"For the crystals," he said. "This land was given to a tribe of Yellows, but not before humans scraped it empty of anzanite."

"What good is land that's been destroyed like that?"

He snorted. "No good. No good at all anymore." He pumped his wings to move on, and pointed. "Over there, they found silphire. That used to be a wide, green valley."

She made a choked sort of sound, and he took some satisfaction in that. "It's so ugly," she said. "Big brown holes all over."

He swooped up high and turned his back. His thirst drove him faster toward the lake. "Not so many holes here as the land past Orman's side of the mountain."

"Who's Orman? Oh! Look! I see the lake! It's so calm and sparkly, like a big blue pillow on a green fir bed."

The thrill in her voice made him smile. He circled the lake once, giving her a long, full view.

"I hope the humans never come up here for crystals," she said.

Her words caught him off-guard. Something in the way she spoke about her own people in the third person. He descended, shaking his head. "The mountains already belong to the dragons. No human leader- what do you call them?"

"Venurs," said Riza.

"No human venur would dare challenge to take our mountains," Kallon said. He landed gently on a bank of soft grass. "My sleeping spot."

She scrambled against him, kicking his ribs as she climbed to drop off. She dangled, then let go, and thudded to both feet, but flopped back onto her bottom. "Oof!"

"You hurt?"

"No," she said, giggling. "Just clumsy." She stood, and brushed at the back of her dress. "Are you going to swim?" Her cheeks were red, and she panted as though she'd just done the flying, instead of him.

"You look tired. Like you can't breathe."

"Not tired. But I was having a hard time getting my breath. I'm better now. It was the most amazing thing that's ever happened to me."

That glow was in her face again. He liked it. He gave her another sniff.

She grinned, and darted toward the water. "Come on. I want to see you swim."

§

Jastin and Blade trudged across his landlord's wilted field. The morning heat was already oppressive, making Jastin feel as though he was squashed into Blade's saddle and held there by a sweltering, invisible hand. "Hotter than blazes," Jastin mumbled, and yanked at the ties of his leather vest. He was curling around to stuff it into saddlebag when Blade snorted.

"Fizzitmeallenwhum," said the horse.

Jastin stared. Were hallucinations the first sign of heat stroke? Instead of pushing his vest into a saddlebag, he pulled out a canteen of water. He gulped a few times and then splashed a handful over his face.

He dug the heel of his hand at his eyes. He stared at Blade again.

His mount swung his head to look back at him, dark eyes bored.

"Thirsty?" Jastin asked, and offered out the canteen.

Blade just lowered his head to nose around in a patch of crispy grass.

"No, didn't think so." Jastin watched a moment longer anyway, eyes narrowed, until Blade stamped a hoof, as eager to get moving as Jastin was. "Fine, let's go. Just let me do all the talking from now on, eh?" He reached to replace his canteen.

"Fizzitmeallenwhum," said Blade.

Jastin launched from the saddle and landed on both feet. "What in the—?" He wrapped his fingers around Blade's bridle and glared into his face. "I don't go for any nonsense. No horse of mine is going to blither like an idiot."

"Uppindesdurance?" Blade's throat worked like he was going to throw up.

Jastin's face involuntarily contorted. He backed up. Then he realized he recognized a word. "Durance? Are you asking about Durance?" Then another thought came to him. He recognized the voice. Far from a guttural bass like his mighty stallion should have, if the animal really could speak, instead the voice was soft soprano, and just taking on the huskiness of age.

"Layce Phelcher? Is that you?" Jastin moved closer again and ran his hand over Blade's snout, searching. "Are you in there?"

"Yes!" Her voice squealed with excitement, which was a pitifully demeaning thing, coming from the mouth of a warrior's mount.

"What are you doing?"

"Ieeetanowhumpwhumpinnarance!"

Jastin rolled his eyes. "I can't understand a blasted thing you're trying to say. Come out and talk or let me get on with my plans."

"Cannomoutimere. Oweringsforvorham."

"Vorham? Is he trying to contact me?"

"Oweringsforvorham."

Jastin growled. "Blasted wizards. Can't ever use conventional means for anything." He led Blade to the line of trees where the field met the dying woods, and tied him off. "I'll be right back," he said, patting Blade's rump. Then he reached for his leather vest again and slipped his arms through.

"Oweringsforvorham!" Layce squealed.

"I'm coming, I'm coming." Jastin felt around in the seam of his vest for the lump of crystal fastened inside. "Can't remember how the thing—"

His legs tingled. His head swarmed with trapped bees, buzzing so loud inside his ears that his head wanted to burst. He clamped his free hand to his forehead, and was just about to shout, when all went dark and silent.

The ground felt hard and smooth beneath his boots. When he looked down, he saw himself illuminated in orange light that rose up like a haze from the hefty crystal in the floor. The familiar scent of dank stone slowly eked its way into his consciousness. Linen clothing rustled a few feet away.

"Jastin?" came Layce's surprised voice. "What are you doing here?"

His eyes adjusted enough to see the outline of the woman's robe. He moved toward her. "You said something about Vorham. I thought he needed me."

Layce snorted and tugged his arm. She led him into the adjoining room, which blinded him with torchlight.

He squinted, trying to recognize the place. Purple velvet hung like thick walls, sectioning the room into three areas. One area held a large mound of purple padding that looked so soft it begged to be slept on.

In another, leather books appeared to have reproduced and mutinied the few shelves meant to contain them. Tomes were stacked in crooked piles atop the shelves and beneath the shelves, and the piles were advancing across the floor toward a puny willow desk that huddled among the mess like a defeated prey awaiting when its time, too, would come.

Jastin thought he'd been in every room in Riddess castle, from the high towers to the foulest dungeon, but this room he didn't know.

"Of course you don't know it, I've never had you in

my bedroom."

"You've never offered," he said.

Layce propped a fist on a bony hip. Her black hair was pulled into a high ponytail that lagged aside as she stared at him. Her face was just starting to lose the battle with age, but the soft blue of her robe matched the soft blue of her eyes, and Jastin often found himself staring more at her eyes than her wrinkles. "Why did you come back?" she asked.

"I told you, I heard you mention Vorham, and I thought you needed me to."

She shook her head, one hand waving. "I was just checking in on his behalf." Then she clasped her hands together. She smiled. "And it worked, didn't it? It's a tricky spell, the connection between amulets is so tenuous." She reached into the collar of her robe and drew out a chip of green stone tied to a leather thong. "Only the finest wizards can manage it." Her chin lifted.

Jastin eyed the necklace. "Was I supposed to understand what you were saying?"

"Of course!" She propped both fists on her hips now. "What's the point of long distance communication if there's no communicating going on?"

"I couldn't understand a blasted thing."

Layce blinked. She straightened her shoulders. "What are you saying?"

Jastin knew he didn't have to say it aloud.

Her face colored in like a blotchy, red tomato. "I'll have you know my father taught me everything he knew. The Phelcher name is synonymous with magic.

Great magic." She whirled and marched toward a purple curtain, threw it aside, and tugged a dusty tome from the top of a pile on the floor. "Must be the spell itself."

"Mm-hmm." Jastin considered teasing her about it, but he'd left Blade too long already, miles away in that dying province of Leland. He pressed his fingers to the back of his stiff neck and rolled his shoulders. "So, if there's nothing you need…"

Layce looked up from her book. At some point, she'd pinched a set of wire-rimmed spectacles to the bridge of her nose. Her blue eyes stared so enormously through them that from across the room he could see flecks of silver within the irises. "I did everything right, according to this. I just don't understand." She tapped a sinuous finger to her chin.

"It's not a scrying stone, is it? You haven't been watching me." Jastin clenched his jaw at the thought. "I wouldn't have agreed to any of this if that's so."

His brother-in-law, Vorham Riddess, had manipulated him into carrying a wistful crystal in his vest, and that was insulting enough. Jastin didn't trust magic any more than he trusted the creatures who wielded it, dragon or human.

"Well. Thank you very much." Layce sniffed. She slapped her book closed.

"Is it a scrying stone?" Jastin repeated, his face warming with anger.

She pursed her lips. She stood, leaning toward him, her eyes looming large and ridiculous through her lenses.

"Layce," he said, trying to sound patient but knowing he didn't.

"Oh, it's not a scrying stone, you big oaf." She plucked her spectacles from her nose and closed them in her fist. "It was just an experiment."

He didn't like that thought anymore than being watched. "I don't like surprises. If you've got any more 'experiments' planned, you'd better tell me right now."

"You take yourself so seriously. I suppose people have told you that."

"What other crystals have you hidden in my things?" He took a step toward her. He would throttle the information out of her if he had to.

"It isn't a healthy way to live, being so serious. In all the time I've worked here for your brother-in-law, I don't believe I've ever seen you smile." She looked right at him, with blue, blue eyes, wide and unblinking.

He felt a nudge somewhere in his mind. An impulse suggested itself, tempting him to grab her arm and wrench it behind her. At first he thought it was his own idea, because he'd already considered doing something similar, but the longer he stared into Layce's eyes, the more he sensed how unnatural it felt. As though she wanted him to do it.

If that were the case, he'd fight it, simply for spite. He held up his hands and turned his head. "I'm not going to hurt you, Layce. I just want an answer."

"Oh fiddle." The disappointment in her voice made him look back at her face. Her bottom lip poked out. "I wanted to try out the irritation crystal I've been working on. You were supposed to touch me and get a shock."

"You wanted me to hurt you?"

She huffed. "Of course not. But it was the only suggestion I thought you'd receive."

Now Jastin really did want to twist her arm behind her back. He clenched his hands, resisting, only to avoid the consequence of her irresponsible magic. "Don't ever get in my mind again."

"No, I didn't quite do it right, anyway. Hmm." She turned, reaching again for a book. "I'm sure I sequenced the descent right. The spell must have been transcribed incorrectly."

She'd been toying with him for so long his anger and surprise and confusion were all twisted together into a thick rope that choked his ability to think straight. He just wanted out of there, where his body and his mind were under his own control.

But first, he needed an answer. "What other crystals do you have in my things?"

She shook her head, finger drawing over parchment. "I won't know until I try a different sequence, of course." She closed the book. "Maybe I'm wearing too many at once. They may be interfering with each other."

"Layce!"

She startled, and looked over at him as though she'd forgotten he was there. "Oh. Oh, that. There aren't any more, just the one."

He didn't believe her.

"Would I lie to you?"

"I can't concentrate on what I need to do if I'm going to be worried about who's watching, or if the trees are going to break into a jig."

"I'm flattered! Only one wizard has ever been able to get a tree to dance. Though it was more of a sway, really." Layce reached her arms over her head, closed her eyes, and rocked left to right. "Legendary."

He didn't have much choice but to hope she was telling the truth. For a split second, he almost wished he did have magic to find out.

Her eyes popped open. "I could teach you. Theoretically. Though a person checking for honesty needs to be righteously honest himself, so, frankly, you'd be a real challenge."

"What's that supposed to mean?"

She sighed. "I could try to explain, but it would be like trying to tell a kutterbug that it's yellow, not brown. First, the kutterbug has to be taught what the color yellow is."

"Now you're calling me a bug?"

She shrugged, and inspected the ceiling.

"I make no excuses for what I do, or why I do it. I know what I am. That's more honesty than a lot of people can handle."

"Of course it is." Her gaze remained fixed on the ceiling.

Jastin groaned. Here he was, justifying himself to this loony wizard. She'd gotten him again, somehow. Time to cut his losses and get back to business. He turned once more from her doorway.

"You remember how to use the wistful crystal?" she called.

He stopped himself from snarling, but he did snap, "I'm not a child!"

When she didn't reply, he considered it a small victory. He stepped into the dark place off her bedroom and moved closer to the smooth lump of orange, glowing stone on the floor. "Just curious, but why did I come back to this room, instead of the place in the woods where you broke off the shard for me?"

She appeared in the doorway. "I had the origin stone dug up and brought here. The shard returns to wherever the origin stone is, and I felt safer guarding it." She looked down at her fingernails. "Not that I'm trustworthy, or anything."

"It's nothing personal."

"No, I know. Once you start trusting people, you might have to believe they could be sincere, which gives them actual merit. Soon, you'd have to completely rethink the color yellow."

"I've had enough lecturing for one day, thanks."

"So go on. You must be worried about your mare."

"He's a stallion."

"Whatever."

Jastin looked down at the orange stone and cringed. He could feel Layce smiling at him, but he wasn't amused. "You're going to make me say it, aren't you?"

She shuffled closer. "Oh, yeah."

"Fine. I don't remember how to use the crystal."

He refused to be embarrassed. He wouldn't let her have that.

"Just climb on, it's easy. Well, not as easy as returning. The shard does most of the work then, because it always wants to come back home, so to speak."

He stepped onto the stone. "Last time we went over this, I don't believe you mentioned the headache that tried to split my brain."

"Didn't I?" she blinked blue eyes and smiled.

"If Vorham asks, this never happened."

"I won't tell him if you won't. He'd be upset to find out my experiment got you off schedule."

"Not an easy man to work for. Why do you stay?"

Layce shrugged, her eyes going unfocused as she considered. Jastin guessed she considered it a lot. "Not many choices. Most venurs don't even keep wizards, with so few dragons to liaison."

"I don't know of any vassal dragons left here in Esra."

Layce shook her head. "No, but there are many dragons in the Leland Mountains, aren't there?"

Jastin didn't know why he was surprised, but his brows went up, anyway. "If you know why I'm going, why are you helping?"

She shrugged again, but her eyes came back into focus. "The future is guided by a hand much stronger than mine. I may not like the part I play, but I do it so I can see the end as it is meant to be."

Jastin nodded. "As it is meant to be."

Layce smiled. "You know, you got a look in your eyes just now that seems almost human. You should try that again sometime."

He let the remark go, and just shook his head. He gripped the crystal shard sewn into his vest. "Can we do this please?"

"Right. Just think pleasant thoughts about why you took the shard where you did. Picture it fondly, and it will whisk you back to the last place you used it."

"My horse is there."

"Good. Use that." She leaned toward him. "There's that look again. Twice in one conversation. Makes me see you a little differently."

Jastin closed his eyes and tried to picture Blade. He truly did want to be back there now.

"Makes me wonder if I was a little younger, and you a little older…" murmured Layce. "Well, not just older, but more mature, too. Gentler, and less selfish, maybe. In fact, if you could become an entirely different person…"

Her voice faded. His stomach wrenched, and he struggled to stay upright. The buzzing flies attacked his brain again, swarming violently and shuddering his head. Then he felt crunchy grass beneath his feet, and a loud, irritated whinny roused him to the present.

Blade pressed his muzzle against Jastin's shoulder, and Jastin gripped it to steady himself. "I told you I'd be right back."

Blade snorted.

The sound reminded him of Layce. He'd forgotten

to ask her where she'd put the stone that let her speak through the horse. He couldn't have that. He had to find the stone and destroy it. He pulled Blade's face close, and looked into his eyes. "Layce!"

"Yes?" came her voice through Blade's open mouth.

"Where's the stone you put on my mount?"

"Fizzitmeallenwhum," said the horse.

§

Kallon shot up from the lake and blasted a stream through his teeth. Water rained down like a thunderstorm, showering the lake, the shore, and the girl. She squealed and ran for cover under a tall elm.

"Not going to swim?" he asked.

She peered out from under leafy branches, suspicious. Then she smiled, and he felt an unexpected churn of warmth in his belly.

"I'd like to," she said. "But I don't want to ruin my dress."

"Can't remove it?"

Her face flared red. He loped out onto shore, and stuck his snout near her nose to get a better look. "Feel all right?"

"Feel fine." She smoothed her hair from her face.

"Thought you were enjoying yourself. Thought you were going to swim with me." He could hear the disappointment in his own voice, and was embarrassed by it. He looked away toward the water.

"I do want to," she said.

There was a long silence as he stared out onto the glassy surface of the sapphire lake. The air was as thick with heat as a forest fire. He was thirsty again, but somehow the thought of swimming had lost its appeal.

"Very well," came the girl's voice again. "Close your eyes."

"Close my eyes?"

"Yes, I'm going to jump in. Close your eyes."

He snorted, but he did so. "When do I open them?"

There was a tiny sound of splashing water, like a pebble striking the water's surface. "Now you can open them," she said.

He found the girl treading water. With a bleat, he charged toward her. Water careened off his chest as he plunged, then he dove headfirst.

He swam deep toward the bottom, beating his wings slowly to let the water above him settle. To let her wonder where he'd gone. When the water cleared, he spotted her waving legs, and rushed them. He blasted a stream as he did before, and jettisoned the girl straight up into the air.

She shrieked, arms and legs flailing. She arched high, higher than he meant to send her, and, still shrieking, she landed with an impressive splash. She went silent, and floated on the water like a wispy patch of fog.

He gulped. He called out as he paddled toward her, "Human? You all right?" No reply. She was facedown. He bumped her with his snout to turn her over.

"Human?"

"Boo!" She sprang at him, latched onto his neck, and erupted into laughter.

"I thought you were dead!"

She released him and pushed off to give him a stern look. "You were the one who sent me flying!" Then her expression fizzled, and she laughed again. "I fooled you."

Despite himself, a smile tugged at his lips. "You did." A quiet rumble worked its way out of his dusty lungs and exploded toward the sky. He laughed.

"Let's do that again," she said. "Except this time, I'm ready for you."

"All right," he said, and turned to plunge. "Here I come."

§

Hours later, Kallon hadn't even realized the whole had day had passed until the girl mentioned. Only then did he notice the fading daylight.

"I should be getting back," said the girl. "If I'm missing another night they might think something's happened to me." She hauled herself out of the water and lay on the shore.

"Who is they?"

"Rusic and Jaspar. Rusic owns the tavern where I work. Jaspar tends the bar." She stood, water cascading down her pale skin. Watching her walk, he realized how thin and fragile she really was. How did humans manage on their own?

"I'll take you as close to the village as I can. I can't be seen, though. Your village has not welcomed dragons for a long time."

"Why not?" she asked, as she stepped into her dress.

"Many human villages do not welcome dragons any more. They do not trust us. We do not trust them. It's the way of things."

"My village, I mean, my first village, the one where I grew up, would not welcome you. I don't even think they believe dragons still exist."

Kallon came onto shore, too. "That's why you were so terrified of me, in the beginning."

The girl lowered her chin. "Yes, I suppose that's why." She drew closer, and touched her cool hand to his leg. "I'm sorry."

He peered down into her face. His snout nearly brushed her nose, but she didn't step back or pull away. The little human didn't flinch or wrinkle her nose; she simply looked up at him with eyes the green of fir trees. He smiled.

"Why don't you ever call me Riza?" she asked.

"Hm?"

"You never use my name. You always call me 'Human'."

"But you are a human."

"Yes. But I have a name. Friends call each other by their names, not by…" She looked away, and reached out to climb onto him. "But, never mind. I forgot."

For a little while, Kallon had forgotten, too. It was nice to spend the afternoon with her, as much as it surprised him. But one day together did not make them friends.

He wouldn't let himself grow attached. He'd promised himself a long time ago not to care about anything so much that he couldn't bear to lose it. No, he dared not risk any friends. Not now. Not ever.

He crouched, prepared to launch. "Just hold tight," he said.

CHAPTER EIGHT

Riza ran through the trees, stumbling. The dark night had come too quickly, and she felt it wrapping itself around her shoulders, trying to suffocate her. She wished Kallon had delivered her closer to the village. Branches, harmless in the day, now curled like arthritic fingers for her hair and throat. She batted at them, trying very hard not to whimper like a terrified child.

Ahead, she saw a clearing. If it was farmland, it meant she was almost safe. Moonlight was bright there, reflected hard off the sun-baked land. She lunged toward the brightness.

A shadow met her in the patch of moonlight, but she saw it too late. She collided into a wall that whinnied and reared back, and knocked her down. She landed hard on her shoulder, wheezing.

"Whoa, Blade," said a familiar voice.

The trod of agitated hooves on dusty ground was joined by a dull thud of boots.

"What is this, a little field mouse?" A strong

hand tugged her to her feet. She met the eyes of Jastin Armitage. The curiosity that had softened his features disappeared. His dark brows wrinkled together. "A beggar mouse."

Riza pulled from his grasp. "I am not a beggar, and I am not a mouse." She pushed her hair from her face and turned away. His hand gripped her again, and he pulled her close.

"But where do you go?" His eyes turned to search the trees. "And from where do you come?"

"I was taking a walk. Let go of me."

He didn't let go. "Such a long walk, to have been gone all day."

"What do you mean? How do you know?"

"Your new boss was looking for you. He said you'd been missing all day."

"I have not been missing. Rusic is the one who told me to spend the day outside, so that's what I did. I like to walk." His gaze felt as heavy as if he'd pressed his hand to her face. She wanted to look away, but lifted her chin. "Let go of me."

He watched her a moment longer. Then he released her. "My apologies, milady." He lifted his foot to the stirrup and swung his leg to drop smoothly behind the saddle. "I'll see you safely home."

She was scooped up by his arm and deposited onto the leather seat before she could react. She gripped the saddle horn. "There's no need for this."

Secretly, she was relieved. Relief didn't last long though. He wrapped his arm around her belly and pressed his chest to her back.

"Hyup, Blade," he called past her ear. He snapped the reins, and swung his mount back around.

She shifted in the saddle and arched her shoulders to force space between them.

"I can't see around your hair," he said. He gathered her dark strands, and snaked them over her right shoulder with a gentleness that surprised her. Then he tugged off a glove, and ran his fingers again over her hair, across her shoulder to the tips. His touch spread a tickle across her scalp, and she bumped about in the saddle in awkward silence.

The silence lengthened as they traveled. She was more than glad to see the hunched buildings of Durance draw closer.

"So," he said, with his breath against her ear, "To what special place did your walk take you, that it kept your attention for a full day?"

"Just the woods. And the meadow beyond."

"Through the woods and to the meadow. Nothing more?" His lips brushed her earlobe. The tip of his nose trailed down her neck. She closed her eyes against the sensation.

"No," she squeaked.

"Because your hair is damp, and there is no body of water outside the village for miles."

Her eyes flew open. "Oh, look, there's the tavern. Thank you for the ride, Mr. Armitage." She shifted to climb down, even though the horse hadn't stopped.

His arm around her waist didn't let her budge.

He held her so tightly she could barely breathe. His mouth pressed hard behind her ear. "There are large and dangerous things in those woods, milady field mouse. If you plan to be wandering them after dark, you might consider an escort."

"I didn't mean to stay so long. But yes, I will." She pushed at his arm. "Thank you, again, Mr. Armitage."

"Jastin." His arm slid up beneath her shoulders. He leaned over and lowered her to the ground.

As her feet touched, she tried to smile pleasantly. She wanted out of there before he started in on more questions. "Yes. Right."

"Say it."

She looked up at him, confused by a soft change in his features.

"My name," he said. "I'd like you to say it."

"Jastin?"

Deep creases in his face arched upward. If the shadows in his eyes had changed, even a little, she might have thought he was actually smiling. "Take care not to wander too far, milady field mouse." He tugged his mount back toward the direction from where they came.

She watched him go. Why should it matter to him how she spent her day? He didn't even like her. And why did all his questions bother her? She touched her hair. It was damp.

She moved toward the tavern and came upon Rusic, whose fuzzy eyebrows were arched high toward his hairline. "Milady field mouse? Were ye captured by a black wolf?" His eyes darted to the departing Jastin

Armitage, and he gave a long wink.

Riza waved her hands. “Doesn’t anyone use names around here? Don’t even know why I bother having one.” She brushed past him and stepped into the stale air of the tavern. “I’ll be up bright and early tomorrow, Rusic. I hope I didn’t worry you.”

“Only a bit. It’s strange territory for ye, I’d hate for something fearful to come upon ye.” He bundled up the front of his apron in his massive fists. “The man’s right, after all. Word’s spreadin’ again of dragons and such. Right in our own forest.”

Riza paused. She peered over her shoulder. “Does that have to be a bad thing?”

Rusic dropped his bundled apron and gaped. “Does it have to be bad? Does it…?” He grunted and shook his head. “Ye young folk, where ye get yer ideas.” He gathered empty tankards and carried them toward the kitchen. “Bad omen, it is. Folks of this village got enough t’worry for, what with the drought and the dying herds and all. Dragons is bad business. Best not t’mention we spoke of it.” He bumped open the kitchen door with his wide backside.

She chewed on her bottom lip. Kallon was right to be fearful of coming closer to the village. She hoped it didn’t mean it would keep them from seeing each other again.

She had so many questions for him. How long had he been living alone? What happened to his parents, that he became so utterly gloomy when he spoke of them? And what was that stone she’d found in her hand last night?

She climbed the stairs, and unlocked the door of her private room. She fumbled for a lantern, but decided she'd just step out of her dress and fall into bed. She was exhausted, but in a good way. She knew she'd sleep well tonight.

She laid her dress carefully across the back of a chair near the window, and pushed open the shutter to let the moonlight guide her path back to bed. A brief flutter of shadow passed over, which caught her eye. She peered through the window.

Again came a flickering shadow that brushed across skeletal treetops before diffusing like a wisp of smoke into the air. Had she seen a glisten of red in that brief moment, or was she only just wishing it? Surely it was a crow, or a fleckowl simply searching for dinner.

She traipsed toward her bed and flopped in. She tugged her covers to her chin, and, remembering the feel of the sky in her hair and the taste of the sun as Kallon flew her high into the mountains, she drifted to peaceful, smiling sleep.

§

Two weeks of working at the Brown Barrel had finally earned Riza enough money to buy new clothes. In her room, she tugged on a fresh tunic and stepped into a bland patchwork skirt. They were both a little too big, but after wearing the same green dress in a tavern kitchen day after day, she'd begun to feel like a walking fertilizer cart. Her new clothes at least felt clean and good, despite their size.

She still needed her dress, though, and planned to take care of it. She'd purchased a cake of lard soap in town, and she used it now to scrub down her dress as best she could. She rinsed it with water from her clay pitcher and then hung the dress in her open window to dry. She watched the thin fabric flutter like an emerald flag against the sill.

What would have happened to her that first day she'd come to Durance, if she hadn't met up with Jastin Armitage? She was afraid to consider it. She still didn't understand why the man had taken pity on her. In fact, the more she got to know him, the more she realized his moment of charity was completely unnatural for him.

Just then, a blast of hot wind pushed her dress from the window, and the fabric sank to the floor. She bent to retrieve it, and caught a glimpse of her reflection. In the early light, the uneven glass held phantom clouds where her eyes should be. She touched her finger to the pane. Maybe someday she would touch a real cloud.

She hadn't seen Kallon since their day at the lake, but today was her day off, and she was going to go looking for him. Along the way, she'd have to work up the nerve to ask him to take her flying again.

She stepped outside her room to hurry down the steps. She heard Jastin's voice and paused, then peered down over the railing.

"There is far more danger to your town than you realize," Jastin said to Rusic. "It's by good chance that

I'm here. I've handled many a problem such as this."

"What problem?" Riza asked, leaning out. Both men looked up at the sound of her voice. Rusic's mouth opened to say something, but Jastin slid off his barstool.

"Milady field mouse," he said, and extended his hand.

She descended the steps. "What problem?" she asked again.

"Nothing that is your concern." Jastin scooped up her hand. "Your generous boss informs me that you are not required in the kitchen today. I would ask you to spend some of your free time with me."

"With you?" Riza stared at him, his face a sudden mask of pleasantness. She hardly recognized him.

"Why are you so surprised?" He bent forward to kiss the inside of her wrist, but she yanked back her hand. She wasn't sure which was more distasteful, his touch, or the unexpected flutter it usually caused.

"Ye dun think the man loiters about the place to visit me, do ye?" Rusic barked a laugh. "I've seen his face more'n Old Yammer's these days!"

Old Yammer lifted his cheek from the bar and stared with glazed eyes. Drool leaked from the corner of his mouth. "On the house, ye say?" He collapsed back into a heap of sweat and clothing.

"But. But I have plans!" Riza stared at Rusic.

"Bah. Another lost day of wandering the woods, I'll wager." Rusic shook his head. "Ye spend too much time alone. Even while yer working, surrounded by noisy folks, yer somehow all alone."

"Very well," said Jastin. He nodded to Rusic, and then turned to Riza. "I'll call for you at four o'clock. That gives you plenty of time to wander the woods before we meet. Until then, milady field mouse." He bowed, and then strode outside.

Riza stared after him. She turned her stare to Rusic. "What just happened?"

"I believe ye just came into a courtship."

§

Kallon arched his heavy wings outside his cave, poised to fly, but his nostrils flared. A familiar scent mingled with, and then overpowered, the musky elms. "Human?"

"It's me, Riza," she called. Brittle underbrush crunched beneath footsteps, and he waited for her to appear from behind the trees. "I hope you don't mind that I came back. I made sure no one saw me leave, or anything." More crunching footsteps sounded before she finally appeared. She paused at the edge of the underbrush.

He regarded her in silence, uncertain if he minded.

She returned his gaze, just as silent. She shifted her weight. "Have you been flying?"

"Was just about to."

She nodded, and glanced down. She hugged her arms around her waist.

"Was there a reason you came back?" he asked.

"Maybe I shouldn't have."

Kallon shook his head. "You shouldn't have, but you're here now, so tell me what brought you."

It wasn't like her to hold back a question, so her hesitation felt uncomfortable. He settled his rump, growing impatient. "Going to ask me something?"

"I've just been thinking about that time you took me to your lake."

"I see." He nodded. "So have I."

"You have?" Her chin lifted and she smiled.

He'd been thinking about it for several days, and regretting it more and more each time he remembered. He'd been really foolish. He wasn't sure why he'd allowed her to go with him to the lake, and he'd realized too late that he'd encouraged her. Here she stood again, just as he'd feared. For some reason he couldn't fathom, the girl kept coming back.

"Oh, I recognize that," she suddenly said, and pointed to the linking stone hanging against his throat. "It's that crystal."

He covered it with his paw. "Yes."

"I've been wondering about that, too. What is it?"

He breathed out. He regarded her for a long time. If he answered this question, there would surely be more to follow. He wasn't going to reply at all, but her expectant face peered up at him with wide eyes. "Was my mother's," he heard himself say.

The girl moved in, and he felt her warmth near his chest. He shifted back.

"You said you heard it speak."

"Yes."

"How does it work?" She inched closer.

He clenched the stone. "I don't know. Didn't believe it really could, until that night."

"Can I see it?"

He tensed. He didn't want her to see it, and didn't want to risk another episode of disturbing whispers. He was just managing to put the last ones out of his mind.

Her fingers grazed the back of his paw. "You said it spoke with your mother's voice, but I didn't hear anything." She gently tugged at his grip.

He finally let her peel his claws away from the stone. It brushed and bumped against his chest.

"How long has she been dead?" she asked.

He really didn't want to talk about this. It wasn't any of the girl's business, anyway. She didn't have any right to be asking.

"Kallon? How long has she been—?"

"Many years," he snapped. "Since I was young."

"What about your father?"

"The same. Many years." The trees grew hazy. His throat closed.

"Is it hard to speak of them?"

"No." Cords of invisible leather seized his insides and tightened. He would not confess.

"How did they die, Kallon?"

He withdrew a step. Memories made his anger begin to sizzle in the pit of his stomach. He had to make her stop talking, to stop poking her questions into his gut like a rusty knife.

"Kallon?" Her squeak of a voice pricked his spine.

"How did they die?"

"They were murdered!" His bellow rumbled the ground beneath his feet. He hoped it trembled the ground everywhere. He hoped it wobbled her feet, and sent her running in fright. "They were stolen from me, one at a time, by puny, pale little humans like you!" Just when he needed them most, they were torn from him as a sapling is wrenched from the ground.

"Wasn't enough to take my mother while I slept, or enough to take my father, too, while I watched!" The spoken words uncorked his anger, and he could do nothing to stop it from bubbling out in broken, hateful fragments. "Had to leave me here! Had to leave me behind to suffer alone!" He slammed his fists into a near elm trunk, and splinters filtered around his shoulders. His wings burst out from his back.

"Kallon, don't fly." The girl's voice pierced his foggy rage. He felt her weight press against his foreleg.

"Release me!" He beat his wings in warning. If she would not let go, he would fly anyway, and let her tumble.

"No. You're hurt. Let me help you."

"I don't need your help!" With that, he pushed off from the ground. He expected her to let go, but the girl would not relent. She just gripped tighter. "Let go," he said, and shook his leg.

"Let me help you!"

"No!" He shook his leg once more, and this time, he felt her slide loose. When she screamed, he swung his head to find he'd risen higher than he realized. The human tumbled toward the treetops, arms flailing. He growled, angry with her for being stubborn, angry with himself for letting her get to him. But he didn't mean to hurt her. He swung around and dove.

Her soft head fell toward a pointed fir branch. She screamed again, and he bolted forward. He caught the edge of her sleeve in his claws, and swung her away from the limb. The motion threw him off balance, and he careened sideways into the very spear he'd saved her from. Pain exploded at the joint of his right wing. He howled. He crumpled, and landed hard.

He could feel nothing but the burning flare in his wing. He didn't move, and wished he wouldn't even breathe, because every jostle stabbed the injury.

"Kallon!" The girl's footsteps pounded toward him.

"Go away."

"I'm so sorry." She knelt beside him, and reached toward his wing.

"Don't touch it. Don't help me." He closed his eyes.

"I will help you, and you'll let me. Stop being so stubborn." She gently prodded his throbbing joint.

He rolled his gaze toward her face, and stared at her from where his chin rested on the ground. "Are you hurt?"

"Just a scrape." She pulled back her skirt to show him a gash across her kneecap. Blood dribbled down her shin. "It would have been a lot worse if you hadn't caught me."

"You should have let go."

"I did let go."

"Should have let go sooner." She clenched his wing. A sudden crack splattered him with fresh pain. "Ouch! Human! Thought you wanted to help!"

"I am helping." She crawled toward his face. "There's no blood, I think it was just out of joint. Can you move it now?"

He feebly lifted his wing. It did feel much better, but he still scowled at her, anyway.

"Now let's see about this." She inspected his knuckles, curling his front paws and turning them this way and that. "Looks like you scraped yourself when you attacked that offensive elm tree. You're bleeding." She leaned across his foot, grabbed a handful of brown moss, and then dabbed it against his knuckles.

"Don't even remember doing that."

She tugged at a string from the bottom of her skirt, and a strip of patches peeled away. This she tore in half, and then wound over and around his digits, each paw in turn. "You were very angry," she said.

He nodded.

"I'm sorry. That was my fault." She tied off the cloth. "I ask too many questions." She sat back against her heels with a sigh.

She did ask a lot of questions. A part of him wanted to blame her. But, looking into her sad eyes, he couldn't even remember what it was that made him so angry. She hadn't meant anything, and couldn't know the years of bottled pain she'd been probing.

She pushed to stand. The hem of her skirt no longer covered her ankles, and thick drops of blood gathered around the top of her boot. She limped backward. "I won't come back anymore. I'm sorry."

He didn't want her to leave like this. It was the right thing, he was sure, but he didn't feel as relieved as he thought he should. "Riza—"

"You said my name!" She burst into a wide smile that dimpled her cheeks.

He didn't know which to react to first, his own surprise, or hers.

"I'm sorry. What were you going to say?" she asked.

At that moment, a gray pigeon tumbled from the sky. It landed with a thud against Kallon's skull and flopped to the ground. A throaty coo burbled from its beak.

"Oh! Poor thing! It's hurt." Riza reached out.

"Kallon Redheart," the pigeon called, then went limp.

Riza flashed her pale face toward Kallon. "Did you hear that?"

Kallon forgot his soreness and thrust to his feet. His wings stabbed the air. "Something's wrong. Orman sounds strange."

"Who's Orman?" Riza knelt beside the bird. She nudged it.

"Is it dead?" Kallon asked.

"I can't tell. I don't think so."

"I must go." He leapt to the air and swerved off toward Orman's mountain. He glanced back to see Riza scoop the injured bird into her arms. Then he raced on, dreading what he might find. He didn't understand the feeling, but he flew hard.

§

Kallon swerved to land on the plateau of Orman's mountain. The wizard's hut had lost its longstanding battle with gravity, and lay as a pile of wood and mortar pebbles. The stone table was overturned. Crystals of onyx and amber and pale blue lay strewn across the ground like a shattered rainbow. Silvery gray pigeons meandered in dazed circles, heads bobbling. Alarm gripped Kallon's spine.

"Orman?" He sniffed at the rubble. Orman's scent was there, but not strong enough that the man could have been inside the fallen hut.

His nose led him toward the overturned table. He recoiled at an aggressive and spicy scent. Dragon. No doubt about it. Another dragon had been here only moments before.

The scent was still strong and easy to follow. Orman's scent mingled with it, but dropped off the edge of the mountain. Whatever dragon had come had either tossed Orman over the side, or carried him off. His eyes followed the logical path, and came to rest on Mount Gore.

Mount Gore. Orman had been there plenty of times, and had even stood beside Kallon's father during council meetings. He was known there as a friend to the dragons. Kallon had no reason to fear for the wizard, and yet, he did fear. Orman's belongings had been destroyed. No friend of Orman's would do such a thing.

Kallon had sworn to never return to that mountain. To follow Orman's abductor would lead him into a world he had long since abandoned. What would he do once he caught up to them? Demand information? Then what? To Dragonkind, Kallon didn't even exist anymore.

Just then, a glare of sunlight caught his eyes. He squinted, searching for the source. He spotted a blurry shape in the distance that, at first, seemed to be a puff of cloud. Then it banked, and sunlight glinted once more, caught on the scales of a white dragon tail. Without thinking, Kallon leapt.

His wings pumped hard to close the distance. He was getting closer, and could just make out a silhouette against fleecy clouds. Then the white dragon veered and plunged into the thick forest below. Kallon lost sight of him.

He growled. He'd come so close! He drew up when he reached the spot where he thought the dragon had disappeared, and circled slowly. He peered down at a town wedged tight among green firs and stout pin oaks.

Wing Valley. It writhed with activity. Greens and Yellows hauled fresh kills onto pallets to dredge them in sauces of red wine and clove. Blues hung artisan-crafted chains and horn ornaments from woven stands. Blacks turned their crystal amulets to glimmer beneath the sun, hoping to catch the eye of passing shoppers. Grays barked prices for dented wing shields and claw cuffs. Browns waved long reeds packed with dried licorice and turmeric, and argued with each other about the logic of gold in weapons, as their smoking sticks choked the air with scent.

It might have only been yesterday that Kallon had last seen the village. After all these years, it seemed like only hours. Remorse threatened to rise in the back of his throat. He stifled it.

He turned away. He didn't have any real proof that Orman was in danger. All seemed normal in the village below, and his wing was beginning to ache again. He'd just head back to Orman's mountain and wait for the wizard there.

Then he remembered Orman's hut, or, the lack of it. He remembered the broken and scattered crystals, and he became uneasy again. A disturbing question filtered from the back of his mind to behind his eyes. What would his father do?

He groaned. Where did that thought come from? Nevertheless, he swung back toward the village, grumbling and practicing the rant he'd turn loose on Orman when he finally reached him. He silently landed on a village path.

He stood eyeing the scaly crowd. Few faces turned. It appeared that no one was interested in the Red who dropped from the sky to shop. He inched forward to blend in, and to discreetly begin his search.

"Look, Father!" came a high-pitched cry from a Blue fledgling. "A Red! You said there were no more Reds."

Kallon jerked his head toward the young dragon to hush him with a glare. Instead, he met the suspicious gaze of the youth's father, presumably, for this massive Blue poked his snout very near to Kallon's, towering like a wall of granite. "That is right, Son. No more Reds."

"They died out with Bren Redheart, the last of the brave," came another voice. Its owner, a thin Green, pushed his way through the forming gawkers.

Whispers and murmurs buzzed around Kallon's ears. He tried to move forward, but the crowd prevented him.

"Was there not a son?" someone asked.

"Yes, but he died," another said.

"I was under the impression he rejected his father's ways, and willingly excommunicated."

"No, he was too young to take the post, I think. No one knows what happened to him after that."

"I was certain he died. I was told he starved to death from grief."

"You are all wrong. He went off to hunt the dragon slayer that murdered his father, and was captured by humans."

Kallon nearly bellowed in frustration. The dragons gathered too near for him to spread his wings, and babbled so distractedly that they would not break up to let him through. He was about to stomp a warning, when a low, vaguely familiar voice called quietly over the din.

"Redheart?"

His eyes came to rest on a petite Brown. The curve of her delicate horns, and her thick lashes rimming glittering eyes revived a phantom memory.

"Brownwing?"

She smiled, and broke through the murmuring crowd. "You remember me." She arched her neck, nearly pressing her snout to his own. "I am stunned to see you. I thought you were dead."

"Others, too, it seems."

"Pay them no mind. Come, tell me why you have returned after all these years." She pressed her shoulder against the wall of surrounding chatter and cleared a path. He followed.

"I am here only for a moment."

"Only a moment?" She paused, and turned. "Then you have not come to claim your station on the council?"

"I have not."

Her head swung around to the path ahead of them. She drew him away from the noisy village path and into the trees. "Then why have you come?"

He didn't reply.

At a near clearing, she lowered her rump to a flattened bed of fallen leaves. She curled around to face him, and cocked her head. In the growing silence, he found his eyes trailing the ridges that followed the gentle slope of her spine to the plump base of her tail.

"I am the only one who still believes you will one day realize your place, and come again to rule the council as destiny intends." One brown paw crossed over the other.

He forced his eyes from her, and gazed instead toward the sky. "There is another who believes this, and he is as deluded as you. I must go now."

She rose. "But you have only just arrived. We have barely spoken."

"Yes, but I must go, Vaya Brownwing." He turned away.

She was beside him in an instant, pressing her shoulder to his collarbone. "You may have lost count of the years since you left, Kallon Redheart, but I have not. Even after all this time, I watch the skies." Her snout pressed to his neck, and she purred, shooting a rumble through his legs to the ground. "I can not let you go so soon."

He closed his eyes, trying to ignore the sweet mingle of her heat and breath. "I may be the only one who really knows you, Kallon. You found the ways of a vassal difficult to understand, and instead of blindly choosing your father's service, you questioned it. I respected you for that." Her paw rested atop his foot.

He could hear her heartbeat. He could feel it, pulsing against his claws and rushing vertigo into his brain.

"It was only natural that you should turn away from all he represented when you lost him," she said softly, her paw caressing. "You were young and hurting, and you misunderstood his death, just as you misunderstood his life."

"You don't know me, to be saying—"

"But I accepted this in you. I still accept it." She breathed across his muzzle. "My father was to speak to your father about promising me to you. We were to be the first crossing of our tribes."

He was losing the sound of her voice to the emptiness between his ears. He couldn't think past her scent. He couldn't gather intelligent words with her pressing so close. "My father? Your father?"

She drew back, and smiled gently. "I see in your eyes, you never knew this. That helps me understand."

Her distance helped him breathe. "Understand?"

"It helps me understand why, when your father died, and when you turned from everything he believed in, you turned also from me."

He tried to speak, but he had no words. It was true that he never knew. He couldn't help but wonder if knowing would have made any difference. Gazing into her golden eyes, and feeling the slide of her scales against him, he thought it might have.

"Go on," she said. She stepped back and waved her paw. "Rush off to whatever coaxed you into the land of the breathing. But…" Her eyes closed to half-lids. "… promise me you will come again."

He shook his head. "I can't promise that, Vaya." Then, afraid she might entice him into promising, he lunged away without looking back.

CHAPTER NINE

Kallon barged through the trees back toward town. He'd allowed himself to be distracted by the Brown, and had lost valuable time. Her words, and her presence, clung to his mind, lingering like the shapeless blotches before his eyes when he stared too long at the sun.

Back on the dirt path, he wound around carts and wooden slabs. There were a few shelters, some woven with branches and vines to hold supplies or food stores. None were large enough to hide a human, let alone a dragon. For all he knew, the dragon was long gone, anyway, and the wizard with him. He did find a meager scent trail, and followed it to the farthest edge of the town. There his nose gave out, weary from sniffing. He could smell everything and nothing. All odors seemed the same.

His ears, however, were strong. Whispers came from behind a near lean-to, and he crept closer to investigate. Through the spaces between woven twigs, he saw movement. Arms of black leather wrapped fat twine around a set of bony, gray shoulders. A white beard was tossed over one of those shoulders. "Orman?"

At Kallon's voice, a pair of dark eyes blinked through the twig slats. "This is no business of yours, dragon," said a voice that must have belonged to the eyes.

"What do you do, there?" Kallon peered around the edge of the structure to meet the dark human's face. A soft sound came from beside him. It was the wizard, bound with twine and sitting on a fat stump. Orman's head rolled aside, and he moaned again. Blood caked in the corner of his mouth.

An emotion Kallon had no name for sizzled through his veins. "Who are you? What have you done?" He knocked Orman's captor off-balance as he pushed forward to free the wizard. Tugging at a knot, Kallon heard the clang of steel against steel. The sound echoed through his memories. He swerved his gaze to the dark human who stood with sword in hand.

"I said this is no business of yours, dragon."

Kallon stared at the gleaming blade and recoiled. Fear, mysterious and murky, chilled him. He felt suddenly small and vulnerable, and helpless against a terror that wrestled for control. He looked to Orman. The wizard's eyes were on him, calm and knowing.

"Now, now, Armitage," came a muted voice. From the trees behind the human emerged a White, whose scales of pearl glinted so harshly with each step that Kallon had to squint.

"What goes on here? Why have you stolen the

wizard?" Kallon asked.

"My dear Red," said the White, as he oozed toward Kallon like a widening puddle of spilled milk. "This wizard has not been stolen."

"I followed you here. I know you stole him."

The White glared at the human in black, who slid his sword back into its sheath. "This wizard is a friend of yours?" asked the White. He circled slowly behind Kallon. "Mind your answer, Red. He is in a dire situation."

"What situation?"

The White sighed, and rested his glittering paw atop Orman's head. "I fear he is accused of passing secrets. Spying."

Kallon reared back. Orman shot to his feet. "Spying!" came dragon and wizard voice in unison.

Dragon heads turned from their business toward the shout.

"Since when have dragons and humans been adversaries?" Kallon asked as Orman struggled against his bindings, paler than Kallon had ever seen him.

"Since humans began sneaking about on our lands, trying to learn secrets and weaknesses of our kind."

Dragon murmurs erupted. Listeners drew closer, shrinking in slowly toward the scene.

"What secrets do we keep, that humans must sneak about to learn them?" Kallon wedged himself between the White and Orman. "I can vouch for the loyalty of this human. He knew my mother. My father served as his vassal."

"Your father?" The White shot a cold look to the human, who didn't react, and then to the growing dragon throng, whose whispers grew agitated. "Your father was Bren Redheart?" He smiled, and lowered his snout, arms widening. "The name is honored, of course." The crowd agreed, and hushed voices echoed the sentiment.

"I am Kallon Redheart. I vouch for this wizard." Kallon reached for Orman's shoulders. The White's paw stopped him.

"Kallon Redheart. Yes, I remember. Is this the wizard your father was defending when he was killed? How many years ago was that, exactly?"

Kallon glanced toward the crowd of dragons, which had gone quiet.

"Many thought you were dead." The White's eyes narrowed. "Have you come finally to claim your place among us?"

"I come for the wizard."

"Ah. Yes. The spy."

"He is no spy!"

Orman slouched back onto the stump, and Kallon reached toward him. The dark human sprang to block.

"Gentle dragons," called the White. He darted a paw to stop the human. "This dragon gives word for the wizard's loyalty, but this dragon is known by name only." Facing the crowd, he extended his arms. "He is no one to us but a stranger, who claims a name long dead to our Kind. Is there anyone among you who can vouch for him?"

Kallon turned to the listeners. Each face was a stranger, each pair of eyes as unfamiliar as the next. Not one did he recognize, not one did he expect to speak.

He looked at Orman, who sat quiet and staring toward the distance. For the first time, Kallon felt ashamed of turning his back all those years ago. He bristled against the feeling, but couldn't make it disappear.

"No one?" asked the White. "Not one of you knows this Red?"

There was movement in the throng. Dragons parted, making room for a Brown. She pressed forward and craned her delicate neck. Kallon again found the gentle smile of Vaya Browning. She remained silent.

"Anyone?" called the White. "Surely someone is willing to claim this Red's sincerity."

Vaya's smile evaporated. The edges of her eyes hardened. "Pardon me," she said quietly to the dragon stranger beside her, and squeezed past. Turning her back, she disappeared into the mass.

"Very well." The White clucked his tongue at Kallon. "I can not accept your vouch for this human, if there is no dragon to vouch for you. You understand." He hoisted Orman, bound and listless, with his forelegs. "Armitage, you know what to do." He soared to the sky.

"No!" Kallon dove. He just missed Orman's legs and tumbled into the lean-to.

The woven structure exploded, raining twigs and straw, obscuring his view. He lost which way was up. Just as he got his legs beneath himself, pain sliced into the base of his tail. He snarled, swiping instinctively.

He struck the dark human's chest, and the man stumbled back, but immediately raised his sword again. The blade captured a flash of sunlight, and as before, Kallon was thrust back in his mind to a place of dim, churning fear.

He knew that sword. He had stared up at it before. The curved handle had been lifted high to strike, and Kallon had closed his eyes and waited to die.

A collective gasp from the crowd drew him out of his memory. He blinked and lurched to his feet. Around him, Greens, Blues and Grays pressed in, growling at the human in warning, surrounding Kallon with protection.

He had no time to thank them; he had to follow the White. He leapt into the air, and pressed hard against the sky. In the distance, he saw the same glitter of cloud-like shine from before. He swerved to follow. Hot pain clamped his spine, twisting him in mid-air. He struggled to stay airborne, but his injured wing drooped, and his tail went heavy and unable to rudder.

He tried to push on, but he could only watch as the dragon, with Orman, faded and then finally disappeared. He lost them.

He managed to hover for a few seconds, but in the end, he knew he'd been beaten. He was wounded and bleeding; he had to give up.

With a roar of frustration, he dropped. He landed too fast, and his legs crumpled. His belly hit hard, knocking the breath from his lungs. His tail flared with pain, but before he could even try to cry out, he was engulfed in darkness.

§

It is four o'clock, isn't it?" Riza asked Rusic. She waited, perched on a barstool in the Brown Barrel, and fervently hoped that Jastin had changed his mind about meeting her here.

Rusic tugged a pocket clock from behind his apron and nodded. "Quarter past, in fact."

"He must have gotten busy. Oh well. I need to check on my bird." She slid off the barstool and passed Old Yammer, who gave her a toothless grin. She hurried toward the stairs.

"Do forgive my tardiness," came Jastin's voice over the heavy thud of his footsteps.

Riza grimaced, and hurried even faster toward the stairs. "Don't be silly," she called over her shoulder. "I'm sure you're busy. I'd just as soon go to my room." She made it to the first step.

"Nonsense." Jastin's hand caught her elbow and steered her around. "I'm here now, and I'm famished. You?"

"Actually, I'm not hungry at all."

"No? More for me, then." Jastin nodded at Rusic, who disappeared behind the kitchen door and returned with a small, cloth-covered box. Jastin tucked this under his arm as he pulled Riza past the bar. "Blade will escort us."

"Where are we going?" she asked, trying not to trip on her own feet as he yanked her outside.

"Picnic." He pushed the small crate into Blade's saddlebag.

Riza blinked.

"What's that look for?" he asked.

She shrugged a little. "I guess I didn't think of you as a picnic kind of person."

Jastin's eyes squinted. Then he hoisted her and sat her hard onto Blade's saddle.

She hunched forward in the seat as Jastin settled behind her. His arm squeezed around her belly. "I feel like a prisoner," she muttered, squirming.

"A what?"

"The way you push me around, and bark at me, and now you're holding me so tight I can't even breathe."

Jastin let go. He switched hands on the reins, and thumped his heels against Blade's ribs. The horse lurched into a trot, jerking so hard that Riza squeaked and flailed, and finally grabbed the saddle horn to keep from falling. She was trying to get her heartbeat under control when he spoke.

"I didn't realize I was barking. I've always thought myself a gentleman with you."

"Well," Riza said, concentrating on squeezing her legs and trying to find Blade's rhythm so she didn't bounce so much in the saddle. "You do order me around."

His voice was soft when he spoke again. "Then I owe you an apology, milady field mouse."

Riza glanced over her shoulder at him. His dark eyes focused ahead. If he saw her glance, he didn't acknowledge.

She looked back to the trail. Blade was carrying them far from town. For a time, she listened to the crunch of Blade's hooves against brittle grass, and to the whistle of sparrow song through leafless trees. The ride might have been enjoyable, if she wasn't so tired already from trying to hold herself steady.

Slowly, in tiny degrees, she began to relax. She leaned back, just touching Jastin enough to stabilize so she could rest her arms from gripping the saddle horn, and to loosen her legs around Blade's ribs. Jastin didn't even seem to notice. Now she could close her eyes and breathe in each dry breeze that tickled her face.

She lost track of how long they'd traveled before she felt a shift. She opened her eyes to find they'd followed the tree line of the mountain forest, and that they were on a slight descent toward a huge expanse of red clay. "Where are we?" she asked.

"Fell Lake." His voice was close to her ear. She realized she'd been resting her head against his shoulder. She bolted upright, and found that his hand had made its way to her stomach and gently pressed there.

"This is a lake?" she asked, twisting to dislodge his hand.

"Used to be. It was the largest body of water in all of Leland, though shallow enough for a horse to walk across, even before the drought." He urged her out of the saddle, and then slipped off, as well. He retrieved a woven blanket and the crate, spread the blanket over the cracked dirt, and sat. "Dinner." Then he bowed his head. "If you find yourself hungry, after all."

"Well. I guess I am, a little." She plopped beside him on the blanket and pulled the cloth from the crate. Warm beef and rolls released delicious steam. She reached for a roll, and bumped hands with Jastin, who'd had the same idea.

"Ladies first, of course," he said, and rested his hand against his chest. He wasn't wearing his gloves, and she tried to remember if she'd seen him without them before. His fingers were thick and dusted with black, curling hair. Scars criss-crossed his skin. Beneath his hand, at the vee of his collar, more curling hairs tangled above a slash of peeking white.

"Is that a bandage? Are you bleeding?" She brushed away his hand and peered close. The bandage was speckled with seeping blood. "What happened?"

"I tangled with a tree in my rush to see you."

She frowned. He was lying, but there was no sense in arguing. She sat back and poked at her roll. "I realize I don't even know why you're here in Durance. What sort of business are you in? Are you something of a warrior?"

"Yes, something of that nature."

"And you're new here, like me."

"Yes, I'll only be here for a short time. Then I'll return to South Morlan, where I prefer to live between journeys." He took a large bite of bread, and Riza watched his jaw work as he chewed. The lines of his face were cleaned of their usual dust, and the gray at the tip of his beard stood out more sharply against glistening black whiskers.

"Do you have family there?" She lifted her roll for a bite.

He swallowed, eyes scanning the horizon. "My wife's family lives near there."

Riza paused, her bread in mid-air. "You have a wife?"

He tore what was left of his bread in half, and tossed the two pieces to Blade. "I had a wife. A long time ago." He tugged a slab of beef from the crate and offered it to her. "Does that surprise you?"

"Yes, actually." She accepted the meat, and sandwiched it into her roll. "Did you love her?"

"Of course I did."

"What happened to her?"

"You ask a lot of questions."

She sighed. "I know." She nibbled at her sandwich. Feeling him watching, she shifted self-consciously. She tried to find the other side of the lakebed, but it disappeared into the hazy distance. She glanced back at him.

He was still watching.

She cleared her throat. "So why did you want me to come here with you?"

His thick brows arched. "It isn't obvious?"

"No." He narrowed his eyes, as though trying to decide if she was lying. "Well," she added. "Rusic seems to think it's something of a courtship, but that can't possibly be the reason."

"Why not?"

She snorted. "Because you don't even like me."

"Why do you say that?"

"First I'm a beggar, then I'm a field mouse. I'm skinny. I'm trouble. You don't know anything about me, but you're always angry with me. You watch me as though I'm going to do something criminal—"

He held up his hand. "All right. I see what you mean." He brushed his palms down his thighs, and then pushed to stand. "You're right. At first, I didn't trust you. I didn't believe your intentions were as innocent as they appeared."

"My intentions? What do you mean?"

He moved to Blade, and opened the leather flap of a saddlebag. "I've since come to suspect that you are genuine, after all. Misguided and foolish, but genuine."

"That sounds an awful lot like you still don't like me."

He tugged a wine bottle from the bag, and two small mugs. He returned to the blanket and sat, offering her a mug.

She accepted.

"Does that bother you?" he asked.

She lifted one shoulder in a shrug. "Not really. Except that you order me around."

He popped the cork off the bottle and poured dark wine into her mug. "Yes, so you've mentioned." He touched the neck of the bottle to his own mug, and filled that, too. "You have to understand, I've spent a number of years alone, traveling from city to city. It doesn't require manners. I suppose I've forgotten how to be with a lady." He sipped his wine, and kept his gaze toward the blanket.

For once, he lacked the dark, intense expression she'd come to recognize. He actually seemed thoughtful. And somehow, younger.

"You must have loved her very much," Riza said.

He glanced up. "Hm?"

"Your wife. You must have loved her very much, if you've chosen to spend so many years alone since she died."

"Yes." He nodded, and looked down again as he sipped. "I did."

"How did she die?" she asked.

He touched the bottom of her mug and urged it toward her mouth. "Aren't you thirsty?"

She sipped, and then rested her mug on her thigh. She stared down into the wine and watched it ripple as the silence between them stretched.

"Fire," he finally said. "She was burned."

"Oh. I'm so sorry."

"She was carrying my child. It was to be our first." His grip tightened around his mug. "She liked to walk, like you do."

"What happened?"

He drained his wine. He drew the back of his scarred hand across his mouth. "I heard her scream. There was a loud explosion. By the time I reached her, she was…" His voice broke. He cleared his throat.

"There was a circle of burned earth all around her. I saw a gold dragon flying away."

"A dragon? But why? For what purpose?"

"I never knew." He poured fresh wine into his mug, and offered the bottle toward hers, but hers was still full. She shook her head. "I vowed after that to hunt every dragon I laid my eyes on," he said. "For the rest of my life."

Riza sucked in a breath. "You're a dragon hunter."

"Yes."

She pushed to her feet, spilling wine on her boot, the blanket, his thigh. "You kill dragons! For money! That isn't even legal!"

Jastin jumped up, too, and growled at the stain on his leather pants. He grabbed the cloth and swiped at the wetness. "A man needs a living, Riza. No one scrutinizes the law when the beasts are destroying livestock and hoarding the land richest with crystal." He tossed the cloth back to the blanket. "Dragons may have served a purpose for humans once, but they have long outlived it."

"I can't believe you're saying that. They are living creatures, with a heart and soul. They have kindness, Jastin. I don't know why one dragon out of so many chose to hurt your wife, and I'm very sorry for you. But not every dragon deserves to die because of the action of one."

"That is beside the point." He stepped toward her. She shrank back, and his face took on familiar, angry shadows. "Things are the way they are, and I am too old to take a different route. I haven't cared in a very long time about right or wrong. I haven't cared about anything. Until now." His hands gripped her waist. "You are caught up in things that far exceed your understanding, Riza. I'm giving you a chance to get out."

She pushed at his hands. "What are you talking about? Let me go."

"That first time we met, in the barn, I recognized the scent on you. I have been watching you; you're right about that. I've followed you. I know where you go when you walk the day away."

Her skin went cold. "What do you mean?"

"That beast you've befriended can not be trusted. You know nothing about him, except what he wishes you to know. Already the town is talking about him, and how dangerous he is."

"He isn't dangerous, Jastin. You are."

"Even so, the town is talking. And if they learn what I have learned about you, you will suffer."

"I don't care. Let me go."

"It doesn't have to be this way. Give him up to me. I'll protect you if you help me."

"Help you kill him? Are you insane?" She pushed with all her strength at his hands, and twisted away from him. "Leave me alone! I won't help you harm him."

"Yes, you will," he said, and captured her shoulders.

She dug her toes into the clay, but it crumbled, and he pulled her close.

One arm wrapped her waist as his other hand lifted her chin. Panic welled as she met his eyes.

"You will help me," he said again. "In one way or another."

§

Kallon felt a sting in his tail and the throb of cramped muscles before he was fully aware of himself. As he came to consciousness the pain only increased, but he couldn't remember why he hurt. He opened his eyes in the gray twilight, and the memory came rushing like a gale wind. His failed attempt at being a hero.

A scrawny White and a human had been his only adversaries, and still he failed. He had missed every cue, had bobbled his attempts to free Orman, and had left his vulnerable hindquarters exposed as a perfect target. Wouldn't his father be proud?

He curled around to inspect the wound. The blade had sliced at exactly the point where his wide tail met his rump, into the sensitive flesh exposed between oddly angled scales. It was too skilled to be coincidence. The human had known just where to strike. Kallon considered himself lucky. The gash had already crusted over and stopped bleeding. Had the slice been deep enough to reach bones and artery, he would have bled to death. Many a dragon died in battle of such a wound. Just like his father.

It had all happened too fast. Why did the White want Orman, and why would he lie about the wizard being a spy? Where was Orman taken?

If Kallon was going to search, he'd have to start in

the mountains, but darkness was coming quickly, and he was too weak. The entire attempt would be hopeless anyway.

If he found Orman, what then would he do? Fight to free him? Coerce the dragon to let Orman go? The White had already proven the name Redheart was only the faded remains of a fallen champion. Kallon was a nobody.

He was a weary and aching nobody who was crusted and thirsty and hungry. He couldn't even remember the last decent kill he'd eaten. Ever since Riza had interrupted his life, he'd been off his schedule for flying and hunting. Of course, he was the one who'd dragged the girl to his cave to begin with, and he was the one who'd taken to nightly sweeps over the dwelling where she worked, just to keep an eye on her.

He still didn't understand why he felt compelled to do that. Nor did he understand why he'd gone after Orman and the White. Humans were complicating his life!

Thinking of it that way, it only seemed right that he ought to get something back for all his troubles. A juicy sow would be just the thing. He'd already visited the human village three times this week without casting suspicion, and the smell of the porkers had watered his mouth even then. It would be easy. Just a swoop and a snatch. Humans owed it to him.

He struggled to his feet, legs tingling. He spread his wings and experimentally pumped them. His right wing ached, but worked. He thrust into the air. His heavy tail dangled and was practically useless. His flight was clumsy and unnatural. He'd never be able to chase down anything in this state, anyway, so, really, his only option was to raid the pig farmer.

Nearing the edge of town, he arched his wings to coast. He spied the farm and the grunting mangle of porkers digging in a mound of dry sand. He circled once to make sure the area was clear of humans. Night was just settling, and offered good cover. Silently, he dropped. He reached out his claws.

A scream erupted somewhere to his left. Startled, he missed the catch, and his knuckles cracked against the wooden fence, knocking a post. The post wobbled and fell, and slammed against his wounded rump. He bellowed in pain.

A woman emerged from a small outbuilding, waving her arms and screeching. "Dragon's got my pig! Dragon!" The farmhouse door flew open, and a man stumbled out. He tripped as he tried to fasten his pants. Squealing pigs charged the broken fence and swarmed and squeaked in a churning, pink tornado.

Kallon couldn't climb fast enough. Blood oozed from his opened tail wound. Even his knuckles were bleeding again. He must have lost Riza's bandages when he hit the fence. He could see the spotted trail of blood he left behind for them to track, but he could do nothing about it. He just flew.

His belly skimmed treetops. The shouts of human voices and squealing pigs faded behind him, but his panic stayed strong. It shot through his veins, prodding him forward, blindly leading. He didn't dare lead them toward his cave, so he veered and rambled over strange lands and fields. He lasted as long as he could, pushed by only his sheer will. Finally, he was breathless and exhausted. He had to land.

He heard no posse of chasing humans. He waited for a time, hunched and quiet. Dreary shadows of knobby trees were his only companions. Chirping wind through hollow branches was the only sound. He tried to relax.

There was no time to rest yet, though. He needed his bearings. He didn't recognize where he was. He loped forward, shuffling through the underbrush toward a clearing, and stepped out into crunchy earth. Orange, crunchy earth. His eyes swept over the dustbowl that was once Fell Lake.

He smelled her before he spotted her. Her scent was infused with another's and it momentarily confused him. He inched forward, seeing only a single silhouette against the failing light. He sniffed, and the silhouette moved.

He continued to advance. Only then did he realize what he was seeing. Riza's back was to him, and arms of black leather gripped her waist. A man in black—that man in black—held her tightly, arching her spine. His mouth touched her mouth.

Kallon had no name for what welled up from deep within him, but it exploded and rocked him senseless. Sparkles of dancing light stung his eyes. He stumbled back, orange dust billowing, threatening to choke.

The man's dark eyes met Kallon's face. They glinted. The man's hands went to his sword, and Riza dropped like a felled bird to the ground. "Dragon," he said, his face twisting into a foul smirk. Then he reached slowly for his horse's reins. "Thank you, my dear Riza. I told you you would help me."

Kallon flew. Confused by the sight and his reaction to it, he careened toward the sky. He forgot the pain of his wound; it was engulfed by the inexplicable pain in his chest. A rumble of chasing horse hooves followed him, but he was barely aware.

"Kallon!" he heard Riza call. Against his chest, the linking stone vibrated to life, and from its glowing depths came Riza's voice again. It was a mere whisper beneath the deafening thud of his racing heart.

CHAPTER TEN

Kallon began to think this aching night would never end. He would fly and bleed and struggle in this forever darkness, until his wings turned to dust and his scales to powder, and he would simply cease to exist, unable to land, unable to rest.

His wings drooped, refusing for a moment to work. He felt himself drop toward the ground, and the jolt of warning that passed through him snapped his mind to attention. Glancing below, he found his crystal glowing against his chest like a miniature purple torch. Startled, he nearly dropped again. He urged his wings into a glide, which turned him, and the crystal's glow strengthened.

He swung back to his original course. The stone faded. He swerved upward, and the flicker of remaining flame blinked out completely. When he lowered and turned his shoulder, the glow returned and bathed his chest. Baffled, he tucked and twisted and adjusted his flight until the radiance of the necklace shone ahead and around him with all the brilliance of a star. Lower and lower he followed it, until his knuckles brushed cool earth.

Setting his weight on his feet shot pain through his exhausted muscles. His burning wings sagged in relief against his back. He nearly crumpled right where he landed, but his linking stone urged him forward with a gently drawing whisper. He managed several steps out across an open plain. Then the linking stone's guiding light transformed from amethyst to white, and burned as bright as daylight. Kallon had to squint to discover he was not alone. There ahead of him lay another dragon.

He wasn't sure at first that he really saw it. He could have been hallucinating, or the quick shift of his eyes from dark to light might have caused him to imagine it, so he blinked. And shook his head. And then stared.

His dragon companion was still there, though appeared completely unaware as it slept soundly, its body curled around the trunk of a thin tree. The boughs of the tree appeared to sprout directly from the creature's shoulder. Its snout rested against twitching hind toes. It was a small dragon, from what Kallon could tell. Perhaps a foundling that had wandered and lost its way.

Except that Kallon had never seen, nor heard of, a Gold. This dragon's scales were rich and vibrant. Even the dragon's snout rippled like jewels in the shine of Kallon's stone. The dragon had no horns, no spinepanels, no curving claws. Kallon sniffed quietly. There was nothing familiar in the scent.

The sleeping dragon snorted, and one eye peeped open. Kallon tensed and eased back a step, but he sensed no fear or concern from the other, so he lifted his chin. "Did you call me here?"

The Gold outstretched his front paws and yawned. "Me? Call you?" Its eyes, the same, golden hue of its scales, dipped to glance at Kallon's necklace.

"Yes. You," said Kallon. "There is no one else here."

The Gold smiled pleasantly, but for some reason, the smile made Kallon feel as though he were a foundling himself, and small and stupid. "Why do you wear that stone if you do not even know how it works?"

Kallon's fist clamped protectively around the crystal, dimming it. "It was a gift."

"That does not answer my question."

"I do not have to answer your question, fledgling. I owe you no explanation."

"Fledgling?" The Gold's lumpy eyeridges arched and he tilted his head. "You assume much. You are well-trained in using only your eyes with which to see."

"Eyes see. Ears hear. Mouths talk. Your mouth talks in circles." Kallon lowered his aching head and closed his eyes. "Too much talk."

"You are wounded and hungry. You want answers, but are not yet open to them. First rest, Kallon Redheart. I will be here when you are ready."

Kallon snapped open his eyes. "How do you know my name?"

The Gold was gone. Kallon removed his paw from the stone to allow its light, searching for the other, but the crystal slowly faded. Darkness enveloped him in comforting silence. Whatever questions he'd wanted to ask of the Gold, if there had been a Gold, anyway, would have to wait. He closed his eyes. He cuddled the ground, and he rested.

§

Daylight filtered through Kallon's lashes, stinging like hot grains of sand. He pressed his knuckles to his eyes and rubbed hard. His belly felt comfortably full, though he had only vague, fuzzy memories of chewing fresh meat. He shifted. His movements felt stiff, but were no longer painful. He opened his eyes and curled around to inspect his wound. It was closed over and only a healed scar remained.

"You are feeling better," came the Gold's voice from behind him.

Kallon swung his head toward the dragon. In the night, the crystal had done little justice to the Gold's blinding dazzle. Now bright sunlight careened off its thick hide, scattering prisms to the ground, to the air, to the tree it embraced. "I thought I dreamed you," Kallon said.

"Most think that. You did not."

Kallon stood, feeling strong. He tipped his head and arched his back, stretching lazily, curling his toes. Energy coursed through him, warming his blood. He even broadened his tail, waving and testing. "No pain."

"No," said the Gold.

"You did this."

The Gold nodded.

Kallon lumbered closer. "Why are you here?"

The Gold tilted his head, and smiled that soft smile that made Kallon feel like an idiot. "Why am I here enwrapping this tree at this particular spot? Or why do I exist?"

After a moment's thought, Kallon replied, "Either."

The Gold lifted his gaze to the wispy branches above his head that reached longingly for the sky. Delicate green leaves fluttered with whispers. The bark was thin and papery, colored brown with splotches of pale blue. Kallon didn't recognize it. "I am here enwrapping this tree at this particular spot because it is the only growth of its kind in Leland Province, and it feeds me while I rest."

"Feeds you?"

"It gives me strength, as fresh meat gives you strength."

Kallon drew closer yet, until the lowest, swaying branches of the tree brushed his skull. The leaves tickled his horns, but offered no energy that he could tell. He narrowed his eyes on the golden dragon. "It is only a tree."

"For those who see only with eyes, that is true."

Again with eyes. What else is there to see with? This dragon spoke in riddles, and Kallon didn't care for riddles. This Gold sounded very much like Orman. Suspiciously so. "You speak like a wizard. Are you a magician?"

A rumble of low sound, like a hum, issued from the Gold's smiling mouth. Was that a laugh? "If I am, would that give you the reason for which you search to dislike me?"

"Grah!" Kallon reared back. "You do know magic!"

The Gold lifted a shoulder. "What is magic? Is it not simply a word we use to explain that which we can not explain?"

"There is much to this world that can not be explained. It is not all magic." Kallon waved his hand toward the parched ground. "Spring time brings flowers that have no master to tell them when to open, yet they do. Trees give rise to tiny buds when the snow is gone and is safe to do so. Sun rises to give us day, and sleeps to give us night. No magic."

"You do not call it magic, because you have lived so long with these happenings that they cease to amaze you. In fact, they are so familiar to you that you have come to rely upon them."

"They happen whether I rely on them or not. I can do nothing to prevent it. I can do nothing to cease it."

"You believe in them."

Kallon growled. He cocked a shoulder and spun his back to the Gold. "I believe in nothing."

"Then why do you wear a linking stone around your neck?"

"It was a gift! I told you that!"

After a time of silence, he peered over his shoulder to the Gold, who was frowning. "You believe that taking risks in life will lead to sorrow. You believe that death is the bitter end to a bitter existence."

"Enough!" Kallon slapped his paws over his ears. "If your healing me means I have to listen to your crazy ramblings, then return me to my wounds and leave me in quiet pain!"

"I speak only the truth, Kallon Redheart!" The Gold's voice grew louder. "Whether you choose to listen or to ignore does not change it. The truth is what it is, and you can do nothing to prevent it, nothing to cease it!"

"Leave me alone!"

"Your wings are strong. If you so choose, you can fly."

Kallon wanted to fly. Every muscle in his body was tensed, poised to do just that. He growled in frustration, trying to escape, even while his feet remained stuck fast to the ground.

"Turn and face the truth," the Gold urged.

"No!" He actually didn't quite know what the Gold meant, but if the Gold wanted him to turn, then Kallon would fight that very idea. Toes twitched in resistance. His neck throbbed, trying to refuse. But in the end, his body betrayed him. It inched slowly in a half-circle to face the Gold, and Kallon's eyes met the unthinkable.

The Gold had risen from his place around the base of the tree. The full stretch of the tree's branches was revealed, as well as the plot of ground from which it grew. "It is the Dandria, Kallon. The only one."

The wishing tree. Kallon's hind legs collapsed and his front legs sank to his knees. Behind the narrow trunk of the Dandria stood his mother's tombstone, erect and courageous as the day he'd placed it there. Beside her stone rested his father's.

"We were both called here," said the Gold.

"No!"

"Why do you resist?"

"Because she is dead! She cannot reach me, cannot speak to me! If she could know my heart then she would know she should have never left me!"

"Death has stolen only her body. That linking stone you wear is what maintains your bond, just as it maintains any bond forged in love."

"I do not want any part of your madness or your magic!"

"Your wings are strong."

This time, Kallon won. His wings obeyed him, and his body pushed from the ground to fly. Again he climbed, higher and higher, until his lungs ached and his head swam with dizziness. He refused to believe.

He'd tried to make the stone come alive, and it had frightened him. If he could really talk to his mother, she would find out. She would discover his anger, his bitterness, his feeling abandoned. He couldn't live with those emotions himself, and he would never wish them upon his mother, or his father. No, it would never happen.

He tore the stone from his throat with a roar that rattled the clouds. He threw the crystal to the ground, and swerved away without looking back. Perhaps it shattered. Perhaps it lodged in a crack in the foothills.

He didn't care. He wouldn't care anymore ever again. He wouldn't care what happened to Orman. He wouldn't care what was happening to Riza.

He dove headfirst toward his beloved cave and swept inside. There he curled up in the darkness, drew shadows up over himself like a cloak, and waited to die, no matter how long it took. He would simply wait.

§

He is lying!" Blackclaw snarled at the flimsy, impotent Whitetail. "What good are you to me if at every turn I must double-back to do your work as well as my own?"

"I have done everything you have asked of me. And more."

Blackclaw turned his gaze from the parchments spread out on the floor in front of him. "What is wrong, Whitetail?" He leaned forward, one stray document skittering like a wrinkled leaf toward the advisor's planted foot. "Feeling unappreciated?"

"I only wish to remind you that I have neither balked nor refused any instruction you have given me."

He lifted his chin! The wimp of a dragon actually dared to lift his chin and look Blackclaw squarely in the eye with that statement.

"Careful, Whitetail, or I might get the impression you are developing a backbone."

Whitetail stooped, his maw sweeping the stone floor. "I mean no disrespect, of course."

Blackclaw gathered his strewn parchments into a small stack. "Intricate planning such as I have in store requires much thought, much preparation. I need to trust you to assigned tasks without your constant interruption." Then he yawned a gaping and pleasant yawn, before he climbed to his feet, stretching slowly. "However, I could use a break. I will visit this stubborn wizard with you." He brushed past Whitetail, and then paused. "By the way, it was an excellent improvisation to accuse the wizard of spying in front of the village."

"Yes, it did have the intended effect."

"It would seem so." Blackclaw swung his eyes toward Whitetail as they walked. It had been quick thinking on Whitetail's part. He wasn't sure he'd have been able to come up with that himself. "Tell me more of this Red that interfered. Is he a vassal, as you predicted?"

Whitetail shook his head. "I am not certain, but I think not. There has been no word of a Vassal Red since Bren Redheart. This other claims to be his son, but I have been unable to prove or disprove it."

"Redheart's son? Our slayer dispatched him when the father was killed."

"That was my understanding. But this Red did claim to be the heir."

Blackclaw paused. "If the Red is the heir, that can only mean that the slayer betrayed us. If the Red is not the heir, he has gone to a great deal of trouble to pretend he is."

"Either way," said Whitetail, "His appearance could

not have come at a worse time."

Blackclaw smiled. "Where is the quick thinking you possessed yesterday? I say his appearance could not have been timed better." He pushed off again, and lumbered for the wooden door at the end of the long hallway.

"Which do you suppose him to be, a true Redheart, or a fraud?" Whitetail asked.

Blackclaw wrapped his claws around the handle of the prison door and yanked it open. "I am sure I do not know. But we have someone we can ask."

§

Riza trudged to her room. Inside, she lit the lamp on her bed stand. Then she leaned back against her closed door, and, relieved to finally be alone again after a long day of silent worry, she closed her eyes.

It had been so hard to keep working. Twice, she'd burned the morning bacon. She'd forgotten to add milk to the biscuits. Rusic had even pulled her aside and told her that customers were complaining. "These folks aren't hard t'please, mind ye," he'd said. "But now they're asking, and I'm worried for ye, girl. What's wrong?"

How could she give him an answer, when she hadn't known, exactly? She'd just been remembering how Jastin had hurt her mouth with his kiss. She'd been so happy to see Kallon when he appeared. She hadn't known how the dragon had managed to find them, but there he'd been, again saving her from something she was afraid to think about.

Then she'd heard Jastin's snide thank-you, and had seen Kallon's eyes.

It was that look in Kallon's eyes, really, that had kept her insides tumbling all day so that she couldn't even manage to eat anything. Thinking about it now, she realized she finally had her answer. She covered her face with her hands, trying to force the image out of her mind, but there it clung like a stubborn spider web.

A bleak little coo made her eyes open. She walked to the box at her bedside, and knelt to stroke the gray feathers of the wounded pigeon she'd brought home from the woods. "Hello, little one," she said quietly. "Are we feeling better?"

Her fingertip rubbed over a spot behind the bird's eye where a feather was missing. Feeling wetness, she looked at her fingers. Fresh blood? But that scratch wasn't there yesterday. "You poor thing," she said. "The more I try to help you, the more you seem to suffer."

She gently cupped the bird and drew it out of the crate. It was so weak it didn't even struggle. "Today I brought some sesame seeds," Riza said. She set the pigeon onto her bed and sprinkled the seeds from her pocket. It stared at her, its beady eyes unblinking. Then, it poked its beak at the food.

"That's good. You need to keep up your strength." She smiled and stroked its soft head. It paused now and again to peer up at her, and each time it did, she felt it studying her. Almost as if there was something quietly wise behind its eyes.

"I don't know how you keep hurting yourself," she said. "Maybe I'll leave you out of the crate tonight, and give you more room. When you've finished dinner, I'll pour you a bath, and clean up all those scratches, and then we'll both rest."

There was no reply from the pigeon, of course. She pressed her elbows to her bed, propped her chin on her fist, and watched it eat.

§

Blackclaw stomped out of the dank prison room. He swung his tail clear of the door and slammed it. The iron hinges wobbled, and granite powder filtered like snowfall. "I am losing my patience with that human."

"He is stronger than we realized," said Whitetail, who had left the room ahead of him.

"You are certain no one has been sneaking him food? No water?"

"I have guarded him myself for many hours. The other dragons posted in my stead I would trust with my life."

Blackclaw pounded his fist against the door. "The wizard is too old to be so resilient on his own. I searched him myself for crystals and powders. He hasn't an orifice left to contain them." He lurched along the hall, back to his quarters. He smelled of human sweat and urine and couldn't wait to rid himself of the stench with a bath. "If he will not give us information about this Red, we will have to discover it ourselves. It is clear the wizard is willing to suffer, rather than cooperate. He is of no use to us."

"It is possible that he speaks the truth," said Whitetail. "Perhaps what you have in your possession is the one true circlet."

Blackclaw stopped, his thick claws scraping the stone floor. He swiveled his head and stared down Whitetail. "It is not possible."

"I have consulted our own conjurers," Whitetail said, his face lowering. "They concur that a pure and intense crystal such as the bloodstone is extremely sensitive to subtle tones of emotion. That which makes it so powerful also makes it complicated to use. The slightest portrayal of dark desires—"

"Are you saying my motives are impure?" Blackclaw could feel the acid heat in his stomach churn. His nostrils flared.

"Not at all, your Honor. That is not what I meant." Whitetail's nose brushed the floor.

Blackclaw shifted toward Whitetail, ringlets of smoke billowing with each word. "You are at death's door. I suggest you stop knocking."

He spun away with a growl. "Announce the wizard's pending execution. If the human will not lead us to the Red, we will bring the Red to us. And Whitetail," said Blackclaw, pausing without looking back. "There is plenty of room on the execution block for those who defy my leadership." He turned the corner of the hallway.

§

Jastin cursed. A boulder the size of his fist had broken loose from the mountain face and crashed against his knuckles, bloodying them. He suckled the wound as he paused to assess. He clung near the base of Orin's Peak, the smallest of Leland's mountains, situated between the dying woods of Durance and rest of the rocky chain.

He'd run Blade hard through the night and day, chasing the Red through withered trees, over brown hills scattered with granite rubble, and over deep chasms once flowing with crisp waters. It had been easier to follow the scent than he'd expected. Mingled with the stench of musty dragon scales was the odor of festering tissue. The dragon had been wounded, after all.

Come dawn, Jastin had found the spotted trail of blood that the Red had been so thoughtful to leave behind. It was this trail he'd followed to the mountain. There was a large splash of blood above him on the rocks. It was dry, but fresh enough that the dragon might still be up there somewhere, perhaps fainted. Perhaps dead.

He dragged himself another foot up the mountain, scrabbling for hold. He couldn't leave the Red's death to chance this time. He had to know, and had to finish the job he was given all those years ago, on his first visit to the Leland Mountains.

The battle with the red vassal for the Circlet of Aspira had been brutal, but he'd been young enough back then to outmaneuver the huge beast. Once the poison arrow had brought him down, Jastin had moved into ground fighting. As with any wounded dragon, it had only been a matter of time until Jastin had managed the fatal blow to the base of the beast's tail.

That's when the fledgling had appeared from nowhere. Jastin had heard a squeal, and then it was there, draped over the bleeding vassal, howling and pleading for his father's life. Jastin hadn't planned on killing the youth. He hadn't been hired for that.

But Blackclaw strode out of the woods. "Quite convenient," he'd said. "Finish them both." He'd tossed Jastin a bag of gold, and then lumbered away.

Jastin had swung his sword for the powerful blow that would separate the young dragon's head from his neck. Then the father had groaned, and rumbled something in dragonspeak. A burst of warm light had suddenly roared in his ears like the surf, and had blinded him with painful jabs like fingers to his eyes. When the light faded, there had been only the dead father.

He'd sliced off the Red's hind toe, as he always did for his trophy. Then he'd spent a few minutes searching for the young one. There'd been no tracks, and no lingering scent on the wind. When he'd heard shouts and running footsteps, he decided it was time to get out of there.

He couldn't have guessed that he'd return to this land, called again to the service of the black dragon. When the Red had shown himself in the dragon village, it had appeared to surprise the White. That's good. Now was his chance to kill the beast before anyone had time to realize the truth.

But he wasn't going to find the dragon this way. He was making no progress up the mountain, and he was only exhausting himself. He really was getting too old for this. He slowly picked his way back down, toes and fingers searching in turn for holds, until he was low enough to jump.

Blade whinnied from afar. He tracked the horse to a field of crunchy grassland. "Ho, boy," Jastin called. "You're going back to town. Wrong way." Blade drew up, shook his mane, and splattered foamy spittle to the ground. "I'm thirsty, too," said Jastin. "But we can't go home. Not yet."

He tugged Blade to follow. As he turned, something glinted at the corner of his eye. He peered into the shadowed crevices. It wasn't glinting after all, it was glowing. Jastin crept forward, sensing a throb of energy pulsing from the object like a ripple of heartbeat. He frowned. Magic.

A purple stone, though. Probably amethyst. Either way, it was a valuable chunk of rock, and he tugged it free. It wasn't very large, only the length of his fist, but it was fastened to a strip of leather as an amulet. There was something familiar about the piece. He dangled it before his eyes.

The wind shifted and brought an acrid sting to Jastin's nose. The Red! He was near. He stuffed the amulet into his pocket, swung up onto the leather saddle, and led Blade in a trot.

After several yards, he came to face a looming wall of rock. He was forced to turn sharply north. There was a patch of level ground just beyond a sandy incline, and he guided Blade upward. There, the dragon stench was so powerful it nearly knocked Jastin off the saddle.

In the times he'd trailed Riza to the mountains, she'd never led him directly to the creature's lair. Now he found it. And the dragon was inside it.

He slid from Blade, both feet landing so softly not even the dust was stirred. He inched forward, drawing his sword. Anticipation of the battle brought familiar emotions, but there was an undercurrent of something less recognized. Uncertainty.

This would be his third confrontation with the dragon. No dragon before him had ever lived for even a second battle. Was he losing his edge? He quickly swallowed this thought, along with the salty taste of perspiration from his upper lip.

He paused at the gloomy cave entrance, allowing his eyes to adjust. He could make out a lumpy, dragon-shaped shadow against the wall. No sound, not even breathing, stirred the darkness. Jastin crouched, ready.

The dragon shifted. His fat tail flopped toward Jastin's feet. A faint shaft of light beamed directly across his rump. Right on target. He would need to split the dragon's artery on the first try, because if the dragon awoke with full strength, it would have the advantage in this dark place.

But the dragon was already awake. Jastin's eyes finally adjusted enough to realize the beast's eyes were fixed straight on him. No teeth bared. No blast of sulfur. Just brown eyes, wide and staring. Jastin hesitated. Was there to be no fight at all? So be it. He swung his sword up high to strike.

CHAPTER ELEVEN

Riza stacked two gravy-smeared plates atop each other and balanced an empty mug in the center. She didn't usually clear the plates from the tavern proper, but business was slow. With few meals to cook, she wanted something else to stay busy with, and to help keep her mind off the last couple of days.

"I'll get those," said Rusic, as he came around from the behind the bar. "Why don't ye go drain the brine from the pickle crock, and re-salt 'em?"

Riza waved him away and moved to another table of dirtied mugs. "I don't mind clearing, Rusic. I drained the pickles yesterday."

He glanced toward the door. "What about the meat pies? Isn't it time to check 'em?"

"I just did. I put them out to cool." She followed his gaze toward the door. Outside, three farmers argued, their arms waving. One of them pointed toward the tavern. "Is that Jemiah Rode? He looks angry about something."

"Never you mind about that. Just take those dishes to the kitchen, and get roasting some chickens for dinner." He tugged her arm, rattling the dishes in her hands. He gave her such a push that she stumbled and nearly dropped them.

"Rusic! What's—"

"Just go on, now. I'm expecting a crowd here tonight, and they're going t'be hungry."

She'd never seen him acting so nervous. But she obeyed, and, frowning, she went into the kitchen.

She plunged the dishes into a half-barrel of hot water. Then she set the spit in the stone oven and stoked the fire. She had the uncomfortable feeling that Rusic didn't really need a lot of chickens for dinner, but it wasn't an unusual request, so she ignored the feeling.

She was just plucking out her third chicken when she heard a shout on the other side of the kitchen door. She wiped her hands down the front of her apron and crept toward the door. She gave a little push, and leaned her ear against the crack.

"The girl's got to answer for what she done." She didn't recognize the voice. She tried to peek through the crack, but couldn't see anything except a shaft of floor and bar shelves.

"The girl's in my keep, and as long as she is, ye'll leave her be. Ye got lies and rumors, and nothing else," she heard Rusic say. "Yer cackling like a brood of old hens! I'll not turn her over t'yer witch hunt."

"She brung a dragon to my farm!" shouted Jemiah Rode. "We ain't seen or heard of dragons around here until she showed up. Now she brung one to my farm!"

"There she is!"

The door swung open. Before she could pull back, hands grabbed her arm and wrenched it. A stranger's face scowled down at her. He forced her around the bar, and planted her in front of a group of several men.

Rusic yanked the man's hand off her arm and wedged himself between. "Yer stark crazy. Look at her, she's a wisp of a thing. What's her profit in bringing dragons down on us?"

"Ask her yerself! Look at her clothes!" Jemiah shook his fist. Clenched in his hand was a muddied strip of patchwork cloth. He held the cloth toward her nose, and his eyes hovered like a swarm of black bees. "How did a piece of yer clothes get stuck on my fence, girl?"

Riza felt the room lurch.

"Up t'yer room, Riza," said Rusic. "Lock the door."

"I don't understand," she started to say.

Rusic spun her around and shoved her toward the stairs. "Now."

She stumbled for her room.

Behind her, the men's voices grew louder. "She's got to answer for what she's done! If she brought one dragon, she can bring two!"

"She's a witch!"

"She's worse than a witch, she's a dragon-lover!"

Riza's temples pounded, and her shaking hands struggled to move the door handle. Finally, the latch clicked, and she tumbled into her room. She slammed the door against the thunder of voices that bellowed up the stairs.

She didn't understand. It all seemed fuzzy and unreal. She should take a bundle of things with her. Where was she going? Her bed wasn't made. Her bird was gone. They took her bird. Odd thoughts jumbled against each other. Her brain wouldn't work. She crumpled to her knees and hugged the empty bird crate to her chest.

The voices pounded up the stairs, and bashed against her door. What should she do? Should she just sit there in the room until the voices broke through the door and reached in to get her? Wasn't there someone who could stop them? Rusic? Even Jastin? Kallon?

"Kallon!"

She heard his name explode into the room with her own voice. The voices outside were suddenly silent, and Kallon's name bounced around in echo. She came to, kneeling beside her bed. She stared at the door, at the bird crate in her hands. Had she tumbled from bed with a nightmare?

Then, outside the door, someone asked, "Did you hear that?"

"Who's she talking to?"

"Someone's in there with her!"

The door erupted again in pounding. She jumped to her feet. She grabbed at the oak washstand and grunted as she tried to force it against the door. The door groaned and began to split beneath the barrage.

A coo whispered. She whirled to find her pigeon calmly resting on the ledge outside her window. She ran toward it and peered outside. A long drop. She'd never survive. Where was Kallon, when she needed to fly? "I need to fly," she told her little bird.

"Mattress," the little bird told her.

She stared. Now she was really losing her mind. She didn't have time to think about it, though, because a wood panel of the door shattered, and an arm poked through, grabbing for the handle.

She ran to the door and swung her oil lamp at the arm. "Bloody 'ell!" shouted a voice, and the arm disappeared. "She broke me arm! The witch broke me arm!"

She tossed the lamp and grabbed for her mattress. She dragged it, lost her grip several times, and left a trail of dust and straw. She paused, wheezing. A jolt knocked the door handle to the floor.

"Push! Almost got her!"

"Shut up, I'm pushing!"

"Something's blocking!"

She hoisted the straw mattress over the sill. It hung like a dead goose, half in the room, half outside. She pushed. Her feet slipped. She slammed her shoulder against it. It caved into itself, nearly swallowing her. She tugged and lifted and screeched! The mattress finally whumped to the street.

She didn't look back. She climbed onto the sill, swung her legs to dangle them, and dropped. For a second or two, her stomach went sick with weightlessness. Then she landed hard. Her ankle slapped to the cobblestones. She lay stunned.

A whisper tickled her ear, rousing her. Her pigeon watched her with a tilted head, his wings flapping. Voices spilled out in a tumble from above, and she looked up to find the faces of the men at her window, leering and twisted like gargoyles.

She rolled over to stand. Her left ankle blazed with pain and she cried out. Her leg crumpled beneath her.

"She's over here," called someone a few feet away, waving a torch. She tried to climb to her feet again, and managed to stand, balancing on her right foot. She couldn't see. Her eyes were fuzzy. It took her several moments to realize she was crying. She hobbled blindly along the inn's wall, away from the stranger and his torch.

"Come on, she's here," he said again.

Her pigeon swooped up from the mattress and dove straight for the man's face.

The man waved his arms, and then dropped the flaming stick as he stumbled.

Then she felt hands gripping and bruising her arms. Her ankle jarred and she screamed again in pain, but her own ears couldn't hear it; it was invisible against the wall of the mob's roar.

So many faces, swirling with shadows and torchlight, mouths open and taunting. So many hands, thrashing and grabbing, tugging her arms in their sockets. A yank at her hair snapped back her head. Her face sizzled from the heat of torch flames. She saw a rearing fist, and then pain detonated her cheek, shooting bright lights into her eyes and rattling her teeth. She whimpered, knowing she was going to die. Her muscles went slack.

Moments later, the hands were gone. The cobblestones were a cold compress against her cheek. As the ringing in her ears faded, she heard a new voice call out, "People of Durance, you're making a mistake!"

She managed to lift her head. The voice belonged to Jastin Armitage. He sat atop Blade, his arms raised. She sobbed in relief, and dragged herself toward him.

Black boots hit the ground and strode closer. Then Jastin crouched, and drew her up to sit. "Riza," he said. "You should have listened to me." He stroked her hair away from her aching face.

"What did I do?" she asked through a pinched throat. Flickering light cast over his features, deepening the lines of his bearded face.

"She brung a dragon to my farm!" came a shout.

"She's a dragon-lover!"

Jastin released her and stood to face the swarm. "You idiots! She's a girl! Look at her!"

Murmurs erupted. Looks were exchanged. "She's a dragon-lover and a witch!" someone shouted. The swarm re-gathered and shifted forward, fists and torches waving.

"You lay another hand on that girl," Jastin said, his sword drawing out from its sheath, "and I will remove it from its wrist." He waved the tip of his weapon toward the crowd, which swept back with a hush.

"Ye warned us," said Jemiah Rode, and he stepped out from the crowd. "Ye said dragons was coming, and they did! Right as this girl showed up!"

"She's brought trouble on us!"

"We got more trouble 'n we need already!"

Jastin waved his sword again. "All of you be quiet! Your dragon troubles are over. The Red is dead."

An invisible wind froze Riza's bones. Kallon? Dead?

"And just how do you know that?" Jemiah's eyes narrowed.

Jastin reached into a pouch at his side. In the darkness, Riza couldn't make out what was in his hand until he pitched it to the ground. It rolled, withered and dusty, toward her knees. A toe. A red dragon toe with a curving claw. She screamed.

Then she went numb. She reached for the shrunken thing, but couldn't even feel it in her hand. She hugged the body part, Kallon's body part, to her chest. She sobbed. It was all her fault. He'd never wanted a friend. She'd pushed him and followed him. And she'd killed him.

She arched forward, pressed her forehead to the ground, and died inside.

From somewhere far away, she heard Jastin again. "Your superstitions have harmed an innocent girl who was only trying to help you. She lured the beast to me, as I asked her to do."

"No!" Riza's voice came out with more strength than she realized she had. She stood and tried to glare at Jastin, and at the mob, even though it welled the pain in her body. "I won't lie! I don't care what you do to me.

I did not, and would not, help anyone harm that dragon. He was my friend!"

The crowd surged toward her, and even Jastin couldn't stop them. They knocked him to his feet and covered him like a swarm of ants over a dry leaf. Riza's legs trembled from the effort of standing, but she held tightly to all she had left of Kallon and watched them come.

Then, near her feet, the ground spat up a tongue of flame. The heat knocked her back to the ground, and the scaly toe bobbled away. Another flame erupted toward her left. Townsfolk dropped torches and ran, pointing and screaming toward the dark sky.

She looked up. A great, black cloud drew in fast on flapping shadow wings. A dragon-shaped mouth opened, and a spout of fire belched out to strike the ground behind her. Then the cloud descended, and was lit up by a wall of its own flame. It wasn't really black, and it wasn't a cloud.

"Kallon!" Riza called through crackling heat. She didn't care if she was imagining it. She reached for him. Then she went limp.

§

Kallon lunged and caught Riza before she hit the ground. She bore scratches and fist marks. Her clothing was torn. She looked just as she had the first time he'd laid eyes on her. He shook with a rage he'd forgotten he could possess. He cradled her, feeling her like a feather against his chest.

"You did come," said the voice of the dark human.

Kallon lifted his eyes. The human limped toward him, his shape distorted through the haze of fading heat and smoke. Around him, villagers continued to scatter, except for those few that beat sticks at a thatched roof that had caught flame.

"Tell me," said Kallon. "How is it that a race of creatures so filled with hate and destruction can produce such a gentle spirit as in this girl?"

"I suppose in the same way that a race of hearty, flying beasts can produce such a miserable weakling as you," Jastin said.

"It's you who didn't save her," Kallon said.

"She didn't want to be saved," Jastin said. "She's being infected by your poison."

Kallon growled. "Poison?"

The human stooped, wrapped his hand around his weapon, and pointed the blade toward Kallon. "You were a fledgling when you first stared up at me with eyes that wanted to die. You looked at me today with those same eyes."

The dark human. The sword. Kallon finally remembered, and his stomach churned. "You."

"And I'm only too happy to oblige."

Kallon's voice roiled out with a billow of smoke. "You killed my father."

"Your father was already dead. I only made it official."

Kallon lunged. He snapped at the human's head,

but the man dodged and spun. Riza was snatched from his arms before he realized what had happened. The human held her, dragging her feet as he backed away.

"You coward!" said Kallon. "You would use her as a shield against me?"

"Oh, no," the human said. "I'm removing her as your shield against me."

Riza jerked and moaned.

"Be careful! You're hurting her!"

"She's no concern of yours anymore." The human laid Riza to the ground and touched his fingers to her pale cheek. "When I heard her voice in the cave, I thought she was there. I thought somehow she'd followed me." He stood, pointing the tip of his sword at the linking stone around Kallon's neck. "What is that crystal, that she called your name through it?"

Kallon touched the stone at his throat. It was still glowing a vibrant purple. It had begun a short time ago, in his cave, when Riza's voice had called out just as the man's sword had lifted to strike Kallon's tail. Both the human and Kallon had been startled.

There hadn't been time to think. The man dug the glowing crystal from his pocket, and he and Kallon had stared, listening, as Riza's voice cried out again, and screamed in fear. *What…?* the man had asked, his face going pale.

Kallon had snatched the stone and pushed the human out into the darkness. *Go!* he'd shouted. *They're hurting her!*

Kallon had been left alone to listen to her strangled

pleas. He'd shrunk farther and farther into the cave's darkness, living her fear through the stone. He'd clamped his claws around it, trying not to hear, trying not to know that the human would be her hero.

Except the man wasn't. Kallon had felt Riza resist. And when she'd thought he was dead, he'd shared her agony. She'd thought he was dead, and she'd shattered. In that moment, his own broken will suddenly set. He'd shot out into the night. He hadn't even needed the stone to guide the way. He'd just followed his heart.

Now he stood watching the human and calculating his distance. Kallon would be able to scoop up Riza in two wide steps. "I should have killed you. I shouldn't have trusted her to you."

The human gripped the base of his sword with both hands. "I left you alive, not the other way around."

"And I was forced to come because you failed!" Kallon shouted.

"Forced? Did you say forced?" The human crept closer. "She stood up to that pack of wolves and told them you were her friend." He poked his sword again toward the crystal. "Did the stone tell you that?"

"I heard it."

"And you're offended that you had to help?" The man glared. "I'll be doing her a favor by destroying you before she has the chance to find out what you really are."

Kallon bellowed and charged the human. As the man parried, the sword slapped Kallon's shoulder. Kallon swept his tail at the man's feet and knocked him flat. Then he grabbed for Riza.

"Leave her!" The human jumped to his feet and stabbed. Kallon felt a sting in his ribs, but ignored it.

Kallon was about to lunge again, when a distant voice cried out, "It's the dragon!" He froze.

The villagers had stopped panicking in time to notice him again. Faces peered from around buildings. "Weapons!" someone shouted.

Chaos broke out as villagers raced to action.

The dark man cursed. "Get her out of here. Go."

Kallon turned, but spotted a red, withered dragon toe on the ground. His father's body had been missing a claw on his left rear leg. He scooped up the toe, and, with a snarl, stuck it in the human's face. "This isn't over. I will kill you."

The man's blade chopped the toe in half. "Not today."

Arrows clanged into Kallon's scales. The dark human shouted and waved his arms. "Be careful! You'll hit the girl!"

Kallon thrust airborne, not wasting another moment. The bedlam faded behind him, and the beating of his wings in the warm night drowned out the shouts. He'd come very close to crunching off the human's head tonight, and still trembled from the thought of it. He was filled with disgust at the violence of it all. At the humans. At himself.

"Kallon?" Riza's fuzzy voice came from near his throat. "Am I dreaming?"

"No," he said.

Her soft arms gripped his neck. "I thought you were dead."

By the sound of her words, he could tell she was crying. He wished he knew what to say. For a while, the only sound between them was the whuffle of air as his wings pumped. Then he took a deep breath. "Riza?"

"Hmm?"

"You told me once that you thought your mother did a courageous thing by just closing her eyes and dying. Do you remember?"

She shifted in his grasp. "I don't really know if that's what happened."

"But if it is. Do you really believe her choosing to die was brave?"

She paused before she spoke. "I believe it can be brave to die when you want more than anything to live," she said. Then her voice grew very soft. "But I think it's just as brave to live, when you want more than anything to die."

After a few minutes, she went still, and he thought she'd fallen asleep. He looked down to find her bathed in the amethyst light of the linking stone. Her eyes were open. "I wish she'd lived," she whispered.

§

Riza awoke to the gentle music of trickling water. She became aware of the cool rush bathing her throbbing ankle, and a damp compress against her eyes. She rolled to her side, but was urged again to her back by a mild nudge. Her foot was guided and submerged again into cold wetness.

She tugged the compress from her eyes. Bright sunlight flooded her face. Above, a canopy of green leaves swayed in a breeze. The ground beneath her back was lush and cool. Bird song twittered playfully, echoing among thick ferns. The pungent scent of honey soaked the air, and when she breathed in deep, she could taste sweetness at the back of her throat.

She sat up slowly to find Kallon crouched beside her at the edge of a meandering stream, his eyes riveted to her leg. She shifted, and he carefully coaxed her ankle back into the water. She smiled, and tugged her ankle from the stream on purpose, only to have him repeat the motion.

"Must keep still if you wish to heal," he said.

"Have you been there all night?"

"Yes."

"Keeping my ankle in the water?"

"Yes." His muzzle swung toward her. His nostrils flared as large as her fist, and the breath he sucked in stirred her hair against her cheeks. "You still smell of blood."

Blood. She'd seen it redden the eyes of those angry faces in the night, and the memory rushed a chill through her heart.

"You're shivering," Kallon said, his nose bumping her chin. "You cold?"

"A little, I guess." She looked around herself at the walls of shifting green. "Where are we? This place doesn't feel real. It's like a little pocket of forgotten magic."

"If there is any magic left in these mountains, it's here. If there was any magic to begin with."

"So we're still in Leland?"

"We are." He yawned, and a drop of his saliva splashed to her thigh. It stung through her skirt like hot bacon grease.

"You're exhausted."

"I'm fine. It's you who needs rest. We have much more flying to do when you're ready." His eyes closed, and his muzzle hung so low it brushed her lap.

"You're not going to take me back to Durance, are you?" Riza asked.

His eyes snapped open. "No. You can never go back there."

"Then where are we going?"

"Not we. You. Home. Back to your father and your people."

She stiffened. "But I don't want to go back there, either!" She grabbed his jaw to look him deep in the eyes. "I would rather go back to Durance than to face my father and admit to him that he was right."

He pulled his face from her hands.

"Please, Kallon," she begged. "Don't take me back there. It will make everything I've been through all for nothing."

"All you've been through has been for nothing. Violence stalks you, Riza, and you are too innocent to recognize its traps. You walk straight into them, and it's me who keeps pulling you out."

"Maybe my place is with you, then," Riza said.

"You really did hit your head hard."

"What?" She leaned forward. "What's wrong with that? Even my father speaks of a time when dragons and humans used to live together as equals, if I serve him enough wine."

"Not equals," Kallon said. "Servants and masters."

"Oh, come on," Riza said. "Dragons served by choice, not bondage."

"What do you know about it?" Kallon sat back with a snort.

"I know what I see of you," Riza said. "I know you keep helping me, and not because you're my servant."

Wispy curls of steam puffed from his snout.

"Dragons could crush us out of existence any time they want, but they don't," Riza continued. "They choose a higher calling. They forfeit their own will for the sake of a greater good."

He poked his snout toward her face. "Human survival is the greater good?"

"No." Impulsively, she stroked his cheek, which she found cool and smoother than she'd guessed it would feel. "Our being together is the greater good."

He pulled from her touch. "Humankind and Dragonkind, you mean."

She withdrew her hand, fingers curling into a fist, which she pressed to her lap. Is that what she meant? "Of course," she said.

He regarded her for long time. "If more humans

thought like you, Riza, you wouldn't be in so much danger among them."

She smiled. "I like when you say my name."

"Lay back and rest now," Kallon said.

She didn't feel like resting, she felt warm and tingly inside and ready to walk, or even fly. But she lay back anyway, and watched him watching over her until the melody of the spring faded from her ears, and the green leaves huddled together in a blanket of darkness against her eyes.

CHAPTER TWELVE

Kallon squinted open an eye. He must have dozed. He didn't mean to, but he felt as though he'd already been tired for days, and his vigil over Riza had drained what energy he had left. His peering eye found Riza staring directly at him. Her thin legs were lumpy beneath his chin. He'd fallen asleep with his head on her lap.

"Why did you say that if Leland had any magic left it would be here?" she asked.

He lifted his head. Then he groaned, his neck gone stiff. Riza wiggled her feet and legs. They must have gone stiff, too, with the weight of his slumbering head on them.

"Why would it be here, if there was magic left?" Riza asked. "And why did you say 'if there was any to begin with'?"

"How long have you been awake?" Kallon gazed up, but the bushy leaves of their green haven blocked the sun. The temperature was no gauge, either, for this place was warm with morning sun and cool with an evening breeze at the same time. It was a comfortable memory of the Leland Province that once was.

"I've been awake for a while," Riza said. "My ankle is better." She held out her foot. Her ivory flesh was pickled from the water, but the black-blue discoloration was nearly faded. "I think there is magic here. How did you know about it?"

The metallic tang of blood still overpowered her scent, which concerned him. Predators of any species knew the smell of the wounded, and he wanted her rid of it. "It would be good for you to bathe entirely," he said.

"But it's so cold!"

"It's good and clean." He poked the tip of his tongue into the bubbling stream. It *was* good and clean, and he drank.

"Well. All right." She crawled forward and dipped her hands into the water, swishing them in lazy circles. "I'll bathe if you tell me how you know about this place."

"I have known about it for years." He waited for her to move further into the stream, but she only pressed her mouth into a tight line and stared back.

"I don't like talking about this," he said.

"You don't like talking about anything." She smiled, and her eyes were rich with the emerald of the velvety grass she sat on.

He sighed. "Very well. Follow me." His weary legs pushed to stand.

"This stream was once a river. Its mouth is near

the top of Mount Gore. It circles the mountain, disappearing into the earth and reappearing again among the trees and boulders." He glanced over his shoulder.

She was following, but was favoring her ankle.

"Can you walk?" he asked.

"Yes," she said. "Please go on."

"Legend says that the river is the heartbeat of the province. It pumps life into the veins of crystal ore that run deep through the land, in all territories, dragon and human."

"Look there," he said, and paused at the edge of a wide pool that parted the lush growth. Here, his eyes traveled upward to the sheared-off top of Mount Krag. Beyond the mountain the sky arched as a tapestry of puffy clouds threaded through turquoise linen.

"Oh. It's breathtaking." Riza came up beside him and rested her palm against his shoulder.

"That trickle was once a waterfall," Kallon said. "Follow the water with your eyes, do you see that ledge up along the mountain, just there?"

She nodded.

"You can't see from here, but there's a place that was once the home of Orman Thistleby. He's the human who helped me when I first brought you to my cave."

"That day you saved my life." Her face turned to him, and her chest rose with a deep breath. "The first time you saved me."

The warmth in her voice stole his words. He simply nodded.

"Where is he now?" she asked. "You said he was in trouble that day the bird fell from the sky."

Shame clamped his chest. "I don't know. I tried to help him but failed."

"What do you mean? What happened?"

He shook his head. He couldn't bring himself to explain.

"Kallon, what happened to your friend?" Riza moved closer. "Is he dead?"

"I don't know," he whispered, in case the trees were listening. "If he is, it is because I failed him."

"Tell me what happened," she said.

He closed his eyes. "He was taken by a White. I followed them to Wing Valley, the first time I have been there since…"

"Go on." Her fingers brushed his scales, and he was embarrassed by the pleasant shudder that arced like tiny lightning down his spine.

"I found him behind a shelter, tied like a thief. When I tried to free him, your human friend in black was there."

"Jastin Armitage?"

He nodded. "Then the White accused Orman of spying, and there was a struggle, and your friend wounded me, and Orman was taken."

"He is not my friend." Such venom oozed from her words that he tipped his head to find her face. He was startled by her eyes. Their inner glow had been snuffed and replaced by shards of ice. She turned away, and stepped closer to the edge of the pebbled mountain pool. Her frozen gaze stared out across the horizon.

A steady dribble of water pocked the surface of the pool, marking time as Riza stood silent. He wondered what she was thinking. He had his own dark thoughts about Jastin Armitage, and guessed, even hoped, a little, that hers might be the same. She surprised him, though.

"Is that Mount Gore?" she asked. "The high, green peak in the distance?"

He turned to look. "Yes."

"Is it wearing a crown?" she asked.

He smiled without intending to. "That's the dragon council arena, where Leland dragons gather for public meetings and celebrations. The council leader lives there, too. Their chambers are carved deep into the mountain, though. You can't see those from here."

"Carved by magic?"

He'd never considered how the arena came to be. It had just always been there. "I don't know," he said.

"Mount Gore is where the river comes from," Riza said. "If the river is the heartbeat, then that mountain is the heart." She spun to face him. "So the blood pumped by the heartbeat must be magic, right?"

He settled onto his haunches and blinked. "The wizard spoke almost those very words."

"The wizard?"

"Orman."

"Oh. Your friend." She moved toward him again. "Where was he taken?"

"To Mount Gore, I think."

"Then that's where we should go look for him."

Kallon shook his head. "No. You have no place there, and I have no place there anymore. I can do him no good. In fact, I would probably make things worse."

"But how do you know unless you try?" she asked.

"No." He meant it. "He's not helpless. He's stronger than he seems."

She pressed a finger to his chin. "You're braver than you let yourself believe. You're a dragon of action. It takes all your strength to resist that."

"I will not go, Riza. That mountain was once mine, but I forfeited my right to it. To return now would be returning as a stranger."

He thought he would find disappointment in her expression, but he didn't.

She only nodded, very lightly, and then smiled in a sad way. Her fingers drifted along his jaw. Then she pressed her cheek to his throat and hugged him tightly.

A flutter of resistance tickled his brain, but he closed his eyes and let the embrace come.

The air flashed cool. He opened his eyes to find himself and Riza engulfed in a shadow. Then the shadow was gone, and the air was warm again.

"What was that?" Riza asked.

"Something flew over. I'll go see."

When Riza moved to climb onto his back, he stepped away and shook his head. "No, you stay here where it's safe. Take your bath. I won't be long."

"Wait, look, was that it? There's a bird up there on that ledge." She pointed.

"No, the shadow was too large. That's probably one

of Orman's birds. He had many like that."

"It looks like the one I was taking care of in my room." She turned to Kallon with a hop. "Will you take me up there? I think I know that bird!"

"First I'll fly. If all is well, I'll take you up there when I get back." He flicked his claw in the water and splattered her. "Bathe, and wait for me."

"Bossy." She kicked a splash against his forelegs.

As he moved to turn, she looked up to the flapping bird high on the ledge, and to the snowfall of pale feathers it released. He paused.

"Don't try to climb up there," he said. "Those rocks are sharp and slippery."

"Don't be silly. I'm going to take a bath." She wiggled her fingers. "Shoo."

"Riza."

"It was your idea. Do you want me to bathe or not?"

Still he hesitated. "I won't be long."

"I know." She turned her back, stepped out of her rags of clothing, and moved cautiously into the pool of water.

He watched for a moment. Then he turned and stretched his wings.

But she squealed, and he darted a look over his shoulder. "Cold," she said, hugging her arms to herself. Then she submerged.

§

Riza popped her head back up out of the water to watch Kallon fly away, up over the treetops and into pale threads of fog still clinging to the morning sky.

He was right to be suspicious of her. She was considering climbing up those jutting rocks where the waterfall was supposed to be. Something was up there. Not just the bird she was worried about—the one who she'd swear had spoken to her in her room—but something more. She sensed a sort of charge around her, the way a looming thunderstorm made the air feel like thistles on her skin.

But just as she was pushing through the water to find her clothes, she spotted Kallon. He was a speck of dust in the far distance but returning quickly. He must have known her curiosity would get the better of her.

She raised her hand to wave at him at the same moment she realized, as the sinewy dragon shape grew larger and closer, that the color was wrong. Not red.

Brown.

She froze. She hadn't even considered that other dragons would be here. Of course they would. The mountains were their home. But friendly? Toward a human? She didn't know. Couldn't think of the right way to react.

As the brown dragon loomed large, their open mouth fierce and steaming, their eyes sharp as daggers, Riza decided to run.

She turned, splashing and pushing against the river. Her ankle twisted, her bare feet slipped on riverbed stones. She sank, flailing. She surfaced again, gasped a breath, and then felt a scaly grip around her shoulders.

The weight of it plunged her under once more, briefly, and she sucked water down her throat. Then she felt the river and the bed beneath it drop away. She was yanked hard into the air.

She coughed water. Went dizzy. She tried to call out for Kallon, or scream, or yell anything at all, but she could only writhe and vomit river water.

§

Blackclaw huddled over a wooden box in his chambers, cradling it with tender respect. He had once believed its contents to be an answer to his desires; a shortcut through the gloomy fog of time. He'd always known his fate was to bring Dragonkind to ruling power. He believed it still.

He lifted the ornate lid to reveal the circlet inside. The once-crimson bloodstone, held by thin fingers of woven gold, had gone black and hollow. He drew the pad of his thumb over the crystal. No spark of life, no hint of power. Even the surrounding metal seemed more gnarled than braided, desperately clutching the bloodstone like the hands of a mourner against the face of a dying hero.

He'd been a fool. A snarl erupted from the depths of his anger, and he threw the wooden box against the wall. So many years, wasted! Too many years to count.

He'd spent them believing in a lie, putting his faith into a trick of art. He thought he'd been holding the future, but there was no future in the twisted, broken circle of gold lying impotent on his floor. No hope in the blackened stone. His future was his own to carve, just as it had always been.

Oh, he would have the circlet. The one, true Circlet of Aspira, created by skilled dragon artisans, that was hidden by the wizard. The one the Red died protecting. He would have it, and not because he needed it, but because it should have been his all along. He would prove to the wizard, to Whitetail, and to all dragons that he was no fool.

"Leader Blackclaw."

He turned to find Whitetail's snout poking through the opened door of his chambers.

"You are summoned," Whitetail said.

"Is it the human hunter?" Blackclaw asked.

"No, there has been no word from him in several days." Whitetail pushed the door open further, and waved snowy claws toward the hallway.

"Do not tell me the Red has finally come in regards to the wizard."

"No," Whitetail said. "But this is nevertheless very interesting."

Blackclaw stared. He crossed his forelegs. One claw tapped against the stone floor. "And are you going to tell me what it is, or shall I continue guessing?"

"Vaya Brownwing has arrived with a human companion she claims to have found in dragon territory. She believes the human to be a spy." The corner of his mouth curled into a grin.

"A spy?" It was all Blackclaw could do not to release a belly laugh. "Well done." He lunged through the door to follow. "Let us go see this spy. And tell me more of this Brown. She is the daughter of Hale Brownwing, is that right?"

"Yes, that is correct."

"Has she been mated?"

"If memory serves, she was to be mated to Redheart's son."

Blackclaw stopped. "Then she would know if this Red whom we seek is the heir." He grabbed Whitetail's chin and yanked it close. "Why did you not mention this earlier?"

Whitetail gurgled. "I only just remembered. I am not even certain I am remembering correctly."

Blackclaw released him. "I have more faith in your memory than I have in these stone walls to prop up the ceiling." He lumbered down the hallway again. "This may be just the opportunity we have been seeking. If we no longer need the wizard, I will be glad to be rid of him. Come on, Whitetail. You are dawdling again."

§

Kallon's instincts told him the only flying creature large enough to create such a shadow was a dragon, but he knew of few dragons that flew near Mount Krag any more. He searched longer than he'd meant, determined to find this dragon and question them. If they had been scouting Orman's home or belongings, there was much he'd like to know.

But daylight waned, and still he found nothing of significance in the sky or in the paths beneath him that wound like yarn through dying lands. The passing creature's scent had been carried off by the wind. Finally, he gave up. He'd left Riza alone too long.

He returned to the river and swung low to the pool. She was gone. He landed at the pool's edge, his thick tail splashing into the water. She was right, it was cold. He withdrew his tail and gave it a shake.

"Riza!" He called, and lifted his snout. Her scent lingered, though it was faded. He followed the waft of dampness toward the wall of rock beneath the high ledge. No. She didn't really try to climb, did she? His foot caught the edge of something soft, and he looked down.

Her tattered clothing. Would she have tried to climb the mountain without her clothing? It didn't seem logical. But then, he didn't really understand humans.

Pigeon feathers floated atop the rippling pool. An eerie feeling skittered across his scales.

He swooped high and fast, up to the ledge and over, and came to the flat of Orman's mountain. "Riza!" He loped toward the mound of wood that was once Orman's home, his nostrils flaring, searching for any sign of strength in her scent. But here there was no scent of her at all. His sniffing grew anxious, his scales tightened against the back of his skull in alarm. Where was she?

§

Blackclaw prodded the human with a foreclaw. "She is all bones, and puny and pale. Even for a human." He swung his gaze to the Brown. "What about this wisp made you suspect her?"

"She was bathing in the stream of Wren Meadow," the Brown answered, her amber eyes meeting Blackclaw's gaze.

"And for this she was brought to me?" He eased forward a step and lowered his chin.

She continued to hold his eyes confidently. In any other female he would consider this defiance, and not tolerate it. But the fading sun lengthened the shadows of her lashes, softening her stare, and the unblemished scales of her face were relaxed.

He could not take his eyes from her. "You're a Brownwing, aren't you?"

"Yes," the Brown answered. "Vaya Brownwing."

He remembered her now. Councilor Hale's daughter. When had she developed into such a beautiful creature? And how had he not noticed before?

"This human was near the wizard's hut," Vaya said.

"Right. But the wizard is here, so they could not be consorting." Blackclaw pressed closer yet, his snout nearly brushing her forehead. "So I must assume that you have further reason for bringing this woman to me."

At that, the Brown's gaze faltered. She nudged the woman who appeared to have lost consciousness by the way she was dangling from the Brown's delicate claws.

The woman moaned, then tried to stand with her own strength. "She was not alone," said Vaya. "She was with a fellow dragon."

"A fellow dragon? Why is this dragon not standing before me as well, then?"

"When I circled back to investigate, he had gone, and there was only the human."

"I see," Blackclaw said. "Did you recognize this dragon?"

"I did."

Blackclaw nodded and awaited the name. He might have grown impatient by now, but he was enjoying the rhythm of their little game. "And it was…?"

"Kallon Redheart," Vaya said.

Redheart. His jaw clenched. He swung a look at Whitetail, who lifted bony shoulders and appeared apologetic. He would have liked to tear the head off his pallid advisor, but instead, he coughed a billow of steam. Then he looked again to the Brown, guarding his expression. "You are certain of his identity?"

"I am. We were once friends," she said.

"But no longer?"

Vaya released the human's arms. "What will you do with this one?"

Blackclaw glanced toward the human. Her eyes had become clearer and more intense.

"What are you to the Red, human?" Blackclaw asked her.

The woman blinked, looked to Vaya and back to Blackclaw.

"She does not appear to know Dragonspeak," offered Whitetail.

Blackclaw closed his eyes. "Thank you, Whitetail. Quite astute of you."

This questioning was accomplishing precious little. What he wanted now was answers. He pressed his knuckles to the painful throb between his eyes. "What are you to the Red, human?" he asked again in her own language, eyes still closed.

When there was no immediate response, he lowered his paw from his forehead and thrust his snout in the girl's face.

She meekly asked, "Why am I here? What have I done?"

He stepped back. "Whitetail, are my questions terribly difficult?"

"No, sir," Whitetail said.

"Why do you suppose my simple questions are being answered with more questions?"

"I could not say."

Blackclaw clenched fists. "What I want to know is why this Red, who claims to be the heir of Bren Redheart and thought to be dead all these years, has appeared from nowhere? Where has he been? What does he want?" He eyed Vaya and the human. "Which of you can tell me?"

Silent stares. He felt the pungent sting of acid bubble against the back of his throat. "Very well. Which of you can tell me where to find him?"

Still nothing.

His jaw clenched so fiercely against his rising anger that it ached. "Brownwing, you have brought me a potential prisoner that I must feed and care for. Explain to me why I should have been bothered with this. Now."

Vaya shifted, glanced at Whitetail, and then focused her sparkling gaze once more on Blackclaw's face. "I can only tell you that Redheart appeared in Wing Valley recently, searching for the man who is imprisoned for spying. This evening I discovered him in the company of yet another human." Her golden stare turned down to the girl, and shifted dark and angry.

Now he was getting somewhere. A female scorned, no doubt. He pressed his palms together, contemplating.

The human could be questioned at any time, and probably had less to do with the current situation than the Brown gave her credit for. She would most likely turn out to be nothing. On the other hand, this Brown and her resentment could prove useful.

He gently spoke. "Vaya, you have done the right thing. Our times are troubled ones, and we cannot risk assumptions. I will get to the heart of this matter, but for now, join me for dinner, and tell me of your history with the Red."

He held up a paw as her mouth opened.

"I insist," he said, and offered a soft smile. Then he turned to Whitetail, his voice low. "Toss the human in with the wizard. I will deal with her later."

Then he turned to Vaya once more. "As for you," he said, as he swept up her soft foreleg in his claws, "I believe you should be rewarded for your initiative. What kind of wine do you enjoy with venison?"

Vaya pulled her foreleg from his grasp. Her golden eyes searched his, and for a moment, he thought she would deny him. He hadn't before known what that could feel like.

But then she smiled. Soft and mysterious. "Mulled raspberry," she replied. She offered out her paw.

"Something we have in common," he said. "I'm sure there is more to discover." He hooked her paw around his foreleg, more gently this time, and drew her toward the Great Hall.

CHAPTER THIRTEEN

Riza struggled to keep up with the pace of the white dragon who dragged her down a long, dank hallway of stone. "What's happening? Where are you taking me?" she asked between tripping up against the dragon's legs and tugging at his painful grip. "I don't understand why I'm here! I haven't done anything wrong!"

Her captor's face could have been carved from the very stone of the walls. When they reached a wooden door at the end of the corridor, he tugged a chain holding it closed.

"Do you understand me?" she asked.

If he did, he made no indication. He yanked open the door, and she felt a sharp slap against her back. She tumbled and fell to her face. Behind her, wood slammed against stone, and the metal chain clanked.

A mouth of darkness swallowed her, and she felt herself sliding down its damp, sticky throat. A lumpy mass pressed up against her face as though she'd landed on a stomach of ice. The stench of the place was an outhouse gone rancid. She curled her arms and legs to herself, shivering. Before, she'd been so frightened she couldn't even cry. Now she was so frightened she couldn't stop.

"There, there, child," came a hoarse but gentle voice from the darkness. Shuffling sounds of movement came near.

Riza bolted up, caught between relief and terror. She crossed her arms against her bareness. "Who's there? What do you want?"

"My name is Orman."

"Orman Thistleby?" Riza asked. "Kallon's friend?"

"Then you do know him," said the voice, growing louder. His presence seemed near her face. She felt cold hands bump her shoulder, then rest atop them.

She stiffened.

"Don't fear," Orman said. "I only wonder if you're the one Kallon told me about. The girl who has been helping me."

"Helping you?" Riza bucked her shoulders to dislodge his hands. If only she could see! The blackness was harsher than even Kallon's cave, and made everything seem immense and threatening.

His hands did leave her shoulders, but she felt them again on her arms, then grasping her hands. "You're frozen! Are you naked?" Soft rustling sounded. "Take my tunic. Mind the pockets." Cloth pressed to her face. The smell told her how filthy it was. Still, it was warm.

She slipped it over her head.

"Kallon said a white dragon brought you." She tugged the fabric into place around her knees, and her hands moved curiously along the seams in search of pockets.

"Yes," Orman said.

"How long have you been here?" she asked.

"Lost track," he said.

She felt his hands again, stopping her searching fingers.

"The pockets are there," he said. "You'll have to trust me on that."

She pressed her hands to her lap. "Why did they bring you?" she asked.

He sighed, and she could hear the creak of his old bones as he shifted to settle. "Fordon Blackclaw doesn't need reasons to do what he does. But if I were to give one, it would be that he's greedy."

"Fordon Blackclaw?" Riza asked.

"Did you meet a monstrous black dragon?" asked Orman.

"Yes," Riza said. Her nostrils still sizzled from his breath.

"That's him."

"He wants to know where Kallon is," she said.

"Did you tell him?"

She shook her head. "I don't know where he is." She drew her knees up to her chest and hugged them tightly. Tears sprang anew, and her chest tightened with trying to hold them back. "I don't understand any of this."

"No. I'm sure you don't." He patted her kneecap.

She suddenly wondered how much more frightening it would be if she were alone. The sound of his voice somehow kept the panic at bay.

"Why does Mr. Blackclaw want Kallon?" she asked.

His patting hand paused.

"...Orman?"

When he spoke, the lilt in his voice led her to think he was smiling. "Where are you from, child?"

"Cresvell, originally," she answered. "Most recently, Durance. Why?"

"Cresvell," he repeated. "Far removed from any dragon territories. Almost not even in Leland Province. Can you see the mountains from there?"

"On a clear day we can almost see shadows of them. We know they're there."

"Is that what you came searching for when you left home? The mountains?"

Riza frowned in thought. "I don't think so. I don't know that I left in search of anything, I only know I couldn't bear to stay."

"You're an adventurer," Orman said.

Riza rested her chin on her bent kneecaps. "If I am, I'm not a very good one."

"No one gets it just right on the first try," Orman said.

She closed her eyes. "I'm sorry for you that you're here, but I'm glad for me that you are. I don't like the dark."

"Don't sleep well in it."

"No. Not anymore." She lifted her head and squinted at him. She could almost make out a faint, fuzzy outline. "How do you know I don't sleep well?"

"I'm a wizard, after all. I'm not without my tricks."

"What kind of tricks? Do you have a way of getting something to drink?" Her throat felt coated in sand each time she swallowed. She pressed her fingertips to it.

"No," Orman said. "Wrong crystals. But we have this."

She felt a ripple of air at her left side, and a yellow light exploded from the seam of the tunic. The glow grew to the size of a fist, then a loaf of bread, and then it burst open to scatter glittering fragments like floating glass around their heads and shoulders. Each splinter cast its own tiny prism flame.

"I save that for when I really want to impress someone," Orman said.

She could see! Orman sat in front of her, his knobby legs folded. Dancing light arced over his scrawny chest, turning sparse hairs to buttery yellow. His beard whiskers took on the same warm tone where they drooped over one knee and puddled onto the floor between his legs. Wild eyebrows perched over sharp eyes. He smiled. Wrinkles collided around his cheeks.

"How are you doing that?" Riza patted the seam at her ribs. "I don't feel a pocket or anything."

Orman lifted a finger. "Doesn't mean one isn't there. Our eyes are as easily fooled as our minds." He leaned closer. "All the times you fed and tended Wager, you never did see the tiny shard around his neck, did you?"

"Wager?"

"My pigeon."

"The bird I kept in my room? How could you know about that?"

"Child." Orman tilted his head, and his eyes narrowed, inspecting her so closely she could feel his eyes like probing fingers. "I thought by the strength of the link that you might have the gift. But you're not understanding easily."

Riza lifted her chin. "Well, maybe if you would stop talking in riddles!"

Orman tsked and shook his head, his beard wobbling on his knee. "Is all of Cresvell so ignorant of the old ways?"

"I'm not one to ask. I thought the only ways we have are old ways."

He smiled again, and tapped a finger beneath her chin. "You feel trapped by them. Bound up in the old ways like leather straps around your dreams."

Riza didn't ask him this time how he could know such a thing. She simply nodded.

"Oh, you have it, all right. Something's inside you waiting to blossom like a hopeful bud on a Dandria branch. You're still young enough to sense it." He patted her knee again. "You got out just in time, Riza Diantus."

She didn't remember telling him her name. Somehow, maybe, he just knew.

Orman gave a long wink. "Now you're learning."

§

A scrape of claws against stone alerted Riza.

Orman doused the light with a wave.

The rattle of the door chain sent a bolt of fear down Riza's spine, and she scooted toward Orman, hands reaching for him.

His leathery fingers closed around her palms, and her panic quieted.

A shaft of flickering light snapped against the floor. Slivers of something oozed like flat snakes through a slot in the door and dropped. Then the light disappeared with a groan of metal, and the retreating clickclick of toenails left them alone once more.

"Dinner," said Orman. "You like dried meat?" He shuffled past her shoulder, bumping her off-balance.

Her stomach burned from emptiness. "I'd like dried leather just about now."

"Isn't much, but you can have mine. I've lost my appetite these days."

"But you should eat, you need to stay strong." As she spoke, the glow from her pocket blinked to life again and exploded around her face.

Orman knelt, offering his meager strip of meat. "Take it. And remind me what I was saying."

She took it. She tore it in half and tried to offer some, but Orman shook his head, so she nibbled it. "You were saying that Kallon's father was your vassal."

"Ah, yes. That's right. A fine and honorable soldier he was, too. It was my pleasure to know him." Orman tugged thoughtfully at his whiskers. "Had such plans for his son. But Kallon is stubborn and still angry."

It did describe him. "He's never told me exactly what happened," Riza said.

Orman stared for a long time at nothing. Then he spoke. "There's no magic stronger than dragon magic. Humans try to duplicate it, attempt to harness a sort of power of our own. But what we do is really all about the crystals in our feeble hands."

"I know nothing about how magic works," Riza said.

Orman smiled. "So you say. But you rise with the sun each morning. You watch clouds dangle from the sky like bits of cotton from thread. You've watched the birth of squealing piglets and bathed in a warm summer breeze."

Pleasant memories, all of them. She smiled. "Of course. But what's that got to do with magic?"

Orman grasped her hand, regarding her patiently. "That's the real magic. Those are the things that defy explanation." He fanned out his fingers. "Miracles." He lowered his hands again. "That's what we try to duplicate with our chants and crystals. That's the power we try to harness for ourselves."

Riza studied him. "I don't think I understand."

"No, maybe you won't just yet. It took someone very special, and wiser than me, to help me understand. You're not eating." He shoved a strip of meat toward her face.

She smiled, and pushed at his knuckles. "I'll eat if

you eat."

"But you're starving."

"So are you."

His eyes went so dark she thought he was suddenly angry. But he bit the meat, tore off a bite, and waved the sticky end at her. "Your turn."

She gnawed at her own food. "How long can they keep us here?"

"As long as they want." He chewed and leaned in, eyeing her. "Whatever you did to get Blackclaw mad at you must have been impressive."

"I don't know what I did at all. I only just saw him for the first time when I got here. I was with Kallon by a river near your house."

"Aris River? In Wren Meadow?"

"Kallon never named it." She hugged herself. The prison's frozen air was leeching into her very bones. "I took a bath, and Kallon went to investigate something that flew overhead, and while he was gone, a brown dragon swooped down and scared me half to death."

"A brown dragon? A male?"

"I think it was a girl."

Orman tugged his beard. "Vaya perhaps. Interesting." He bobbed his chin. "Go on."

"She grabbed me and flew off so fast I couldn't even get my clothes."

"She didn't say why?"

Riza shook her head. "It's as though she was already mad at me before she even met me." She pulled her arms in from the sleeves of her tunic, and huddled beneath the thin cloth as though it were a blanket. "We landed here, and everyone spoke a language I don't know, except at the end, when Mr. Blackclaw asked me about Kallon."

Orman tore off another bite. "Goes round and round, just like the circlet that started it all."

"What circlet? Started all what?"

Orman rocked forward to his hands and knees. Then slowly, creaking and groaning, he pushed to his feet. His arms stretched up, out of the crystal's light, and eerie shadows crawled across his face. "It was while I was dragon liaison to Venur Romas of Shornmar. You probably don't remember dragon liaisons. Few people do."

"No," said Riza. "What is it?"

"It's how most wizards got the best training. We served a land owner, managing the dragon soldiers in his service, and in turn, we were allowed to study his vast library, and were given crystals mined from his land." He crouched, his face near. "We got the discards. No venur would sacrifice the best crystals for a liaison wizard. But sometimes, Venur Shornmar would take me to the mining site, and I saw them pulled from the ground in their purest state." His eyes drifted aside, and Riza could almost see his memories in his cloudy gaze. "Bluest quartz, pink crystals like peppermint, and bronze-speckled chunks of clear ice."

"You never kept any of those?"

"Oh, no. I hadn't anywhere near the skill needed to wield pure crystals such as those." He shook his head.

"I was a new wizard, and a mediocre one at that. I came into the trade late in life, you see."

"Was it your first post?"

"It was!" Orman pointed a finger. "It's why I didn't recognize the power of the circlet when first I saw it. I sensed something. I could tell by the way Venur Shornmar whispered its name. He never touched it directly, only gestured with the box containing it." He drooped like a grieving buzzard. "Don't know how I could have known, but I somehow should have."

"Known what? What circlet, Orman?"

His voice hushed. "The Circlet of Aspira. Only one of its kind. Crafted by dragons, with bloodstone dredged from the very vein that courses through Mount Gore." He let out a low whistle, and patted the stone floor. "Perhaps right beneath us, even now.

"I don't know how it came to be in Shornmar's possession," he answered to Riza's next question before she had a chance to voice it. "Didn't ask. Didn't want to know."

He formed his fingertips and thumbs into an oval, and then pressed them to the top of his head. He closed his eyes. "To grant the wearer the desires of their heart."

"What happened to it? Where is it now?"

He lowered his hands. "As a friend to Bren, I finally told him about it. He said the circlet was supposed to have been destroyed years ago, but had been smuggled out from dragon possession, and lost."

"Did it really grant wishes?"

"Yes. It did. But bloodstone is a very precarious

crystal, and if your focus is even a little off balance, there are far-reaching consequences. Not to mention the fact that most people don't really know their deepest desires. You can imagine why it was considered so dangerous."

Riza's feet were falling asleep from sitting so long. She stretched out her legs. "What happened to it?" she asked, after she'd gotten comfortable again.

"I decided to relieve Shornmar of it. I thought it would be for the good of everyone to get it back to the dragons, where it belonged." Orman sighed, and the lines of his face deepened. "Didn't know I'd been tracked. When I found Bren in the woods of Mount Gore, we were attacked. I scrambled to hide the circlet in the knothole of a fat tree, and Bren fought my battle for me."

He sighed again. "I came around a hill to find Bren wounded and bleeding, and dying at the feet of a man in black. So had Kallon. He'd thrown himself across his father, and I was too late to stop him." He paused, pressing his fingertips to his eyes.

"So Kallon watched his father die," Riza whispered.

Orman nodded slowly. "Kallon would have died, too. The man had his sword raised high, and Kallon was too frightened or too desperate…"

"What happened?"

"Bren cried, 'May vita en dae!' I was blinded by a kind of light I'd never seen before. When I could finally see again, everyone was gone. Except Bren."

Silence settled like a heavy cloak.

Riza watched the memories in Orman's eyes, and

touched his hand. "Poor Kallon." She wished he were here now, so she could touch him, too, and tell him that she knew, and that she understood. But she was buried deep in a chamber of the heart of Mount Gore, and he'd sworn that he would never return to this place. She wondered if she'd ever see him again.

"No magic's stronger than dragon magic," Orman said. "They are born of the same power we try to grasp, but so pathetically mimic." He turned and rested his wrinkled face against the wall.

Riza crawled toward him just as the pocket crystal blipped out. If she hadn't been beside him, she might have panicked. But she could hear his breathing, and could feel his bony kneecap against hers.

"Orman? May vita en dae, what does that mean?" she asked.

He shifted. His voice came nearer to her ear, though it was very soft. "It means, 'My life for his', child. Bren said, 'My life for his'."

§

Kallon sat on the plateau of Mount Krag. He felt as though he'd been there for hours. Not a muscle twitched, for fear he'd disturb the gentle current of air that might bring a clue, or a familiar scent, to lead him toward the place where Riza had disappeared. His ears were primed, and his nostrils wide.

His neck ached. His shoulders cramped. Frustrated, he opened his eyes and nearly called her name again, but something pressed to the inside of his gut and warned him to stay. Be still.

"Kallon Redheart!"

Kallon snapped his gaze toward a pebble-eyed pigeon that blinked impatiently up at him. "Orman?" he asked.

"Of course," snapped the little bird. "What are you doing loafing about when you are needed?"

"Was not loafing! Where are you? Are you all right?"

"No thanks to you. But we're tired of the place. Wing your carcass over here and get us out."

"Us?"

"Your lovely friend, Riza, is here with me."

Kallon shot up to all fours, his wings wide and ready to fly. "Tell me where you are."

"You know where we are," said the little bird.

His wings sank as his heart dropped low in his chest. "Mount Gore. Why is Riza there? Who took her?"

"Doesn't matter. She's here, and she's cold and hungry."

"And frightened," Kallon added quietly as he turned his eyes to the towering peak in the distance. "But I have no power to release her. I'm no one to them now."

"You are, and always will be, the son of Bren Redheart. You have authority over all dragons in this province, whether they acknowledge it or not. Claim your place and you will see them know you."

He didn't believe Orman, and he wasn't sure he wanted to claim his place, even if the dragons were willing to listen.

What would he say to Blackclaw? How could he convince the leader to release his friends? He would be flying straight into the most humiliating experience he'd ever know. But Riza was there, and in trouble again.

He groaned. "Orman," he finally said. "Tell her I'm coming."

§

"What did he say?" Riza asked, as Orman turned. She'd been watching the wizard speak to the air.

"He's coming. I told you he would."

She clapped her hands together. "I don't believe it! Can he make Blackclaw let us out?"

"He can try."

"How did you use the bird to speak to him?"

"A link through a small crystal around the bird's neck. It's a similar version of Kallon's stone. The one that was his mother's."

"Yes. I've seen it. But I never saw the one around Wager's neck."

Orman pressed his cold hand to her cheek. "A crystal that can be seen can be removed. I can't have that, can I?" He patted her face, and Riza smiled at the warmth in his voice.

She rummaged in search of the pocket crystal. "Can't we have the light?" Her eyes had adjusted to the darkness enough to see a shadow of Orman's face, but madness had begun a slow and ominous churn through the back of her mind.

"Almost emptied. The weaker the crystal, the more often I have to recharge its energy."

"But Kallon will be here soon, and we'll be released. We only need a little more of it."

Orman shifted in the darkness, but didn't reply.

"At least keep talking to me, then." Her voice squeaked high. "Talk to me about the crystals." Anything. Just keep the shadows away."

"Very well," said Orman. "I have no student, as Kallon has resisted my teachings for years. Consider yourself his replacement."

"Really? You'll teach me about magic?"

"Yes. If..." he said, tapping a crooked finger on her nose. "...if you have it within you to learn."

She drew in a deep breath. "I want to learn."

He slapped his hands together. "Very good. Your first lesson will be an easy one. Remove the light crystal from your pocket."

She fumbled along the seam. "I don't feel it."

"Now there's an interesting choice of words. You don't feel it." Orman leaned so closely that she felt his breath on her face. "Magic is all about feeling. The crystals are only the tools. They gather energy and store it, but it is the wielder of the crystal who must direct that energy."

"Direct it how?"

"From deep within yourself. We are wellsprings of

emotion, each of which evokes real physical reactions in our brains and tissues. This reaction is the catalyst that sends our energy out into the world." He shifted back. "Now, that seems less like magic and more like science, doesn't it? But don't let on. Wizards have too little respect as it is."

"I won't." She was eager to hear more, if only to light the crystal again. "Emotions send out the energy that is stored in the crystal," she repeated.

"Yes. The energy trapped in the crystal is neutral. The emotion we use to direct that energy, positive or negative, will dictate whether the magic will create and heal, or weaken and destroy. The slightest twinge of anger can make the purest spell go dark."

"But what if we don't feel anything at all? Wouldn't the best spell be the kind untainted by any emotion?"

He gently grasped her chin in his fingertips. "That spell would be as dry as a desert, with no energy to go anywhere. You must know your emotions and feel them stronger than ever, but you must control them. Now, reach again for your pocket, and don't trust your senses. Don't just feel for your pocket. *Feel* for it."

She closed her eyes. Her fingers crawled slowly along the seam. She felt a tingle, like the silent buzz of a bumblebee, and paused. "Something…" she murmured. Her fingers dove into a flap of fabric, and closed around a smooth pebble. "I found it!" She withdrew it, and waved it proudly.

"You're quick! Now we'll use what's left of the crystal's energy to—"

The scrape of approaching feet cut Orman's words. He guided her hand to the pocket and urged the crystal again into hiding. "Ssh."

"Humans!" blared a dragon voice from the opposite side of the door. "Step away and press against the wall!"

Riza scrambled to comply, but Orman only planted himself more firmly where he sat.

"You are summoned to appear before Council Leader Blackclaw," said the voice. "You will bind your wrists with these chains."

With a grating squawk, the door swung wide, and metal hit the floor and slid toward them.

Riza reached for the chains, but Orman stopped her.

"We'll do no such thing," he said. "If Blackclaw wants us bound in chains, he can come in here and do it himself."

What was Orman doing? Riza opened her mouth to ask, but his grip tightened on her arm.

A moment later, the door slammed closed. Heavy footsteps retreated.

Orman released her arm. "Never give them your dignity, child. Always give it a good fight. They'll be back soon, but don't be frightened. Whatever happens next, you hold tight to your dignity."

§

"They refuse to chain themselves, Leader Blackclaw."

Blackclaw pressed a knuckle to his forehead, his teeth grinding, as an incompetent Gray whined about the prisoners. "And this is my concern how?" Did he have to be everywhere, doing everything himself?

A rap at the door echoed through the chamber.

Blackclaw looked up to find Whitetail's jutting head.

"We have been contacted," the advisor said quietly.

Finally. Blackclaw heaved to his feet. "Leave the prisoners to me, I will deal with them. Be gone." He waved the Gray outside, and beckoned Whitetail to come closer.

As the tip of the Gray's tail disappeared, Whitetail closed the door.

"The human dragon hunter?" Blackclaw asked.

"Yes," Whitetail said. "He is here, awaiting final word near the arena."

"He certainly took his time. I had begun to think he had run off in shame," Blackclaw said.

"I have chosen the target," Whitetail said. "As the council members filter in this evening for tomorrow's meeting, I will draw him out for the human."

"Do not tell me any details. I want my surprise to seem genuine." Blackclaw stood. "The timing could not be better, I will be able to deal with the prisoners as well, and have this whole fiasco settled nicely by dinnertime tomorrow. Does the hunter know of Redheart, and that we are aware he is alive?"

"I did not mention."

"Good. Do not. The human dragon hunter will pay

for his carelessness, but first he will serve me. Go give the prisoners a warm meal, and meet me at the arena in one half hour."

"Very well." Whitetail moved outside, closing the door behind.

CHAPTER FOURTEEN

Kallon circled for a while over Mount Gore, staring down at the arena, trying to figure out what he was going to say. If he demanded Orman and Riza be released, he would be laughed off the mountain. If he argued in their defense, he might cause them to appear guilty, and only feed the flames already lapping at their withers.

Frankly, he didn't know what he was going to do, short of sneaking into Blackclaw's manor and stealing them both. How he could manage that was beyond him.

The arena below seemed particularly active. The place was dormant between council meetings, wasn't it? Yet, he could see the crawling spines of several hues of dragons. From this height they appeared as patches of color, writhing like rainbow larvae in the core of a rotting apple. Was it time for a council meeting? He veered off to land inconspicuously behind the arena.

Hearing voices, he ducked quickly behind the branches of a group of firs. He peered out from behind his cover.

There stood Blackclaw himself, speaking quietly to a White, who nodded and bowed low. Was this his chance to approach? He was still trying to make up his mind when the White shifted aside. Standing between Blackclaw and the White was a human. Armitage.

The urge to charge and trample the human took Kallon's breath. He gripped a branch and willed himself to stay put. What could the three of them possibly be discussing? Why did Armitage hold a pouch that bore the crest of the Mount Gore Manor?

Then Blackclaw snorted and stalked off, his ribs disturbing the low branches of the firs to scatter needles in a grassy shower. Whitetail followed, leaving Armitage alone.

Kallon skulked toward the human, trying to take him by surprise, but Armitage swung to face him, his hand on his sword, before Kallon even got close enough to breathe hot air on his ugly face.

"Well, well," Armitage said, and relaxed his grip on the sword handle. "You do have a gift for entering in the middle of a show."

"What show?" Kallon growled. "What business do you have with Blackclaw?"

Armitage flipped the pouch in his hand, and caught it by the strings with a satisfied smile. "I can only guess why you're here, Red. Seeing as how the girl is on the mountain, it only follows that you would be hanging around, bemoaning your need to play hero again."

"What do you know of Riza?"

"I know this time, you're too late."

Kallon's legs tensed.

"Oh, calm down," said Armitage, and held up a hand. "The girl is my responsibility now, so you don't have to worry about her. That should make you happy."

A sound erupted in Kallon's throat and growled through his words. "You will tell me what you know of Riza." He shifted a step closer.

"I know she didn't come cheap." Armitage slid his money pouch into a hidden pocket in his vest. "It took nearly half my usual payment to free her. Whatever your plans, you needn't pursue them. Riza will be coming home with me."

It took all of Kallon's effort not to engulf the man in flames. "She won't want to go home with you."

"No?" Armitage took a step closer this time. "Whom do you think she would rather go home with, then, you?" He laughed. "I don't believe what I'm seeing in your eyes. Are you jealous?"

"I know her better than you. She was cast out by your kind. Made to suffer. All for the simple act of accepting a friend by what she sees in his soul, regardless of the hide he is wrapped in."

He sneered. "I think you're more than jealous. I think you love her. I'm going to be sick."

"What do you know of love, human?" Kallon roared, coating the man with haze.

"What I know is the deeper you feel it, the more painful your grief when it's stolen! I hope against rational thinking that you are one creature among your kind that *can* feel love, Red. I hope you love her, and that you spend the rest of your days grieving for her while she forgets you and bears my children!"

Kallon lunged, his vision stained red. He swung his claws, but felt only air. Suddenly, a stab of pain cleared his senses. He froze. The tip of the human's sword was wedged between the scales of his throat.

"Kill me, and she will never see the light of day again," said Armitage. "I am her freedom now. Not you."

Kallon couldn't catch his breath. He couldn't control his frenzied heartbeat. He tried to think of Riza. This human knew more about her condition than Kallon, and perhaps the man had made a deal for her freedom. Could he risk destroying that? Kallon stared into the man's face and quietly despised him.

"You, on the other hand, are quite expendable," Armitage continued. He shifted his grip on the end of his sword, eyes flashing with death.

Behind them, a bleat rang out from arena. Neither of them moved. It bleated again. It was the ceremony horn, calling for the assembly.

Jastin cursed. "How you manage it I don't know!" His glare burned into Kallon's eyes.

Kallon returned the bitter stare.

"Soon your invisible guardian, or whatever it is that keeps you alive, will misstep." He lowered the blade. "This sword will be your destroyer. On my oath."

"Fate will take me when it will. If your weapon is the tool, so be it." Kallon breathed a coil of smoke into the man's face that slithered around his throat and dissipated. "But not today, human."

Armitage stabbed his sword into its sheath, glaring hatred. He disappeared into the foliage.

Kallon gripped the earth to stop shaking. He didn't even know where his words had come from. He didn't believe in fate! He didn't believe in magic, or in invisible guardians, or in the place beyond the limits of sky where dead dragons lived on.

Warmth against his collarbone drew his eyes downward. His linking stone glowed so brightly that it cast a white sheen to the ground, even in the light of pale dusk. He wrapped his clawed digits around the shimmering crystal, and somehow, he felt less alone.

A snort caught his attention. He slid back into the trees to hide.

"Nothing but more of the same rhetoric, I am convinced." Kallon peered out to find a Blue speaking to a Gray. "I do not even know why I waste my time coming. There is talk, but no action!"

The Gray replied. "I will try to speak with Blackclaw during the opening ceremonies. If he does not address our concerns, I will make the motion." The Gray's wings scraped past the branches of Kallon's cover. "Hurry, they have already sounded the horn."

Kallon lost sight of the pair. Their footfalls grew softer and softer until they were gone.

Kallon used to feel so proud watching his father during the opening ceremonies on the night before each council meeting. His father would carry in the colors of the tribe and place them in the coveted center of the presentation stand.

Banners of every tribe would line up in brilliant, fluttering array, and for as long as memory served them all, red had been the prominent leader. But not tonight. Tonight, the presentation stand would hold black in its center.

Tonight! Of course! The manor would be deserted. No dragon on Mount Gore was allowed to miss opening ceremonies. At least, that's the way it used to be. Kallon had no idea where Riza and Orman were being kept, but he'd lived there, once. If he snuck in, he ought to remember his way around.

He eased out of the mass of trees and carefully picked his way past the arena toward the manor.

When darkness finally fell, he would slip inside. He hoped more than anything that he would find Orman and Riza before Armitage had a chance to touch her.

§

"The girl comes with me." The voice sounded into the darkness from the other side of the door like the low peal of a massive bell.

"Orman?" Riza reached for the wizard and clung to his arm.

"Now," said the voice.

A grind of metal slid open the grate on the door. Torchlight spilled in through the slats to cast flickering rectangles of yellow-orange to the floor.

"Orman, I'm afraid," she whispered. She felt the

familiar touch of wrinkled fingers on her hands. Were they trembling?

"Come with me now and you will not be harmed." The voice sounded oddly patient. Not the usual snarl of the voice that brought food. She looked toward the door.

"Maybe Kallon is here," she said to Orman. "Maybe they're going to take me to him."

"Just remember what I told you. Dignity. You keep your chin high," said Orman. He peeled her fingers from his arm and nudged her toward the door.

She crawled on stiff hands and knees. If she were nearing freedom, why did her heart grow heavier the closer she drew? She kept moving, but her weary arms and legs propelled her slowly, resisting. Then the torchlight bathed her face and stung her eyes.

"Open the door." She saw the movement of a white jaw through the grate as the voice spilled in again.

She managed to climb to her feet, and pressed herself against the door. It wouldn't budge. "I can't."

"Come now," wagged the jaw. "Give a push."

She pushed. She grunted. The door gave by an inch and stuck fast again. "I can't!"

"Very well. Give another shove, and I will help you."

If the white dragon on the other side of the door wanted to help so badly, why didn't he just do it himself? She was about to ask just that, when a quick flash of green startled her. The bitter taste of sulfur stung her mouth.

"Well? Go on," urged the jaw.

She sighed and pressed her palms to the door. The door gave way and slammed to the floor in a thud that rocked the walls. Granite dust billowed.

"There, you see?" The white dragon grinned, his paw waving at the filtering dust. "No need to look so frightened. I am taking you to a friend."

Riza sucked in a breath. "He came? He's here?"

"He is anxious to see you, and we are anxious to be rid of you." An eyelid as big as her fist wrinkled up in a wink. "Watch your step. We must be quiet."

Her strength redoubled at the thought of seeing Kallon again. She scrambled over the door and followed the dragon. "What about Orman?" she asked. "Why isn't he coming with us?"

"The wizard was not negotiated."

"Not negotiated? Why not?" Why wouldn't Kallon have tried to free Orman, too? The dragon stopped and held up a paw in warning. She stopped, too.

The dragon peered around the corner at a crossing hallway. "It is safe. Hurry now. All dragon eyes should be in the arena, watching the opening ceremonies. It is growing dark, but your friend will guide you."

"Guide me where? Can't I take Orman, too? Where am I going?"

The dragon smiled, and patted a scaly palm on top of her head. "So many questions. Such a poor time to ask them. Rush now. Turn left and right, look for a torch in the trees to the east. Go."

"But I—"

"Go, girl!"

She darted into the hallway. She didn't want to leave Orman, but perhaps Kallon had a plan, and knew what he was doing. Perhaps two prisoners at once were too much to ask. Poor Orman. She hoped he would be released soon, too.

She paused at the next hallway convergence. Left, then right. She inched around the corner to the right and found the exit, looming like the open mouth of a hungry beast. She couldn't see the arena from this distance, but she could hear it. The thrum of distant voices filtered through the trees and carried fear to her feet.

She glanced back from where she came. The white dragon trailed behind. He nodded and flicked his paws, shooing her toward the night. "Thank you," she called quietly.

He stopped. "Do not thank me. Just go."

She ran. Outside, she stumbled on weak legs and nearly fell. How long had she been cramped in that dank prison? One day? Two? Maybe more. Time had lost its meaning in the blackness.

She veered for the trees, searching for the promised torch to guide her. Just as she reached the branches of the tree line, she heard the voice of the white dragon again. This time, he shouted. "The human girl has escaped!"

Did she hear that right? She pushed away the limbs blocking her view and stared at the dragon some yards away on the top step.

He spotted her. He shooed her again toward the trees, then cupped his paws around his mouth. "She has escaped!"

Where was Kallon? Where was the torchlight that was supposed to lead her to him? She didn't know, and didn't understand what was happening. But when a rush of angry voices surged toward her, she knew enough to run. She dove into the forest.

Branches clawed her face. Needles stung her arms and calves. Her bare feet tromped hard on sticks and pebbles. She was almost grateful that her fear numbed the pain, but it did nothing for her stamina. Her body gave up before her mind was ready, and she dropped to her knees, her breath raspy. She clutched at the pain in her ribs.

Movement rustled behind her.

"Kallon?" she whispered.

No response.

A stick snapped, and she whirled. "Who's there?" she said.

A hand clamped over her mouth. She was crushed against a chest and ribs, and dragged backward across scraping underbrush.

"What are you doing? You were told east! East, not west," said a harsh voice in her ear. She recognized it, its whisper was no disguise. Jastin Armitage.

She clawed at the gloved hand over her mouth and tried to kick backward. When she couldn't find his legs with her feet, she clamped her teeth on whatever she could grip.

"Holy—!" he wheezed. His hand dropped.

Before she could suck in a breath to scream, the hand was back, choking her.

A stampede of heavy feet closed in.

She was lifted.

Her captor threw himself against a mound of boulders, pulling her with him. They fell onto the floor of a small cavern, and she landed on top of him with a grunt. Behind them, rumbling footfalls shook the ground and rushed past the slim opening of their hiding place.

He removed his hand from her mouth. "Go ahead," he whispered. "Scream now."

Oooo, how she burned. She'd rather be trampled than to have to look at him. She tore away and flung herself at the fissure opening.

He cursed. His hands latched around her ankles.

She fell hard on her face and saw sparkles. When she felt his hands on her shoulders, she sprang to action again, kicking and clawing at him.

He pulled her to her feet anyway, and slapped her to the rock wall. "Stop fighting me," he snarled. "I'm trying to help you!"

"I don't want your help!" Riza shouted. "Where's Kallon? What have you done to him?"

"I've done nothing to him. He isn't coming for you."

"Yes, he is! He said he would!"

"Get it through your head, woman. I'm your hero. I always have been." He pressed her arms above her head, and his voice came near to her mouth. "Your dragon is a coward."

"I never asked for a hero. Only a friend." Something stabbed her ribs. She writhed, trying to pull from his grasp. "You're hurting me."

"Where were they keeping you? You stink like a sewer. It's going to take a month of baths to get the stench out of your hair."

"If it means you'll stay away from me, I'll be happy to never bathe again."

He released her. "There are thirty dragons out there searching for you right now. Come dawn, there will be more. They will all want to find you, and without me, they will. Hate me if you want—"

"Fine. I will," she snapped.

He moved away. When he spoke again, his voice was soft. "Hate me tomorrow, but tonight let me help you." He sounded so weary.

She'd have never guessed the man was capable of being tired. And he sounded hurt. She'd have never guessed he was capable of that, either.

She wanted to see his face. She slipped her hand into her pocket, and her light crystal ignited. Sparkles lifted toward the low ceiling of the hiding place and cast yellow light over his hunched shoulders and surprised eyes.

"How are you doing that?" he asked.

"Orman taught me." She stepped closer and studied him. He did look weary. Even beaten. She almost felt sorry for him. Almost. "Fine. For tonight I'll let you help me, if you tell me where Kallon is."

He wrapped thick fingers around her hand and turned to lead her outside. "That light trick is handy, but douse it a little, will you?"

She held her ground. "Jastin. Where's Kallon?"

When he tugged her, she had to shuffle her feet to keep from falling over. "I don't know," he said. "I don't know where he is."

§

Kallon peered around from the corner of the manor. He'd been crouched, listening for the fall of dragon steps, for what seemed hours. In, out, up the stairs, down the stairs, herds of feet trounced the ground until he thought the ceremonies were never going to start.

Twice, he'd circled in back to the place where the manor and mountain became one. By design, none of the windows were large enough to climb through. All dragons had to enter through the arch. He'd considered climbing up the windows, though, and perching on top.

It was on his second circle that he'd heard a shout. He'd scrambled back around to the front of the manor.

Now, peering around the corner, he saw herds of dragons split off from the entrance to the arena and rush into the surrounding trees. Snorting dragons stomped past without seeing him. Claws kicked fir needles into the air in a chaotic blur. The earth shook. Then all was quiet.

His chance had presented itself. He rushed up the granite steps of the manor and ducked inside. He pressed against a far wall, whisking his tail in to wrap it around his feet.

Riza's hazy scent found his nostrils. He barely recognized it, it was so infused with the sour tones of human waste. He must be close.

The hall was clear. He inched his way forward. He reached the doorway of the Great Room and peeked in.

The sloping curve of the high ceiling, detailed paintings of dragon battles on the stone walls, the plush, woven flooring beneath his feet; all were reminders of the time when this place was his home. Great feasts and celebrations had been held here. Suddenly, his memory echoed with his father's laugh that ricocheted like thunder off the walls, drowning out the chatter of dining guests. The sound was so convincing, he had to look around himself to make sure he hadn't really heard it.

He moved on, shaken. He was afraid to go further for fear of what other memories might surface, but he willed himself to continue. He would find Riza and Orman and steal them away to safety. His heavy footfalls were silent against the cushioned floor.

"Kallon!"

He drew up. "Orman?" he asked, eyes searching left to right for a trace of the man.

Orman emerged from the shadows of a long hallway, arms outstretched. His beard, brown with filth, spread stains across his scrawny chest. He limped.

When he reached Kallon, he collapsed against Kallon's ribs.

"Where's Riza?" Kallon turned toward the dark hall, expecting to see her green eyes and smiling face. He didn't.

"Gone," said Orman. "Whitetail took her, left the door open."

"Left the door open? He took Riza and left the door open?"

"Yes. Yes. Go, we must get out of here." Orman pushed off from Kallon and limped past. "Hurry. I've a feeling—"

"He will be back?" finished a voice for Orman.

Kallon spun around. He stared into the face of Fane Whitetail.

CHAPTER FIFTEEN

"Whitetail," said Kallon, not knowing where the firmness of his voice was coming from. "This human has done no wrong. You are holding him prisoner against the Dragon-Human Relations Pact guidelines for non-war conflicts."

"This human is a spy," Whitetail said. "There are no guidelines which dictate this situation."

"Hawk spit! I'm no spy, you pale runt!" Orman balled his fists and shook one at Whitetail. He swung flashing eyes to Kallon. "All they asked me about was the circlet. They think the real one is out there somewhere."

"The Circlet of Aspira? Is that what all this is about?" Kallon looked from Orman to Whitetail, and back. "What does that have to do with Riza? What does that have to do with you, Orman?"

"Kallon, that circlet is what your father was defending when he died." Orman sighed, and looked older than Kallon remembered him ever looking.

"But, you always told me he died defending you."

"Yes. I was bringing it to him. To return it to the dragons." Orman closed his eyes and withered against the wall. "We were attacked, and I never did find the circlet after that. We failed to protect it."

"Do not say failed!" Kallon reared back, his anger blasting to the ceiling. "He was not a failure! He was a hero!"

"Yes." Orman held up his hands. "You know that's not what I meant."

Kallon felt Whitetail's eyes boring into the side of his face, and he swung his narrowed eyes to the White.

Whitetail crossed his forelegs and arched back. "So. You are the heir of Bren Redheart after all."

"Of course I am. I am the last Red," Kallon snorted, and surprised himself again with his tone.

"We thought you had died with your father. That is," Whitetail added, "…we dragons. You will forgive us our surprise at your sudden and unexpected return."

"What have you done with the girl?" Kallon asked.

"Me?" Whitetail looked between Kallon and Orman. "What do you mean, what have I done with her?"

"The wizard said you took her and left the door open. What have you done with her?" Kallon asked again.

Whitetail shook his head, paws uplifting. "No, you are mistaken. I have only just come from the woods, where we have been searching for her. Your wizard here is the one who opened the door and helped her escape."

"You're lying!" Orman puffed his chest and glared

up at the white dragon.

"Am I?" Whitetail's eye ridges lifted, and his paws fanned open. "You will have the opportunity to refute the accusation tomorrow, during the council meeting. In the meantime, we will investigate. You will have to be kept in chains in full view of a guard at all times. You can not be trusted to stay put."

"I'll do no such thing," Orman said. "You've gone too far this time, Whitetail. The others will see right through you!"

"We will see." Whitetail waved a paw, and from nowhere, a Gray appeared with chains in his paws, dragging them noisily across the floor.

"No!" Kallon roared. He lowered his head and rammed Whitetail in the shoulder. The frail dragon grunted in surprise and careened back against the wall with a thud. Kallon spun for the Gray.

The Gray dropped the chains and tensed, but before he had a chance to pounce, Kallon dove. His headbutt found the Gray's jaw.

The Gray's head snapped back, but his forelegs jutted out, clamping around Kallon's throat.

Kallon yanked back, trying to pull the Gray off balance, but the Gray only stumbled and caught his footing again. Kallon couldn't breathe.

The Gray loomed over him, face twisted.

Kallon worked his tongue, and then spit a pathetic spout of flame into the Gray's face. He knew it wasn't strong enough to singe anything, but he hoped it was enough to sting his eyes.

The Gray recoiled with a growl and the grip around Kallon's throat loosened. Air rushed into his lungs.

Kallon chopped his foreleg upward to break the hold, and then rushed. Desperately, or, instinctively, Kallon went for his throat. His jaws clamped around the Gray's thick neck, and Kallon threw all of his weight into flipping the other onto his back.

Gray claws flailed. His opponent slammed into Whitetail with the rumble of an avalanche.

"Hurry," said Kallon, and nudged Orman with his snout. The rooms of the manor weren't large enough to allow full wingspan, so he and Orman couldn't lift until they were outside. Only a few feet to go.

When Orman struggled to run, Kallon gently nudged him again.

"Get off me, you oaf!" Whitetail was heard above the scratching din of two dragon bodies scrabbling for balance.

They reached the arch. Kallon clutched Orman to his chest. His wings sliced the air, and they flew. Kallon pivoted to look behind them. They weren't being followed.

"What about Riza?" Orman called over the wind.

Kallon dipped to catch a cross draft, and his billowed wings shot them sharply forward. "Whitetail said she is in the woods. If we try to look for her now, we might lead more dragons to her."

"Why would Whitetail help her escape, only to abandon her to the wilds?"

"I do not think she was abandoned, I think she was

delivered to someone. A human."

"A human?" Orman asked, his voice weakening.

Armitage. That human in black was at least competent to keep Riza safe in a wood full of searching dragons. Kallon seethed at having to leave her to his company for the night, but he wasn't exactly given a choice.

"We'll need to go back. This isn't over, you know," said Orman. "They're using that girl. I have a bad feeling."

"I'll go back once you're safe," said Kallon. While he spoke, his eyes scoured the darkness below. Armitage had better take care of Riza. Or he'd kill him.

§

Riza was tugged through the cutting underbrush, trying to keep up. "How much farther? Where are we going?"

Jastin didn't respond. He only yanked her arm harder.

She stumbled, and the glowing crystal dropped from her hand and winked out.

Jastin stopped. "Now what?" He crouched and sifted his fingers through the thick carpet of fir needles. "We could really use that light." His face hovered somewhere near her knee.

She wanted to kick him. "I'm tired. I'm hungry. I'm scared. I think my feet are bleeding."

He rose up, and though she couldn't make out his

features in the darkness, she felt his face close by. "I'm sorry, Riza. I know I'm pushing you hard, but we're almost to Blade, and then you won't have to walk."

"But then what? Where are you taking me?"

"To a safe place, where the dragons won't find us. We'll need to spend the night there, then we'll leave the mountain tomorrow." His hand drew down her arm and clasped her fingers. "Forget the light. I can hear Blade. Come on."

She couldn't think of what else to do, so she followed. Leaving with him tomorrow would be a different story, but she didn't mention that. She trudged along, her feet aching as though on fire, her legs as heavy as timber logs.

"Ho, Blade," Jastin called.

Hooves rustled and a soft whinny sounded.

"Up you go," Jastin said.

Riza was whisked from her feet and deposited onto Blade's saddle.

Jastin hoisted himself behind her, wrapped his arms around her to grasp the reins, and clicked his tongue.

What a relief to be off her feet. She sagged against Jastin despite trying not to. "I feel like I've been hungry and tired for weeks," she murmured. "Always running. Always dark. I want to see the sun again."

"You rest now," he said, and pinned her gently back with his left arm.

In the next moment, he was rousing her. "We're here, Riza. Look."

She peeled her eyes open and tried to find what

she was supposed to be seeing. A blur of flickering light floated somewhere in the distance. Everything else was just darkness.

Jastin slid from the saddle, then eased her down onto her feet. The moment she touched down, sharp pain shot through her legs. She hobbled a few steps, then crumpled, her body refusing to work.

Jastin's arms came around her and scooped her up. "We have food and water and shelter for the night. You'll feel better soon."

He carried her into the mouth of a cave, where torchlight bathed them both. Jastin's face was pinched and dusty.

Her borrowed tunic crumpled around her thighs, torn and muddied. Her arms oozed blood from hundreds of tiny scratches.

He laid her onto the ground.

"So many caves," she mused aloud. Then she saw the crate beside her. She pulled back the cloth. "Food! Bread and cheese!" She didn't even wait for an invitation. She broke off a handful of white cheese and gorged.

"Help yourself." Something in his tone sounded amused, though he didn't smile. He crouched beside her and broke off some bread for himself.

"How did you know this would be here? Did you bring it?"

"No," Jastin said. He chewed.

"Then who did?"

He only watched her, then rose up and stepped outside.

"Jastin?"

He returned with a saddlebag. Opening it, he laid out an empty water bladder, two piles of cloth, a cake of lard soap, and small tins that were bent and tarnished.

She finished her cheese and broke off a thick piece of bread while she watched. "Are you going to tell me anything about what's happening?"

"What's happening is that we're eating. And drinking, hopefully." He leaned over the crate and rummaged through it. "Ah. Perfect." He withdrew a clay pot and two chipped cups. "This will help you feel better." Red wine splashed into the cups, and he offered her one.

She accepted. She was so thirsty that she drank it dry, and then held out the cup for a refill.

"Not too much on an empty stomach," he said. "Just sip." More wine poured.

She sipped. Warmth filled her weary body. She did feel better. She finished her bread and reached for more. "Someone knew we would be coming here tonight, and left food and torchlight. Why?"

"When you're able, you'll bathe." He set the soap and the pile of cloth beside her. "Scrub your feet, even though it will sting. You can have one of my tunics."

As much as she detested the thought of bathing anywhere near the man, she was looking forward to a good soak. Filth and grit felt caked into her skin, as though she'd been lifted by her heels and dunked headfirst into a vat of grime. "I'm able, I think, if it's not far," she said.

He whistled, and Blade appeared at the cave opening. “I’ll lead you there. Blade will wait for you and lead you back.”

A few aching minutes later, she was perched atop the black mount, watching the sky as she was carried. “I see stars. Look, Jastin.”

“A clear night,” he said. “Hot.”

“Yes. Always hot.”

Water splashed around her feet as Blade moved into the water. Her feet did sting as they submerged, and she sucked in a breath. Then she slid off the saddle and plunged into the cool water.

Blade waited while she soaked and scrubbed her stinging feet, her scalp, and her face.

When she finally climbed back onto Blade’s back, she breathed in deeply of the clean mountain scent mixed with lavender and damp hair. Then she slipped Jastin’s black tunic over her head and tugged it into place.

“Ho, Blade,” came Jastin’s voice, and the horse turned to follow.

She stiffened. “How long were you standing there?”

No reply. She wished she’d kicked him in the head when she’d had the chance.

Back at the cave, she rested against a scratchy wool blanket from another of Jastin’s saddlebags.

He was tearing a second tunic into strips for her feet.

“Why did that white dragon help me out and then tell the others that I’d escaped?”

Riza asked. "And how did you know I was supposed to go east? Why was this food waiting here?" She leaned up to peer at him. He silently wrapped a strip of cloth around her swollen wounds. "Jastin?"

He tied off the cloth. "I do like the sound of my name from your mouth. A mouth that asks too many questions, though."

She lay back with a huff. "Kallon answers my questions."

"How nice of him."

"He is nice. If you'd give him a chance, you'd find out for yourself." His hands were gentle as they wrapped her other foot, and she peeked across her belly at him.

"I think you and that white dragon worked something out together," she said. "If you can trust him, why can't you trust Kallon?"

He moved closer and stretched out on his side, his dark eyes regarding her. "I don't trust any dragon. What I worked out with the White was done out of a higher purpose. He's giving me a chance to be a part of something larger, and I am taking it."

"Something larger?"

He tucked his arm beneath his head, his cheek resting on his forearm. "You have charmed the Red, you know. He's smitten, somehow."

"We're just friends. We care about each other."

"I've protected you, and I've fed and clothed you. Yet you don't call me a friend. What do you see in that red beast you don't see in me?" His hand reached out for her cheek.

"Don't." She rolled over, turning her back.

What did she see in Kallon that she didn't see in Jastin? Why did she prefer Kallon's scaly touch? These questions, and others, circled her mind like a mouse running in a barrel.

Despite her exhaustion, and her eagerness to sleep, she didn't. Around and around the questions looped. She wrestled with them deep into the night.

§

Riza opened her eyes to find her wish had come true. She could see the sun again. At least, she could feel it, because it reached warm fingers into the cave that caressed her legs and soothed her stiff joints. How she'd missed the light! She sat up and stretched, lazily content.

And alone. "Jastin?" She tried to stand on puffy, aching feet, but was forced back to her knees. She crawled forward, inching her face out into the day. "Jastin? Are you out there?"

Four gray feet landed on the soft grass outside the cave. Then four green feet. And four more white, clawed feet dropped to land in front of her face.

Riza clutched the trembling ground.

Three fierce dragon muzzles lowered, snorting hot breath.

She felt the air seep from her lungs.

"Where is your mate?" Whiteclaw's familiar snout moved to within inches of her nose. "Has he abandoned you?"

"My mate?"

"The other human," Whiteclaw said.

She scowled at the white dragon. "He's not my mate."

Blade's clopping gait sounded from near the water.

"I'm not even her friend," came Jastin's voice from behind the dragons.

They turned, tails swinging wide, to face him.

"Seize him," said Whitetail.

The Gray and the Green rushed Jastin, dwarfing he and Blade between them. Claws gripped his arms and forced them away from his sides.

Blade whinnied and thrashed.

"What the…!" Jastin shouted, his face flaming red. His thighs gripped his mount, trying to settle him. "We had a deal, Whitetail!"

"Deal? I am afraid I do not know what you mean." The white dragon oozed toward the group around the frightened horse. "Where have you been this morning, human?"

"You know where I was." Jastin's mouth curled into a snarl. He struggled to yank his arms from the dragon claws.

"Let me guess. Somewhere in the vicinity of the council arena?" Whitetail daintily reached for Jastin's sword at his side. "That is where we found the murder victim. A crossbreed of blue and green."

The sword drew out slowly from its sheath. Thick blotches of crimson clung to the blade. "Would this be dragon blood on your sword, human?" Whitetail asked.

Watching the scene as though it were a dream, Riza felt her color drain from her face. She choked on the urge the retch. "Jastin." She heard her own voice as a whisper. "What have you done?"

Four sets of eyes turned to her. She could only stare back. "Ah, yes. The accomplice," said Whitetail.

"No," said Jastin through clenched teeth. "Not the girl. You leave her out of this."

"Tsk, tsk. I would be remiss in my duties if I did not bring you both to the council for sentencing," Whitetail said.

"No!" Jastin suddenly bolted up and out of the saddle. He swung his feet, flipping them over his head to spin within the dragons' grasp. As his feet came down, he planted them against Blade's rump and kicked him forward.

The horse bolted.

"Take him, Riza! Go!" Jastin shouted.

She didn't have time to think.

Blade bore down on her and she stood.

Pain screamed from her feet, but she didn't have time to feel, either. She leaped at the horse, grabbed at the saddle, and caught. Her fingers clawed, trying to pull up, but Blade's run threw her against his ribs, and it was all she could do to hang on. Her feet smacked the earth, bounced up with a jerk, and smacked again. She cried out.

Just as her grip gave way, a suffocating pinch of green claws snatched her from the horse. Her stomach lurched as she was yanked skyward. Blade continued his frenzied bolt, and she watched him plunge through the thick firs as he became smaller and smaller. The world spun. Her stomach emptied.

§

"Orman, the sun is up. I'm going back to Mount Gore." Kallon nudged the sleeping wizard with his snout.

Orman grunted.

"What do you need before I go?" Kallon asked him.

Orman rolled to his back, knuckles circling at his closed eyes. "Mount Gore, you say?"

"Yes," Kallon said, impatient to get going.

"Yes, yes. We must go. The wind was calling to me in my dreams." Orman pushed up to sit, hunched and bewildered-looking, with his white hair turned wild from sleep, and his gray eyes hazy. "But not yet. Let me gather up my things." He suddenly blinked. "Where are we?"

Kallon hung his head. He'd brought Orman to the first place he could think of that might mean rest and strength to the human, and had quietly hoped that he'd be able to slip away before Orman realized.

Kallon had spent the night rationalizing that his cave would be too risky, that Orman's hut had been out of the question, and that he could think of no other place. But the truth was that Kallon had originally brought Orman to this place without conscious thought at all, except for the vague memory of a mysterious dragon helper that had once healed and strengthened him here.

Kallon watched Orman's eyes trail the burned landscape. He watched Orman's expression shift from confusion to surprise, then to astonishment, as the wizard's gaze found the erect headstones of his father's grave, his mother's grave, and the Dandria tree.

Finally, Orman's eyes returned to Kallon, and glanced briefly to the dull linking stone before meeting Kallon's eyes.

Kallon shrank smaller and smaller in shame. At least, he tried to shrink. The fact was that he actually felt larger and larger, growing in embarrassment and stupidity. He shifted his weight. His throat rumbled. In the end, it was he who broke the silence. "I don't know why I brought you here."

Orman's wrinkles caved in around his mouth and bunched up into a wide smile. "I think you do."

He couldn't meet Orman's eyes. "It doesn't matter. No help came to us. I don't know why I allowed myself to think it might."

"In other words, you came here in a time of need, seeking instant help from someone you don't even really believe in, and because you didn't receive exactly what you wanted, you feel justified in your denial."

Kallon lifted his eyes to stare flatly at Orman. Fine. He'd play. "Yes," he said. "Now if you don't need anything from me, there's someone out there who does."

Orman climbed unsteadily to his feet. He made

his uneven way to the Dandria and stroked his fingers across the mottled bark. "You met him. You actually stood in the presence of the Gold, didn't you?" His face swung to Kallon. "And still you managed to deny it all to yourself. That is some feat, Kallon Redheart. Few are able to do that."

Kallon snarled. "You're mocking me."

Orman's hand shot up. "No, not intentionally. I actually admire the depth of your stubbornness in a way one might stare in fascination at a starving salamander, gobbling up its own tail in attempt to survive."

Kallon growled, but Orman waved him to silence. "I'll save the lecture for later. You did the right thing, bringing me here. Thank you. Now we have business with a certain black dragon. And your fate."

"The only fate I am concerned about now is Riza's," Kallon said. "You don't need to come if you're not strong."

"I'm not strong. But I'm needed." Orman beckoned Kallon to crouch, and he sprang up to clutch at Kallon's spine. Bare feet kicked at his ribs, and hands pinched his scales as Orman tried to swing his leg over.

Kallon winced. If his friends didn't get better at mounting, he might have to invest in a saddle just to spare the pain of each climb.

Orman paused. He looked at Kallon with upraised brows.

Kallon glared back. "Don't even think about it."

"Wasn't my idea," said Orman. The wizard finally settled across his shoulders. "Anything left of my home?

My crystals? My workshop?"

Kallon almost didn't have the heart to break it to him. "Nothing but rubble."

He could feel Orman's sigh draw right up through his scales. "Alas," said the wizard. "We'll have to use our wits, then. I've never had much confidence in mine."

"Nor have I," Kallon said.

"After all," Orman continued, and patted Kallon's shoulder. "Look who I'm counting on to be the hero of the day."

CHAPTER SIXTEEN

My fellow dragons," blared Blackclaw's voice above the buzzing swarm of murmurs in the arena. "You have all heard the rumors of the senseless murder of one of our own at the hands of a human dragon hunter."

"We have heard!" came a rasping shout from the crowd. "Tell us the truth!"

A dramatic pause urged the murmurs to complete silence. A breeze swept through the fir trees at the arena opening, rattling the soft needles.

Orman's hand gripped Kallon's shoulder tightly, and they shared a nudge of alarm from where they'd paused, hiding, to listen.

"It is true," Blackclaw finally said. "Delt Bluecrest, the council's own appointed recorder, was found dead this dawn."

The arena erupted in frenzied ramblings and shouts.

Orman spoke, but Kallon couldn't understand his words beneath the crushing volume spilling over the arena walls.

"Your anger is acknowledged, good dragons! As is mine," came Blackclaw's voice again. "The murderers will not go unpunished!"

"Did he say 'murderers'?" Orman asked, eyes narrowing.

Kallon stared back at Orman, his mouth gone dry as Fell Lake. His mind skipped through the words... human dragon hunter…dead this dawn…murderers. It couldn't possibly mean what his brain was trying to puzzle together. It couldn't possibly be.

"Councilors! Representatives!" Blackclaw's shout brought the crowd to attention, and the voices dulled. "We are a reasonable Kind. We do not seek revenge for the sake of anger, but justice for the sake of righteousness. I will present the criminals to you, and we will hear them!"

Kallon managed to hear the rattle of chains above the shouts.

Orman rushed forward to peer around the wall of the arena, but Kallon was held in place by a fist of fear.

He didn't want to see. He didn't want to know.

Orman gasped, and turned wide eyes to Kallon. "It's the girl."

Kallon pressed clawed digits to his eyes. He was suddenly dizzied by the sensation that this was all some freakish joke; he would peer around the arena wall with Orman, and find Riza and Blackclaw and the others smiling and waiting to shout, "Got you!"

Breath held, he lurched forward. Slowly, his snout

rounded the wall, and his eyes found the platform at the front of the stadium.

Jastin Armitage, shirtless and scarred, jerked violently against his chains. He ranted. He stomped his feet. But the din of the raging crowd gulped up his threats, and dragon fists pumped the air before him.

Beside him stood Riza, her hands bound behind herself, her black tunic fluttering like ghostly feathers against her legs. She lifted her chin. Her eyes met the gale force of dragon fury without wavering. She was a dignified queen, facing down her unruly subjects with gentle benevolence. His heart clenched.

"Look at her, Orman. She's beautiful."

"She is," Orman agreed.

"I haven't really known her until now, have I?" Kallon said.

He felt Orman's hand against his chest. "If you don't do something to stop this nonsense, you'll lose her."

"I don't know what to do."

Orman swatted his throat. "Get in there and tell them who you are."

"State your name for the record, and tell us why you are here."

Kallon blinked.

Fane Whitetail waved his paw toward Armitage.

"I am Kallon Redheart!" Kallon's own voice startled him.

Pairs of eyes darted to him. Then others followed, nudged dragon by dragon. Each new set of eyes stung him like nettles.

His throat burned. "My mother was Sera Redheart, my father was Bren Redheart. They both died in honor and service to you all!"

"Well, well," Blackclaw said as he rocked back and crossed his forelegs. "The rumors are true, then. The Red has returned."

Voices began to rise again, but Blackclaw swept out a paw to halt them.

"Tell us," Blackclaw said, "Great and honorable Redheart, where you have been all these years. Why did you choose to abandon your responsibilities at a time when your Kind needed you most? And why have you chosen this time to come forward from your silence?"

Within the multitude of hovering eyes, a pair of green prisms, wet with tears, pled silently. Riza's eyes.

He focused on these, and the clammy grip of fear around his throat loosened. "I have come for the woman. She is innocent."

Dragon faces swung to regard Blackclaw.

"Do you have some sort of proof that this is so?" Blackclaw asked.

"Do you have proof that she is not?" Kallon replied.

Blackclaw turned to address the dragons. "She was in the company of the dragon slayer. The dragon slayer was found with Bluecrest's blood on his sword!"

Dragons roared in response, waving their tails.

Armitage shouted, "The girl is innocent, Blackclaw! What is she to you?" He struggled against his chains again, but his outburst was lost in the tide of dragon cries.

Blackclaw continued, waving his forelegs toward the crowd. "We have one innocent here, and that is Bluecrest! If the girl did not swing the blade to murder Bluecrest herself, did she raise a hand to prevent it? It is by her lack of action that she is responsible!"

The dragon horde swelled toward the platform, squeezing in against the granite steps on either side, scaled fists pummeling the air. "Execute her!"

"Kill them!"

"They can not get away with this!"

"They will be examples to all humans!" Blackclaw swung a fist toward the sky. "We dragons have lived quietly for too long! We have been disrespected, feared, and systematically murdered. We have had our lands stolen. We have dwindled to handfuls of proud, but powerless, tribes. Is this the legacy for which our leaders fought and died? Are we weaklings? Or are we warriors?"

A rumble shook the ground as dragon heads lifted and scaly mouths parted. Words broke loose and poured from their tongues in deafening unison, "Warriors! Warriors!"

Blackclaw raised both fists and pumped the crowd into a chant.

"Warriors! Warriors! Warriors!"

When the voices softened to a hum, he spoke again. "We are warriors. Humans were once our cause. We befriended them. They betrayed us." He surged to the edge of the platform like a shifting thundercloud. "It is time for a new cause!" His fists opened to splay wide, powerful digits. "Supremacy!"

Shouting again buffeted the air. Kallon had to cover his ears to prevent his brain from shriveling.

A new chant took over. Dragons growled, "War! War! War! War!"

Kallon could only stare as dragon eyes reddened and dragon mouths foamed. Were these the peace-loving creatures his father once led? Were these the companions and mentors he remembered as a child?

The faces he looked upon twisted grotesquely, puffed and disfigured by rage. A haze of sulfuric breath filled the arena, stippling the scene in an opaque nightmare.

He glanced at Orman, who was staring in shock at Kallon above two fingers pinching his nose. Kallon looked for Riza on the platform.

She'd gone pale and listless, staring off toward the far wall of the stadium.

For a moment, Kallon thought she'd lost consciousness on her feet, until Armitage moved beside her to touch her shoulder, and she jabbed her elbow at his stomach.

Kallon tried to find the end of the chains binding Riza's wrists. If she wasn't attached to anything, he might be able to swoop over the distracted council members on the platform and escape with her and Orman to safety. Once done, would the council bother to send chasers after them? With more important tasks to concern themselves with now, such as war, Kallon would be a speck of a problem. A nuisance. He could continue to live quietly in another province. One that had long since lost their dragons. A place where neither he nor Riza were known or noticed.

His fellow Kind roared on. Blackclaw hollered loudest. But within, Kallon heard a still, small voice. His eyes darted to Orman.

Orman seemed to have heard it, too, for he lowered his hand from his nose and smiled.

Kallon almost fought it. He wanted to fight it. He wanted to drown it out with shouts of his own, but again the voice came, not from outside his ears, but from between them. Right inside his own brain. It said, "no."

"No," he repeated aloud. Softly.

"Again, Kallon," said Orman. "Tell them."

"No." Something broke loose inside him. It broke loose from somewhere deep where he carried his unshed tears and forgotten emotions. He felt a crack, as real as the peal of breaking stone. He threw himself at the throng of dragons blocking passage to the platform and shouted, "No!"

Startled, one Green clamped his mouth shut to stare. Kallon wedged his way through, squeezing between scaled shoulders and ribs, heaving this way and that to force openings. "No! No! You are wrong! Our leaders would not want this! My father would never want this!"

A Gray moved aside to let him reach the platform steps.

He climbed them.

Whitetail appeared from behind the council members to wave them forward and block his path, but Kallon shouted again.

"I have the right to speak!"

That captured Blackclaw's attention, because he swung his gaze over.

Council members of green, brown, blue, and ginger exchanged looks.

Kallon repeated, "I have the right to speak! I am Kallon Redheart, son of Bren Redheart, grandson of Arin Redheart!"

Blackclaw glared, gesturing for Whitetail to stop him.

When Whitetail pressed forward with an outstretched palm, Councilor Hale Brownwing reached out his own paw to Whitetail's chest. "He is Kallon Redheart. He has the right to speak."

Whitetail peered pitifully over his shoulder to his leader.

Kallon realized the crowd had ceased shouting. All eyes were on him once more. He faltered back a step, feeling the weight of those eyes as an oncoming boulder. A rattle of chains roused him, and he turned to find not a boulder, but an oncoming Riza.

Her young face was tight, her eyes dark with shadows. With arms pinned behind her back, she ran to him, but was stopped violently short by the wooden post to which she'd been fixed. She nearly toppled over.

He lunged toward her and caught her in his claws. He steadied her with one paw on each shoulder and lowered his gaze to find her eyes. "Be strong. I'll fight this."

"You see?" came Blackclaw's now-familiar, rumbling voice. "Before all as witnesses, he consorts with the prisoner! This one who claims the right to speak is a spineless traitor who keeps murderers as friends." Blackclaw pointed a menacing claw at Orman, who lingered at the side opening of the arena. "And spies as company!"

Gasps broke out, but Kallon turned from Riza to speak again.

"Fellow dragons, I urge you to think. Many of you know Orman Thistleby as a wizard and friend. My own father trusted and protected him, even died in service to him. What purpose would he serve to gather secrets from us?"

"Bah! I already know all your carnsarned secrets anyway, you fools," Orman said. He crossed his arms and scowled.

"You use the word 'us' as though you belong here, Redheart," snorted Blackclaw. "One claim to heritage does not a leader make."

Kallon found Armitage's eyes on him, and for a moment, he was so filled with outrage he nearly forgot himself. He managed to peel his gaze from the man to respond. "I am only here to remind you of the hopes of our leaders. They believed their purpose, our purpose, is to serve, protect, and above all else, honor the ways of peace between Mankind and Dragon."

"A sentimental and outdated view!" Blackclaw

addressed the crowd once more. "This was a respectful purpose at a time when both sides honored and valued the agreement, but it has long since lost its meaning. Humans do not want our friendship! They want our land, our crystals! They want our extinction!"

"So we retaliate by causing theirs?" Kallon faced the dragons as well. "Is this what our leaders would have wanted?"

Blackclaw turned to Kallon, his upper lip snarling. A tuft of blackened smoke escaped across the tip of his tongue and slithered upward. "There is that word 'we' again, Red. You are not a part of this community any longer. It was your choice to abandon it. It was I who stepped in to fill the responsibility." His dusky eyes turned to his citizens. "The Red forgets that I am your leader now! I say we have bowed to tradition for so long that it has broken our backs!" Up went a clenched fist again. "I say no longer! I say our time has come!"

"Our time has come!" echoed scattered voices.

"I want my territory back!"

"I want their territory!"

Kallon's chest fluttered in panic. He searched for Orman over the crowd, who only stared back with steady eyes. He looked for Riza, who had drifted to her knees on the platform.

Armitage's chained wrists reached for her, and this time she didn't even flinch. He looked over his shoulder to Kallon, and slowly drew her in against his bare chest. His chains groaned as he stroked her hair.

"No!" came Kallon's cry before he was even

conscious of it. "It can not happen!"

"It can happen, and it will!" Blackclaw lumbered toward Kallon. "You have had your chance to speak, now go back to your hiding place and stop blundering in things that do not concern you."

"No," Kallon murmured, falling back from the approaching Blackclaw. "Not right. This is not right." He searched again for Orman, but failed to find him.

Armitage kissed Riza's forehead, and she quietly wept.

Blackclaw's face loomed ever closer, joined by Whitetail's, and even Brownwing's. They closed in to run him off the platform. He'd failed again!

"Kallon."

Kallon looked down to find that Orman had managed to squeeze through the throng and now stood near his feet. Their eyes met, and in that instant, Kallon's mind was filled with ancient words.

In desperation, he shouted them. "Fordon Blackclaw! Your ways of leadership are not commensurate with the long-held beliefs of your citizens. Your aspirations for their future are counterfeit, and your ambitions are self-seeking. I challenge your post!"

Chapter Seventeen

The three approaching dragons halted and exchanged looks. Council members gaped. Mount Gore's arena went silent.

Kallon was as surprised as the others. He didn't even know he remembered the words. What's more, the challenge wasn't only a desperate act, he believed in it.

Blackclaw didn't take long to recover. He laughed. "Are you serious? How can you possibly think yourself a better leader than I? You do not even know your fellow dragons! How can you know their long-held beliefs?"

"Nevertheless," said Hale Brownwing. "The challenge has been issued."

"That challenge is as outdated as the notion of peace, Hale. This whelp thinks he can appear after all this time and challenge a leadership he knows nothing about? That challenge no more applies to him than to a dragon stranger from Esra Province, or from Manent!"

"I am not a stranger from a distant province, Blackclaw. I am a citizen of Leland," said Kallon. "And more than that, I am the rightful leader."

"Yes. So you say. I have yet to hear one other dragon speak out for you. We do not really know who you are, do we?"

Hale Brownwing thumped a fist to his chest. "I will speak for him. I know him, even after all this time." Brown claws gently gripped the back of Kallon's neck and gave an encouraging squeeze. "I have often thought of you, son. Vaya has never stopped believing this day would come." He swept his open paw toward the backdrop of seated council members. "Most of us served beneath your father. I am not the only one who remembers you."

Colorful dragon heads nodded.

Kallon lowered his chin. "Thank you." He looked at Blackclaw, whose face swelled and darkened so that Kallon thought it might pop like a ripe blackberry. Blackclaw's eyes swirled with something vicious, but when he spoke, he sounded perfectly rational.

"Brownwing, it sounds as though you have already given this Red your vote. That could be considered inappropriate, but never mind. If you insist on playing out this little challenge game, so be it. Whitetail, find the particulars in our scrolls, please. I believe there to be something about the challenger having to prove his accusations, and the challenged allowed to issue a quest."

Whitetail turned to descend the platform.

"I will go with him," Brownwing offered. Silent onlookers moved aside to let them pass.

"This challenge ritual is a part of our history,

Fordon, and our law. We should not look upon it as a game," said Shera Yellowfang. "As Herald of the Yellows, I should be happy to step aside and let another serve in my stead if it were to serve a higher purpose for my tribe."

"Yes, of course, true words," said Blackclaw. "And if it were to serve a higher purpose, then I would step aside without hesitation. I only remind you, Yellowfang, that this Red is a stranger to our ways."

"So if he is not fit to replace you, the ritual will show that. Our laws are not arbitrary. They are precise for exactly the reason you describe." Yellowfang rose from her place on the council pallet. "The Red will have to prove his accusations, and prove himself. In the meantime, perhaps we should dismiss the meeting, to reconvene later?" She looked out across the shifting crowd. "They need not be a party to all of this."

Blackclaw narrowed his eyes on Yellowfang. "That would be my decision to make." He moved beside her and raised his voice. "I, for one, feel the citizens have a right to witness all that pertains to them. I say let them stay, if they so wish it!"

A ripple of murmurs moved out across the gathering. The atmosphere tightened. Dragons spoke among themselves, but quietly.

Kallon remembered overhearing many arguments between council members in the manor chambers, but that dissention was strictly kept from public view. Now he understood why. This conflict tested confidence and broke apart the council into individual dragons, forcing the onlookers to choose loyalties. He could see the result on their faces. They didn't want to choose.

But no one was watching him, so he slowly made his way sideways to Armitage and Riza and growled, "Get away from her."

Armitage glanced up. His jaw clenched. His arms tightened around Riza. "You stinking beasts. You're all going to die. Every one of you. I only hope I'm still around to watch."

"Your words are the buzz of a tiny fly, Armitage. Release Riza. It will be hard enough to convince the others she had nothing to do with this, without your cradling and kissing her like a lover."

"You assume we aren't lovers."

"I needn't assume something I know for certain."

"Stop it, both of you," Riza said, eyes darting to the dragons behind them. She squirmed. "Jastin, let me go. Kallon's right."

Armitage let her go. He gave her a push, and she bobbled and fell. "You smell like one of them, anyway," he said. "Even after a bath. Even wearing my tunic. You smell more dragon than woman."

Kallon helped Riza to her feet and she pressed against his chest. "I don't understand what's being said," she whispered, turning up her face to him. "But I know about your dragon friend. You know I didn't have anything to do with that. I never wanted to go with Jastin."

"I know, Riza. Jastin knows. I think even Blackclaw knows, which is why I don't understand what he's doing."

"Blackclaw knows," said Jastin. "But to him, she's just one more human he can kill, and not only will he get away with it, he'll be idolized for it." He sneered. "Isn't that what you dragons do best? Kill humans?"

Riza spun around to stamp her foot at the kneeling man. "Listen to yourself! You murder dragons for money!"

Kallon blinked. "What did you just say?"

"It's his job," she said, nudging Armitage with her foot. "He's a dragon slayer."

Kallon slapped his paw to his forehead. Finally! It made sense! "Armitage, what happened to your shirt and vest?"

He shrugged. "A Gray took them. I don't know what he did with them."

"When he took them, was the pouch still in your vest? The money pouch that—"

"Whitetail and Brownwing have returned," said Councilor Orangepaw.

Yellowfang and the other council members turned to face them, then swept gracefully back to their places along the honored stone pallet. The crowd focused fresh attention on the platform.

Orman joined Kallon and gently nudged him away from Riza.

Kallon tried to catch her gaze as he stepped back, but Yellowfang passed and blocked his view.

Whitetail approached the massive podium and settled a large wooden box on it. "Our laws and edicts,

Council Leader Blackclaw, as pertains to the Ritual of Challenge."

Kallon could see Whitetail's pawprints in the layer of dust coating the box. Whitetail and Brownwing had obviously already broken the spellcatch protecting the lock, judging by the smear of marks there, too.

"Well. Be on with it, then," said Blackclaw, his forelegs crossing. "Our feast of celebration grows cold in the manor."

Whitetail opened the lid. He withdrew a length of parchment, yellowed with age but otherwise flawless. He cleared his throat and then read aloud, "Any citizen of Leland Province who feels the chosen leadership is failing in its responsibilities to the greater whole may challenge any council seat to be replaced."

Kallon felt Blackclaw's intense stare. Kallon kept his gaze on the White, afraid he might cave in if he dared to meet Blackclaw's raging eyes.

Whitetail continued reading. "The challenge must be stated before two or more witnesses, and spoken as thus: Council Member Name, your ways of leadership are not commensurate with the long-held beliefs of your citizens. Your aspirations for their future are counterfeit, and your ambitions are self-seeking. I challenge your post."

"Word for word," whispered Orman. "Got my wits about me so far!"

"The challenge was spoken correctly, and satisfies me," said Shera Yellowfang. She addressed the others. "Any disagreements?"

Looks were exchanged, heads wagged. "Very well, please continue, Fane Whitetail."

He did. "Upon issuance of the challenge, the confronting citizen must offer irrefutable proof, A, that the confronted council seat—foregoing amendment procedures—votes, or coerces others to vote, contradictorily to established edicts, and B, that the confronted council seat has misused the authority and/or stature of the station by supplanting the goals of the community with personal gain." Whitetail glanced to Blackclaw.

Kallon thought he saw the scrolls trembling.

"Is that all?" Blackclaw asked of the White, with a warning shot in his eyes.

Whitetail took a deep breath and gathered himself. "No, it goes on to explain that you have the right to issue a quest, if Redheart wishes to replace you himself."

"Let us hear it, then," said Hale Brownwing.

Whitetail glanced to Blackclaw again and tugged the parchment straight. "The confronting citizen, if wishing to replace the council member himself, must prove his honor and loyalty by completing a task commensurate with the level of responsibility to the seat. This task may be assigned by the challenged council member."

Kallon held up his paw. "That will not be necessary. I do not intend on replacing Blackclaw as council leader."

"Yes you do!" said Orman, and slapped Kallon's shoulder.

"No, I do not," Kallon said, and waved for the proceedings to continue.

Orman grumbled. "When you issued that challenge, you meant to reclaim your rightful place as heir to the council!"

"No, I didn't. One of the other council members is a better choice."

"But," Orman said. "It's your duty! Your destiny!"

Kallon sighed heavily. "Orman, you have to let that go. I'm not my father."

Orman snorted and crossed his arms. "No. You aren't." Orman moved to Riza and put his hand on her shoulder. "I'm sorry. I thought he would do the right thing."

"What's happening?" asked Riza. "What's the white dragon saying?"

"Kallon has challenged Blackclaw as leader of the dragon council, but he doesn't intend to replace him. I'm afraid that doesn't bode well for you, my dear."

"Now wait a minute," said Kallon. "Any council leader can free her. It doesn't have to be me."

"Any council leader convinced of her innocence." Orman raised his voice for the panel. "How many of you just now would say without a doubt that the girl should be released?"

Council members regarded one another. No one spoke.

Orman turned hard eyes to Kallon.

"We all agree that a murder has been committed, Orman Thistleby," said Shera Yellowfang. "We know the human in black is responsible, and the girl was in his company when he was found. We have not seen enough evidence to convince us she is innocent."

"Though her respectful conduct during our proceedings has impressed us," said Hale Brownwing.

"What are they saying, Orman?" Riza asked quietly.

He patted her shoulder. "They appreciate your respect, but in order to be released, Kallon is going to have to pardon you as council leader."

She began a small smile for Kallon, but it froze on her face. Instead, she looked fearfully toward Orman.

"Riza..." Kallon began to explain, but her eyes wouldn't let him finish. He watched her in silence. Then he turned to the council members. "Very well. I include, in my challenge, the claim to the council leader seat."

Orman clapped his hands together in a single beat, and grinned. He hugged Riza, who couldn't hug back.

"Did he say he would do it?" she asked into Orman's shoulder.

"He did," said the wizard. "I feel a change in the wind."

"There's a change all right, but I wouldn't lay odds in your favor." Jastin yanked his chains. "How long are we going to stand here? How long is this challenge going to take?"

Orman looked at Jastin with raised brows. "You understand Dragonspeak?"

Jastin rolled his eyes. "What kind of soldier would I be if I couldn't understand the language of my enemy?"

"Enemy!" Riza said, hushed. She glanced to the

dragons all around them. "Mind your words, Jastin, they may decide your fate."

"My fate's already decided," he said. "I'm only sticking around now to make sure the stinking beasts don't really hurt you."

"Jastin!" Riza chastised again, and moved away from him to the length of her chain, which took her near Blackclaw. When she looked up to find the black dragon glaring at her, she startled and inched back toward Orman.

Kallon had plenty to say to Armitage, but it would have to wait. Council members were fidgeting and glancing toward the exit. Except Blackclaw, who stood like a lump of black mountain. He seemed relaxed, confident. It made Kallon very nervous.

"So what happens now?" Kallon asked.

Brownwing shifted. "Fane Whitetail, do the edicts prescribe the order of proceedings?"

Whitetail skimmed the print. He shook his head.

"In that case, I am ready to state how Blackclaw has abused his post and lied to us all," Kallon said.

The dragons in the arena turned their attention again to the platform.

"Certainly, Red. Be prepared to back it with proof," said Blackclaw, as he inspected his curled claws.

"I will need permission for the human male to speak."

Blackclaw paused. His dark eyes slid slowly to Kallon's, and Kallon met his gaze with something he hoped would pass as confidence. "This man is here as a prisoner," said the leader. "What could he possibly have to say that pertains to these proceedings?"

"He could tell us how he came to be at Mount Gore, and why," Kallon said, turning to the council members.

"He came to be here because the woman gained your trust and led him here!" Blackclaw countered.

"He is a hunter," said Kallon. "For hire." He swept his arm toward Riza. "The woman is no one to us. Only a hunter benefits from the death of a dragon."

"Are they talking about me?" Kallon heard Riza whisper to Orman.

Orman patted her shoulder and nodded, his eyes transfixed on Kallon.

"Are you saying that this human was hired to kill Bluecrest?" asked Yellowfang. The murmurs of the dragon crowd grew louder.

"But who here would hire this human?" Orangepaw strode forward, eyes sweeping over the gathering. "Who here would murder his own Kind?"

"Only someone who has supplanted the goals of the community with personal gain," said Kallon. He stared at Blackclaw and felt a sweeping wave of dragon eyes follow.

Heads turned. Orman spun to look at him. Jastin watched Blackclaw with a flat smile. Even Riza followed the tide and blinked at the black dragon.

Blackclaw pressed his paw to his chest and looked back at everyone in surprise. Then he smiled. "Shera, I like your suggestion that we dismiss the meeting to allow the attendees a rest. The morning has dragged long and weary. We will eat, and reconvene this evening."

"You can not dismiss them now!" Kallon took a step toward Blackclaw.

"I am leader of the council. I can."

"I am not finished!"

Blackclaw lowered his snout, his black eyes sizzling. "But I am. In fact, I am here at the finish line, waiting for you to catch up and realize that I have already won."

Kallon's stomach churned. He turned to the council members. "He manipulates his power to avoid the truth! He is a deceiver and a murderer!"

The council stared back in a moment of collective hesitation. Yellowfang spoke. "That is a serious charge, Kallon Redheart."

"Blackclaw is still our leader and he can dismiss the meeting at will," said Hale Brownwing. "Until you have proven otherwise, we are directed by his management."

"How can he prove otherwise, if the carnsarned leader he's trying to do away with won't let him speak?" Orman rattled a bony finger at Blackclaw. "He's vicious, I tell you!"

Blackclaw grunted a short laugh. "The spy speaks." He turned to the crowd. "May I remind you all that this wizard is an escaped prisoner, broken free from our cell just last night, aided by the same dragon who now wishes to depose me?"

Voices erupted into quiet chatter.

"I have allowed the Red his babble," Blackclaw continued. "I have given him his day to speak out against me. Out of respect for our laws, and the ritual of challenge, I will abide the insult." He pressed his palm to his chest. "I have given you no cause to distrust me. I have led you, and the council, with dignity. We stand before you, wise and unblemished. Let his preposterous accusations come.

"But I submit to you all, where is his gall, that he should arise from silence into our community? Has he worked alongside us while we have struggled to make a life from our pitiful resources? Has he suffered our humiliation at being denied our rightful land to expand and prosper?"

Chattering voices grew louder.

"Who is he, that he should disrupt our harmonious cry for justice with sour words of ancient beliefs? Beliefs to which he holds us, when he, himself, has abandoned them?" Blackclaw raised his forelegs and the mumbles surged into a unified shout. "Who is he to us, that he should challenge us? I say, let him prove himself!"

"Prove himself!" echoed a sharp voice.

"Quest!" chirped another.

Kallon blasted a look at Orman, who gave him wide eyes and a limp shrug.

"Do what?" Orman mouthed.

"What's happening?" He heard Riza's small voice.

"Your dragon friend is regretting he opened his oversized mouth," said Armitage.

The council members were either enraptured by Blackclaw's speech, or simply ignoring Kallon. Some of them were quietly clapping.

"Quest!" shouted Orangepaw.

Inside, Kallon shrank into a tiny lump of despair.

Blackclaw waved his paws to dim the crowd's shouts. He waited for complete silence, and then he extended an ebony claw toward Kallon and smiled. "Bring me the Circlet of Aspira."

Orman yelled. "That's impossible!" He shook his fist.

Hale Brownwing emerged. "Fordon, no one is even certain the circlet still exists."

"The Red can withdraw his challenge if he doubts his ability. Until then, my task stands." Blackclaw waved toward Whitetail. "Send for Grayfoot." He faced the onlookers again. "In my benevolence, I will allow the Red time to consider while we feast and proceed with our schedule. He has returned the escaped prisoner to us. For that, I commend him."

The hulking Gray appeared from nowhere and squinted a bruised eye at Kallon. He snapped cuffs around Orman's skinny wrists before there was time to react.

"Blast you, Blackclaw! You can't get away with this!" Orman flailed his legs, jumping like a jigging grasshopper. "The truth will come out!"

The Gray yanked Orman's cuffs, gathered up the chains of Riza and Armitage, and dragged them all off the platform to the side exit.

"What are you doing, Blackclaw?" Kallon growled. "Your quarrel is with me, not my friends."

"Do not be so arrogant. They will pay for their

crimes, when this quarrel between you and me is settled. As will you." Blackclaw spoke to the council members. "This Red has abetted an escaped prisoner. For now, I am willing to set aside his criminal proceedings until the challenge ritual has been satisfied, but his place is in a cell, with the others."

"I do not believe the Red will avoid his responsibility," said Hale Brownwing, drawing near. "Imprisonment is not necessary."

"I will go," said Kallon. "Blackclaw is right about one thing only. My place is with my friends."

Blackclaw nodded. "See to it, Whitetail." He moved away to address his citizens.

"I am certain Councilor Brownwing is capable of seeing me away." Kallon caught Brownwing's gaze and urged him silently.

Brownwing briefly hesitated. Then he gestured toward the side exit, and turned to lead Kallon off the platform. "Your accusations of Blackclaw's treachery are difficult to believe, Kallon Redheart. They ring with the sound of desperation."

"I am not insulted that you do not believe me, Brownwing, but there is proof what I say is true. Blackclaw protects that evidence now by keeping me from it." He glanced over his shoulder to find Whitetail approaching. "Find out what happened to the human's clothing when he was captured. Keep Blackclaw from destroying it."

"Council Member Brownwing is being summoned to the platform," said Whitetail. "I will lead you myself,

Red, and do not make me chain you."

"That is not necessary." Kallon looked at Brownwing. "If not for me, for my father," Kallon quickly whispered.

Whitetail's claws captured Kallon's left forearm and yanked. "It has been some years since you have seen the manor." The White's tone was as pleasant as a tour guide, but his grip was iron.

"Actually, I was just there yesterday." Kallon turned his head to look for Hale Brownwing, who was just disappearing inside the arena. Then his eyes moved to Whitetail again. "You are hurting me, despite my willingness to go with you. You might keep in mind that you will soon be working for me."

"That would be some trick," said Whitetail with a sniff. But he released his grip.

CHAPTER EIGHTEEN

"I still don't understand what's happening," said Riza, trailing behind Orman and trying to stay as far from Jastin as she could. "Why are we going back into the dark?"

"Your dragon's attempted overthrow just got thrown back in his face," said Jastin, looking over his shoulder at her. "I thought he had them for a minute. But of all the conniving dragons I've met in my time, Blackclaw is the most genius."

"Is that admiration in your voice?" asked Orman.

"Some. I knew better than to trust him, but he still managed to keep me here by playing a hand I wasn't expecting." Jastin watched Riza a few steps more, then faced forward. "I betrayed a weakness, and he masterfully wove it into the whole scheme."

At the door to the cell, Riza clutched at Orman's hand. "I don't want to go back in there. I'd almost rather they just kill me now than to have to go in there."

"That can be arranged," rumbled the gray dragon,

who turned the key in the lock, pulled the door open wide, and then actually smiled.

Riza's spine quivered.

"New door, I see," Orman said, and passed the dragon. "Looks flimsier than the last. How's that eye?"

The gray dragon squinted his black eye, and then pushed Orman into the cell so hard that he stumbled.

Riza hung back, staring into the blackness.

The dragon nudged.

She resisted. "I don't want to go in there."

"Human, you will go in there by feet, or flight. You choose."

The grating voice of the white dragon echoed in the cool hallway.

Riza didn't understand what he said, but she recognized a chuckle when she heard one. She turned to find Kallon beside him. "Kallon!" She ran to meet him, but her chains wouldn't let her close. "They're letting you visit?"

"We're allowing him full lodging, my dear," said the White, and gestured Kallon on.

"With dinner, I presume." Kallon slowly made his way toward the cell. Too slowly.

Riza bounced on her toes. She wanted to touch him, to make sure he was real.

The Gray gripped the back of her neck and spun her around to face the door. "Go."

"But I—" Her feet lifted from the floor. She shrieked. Claws stabbed like knives around her throat, squeezing out her air.

"Put her down!" Kallon shouted.

"Let her go!" Jastin's voice joined Kallon's.

She heard, and felt, the grumble of the Gray's reply just before she saw swirling dots in front of her eyes. There was a moment of weightlessness. Then she hit the floor with a jolt that snapped her jaw and blasted sparkles through her brain. She groaned. Someone touched her and rolled her aside.

"Kallon?" She thought she opened her eyes, but she still couldn't see anything. She recognized the rasp of Jastin's grunt, and his hands left her.

"Riza," came Kallon's voice.

She strained to sit up. "My shoulder," she whispered. "It hurts."

"I can't believe he just threw you in here like rubbish," Kallon said.

"Let me see," said Orman. Hands pressed to her arm and gently squeezed their way to her shoulder.

Hot pain sliced her arm. She yelped.

"Blast it all. I think it's out of joint," said Orman.

"I can fix that," said Jastin. "But not with her arms behind her like that. We've got to get those chains off."

"I haven't any way." Orman settled beside her, his bony hip pressed to her belly. "I haven't any crystals, any powders, any herbs. Without them, I'm no wizard. I'm just an old man." He stroked her hair away from her face.

Kallon's voice was soft, and very close. "You've told me time and again, Orman, that magic isn't something you carry in a pouch. Tools are carried on the outside, but belief is carried inside."

"You were listening, after all." Orman sighed. "But you missed the lesson, as usual. You dragons have your own magic, like the fabric holding this world together. I'm just a bumbling, fumbling human. I need my tools."

Kallon settled his immense weight beside her.

She couldn't roll to face him, but she turned her head and nuzzled her cheek to his paw. She wasn't so frightened now.

Jastin's chains clanked as he moved away. "Dragons created from magic fabric," he said with a huff. "Dragons are lizards, except bigger, and more dangerous, because they can think."

An orange glow emanated from Kallon's muzzle that illuminated his scowling face. "You have no sword now, and no one in here would grieve if I burned you alive."

"If it weren't for you, Jastin, none of us would be here right now!" said Riza.

"Don't give me so much credit," Jastin said. "I'm just the speck of dust in the master plan." He grunted, settling to the floor in the dark.

"What master plan?" asked Orman.

"The plan between him and Blackclaw to murder Bluecrest," Kallon said.

Riza's pain must have been dulling her senses. "I thought I just heard you say Blackclaw and Jastin murdered Bluecrest together."

Kallon's face swung toward Jastin's voice. "That was what I saw in the trees outside the arena, wasn't it? You said you took less than your usual fee to have Riza, too."

"You saw Blackclaw and this man together?" Orman asked.

"Yes," Kallon said. "I didn't realize it at the time, but it makes sense now."

"Treachery abounds," said Orman. "I never have trusted Blackclaw. When he was appointed leader, I protested. I tried to tell the council that he had a viciousness inside him that would be their ruin someday."

"You have no idea," said Jastin.

Riza was having trouble following the conversation. Voices competed with her buzzing headache. Every move she made twisted her shoulder. She couldn't decide if she was hungry or nauseated. Her throat felt swollen. "I can't remember feeling normal," she said. "I can't remember anything but darkness and pain, and I don't even know why I'm a part of all this." What bravery she'd managed so far began to leak out in thick, warm tears. She couldn't even wipe them away.

Orman patted her hip. "You've been quite courageous. You've been through more than any of us."

"The council mentioned they were impressed by your respectfulness," said Kallon.

"They did?" she asked, and sniffled.

"Yes," said Orman. "You were very dignified." He leaned down to whisper, "Kallon said you were beautiful."

"He did?" Her eyes moved to where she thought Kallon's face must be, but she couldn't find him in the dark. She could hear him breathing, though, and could feel the warmth of it drying her cheeks. "I wish I could see you," she whispered.

"I'm here," Kallon said.

She tried to smile. "Your dragon language sounds like poetry."

"Does it?" Kallon asked.

"Yes. I might have actually enjoyed it, if I hadn't been so afraid."

"Then I'll teach it to you, after all this is over," Kallon said.

"I'd like that." She peered into the thick blackness, trying to make out the shape of him. Suddenly there was an orange speck of light before her eyes.

As Kallon released a long breath, the speck swelled from his throat to illuminate his open mouth, his snout and his eyes. He smiled.

She forgot her pain. "When this is all over, will you take me flying?" she asked.

"When this is all over," Kallon whispered, "I'll teach you to fly."

The room echoed with Jastin's harsh laugh.

Orman shushed him.

Riza had forgotten about the others. Jastin's laugh brought a swell of embarrassment, and she shrank into her cocoon of pain.

The flame from Kallon's mouth snuffed. "You've been warned, human, of your words."

"Yes, yes." Jastin's chains rattled against the stone floor. "I was merely appreciating the entertainment. Do go on."

Kallon rose up. The paw Riza was balanced against shifted, causing her to roll aside to her shoulder.

She stifled her cry behind clenched lips, but Orman's hands reached to steady her anyway.

Kallon's claws clicked against stone as he moved toward Jastin's voice. "I am struggling for a reason not to kill you."

"With the girl as witness? Unable to defend myself?" Jastin clicked his tongue. "Why, that would only prove what I have been saying all along."

"What have you been saying all along?" asked Orman.

"Do not let him goad you into talk," Kallon said.

"This dragon is spineless," Jastin said. "He expects everyone else to do their duty but him."

Orman released Riza and shifted. "I hate to say he has a point, Kallon."

"I warned you against being goaded into talk!" Kallon said.

"He's no better than Blackclaw," Jastin said. "He'd rather kill me than listen to me."

"The way I'd swat a fly that pesters my ear," Kallon snorted.

"Now who's being goaded?" Orman asked.

"And you wonder why I despise your kind?" Jastin's voice grew louder. "Your first instinct is to kill whatever annoys you with no more thought than squashing a bug!"

Orange light began to churn from Kallon's words.

"How many dragons have you murdered with that same ease?"

"That's business!" Jastin said. "I don't kill for the mere pleasure of it."

Kallon snarled. "So murder for money is a nobler cause than murder for pleasure?"

"Killing a dragon is a noble cause!" Jastin shouted. "Why not make a living at the same time?"

Flames licked out from Kallon's throat, engulfing Jastin's bearded face with yellow heat.

If the man sensed his near death, he failed to show it. He stood before Kallon's gaping mouth, chained arms flexed, feet planted, and glared.

"You killed Bluecrest!" Kallon showered Jastin with sparks.

Jastin didn't even flinch as the sizzling pinpricks turned to ash against his bare chest. "It was business!"

"You murdered my father!" Kallon belched fire, his eyes gone wild.

This time, Jastin had to duck to avoid it. The cell was filled with the stench of sulfur and singed hair.

"Stop it!" Riza screamed. She clamored to get to her feet, tumbled, and tried again. "Kallon, stop it!" Through her haze of pain and nausea, she knocked aside Orman and rushed toward the heat. "Don't do it!"

"He killed my father!" Kallon roared.

"Not here! Not like this!" Riza ran blindly. She collided into what felt like a solid wall, and only registered the scratch of rough scales a split-second before an explosion of pain in her shoulder came so quickly she couldn't even gasp. She fell back and twitched helplessly. Little specks of light floated around her eyes.

"Riza!" Orman's voice came from somewhere very far away.

She felt hands cradling her. She thought she heard the click of Kallon's claws, but the sound bounced around her ears in echoes.

Again came Orman's voice from some dark, resonant hallway. "So it was you."

Jastin's reply faded like a ghost down that same hallway. "It was business."

§

Fingers roused her, stroking her cheek. She stirred and opened her mouth, but a hand pressed over it.

"Sssh. It's Jastin," he whispered. "Be still."

She mumbled against his hand.

He removed it, but his breath remained close to her ear.

"What happened?" she asked. "Where am I?"

"You're still here, where you fell. The wizard tended you for a while, but he sleeps now." He chuckled softly. "You managed to fix your own shoulder when you ran into that lummox. Must have hurt like a bugger."

"Where's Kallon?" Riza asked. "What did you do to him?"

His hand clamped to her mouth again. "Ssh. You

think I'm able to do something to him in the dark, and with no weapons? I don't even have free arms."

She tried to turn her head, and to pull her mouth out from beneath his grasp, but his fingers only tightened.

His chains scratched her chin as his other hand cupped her cheek. Now his voice came from above her. "Listen to me. Your stubbornness is going to get you killed. You can't leave your fate to the dragon."

She yelled into his hand.

He clenched her face so hard she struggled to breathe. "No, listen," he hissed. "The dragon can't save you. He can't prove Blackclaw's involvement, and he can't retrieve the circlet. When the Red fails, Blackclaw will kill us both."

Circlet? What circlet? She didn't understand what he was talking about, but she wouldn't believe him, anyway, if she did understand. She tried to tell him that, but his hand choked her words. She arched her neck and tried to bite him.

"Missed me," he whispered. "I'm not trying to hurt you. Stop fighting me."

She wished she could see him, so she could at least glare at him.

"I'm going to say this one more time. The dragon will fail. When he does, you will die."

She stilled. She tried to ask a question, but only garbled against his hand again.

He loosened his grip.

"How can you know he'll fail?" she asked.

"Blackclaw has challenged your Red to retrieve the Circlet of Aspira. But I delivered that circlet to him years ago. He already has it."

"Oh. That circlet." Now she remembered Orman's story. "Why don't you tell them? If the others see that Kallon was tricked, won't that show how Blackclaw really is?"

Jastin touched her hair. "Blackclaw isn't stupid. While we're here, out of his way, he's taking care of all that."

"But how can you know?"

He pressed his mouth to her temple and spoke words against her skin. "It's what I would do."

She closed her eyes. "Please stop touching me like that."

"Why do you resist me, Riza?" His mouth drew down the side of her face and he pressed a soft kiss to the corner of her mouth. "Even if this whole challenge weren't already doomed, you could never fit into his life."

"I just want to be his friend. I don't see why we can't be friends."

"Where? Here? You see how they've accepted you already. They despise us as much as we despise them." His lips pressed to the side of her neck.

She clenched against the rise of goosebumps.

"A war brews, Riza."

"No."

"There won't be anymore friendships between humans and dragons. When the fight comes, it will be us against them. Live or die. One side or the other."

"No." Fear clenched her belly and squeezed tears to her eyes. "It doesn't have to be that way."

"It's already that way. You just refuse to see it."

"If Kallon becomes leader instead Blackclaw, he can change that."

Jastin was silent for a long time.

She felt his breath against her throat, smelled the bitter remnants of sulfur and perspiration. She was almost certain he could see her in the dark, and that his eyes were roaming her face for which piece of flesh he might tear off with his teeth.

But when he spoke again, his voice was tender. "I think your Red wants to show the others that Blackclaw paid me with a pouch that bears the manor symbol." His chains scraped over her shoulder as his fingers guided her face toward his voice. "That pouch is already gone. It was long gone before we were captured."

"But if you tell them where it is, won't it be enough to prove Blackclaw was in on it?"

"It's miles away."

"When did he give it to you?"

"Before the opening ceremonies of the council meeting. The night I took you to the cave in the woods."

"Then when did you have time to travel so far to hide it?"

He growled softly. "You are the most obstinate woman that breathes. I thought my wife was the only one who could argue a snake into thinking he was a leather belt, but she had nothing on you."

"Well, I just don't understand!"

"Do you have to understand something before you can believe it?" He slid his hand into her hair and gripped gently. She could feel his lips against her mouth as he spoke. "Understand this, then. I am trying to save your life. I can't think why, with all the trouble you've given me." He drew in a long breath. "When I get my vest back, I can take you to safety in the time it takes you to blink. We can be miles away. Just like that pouch."

"Are you talking about magic? Are you a wizard?"

His quiet laugh held more frustration than amusement. "I'm not a wizard. But I work for someone who knows one."

"You mean Blackclaw?"

His fingers traced her cheek. "Let me take you with me, just to see you safe." His voice dropped so low, she could barely make out his words. "You don't have to stay with me. Just let me save you."

She let herself see deep inside to all the resistance, all the straining she'd ever done against the world and its confines. Jastin was right, she was stubborn. But she'd had to be. In a world of selfish, small-minded thinkers, she'd had to fight with everything she had not to become one of them.

But for what? To be laid out on a cold floor of a cell, buried alive. She'd changed nothing. She'd accomplished nothing. Every small step from home had only carried her further into the mouth of darkness, and she'd been swallowed by it. She searched now for the fight inside her, but only found weariness.

She would have liked to cry a little, but couldn't

work up the strength for even tears. She closed her eyes. "What about Orman?" she asked.

"Let him save himself," Jastin whispered. His kiss pressed hard to her mouth.

She couldn't immediately react. She'd gone numb. It felt like all those times when she'd slept and had somehow known she was sleeping. When her dreams didn't feel like dreams at all, but like moments when her soul had escaped to fly, soaring and fearless, into adventure.

Was she sleeping now? Her body lay unmoving. The weight of his heavy leg swung across her thighs and pinned her to the floor. It hurt, but she couldn't squirm. He pressed harder against her.

Her mind was foggy, full of the shadows of things she once dreamed about in places she thought someday she'd discover. Those things would never happen if she died here on the mountain. Maybe a life with Jastin was better than no life at all. Maybe he was right about that too.

Then she heard someone call. At first, she thought the voice echoed in her mind, but when she listened closer, she realized it murmured from that place in her soul where her fight was hiding. Wake up, Riza, said the voice. You want to fly.

She instantly awoke. Strength flowed into her arms and legs. She cried out against his mouth, and bucked against his weight.

He pulled back, his voice thick with breath. "You're right," he said. "I'm sorry. Not here. Not like this."

"No, Jastin," she said, twisting to push him away. "Not ever."

She could feel his angry stare pierce right through the blackness to her face. "Am I really so repulsive you'd rather die?"

"It's not you. It's everything I've ever believed. I can't give up now. If I'm going to die, I want to die flying."

"No." He gripped her chin again and pressed his mouth to her cheek. "No, I won't let you."

"Let me go!"

Orman snorted awake, and she heard his groggy voice. "Hm? What was that?"

"Riza?" It was Kallon. His voice was so clear she had to wonder how long he'd been awake.

"Stupid woman," Jastin spat into her ear. "Stupid, stubborn, infuriating…" He pushed off, making her grunt. He continued his babble of adjectives as he skulked away.

"What happened? Did he harm you? Are you quite all right?" Orman was there, his hands smoothing her hair, stroking her arms, searching for injury.

"Riza?" Kallon asked again.

"I'm fine. He didn't hurt me." She struggled to sit, her hands still useless and aching behind her back. Orman helped. "I have to tell you about the pouch."

The door suddenly groaned open and blinding torchlight swung in front of her face. She turned her head, seeing white splotches in front of her eyes.

"Time to go," said the talking wall of gray scales

that lumbered into the room. "Just the Red. The rest of you get to stay."

"Wait," she said, trying to get to her feet. Orman was there again to help her. "Kallon, Jastin's pouch—"

"Quiet, you," rumbled the Gray, and pushed her.

She was still trying to see past the floating splotches when Kallon's muzzle brushed her cheek. "It's all right, Riza. I know."

"No, you don't!" She stumbled forward. The massive door slammed shut. "Wait! It's not there! Kallon, the pouch isn't there!" She fell against the door, scratching her forehead.

"We've got to get out there," said Jastin, coming beside her.

"What pouch?" asked Orman.

"Do you think he heard me?" She turned toward Orman, her voice tight. "I don't think he heard me."

"Doesn't matter now, anyway," said Jastin. "We've just got to get out there."

CHAPTER NINETEEN

Kallon paused in the hallway. "Why are the others not coming?" he asked. He could hear Riza's panicked voice, distorted through the thick wooden door.

The Gray kept moving. "I was told to bring only you."

"Blackclaw is violating numerous agreements in the Human-Dragon Relations Pact. You will be held accountable for following orders that defy them."

"By whom?" The Gray gave Kallon a casual glance, and then, instead of veering left toward the exit, he turned right.

Kallon hung back. When the Gray was out of view, Kallon yanked open the metal slab on the prison door. "Riza?" he called.

"Dragon." Armitage's face appeared, covered in soot. "Get us out of here."

"Riza was trying to tell me something."

"You won't find the pouch where you think,"

Armitage said. "I need my vest. Get me out of here and get me my vest."

Kallon snorted. "And I should trust you because…?"

"There was a time when prisoners just quietly did as they were told," came a voice in the hallway.

Kallon turned to find the scowling Gray, who was holding a wickedly pointed shortstaff imbedded with dark blue crystals.

"Fear was enough," continued the Gray, staring down at the staff and twirling it slowly. "There was no need for threats and violence. I liked my job much better then."

Kallon sauntered toward him. "Have you tried asking nicely?" he asked, keeping an eye on that shortstaff.

They turned right. Kallon strained to remember where this hallway led, until he caught sight of an iron door. He paused. Ivy leaves climbed the door and met in the center. There perched a metal dragonfly, watching the hallway with a cocked head. He ran his thumb over the dragonfly's wings, and remembered. His mother's room.

"Go on." The Gray waved his staff.

Kallon pushed open the door. In the center of the room stood a thick slab of desk, with massive legs carved into claws that gripped the four corners. A neatly folded black tunic and leather vest lay on top of the desk, with a sword, several cloth pouches, and a crossbow with arrows, all arranged in a tidy half-circle.

Behind the desk stood Fordon Blackclaw, his

palms pressed to the wood. His dark head loomed over the desk.

"You understand, of course, that the tarnish you are applying to my good name will not easily buff away," Blackclaw said, his tone offensively patient. "You've introduced doubt into the minds of the masses, and it will linger. I will have to work hard to regain their trust."

Kallon straightened his shoulders and met Blackclaw's gaze. He was closer to the council leader than he'd been before. Kallon had thought Blackclaw was larger, somehow. Of course, his head still towered over Kallon's, and the leader's paws were half again the width of his own. So why did he seem so much smaller?

"A great leader should have to work at keeping trust," said Kallon. "He should have to prove himself again and again to those who place their faith in him."

Blackclaw leaned back. "Such conviction in your words." He shifted around to the side of the desk, moving like liquid shadows. "Almost convincing. In fact, your performance this morning made even me wonder if you actually believed the things you were saying."

"Do not pretend for my sake, Blackclaw," Kallon said. "We both know the truth."

"And it was because of those thoughts that I found myself curious about the evidence of which you spoke," Blackclaw said. "It is feasible, after all, that the human male convinced you of a plot by having this 'evidence' in his belongings."

Kallon's stomach lurched. "You destroyed it."

"No, I assure you, I did not. Now, tell me, just

between you and me, Redheart," Blackclaw said, coming in front of the desk. "Why is it that you have come? What do you really want here?"

Kallon regarded Blackclaw for a long moment. What did he really want? All morning, and until just now, he hadn't been thinking. He'd been acting on impulse, responding by instinct.

"Come now, Red. It is the time for truth. What is the real reason you came back?"

"I came back for my friends," Kallon finally said.

Blackclaw snorted. "But what do you want?"

Kallon moved a step closer. "I want Leland dragons to see you for who you really are. I want them to be guided by a leader who cares more for them than he does for himself."

"Or to infiltrate this community with your lies?" Blackclaw said.

"Very well, Fordon," came the resonant voice of Hale Brownwing.

Kallon turned to see the council member emerge from the adjoining room. Shera Yellowfang followed.

"We have heard enough," Hale Brownwing said. "The Red has said nothing to discredit himself, and I believe he speaks in truth."

"As do I," said Yellowfang. "Whether his accusations are true remains to be seen. But I believe that he believes them."

"What is this?" Kallon asked, eyes moving from Yellowfang to Brownwing, to Blackclaw. "Some sort of test?"

Blackclaw opened his mouth, but Brownwing held out a paw and spoke instead. "Forgive us, Kallon. We represent the council members who are at a loss as to what is really going on here. We sense wrongdoing, but are uncertain as to the cause."

"So by presenting me with the human's belongings, which have been cleansed of evidence, you thought I would confess to lying?" Kallon asekd.

"Fordon thought you would betray yourself in some way, but only if you believed you were alone with him," said Yellowfang. "Frankly, I agreed. It does seem an underhanded way of going about it, but you must realize we are only seeking the truth."

"The truth is your leader is the one with the power to manipulate all this," said Kallon. "He can hold me prisoner while he tidies up his secrets. He can keep innocent humans behind bars to protect his own lies." Kallon turned to Blackclaw, a wisp of steam curling from his lip. "As long as you continue to give Blackclaw his full leadership power, he will continue his wrongdoings without consequence."

"We have considered this," said Brownwing. "But we have failed to find a reason to doubt him."

"Then perhaps you should be trying to find a reason to believe him!" Kallon spun to Brownwing. "His accusations of Orman Thistleby as a spy are ridiculous, and you know it. What proof did he give? And yet, the wizard starves in a cell that hasn't been used since the Anodine war. Are we at war?"

"Yes," snarled Blackclaw. "We are at war with

injustice. As such, that wizard is a war criminal."

"By whose judgment?" asked Kallon.

"By mine!" Blackclaw slammed his fist to the desk, rattling Armitage's sword to the floor. "I am the leader here! I need no other judgment!"

"Now see here, Fordon," said Brownwing.

"The council is many members for a reason," said Yellowfang. "We have no dictatorship here."

"Do not lecture me, Shera, on the miniscule edicts of the council." Blackclaw pointed a claw at the Yellow and pressed it to the tip of her chin. "Lest you forget the edict that empowers me to invoke Primacy."

She pulled back from his touch and scowled. "Do you threaten me, Fordon?"

"Primacy!" Brownwing sputtered, his wingtips flaring. "That is no threat, that is an outrage! A difference of opinion is no basis for expulsion from the council!"

"It is if her loyalty is suspect," Blackclaw said, pushing away to swerve toward the door.

"You are betraying yourself, Blackclaw," said Kallon. "If you are not careful, you will show them your true nature, and save me the trouble."

"Thank you for your concern, Red," Blackclaw said. "But should you not be resting in the guest room I arranged for you and your criminal friends? You do have a difficult task come dawn." His onyx claws gripped the door handle. "And be prepared to make room there, would you? I suppose it is getting crowded, but there ought to be enough room for one more." His eyes shot to Yellowfang. Then he yanked open the door and slithered through it.

Yellowfang clenched her fists. "He has really gone too far. Someone should keep an eye on him."

"My nephew has been instructed to do so until I tell him otherwise." Brownwing reached down to the fallen sword and replaced it onto the desk. "However, I am not sure that is enough. We need to gather the council to discuss what the by-laws say about this."

"It is his word against ours," said Yellowfang.

"We are the two longest-serving members on the council." Brownwing put his paw on her shoulder. "It should count for something."

Yellowfang nodded and turned amber eyes to Kallon. "Perhaps completing your quest will help untie this tangle."

"Perhaps," said Kallon. "But I still have to prove Blackclaw's connection to Bluecrest's murder. His removing the evidence has taken care of that."

Yellowfang and Brownwing exchanged glances.

"What is it?" Kallon asked.

"Kallon, Hale did as you requested outside the arena. Out of respect for your father, he sent his nephew to find the belongings of the male human, and to keep watch over them."

"He discovered where they were kept," said Brownwing. "He stayed to guard them, and Blackclaw did show up, as you seemed to suspect." He looked again to Yellowfang.

She continued, "Hale's nephew didn't allow him

to touch anything before he alerted us. The belongings came straight from that room to this one, and have not been altered."

"But I saw him give the pouch to the human! It had the embroidered crest of the manor!" Kallon dove into the items, searching. "Why else would Blackclaw have gone to them if he did not also remember the pouch?"

"I can not say," said Brownwing. "He claims he was curious as to why you seemed so convinced of his guilt."

Kallon closed his eyes. He clutched Armitage's leather vest into his fist. "As long as Blackclaw remains one step ahead of me, I am doomed to fail."

Brownwing reached for the vest in Kallon's grip. "Sometimes, what we believe does not need to be proven, as long as we know in our hearts we fought well for it." Brownwing folded the vest neatly and returned it to the desk.

"She is slowly going mad in that place," Kallon said quietly. "If I can do nothing else for her, can you simply grant me that she not spend another night there? Surely the council can search the bylaws."

Yellowfang bunched her eyeridges. "Her? You mean the human female?"

"Yes," said Kallon. "I assure you she is innocent. And yet she suffers. She is hungry, and cold, and frightened."

Yellowfang looked for Brownwing's reaction, but the Brown only stared at the floor.

"Five of the seven current council members believe

you have spent the last several years going slowly insane," Brownwing said. "They have utmost faith in Blackclaw, and his dictates." His sad eyes lifted and he settled them on Kallon. "I am certain we are on the cusp of change, Kallon. From this day forward, our future will veer from the path we have known since the dawn of our time."

Yellowfang inched forward a step and laid her paw on the back of Brownwing's knuckles. "Hale and I have sensed this coming. The wind murmurs in warning, and we have argued for reason, but our words are empty."

Kallon tilted his head. "You have known all along that Blackclaw intends to draw humans into war."

Brownwing shook his head. "We did not realize the depth of his conviction until today. But he has been fueling unrest and speaking more against humans with each passing year."

"Then you must believe me," Kallon said. "You must see how this obsession makes him capable of murdering his own Kind."

Brownwing's eyes moved to gaze off across Kallon's shoulder. He stared for a time, his throat clenching in a deep swallow. Then he pressed his paws to the desk. "Son, what I believe I dare not say aloud."

Kallon watched Brownwing's claws dent the human's vest. Armitage's vest! Hadn't the man tried to warn him the pouch wasn't with his clothes? He'd said he needed his vest. But why would the human warn him?

Brownwing grasped Kallon's shoulders. "What

I will say is this. How you fare on this quest will determine the new direction of our Kind. You have come back to us after all this time, just when we need you most. It cannot be coincidence."

Kallon sighed. "I wish I could encourage you. I wish I could be the bold champion you want me to be. But I am the fledgling who ran in fear from life and responsibility. I am not bold. I am no champion."

Brownwing's grip tightened on his shoulders. "I see no fledgling," he said. "I see a Redheart."

Kallon looked at Yellowfang.

She smiled.

Kallon couldn't bear it. He pulled from Brownwing's grasp. "What do we know of Blackclaw? That he is a conniving, destructive murderer bent on domination at all costs. What makes you believe that this quest is even possible? Would it not better suit his plans that I fail, and fail miserably?"

Brownwing started, "Yes, but—"

"Perhaps is he confident I will fail because he knows something we do not," Kallon said. Suddenly, the whispers he'd overheard between Riza and Armitage in the prison cell began to make sense. He hadn't eavesdropped on purpose, of course, but with his sensitive hearing, he couldn't help it.

He hadn't believed what Armitage had said at the time, and that the pouch was miles away somewhere and that Blackclaw already had the circlet. However, considering things now, Kallon began to see that Armitage might have been on to something after all.

"What could he know that we do not?" asked Yellowfang.

"The dragon hunter thinks that Blackclaw has the circlet already," Kallon said.

Brownwing scoffed. "And you believe him?"

Kallon regarded the two for a moment. "I believe Blackclaw would not send me to find something if there was a remote chance I would succeed."

Yellowfang turned to stare through an octagonal window.

"Shera?" Brownwing stood beside her, and stared out into the bleak sky.

"Dawn," she said. "We are no closer to an answer than when we began."

Brownwing touched the back of her knuckles. "Our answer is before us, as it has always been. We must trust. In those matters that are beyond our control, we can only trust in the divine force that brought him to us."

Were they discussing Kallon as though they'd forgotten he was there? "Forgive me if I fail to see any working of the divine here," he said. "I see only the broken remains after a stampede of darkness."

Brownwing and Yellowfang turned to face him.

Brownwing spoke. "There has been no stampede, Kallon. Many of us still hope that in the end, right will prevail."

"Perhaps we are wrong about Blackclaw already having the circlet. Perhaps it really is out there somewhere, and he is just desperate enough for it that he is willing to risk your success to get his claws on it," Yellowfang said.

"There is only one way to find out." Brownwing came around the end of the desk and stood before Kallon, regarding him.

"I have not come this far to run now," Kallon said, lifting his chin. "But I can not allow my friends to suffer for my failure. If my going serves no other purpose than to provide them a way out, I will feel satisfied that I have done what I can."

"What do you mean?" Yellowfang asked.

"If I return without the circlet, they are as doomed as I am. And they will be mistreated while I am gone, however long that should be."

"Perhaps we can convince the council to provide them with proper privileges," Yellowfang said.

"Thank you, but not good enough. I need them out from under Blackclaw's threat completely," Kallon said.

Brownwing turned up his palms. "But how?"

"I have to risk them into the hands of the one creature I trust less than Blackclaw himself." Kallon clenched his teeth, grinding them painfully.

A knock rattled the door in its hinges.

"Dawn."

Without invitation, the door swung open, pushed by a gray paw. Grayfoot had to crouch to squeeze under the frame.

"Give those belongings back to the human," Kallon said to Brownwing. "Once my friends are safe, I will search for the circlet."

"Come on," said the Gray, yanking Kallon's foreleg nearly from its socket. "I get no breakfast until this is over."

Instead of grimacing at the pain, he eyed Grayfoot's belly. "You could spare one less breakfast."

"Red, I am looking forward to the part where you come back, broken and disgraced," Grayfoot said. "It makes for a softer beating, but we do have to take the bad with the good."

"You and I are spending far too much time together. I think you are starting to like me."

The Gray only laughed, and dragged him out the door.

He stumbled alongside the guard, watching the hallway pass, each step bringing him closer and closer to the exit. His heartbeat surged louder and louder between his ears and his footsteps became heavier and heavier, until he finally came to a dead stop, staring out through the entrance arch. "Grayfoot," he said. "I have no idea what I am doing."

The Gray snorted. "And here I thought we would never agree on anything."

Chapter Twenty

Once again, Kallon climbed the steps of the granite platform and looked out across a gathering of colorful spines, wings, and dragon heads. There were more dragons now than before. The place was packed tight, and some onlookers even perched on the walls of the arena, peering around pine trees.

Dawn had come to the mountain, but hadn't yet reached into the stadium. Evening torches still blared from their wall sconces in two leering smiles full of jagged, flickering teeth. Wispy mist hung like ghost entrails over stones.

The only sound was Kallon's shuffling feet as he was led to Blackclaw. The nearer he drew to the leader, the thicker the silence became. The arena swelled with anticipation like the moment after a lightning flash when the thunder is due any moment.

Most council members were already there, seated along their exclusive pallet. Glances passed between them. Blackclaw kept to himself, though his stare burned into Kallon's face.

As Kallon faced him, Blackclaw rose. He shifted forward, his forelegs reaching for the crowd.

Kallon watched torchlight dance with shadows across Blackclaw's face, competing as to which could more eerily distort the leader's features.

"My fellow citizens." Blackclaw's voice punctured the silence, and air rushed out of the crowd in a stream of whispers. "It has been an arduous time. Suspicion and accusations have rocked the foundation of trust between leader and followers. Strangers have infiltrated our community, bringing death and dishonor. And one of our own," his fist unfurled toward Kallon, "has come against me to manipulate tradition for his own desires."

Blackclaw's eyes moved past Kallon to something behind him.

Kallon turned to see Hale Brownwing climbing the steps of the platform, Armitage's bundled belongings pressed against his chest.

Blackclaw urged him forward, and pointed for Brownwing to display the items.

"Behold, dragons! The murderer's possessions," Blackclaw said. The crowd gasped, and surged forward to get a better view. "As you know, the Red has challenged my post, accusing me of using the power of my position for personal gain."

Heads bobbed. Tails waved.

"The Red was given the opportunity to prove these charges," Blackclaw said. "He could not!"

Murmurs rippled across the sea of scales.

Brownwing laid out each of Armitage's effects slowly. He seemed to be taking great pains in arranging the pouches just so, in laying the covered sword out in such an angle as to showcase it. The final item, the folded leather vest, was placed at the back of the display. Brownwing turned for his seat without looking at Kallon.

Blackclaw continued, "The Red tried to convince you that I had some part in the plan to murder Bluecrest. How, I ask you, could I possibly profit from this?"

"To stir dragons to hatred for all humans!" Kallon didn't even realize he was speaking until he heard his own voice.

Blackclaw's face swelled. "He speaks out of turn! Still he holds to this foolish notion that I hired the human to commit this act!" Blackclaw pointed to the display of items near their feet. "I submit to you that each of these items has been thoroughly searched by honored members of our own council. There is no evidence to be—what is this?" Blackclaw's eyes narrowed.

Kallon once more turned to find someone climbing onto platform. This time it was Orman, Armitage, and Riza, led by Grayfoot. His heart broke at the sight of Riza.

Filth clung to her hair, her cheeks, her scuffed knees. Her spine curved forward, shoulders slumped in defeat, and her eyes stared, dark and listless, at nothing.

He knew she couldn't take much more, despite her

fight to stay strong.

Shera Yellowfang brought up the rear, and she bowed her head as she addressed Blackclaw. “We thought it best that the prisoners should be allowed to hear the deliberations of their fate, and to stand as reminders before the citizens.”

Blackclaw brushed past Kallon to bear down on Yellowfang with a scowl. “We?”

Yellowfang looked up at the oncoming leader, and glanced at Brownwing. Brownwing stepped between her and Blackclaw, bowing his head, as well. “Those council members that we were able to consult quickly, Fordon. A majority.”

Blackclaw drew up short. He breathed silently for a moment. When he turned to the other council members, his scowl had vanished. “Very well. I concur. Let the criminals serve as examples!” He scooped up a handful of leather and pouches and shook them at the crowd. “They are the first, but they will not be the last. As we establish our new order, we will no longer be disrespected! There will be judgment!”

Just as the dragons broke into a shout, the sun stabbed hot filaments through the tall trees. Blackclaw raised his fist, and Armitage’s balled leather vest caught a stream of sunlight. The vest blazed as though on fire.

Kallon cut his gaze to Armitage, who was staring hungrily at it. He strained against his chains, his fingers twitching.

“Humans are weak and pitiful, even as they try to stand against us!” Blackclaw threw the vest and pouches.

The jumbled mass skidded and rolled to a stop at Orman's feet.

Armitage tensed to jump at it, but lifted dark eyes to Kallon. The man needed a distraction.

Kallon blurted, "Humans need us! There is benefit to mutual respect!"

Dragon eyes converged on his face. He felt them more than he saw them, for he was watching Armitage inch his toe toward the crumpled vest.

Armitage grumbled something to Orman, but Orman only stared back as though he were deaf.

"What mutual respect?" Blackclaw asked of everyone.

Armitage managed to hook the tip of his boot under a lump of leather and dragged it closer. He touched Riza's arm. He spoke softly to her, and for the first time, Kallon saw softness in the human's face.

Kallon hadn't thought him capable.

Kallon didn't know what to expect, exactly, but he was overcome with heart-wrenching sadness as he watched Riza, wishing he could tell her goodbye. A part of him knew he would never see her again. If the human really had some sort of magic in his vest and could take Riza safely away, there was no need to go through with the quest. He would leave the mountain, of course, and pretend to search, but he would have no reason to come back. This time, he would stay gone forever.

"The Red has no answer!" Blackclaw's voice crackled over the crowd.

Riza seemed to steel herself, and at Armitage's

quiet words, she glared. She tugged her shoulder away from his touch. What was she doing? Let the man save you, Riza! Go with him!

"Silent." Blackclaw's gesturing paw caught Kallon's attention. "Perhaps you have finally learned your place," snorted the leader.

Kallon said the first thing that came to him. "It is you who needs to learn his place, Blackclaw! A true leader is a servant, not a master!" He looked back at Armitage.

The human was gone.

There stood Orman, arms crossed and scowling at the empty place between him and Riza.

Armitage was gone! The human had saved himself, and left the others!

Kallon couldn't believe that he was surprised. He felt a little sick.

"We are not here to discuss your leadership philosophies." Blackclaw faced the onlookers. "We are here to give the Red the opportunity to rescind his challenge!" Blackclaw strode toward Kallon, and outstretched his paw. "There is no need to go forward with this quest, if the Red will admit his defeat now."

"What do you mean?" Brownwing asked, coming to stand beside Kallon.

Blackclaw gave a wide, unsettling grin. "I have, from time to time, found myself caught up in zealous beliefs, Hale. I am not so unforgiving I cannot see past the Red's insults into the heart of the matter. However," he said, pointing a claw. "He has spoken falsehoods against me. He must withdraw them if I am to consider a gentler judgment."

Kallon was suddenly alert to Blackclaw's words. "How much gentler?" he asked. "What about my friends?"

"What about them?" said Blackclaw. "They stand for their own crimes."

"But if I were to tell you it was I who was working with the human hunter, not the girl, would you release her?"

"Kallon!" Brownwing touched his shoulder.

Blackclaw blinked. "I could not allow you to live, Red, if you were to admit such a thing."

"Nevertheless, would my confession release the girl?" Kallon asked.

"He does not know what he is saying!" Brownwing shook Kallon's shoulder as though trying to wake him. "You still have the quest! You have the opportunity to redeem yourself."

"But what is the point?" Kallon asked. "I needed to prove Blackclaw's wrongdoing, and I failed."

"The Red finally speaks the truth!" Blackclaw opened his palm and thrust it toward Kallon. "His attempts to prove his accusations were in vain!"

There came a gruff shout in perfect Dragonspeak. "That is only because you were all searching in the wrong place!" It was Armitage's voice.

Kallon turned.

There stood the dark human, wrists still bound in chains as before, feet planted wide on the platform. He wore his vest. "If I had been allowed to speak before now, I would have concurred with the Red."

"You are our prisoner! You would say anything to save yourself!" Blackclaw waved Grayfoot toward Armitage. "Gag him."

"I say let him speak," said Yellowfang. She lifted her chin, and stared directly at Blackclaw. "If he speaks only lies, let them be added to his judgment."

Council members rose from their places, jaws working and paws gesturing. The crowd was awash in frantic mumbling.

Blackclaw, for the first time, appeared shaken. His jaw moved for a moment without words, and then he blurted, "Of course he will only speak lies!"

"Let him speak," said Brownwing.

"Let him speak," came a voice from the crowd.

"Let him speak!" Orman shouted, and clapped Armitage on the back.

Armitage held his bound wrists over his head.

Grayfoot approached, scowling.

"Search my waistline for a hidden pouch," said Armitage. "It is payment for services rendered."

Grayfoot paused. He glanced at Brownwing, who urged him on. Then he glanced at Blackclaw, who came blundering toward him.

"Enough of this nonsense!" Blackclaw shouted. "Gag the prisoner and take him back to his cell."

"Services rendered?" Orman himself reached toward Armitage's waist, his palms patting, patting, patting. "Well, I'll be." He fished out a pouch tucked just behind Armitage's hip, and held it up.

A shaft of morning sun drenched the velvet pouch. In the sudden silence, Kallon could almost hear the crackle of the flames in the crest of Mount Gore Manor embroidered into the fabric.

Someone's tail dropped to the dusty arena floor. Leathery eyelids slid over dry eyes. Even the early clouds slammed into each other in the silence, knocking about in the pink dawn.

Then Kallon pointed, and his soft voice rippled like thunder. "Fordon Blackclaw murdered Bluecrest to stir hatred for humans and enrage us into war with them."

"No." Blackclaw stared in disbelief. "He is lying."

Grayfoot looked from Armitage to Blackclaw. "But I searched him. I searched every inch of him."

Things began happening very quickly. Kallon reeled, staring at Armitage, while the council lapsed into chaotic shouting. They gathered around Blackclaw, who raged and bullied. Behind him, the crowd was still eerily quiet, and Kallon had to peer over his shoulder to see if they were still watching. They were. Eyes stared in confusion and sadness.

Yellowfang's voice rose up over the din. "The evidence is enough to convince me. Blackclaw must immediately be removed from leadership."

An orange paw waved. "I second."

"This is an outrage!" Blackclaw's stomping feet rumbled the platform. "The human is a liar, a thief, and a murderer!"

"I am no thief!" Armitage shouted.

Brownwing gestured for the council to quiet. "Shera Yellowfang will serve as interim leader until the Red returns from his quest."

"I am leader! The Red will fail his quest. I am still your leader!" Blackclaw dove for Armitage's belongings. His claws knocked the crossbow off the granite and it hit the ground in a puff of dust. Vials scattered. Blackclaw swung about, Armitage's sword held like a dagger in his fist. "This Red will not be my undoing!"

The council fell back in shock.

Kallon barely had to time to react. The oncoming swing of the blade dropped him back. He blasted flame at Blackclaw, but his foot caught up in Armitage's chains, and he stumbled. His face, and his flame, skewed off to singe the council members, who were shouting and waving madly to Grayfoot to subdue the leader.

"You will not come into my territory and knock me aside, Red!" Blackclaw swung the blade again, his features engorged with fury.

For a moment, Kallon froze at the sight of the gleaming metal, and just then, for only a moment, considered how much that sword was determined to destroy him. Perhaps the blade was his fate, after all. Then the sharp edge of the metal split the air at his face.

He dodged. Fate or no, he would fight.

He rolled. He slammed against something hard and uncurled to find he'd collided with Grayfoot.

The dragon's stunned gaze hovered between Kallon and Blackclaw, whose footsteps were approaching. The Gray was going to be no help.

Kallon saw Grayfoot's shortstaff, recognized it, and grabbed for it.

Yellowfang's screech of pain sounded.

Kallon spun. Yellowfang had obviously leapt at Blackclaw to stop him, but had fallen, and her blood stained the blade that was now swinging for Kallon's throat.

Kallon blocked the swing with the staff. "This is futile, Blackclaw! They are seeing you for who you are, regardless of my quest!" He forced the blade toward the ground and spun, swinging his spiny tail at Blackclaw's face. He felt contact, and continued through the spin.

Blackclaw staggered aside.

Kallon sucked in a breath to spew fire, but orange and brown and green paws of council members pounced onto Blackclaw to subdue him.

"Kallon!" Riza's voice came from somewhere to his right. He found her squeezing through the chaos, her frightened eyes fastened to his face. Her hands were still bound behind her.

"Stay back, Riza!"

Just as he shouted, a roar exploded from the center of the council members. Blackclaw erupted, and stripped Brownwing from his back with a clawed foot.

Kallon stabbed the crystal end of his staff into Blackclaw's gut.

The leader grunted and buckled.

Kallon jabbed again.

Blackclaw dropped, heaving.

The Green toppled onto Blackclaw, and blocked

Kallon's final thrust.

A black paw latched onto Kallon's ankle and ripped him from his feet.

As he fell, he was blanketed in fire. His scales sizzled, and despite their resistance, pain burrowed like mites into his skin. He landed hard against the platform, knocking out his breath. He blindly clawed the air, unable to see past the wall of sweltering flame. He smelled the charring of his face. Then, what felt like a searing bolt of lightning split the base of his tail. He screamed in pain and rage.

He launched himself toward the direction he'd last seen Blackclaw. His smoking paws felt the tender scales of a throat, and he squeezed. The fire died. He stared into the face of Fordon Blackclaw, whose mouth was wrenched into a grin. Kallon howled, and twisted his grip tighter. "Die!"

"You first!" Blackclaw wheezed.

Kallon couldn't hold him any longer. He tried to squeeze, but his digits went slack. Then his forelegs sagged. He felt himself drop to the platform with the weight of a fallen oak.

"Kallon!" Riza's voice came again from a distance.

"Chain him, Grayfoot, now!" shouted Brownwing.

The council members had finally overcome Blackclaw. The leader's forelegs twisted, his tail and feet imprisoned by council members and dragons from the crowd. Several dragons had stretched Blackclaw's thick wings and sat on their tips.

Kallon could only watch as Grayfoot clasped irons

around Blackclaw's legs.

Blackclaw didn't even struggle. He only grinned that depraved smile down into Kallon's face.

Grayfoot pulled Blackclaw toward the cell.

Kallon wished he could follow. He wanted to hear the cell door slam behind the dragon, wanted to watch him recoil at the smell. But Kallon could barely turn his head. Had Blackclaw's flame really done so much damage? He tried to lift his forelegs to inspect, but couldn't.

Orman was there. The wizard knelt. "Hold still, my boy." His craggy face bunched with sadness.

"Kallon!" Riza shrieked, and dropped to her knees beside Orman. "No. No, please."

Other faces gathered around, bereaved and silent. "What's wrong with me?" Kallon tried to ask, but he wasn't sure if his voice managed to squeeze out of his throat.

Armitage appeared with the others, and his face held a dark smile, so much like Blackclaw's. He leaned toward Kallon's ear. "I did warn you that my sword would be your destroyer. I wish it had been my hand upon it."

Kallon's thoughts were fuzzy. He had to force his tongue to work. "But you came back."

Armitage sneered. "Not for you, Red. Though I am glad I'm here to witness this." Armitage leaned back and looked solemnly to Orman. "You should pull the sword free quickly."

Orman's gaze turned toward the base of Kallon's

tail. "But…he will bleed to death almost instantly."

"He's already dead, Wizard. You'll just make it official."

"No!" Riza shouted. She flung herself across Kallon, but he couldn't feel her. "Don't you let him die, Orman! Do something! Please…please, do something." She sobbed and pressed her cheek to Kallon's jaw. "Kallon, you can't die. Please don't die."

He tried to speak. He tried to say her name, but his strength seemed to have seeped into the stone beneath him.

"Don't you leave me." Riza's tears dampened his face. She kissed his snout.

He didn't want to leave. He wasn't ready. He didn't know what would happen to Riza, didn't want to go without knowing she'd be safe, but he was helpless. He couldn't even manage to hold open his eyes.

"Kallon. Kallon!" Riza called to him again. Or, was it Riza? Her voice seemed different. It sounded like his mother's voice.

He thought his eyes were closed, but somehow he managed to see the clouds part. They offered a warm glow that beckoned him to fly. It would be nice to fly.

"Kallon!" Riza's voice was soft and very far away. "No! Take me," she begged of someone he couldn't see. "Take me! May vita en dae!"

The clouds slammed closed and Kallon was bathed with new warmth. A golden shower of sparks settled over him in soothing waves. Everything was going to be all right. He just knew it.

He remembered the feeling once before. It had happened while he lay over his father's wounded body, and had stared up at a sword that was about to swing and end his life.

His father had shouted the same words, "May vita en dae". Kallon had been blinded by a brightness that had sliced the sky and had immersed him in pleasant comfort.

He suddenly realized what Riza had done. He fought against the light, struggling to move, to wake.

"No!" he cried, and pushed against the sweet lullaby of calm that coursed through his blood. He thrashed. He managed to lift his head and force his eyes open. "Riza, what have you done?"

"No!" Armitage's own shout exploded, and the man dropped to his knees.

Riza lay across Kallon's front legs.

Armitage lifted her carefully and cradled her against his chest. "No." He tenderly kissed the top of her head. "Don't do this, girl. Not for that dragon."

Kallon was numb. He wanted to reach for Riza, but couldn't feel his legs. He wanted to shake her hard and wake her, but he couldn't even blink. All the fear and worry and fighting for Riza over the past few days and weeks had infused new life and feeling into his very soul, had given him a reason to rise, and had given him purpose. He was supposed to have saved her. Not the other way. His shock wouldn't let him believe.

Armitage lifted his chin and snarled into Kallon's face. "I didn't come back to watch her die, I came back to this stinking, filthy place to watch her live!" He thrust Riza's limp body toward Kallon's face. "You did this!"

Kallon recoiled. "I didn't ask her! I wouldn't want this!"

"You may as well have been a dagger in her heart! You did this!" Armitage crumpled and held Riza with trembling hands. He wept against her throat. "Not for a dragon. Not for a dragon."

Kallon watched Armitage express Kallon's own grief; a grief Kallon was too broken to feel. "I didn't ask her," he quietly repeated.

Orman's craggy hand found Kallon's shoulder.

"I would not want this," Kallon said. "I didn't even know she was capable."

"I knew she was different before I even met her," Orman said. "Love has a power all its own, Kallon. It can do miraculous things."

"No," said Kallon. "She trusted me, and I tried to protect her. But she didn't love me. It's not possible."

"Of course it is," Orman said, his hand patting. "It's why she did this."

"But I didn't want her to do it!" Kallon cried. "She needs to live!" A drop of pain oozed out through the crack in his heart. "She can't die! Do something, Orman. Fix this!"

"Me?" Orman pressed his hand to his chest. "Who am I to undo a miracle?"

Armitage seethed. "This is no miracle. This is wrong."

"If it's a miracle," said Orman, "It can't be wrong."

A voice came from the crowd. "What about the Circlet of Aspira?"

"Yes," said Brownwing, and drew close to those huddled around Riza. "Your quest would serve you well if you go. Perhaps the magic of the circlet can right the wrong."

Orman stretched his neck, his eyes narrowing on Brownwing. "Kallon Redheart, your would-be leader, was dying before you. She saved him. How can that be wrong?"

Brownwing looked from Kallon to Orman. "I only meant—"

"Stop it!" Kallon shouted. "She lies dead and you argue!" The hidden pain in Kallon's heart finally erupted. "I do not care if her death is righteous or miraculous! I want her to live!" He rose to his feet. "If the circlet can grant wishes, I will wish her back."

"But Kallon," Orman said. "We don't even know if the circlet still exists."

"Blackclaw has had the circlet all along," said Armitage. "There is no quest. It was another lie."

"We could all be wrong. If I do not search for it I will forever regret doing nothing." Kallon moved to Orman. "Tell me what to do."

Orman looked at Armitage, at Riza's pale face, and at the staring crowd of dragons. Finally, he turned his eyes to Kallon. "I don't know what to do."

"Orman," Kallon pleaded.

"I'm only a wizard, Kallon. I don't have all the answers." Then he pressed his lips together. "But I know someone who does. But…"

"But what?" Kallon gripped Orman's beard and tugged him close.

Orman slapped at Kallon's paw and drew up his shoulders. "But you will have to seek him beyond the boundary."

Brownwing sucked in a breath. "Do you mean the Gold?"

"I do." Orman replaced his beard against his chest and smoothed it.

The crowd gasped.

Brownwing shook his head. "That is legend. No one has ever flown beyond the boundary. No one has met the Gold."

"I have met him," Kallon said.

Brownwing gaped. "What you say can not be so."

Orman shook his finger at the brown dragon. "It is so. Simply because you have never experienced it does not make it untrue."

"It is suicide," Brownwing said. "There is nothing beyond the limits of sky but death."

Kallon lowered himself before the kneeling Armitage. He stared down into Riza's face, white as the moon. Even her lips were pale slivers, and he brushed a digit across their failing warmth. His pain wrenched every muscle of his body. But he would not give in to it. Not now. Not yet.

He clutched Armitage's shoulder. "You tend to her. Take care of her."

Armitage nodded, but hatred seethed behind his

eyes.

Kallon rose again and faced Orman. "Tell me I can find this dragon beyond the boundary. Tell me this without a doubt, and I will go."

"Kallon," said Brownwing.

"I have no doubt," said Orman.

Kallon flew.

CHAPTER TWENTY-ONE

Kallon blasted like a pebble from a slingshot, slicing into the clouds. He didn't know where he was going, didn't know what he'd find when he got there. He didn't know if he'd get there at all. He refused to consider that, and concentrated on his direction. He focused straight up and pumped his wings.

He climbed higher and higher. The sky began to resist. Gently, at first. Then, with each surge forward, it began to push back. He felt he was battling a thick membrane that refused to let him pass. He closed his eyes. He had to keep straining…pushing…to that place no other dragon dared go.

Soon his heartbeat throbbed in his ears. Fingers of fire gripped his lungs. His wings grew sluggish, despite his fight to push them faster. The overstretched boundary closed in, squeezing him in a sticky shroud.

He was losing. The boundary was too strong. He pried open one eye and tried to swing his head to judge how far he'd come, but his movement only brought the boundary's redoubled strength against him. He was forced nearly immobile.

His feet paralyzed against his belly. The eye he'd opened was forced to stay that way. He clenched his teeth, and felt his mouth freeze into a gruesome smile. Finally, his left wing was forced against his back…and stopped completely. His other took a futile stab at the air before it, too, could move no longer.

Kallon would have cried out if he'd had the voice to do so, but he could only stare ahead at the sky that still went on forever. There was no way through the boundary. He'd flown as far as his body could take him, and there was no golden dragon to meet him. He was alone. He was dying.

For what seemed an eternity, he hung there in the clouds. He sensed them brushing his tail, mocking his attempt to imitate them. Anger rose up.

Orman was wrong! He'd told Kallon there was no doubt! He'd sent Kallon chasing after a fantasy! It was hard enough to wake up and find Riza dead, without having to return to her again as a failure. The thought of having to face Armitage and the others, with their twisted, sneering faces, only enraged him further.

Then Riza's memory flooded him. She'd given him the very gift of her breath. It had all happened so quickly, so quietly, it still felt like a dream. Kallon was alive and flying, and Riza was dead. Thick tears filled his eyes, but had nowhere to fall.

Why? Why had she done such a foolish thing? Didn't she realize he would have died a thousand times over to keep her safe? Her life was the one worth saving, not his. He didn't care if he did die up here, suffocated by the sky that was supposed to give him answers. If he had to return to a world without Riza's smile, he'd rather not go back, anyway.

His head suddenly lightened. He couldn't feel his curled legs. His entire body felt numb with cold. This was his last chance to release, to let himself drop to where he could blink his eyes and let his lungs fill with sweet air.

No. He would not turn back. He'd come for a reason. So he met the sky with his one, opened eye and glared. He couldn't lift a wing tip to push an inch more, couldn't stretch out his neck to reach a fraction further. So he leeched the last of his strength into an angry, determined glower. And for one moment longer, he stayed.

§

A voice swept through his mind like a summer wind, warming his face and opening his eyes. He must not have responded, because the words came a second time, with more volume. "Kallon Redheart, why have you come?"

Kallon tried to find the owner of the voice, but he couldn't see through the shimmering cloud of white-gold that surrounded him. He floated without flying. Without falling. "Am I dead? Am I dreaming?" he asked.

"You are neither. Are these the questions you came to ask me?"

Kallon tried to turn, but the bright cloud offered no resistance to push against. He poked out a claw and it disappeared into the churning mist. "Where am I?"

"You know where you are."

"Through the boundary? I made it?" Kallon asked.

"You seem surprised," answered the voice.

"I thought I was going to die," Kallon said.

"And yet you came anyway. There was a moment you could have turned away to save yourself."

But he hadn't. He had managed to break through the boundary. Just as Orman said he could. He still wasn't sure he wasn't dreaming.

"You are not dreaming, Kallon Redheart. For a dragon determined to know the truth, you are stubbornly resistant to it."

"I'm resistant to believe because it brings disappointment."

"There are worse things in life than disappointment. I ask you again why you have come."

Kallon was finally orienting himself to the strange, floating feeling in this bubble of brightness, and speaking to a disembodied voice from somewhere he couldn't see. "I wish to know the whereabouts of the Circlet of Aspira."

"The circlet has been destroyed."

No! "How? Can it be restored?"

"It cannot. The same dark desires that have skewed the magic of Leland Province have drained the bloodstone in the circlet."

Kallon crumpled into a ball of frustration. "There must be a way! I have come so far!"

Silence.

Kallon uncurled. "Are you there?"

"I am."

He drew in a deep breath. "Are you the one I met at my parent's graves?"

"I am."

"Are you the one that was there the day my father died?"

"I am."

"And were you there when Riza spoke the words of my father, and died in my place?"

"Yes."

Kallon's tears welled again. "But why? Why would you let them do such a thing? Why Riza? She was so young, and gentle, and generous!"

"You are young, and gentle, and have learned to be generous."

"But I don't deserve to live. She does! I should have died!" Kallon cried.

"Riza did not think so. She made her decision."

"But you allowed it! You could have stopped it!" Kallon shook his fist. "She didn't know what she was doing!"

Silence.

Kallon withdrew his fist, but his anger remained balled and hard in his chest. "It's not right."

"Your destiny must be fulfilled."

Kallon reared back. "I don't want my destiny! I'm not a leader like my father! And even if I were, I wouldn't want to lead in a world where I was only there because someone else died for me!"

A pause. Kallon felt a shift in the cloud, and when the voice returned, it came closer to his ear. "You have a far greater destiny, Kallon, than to simply lead as your father did."

"What?" He tried to peer through the curtain of mist that boiled around him without being hot, and glowed like the sun without blinding him.

There was another shift in the cloud, and the voice spoke into his other ear. "This force that holds you without letting you fall is a power called upon by humans and dragons, most often in the time of need."

Kallon turned toward the voice. "You mean magic?"

"Your friend, Orman, is correct when he says dragons are formed from the very fabric that fashioned this world. You have a power that exceeds even your own understanding. The same force that forged the mountains, carved the valleys, and set the sun in the clouds is yours to wield, Kallon Redheart."

"But, how? How do I find this power?"

"It is already inside you." A golden claw broke through the swirling mist to tap gently against Kallon's chest. "Here. It was your gift at your birth." The claw withdrew. "You know what your destiny is, Kallon. You know what you must do."

He knew. He closed his eyes. "I must believe."

Kallon couldn't see the face of the Gold, but he

could feel its smile right through the glittering vapor. "Now tell me why you have really come to find me."

Kallon lifted his chin. "I have come to beg for the life of Riza Diantus."

There was another pause. When the voice spoke again, it was soft. "Would you have come to me any other way?"

Kallon hung his head. He clutched a fist to his heart.

"But do not fear," said the voice. "She is only sleeping. You have forgotten the linking stone."

He darted his hand to the stone around his neck. It was pulsating. He could feel her, almost hear her, somehow.

"Riza waits in that place between waking and dreaming, where her soul has often visited in the darkness."

Kallon tightened his grip on the stone. "How can I reach her? Where do I go?"

"Search your heart, Kallon. Bloodstone aches to restore Leland's balance. You do not need a circlet. You have the power to change things."

The cloud of glitter evaporated.

Kallon tumbled, tail and wings akimbo, toward the earth. He fell so fast he struggled to breathe. Then his legs came to life, and he could move them. He thrust his wings to the wind and slowed his descent. His tail ruddered, and he righted himself. He was back in control of his body and mind.

Had he imagined it all? Had his struggle with the

boundary played tricks with his mind? He searched his heart. It had happened. It had all happened. He believed.

He pivoted. He aimed headfirst for the heart of Mount Gore, stuck out his front claws like daggers, and dove.

Kallon plunged toward the earth with a single purpose; to split it open. The arena was carved from Mount Gore, designed to encircle its heart. If bloodstone crystal pumped through this heart, the crystal would be nearest the surface at the arena floor.

It swelled into view below him. He bowed his head to thrust his crown of spikes at his target. Closer the ground came. He strained to move faster.

Voices filtered through the whistling wind in his ears. "Look! Kallon!"

"Is he falling?"

"Move aside! He is heading for the crowd!"

The gathered dragons frantically scattered out of the way. A patch of trampled dirt cleared directly below him. He aimed for this. Then treetops and stone walls and sparkling dragon scales blurred past. He hit.

A thunderclap burst between his ears and reeled him senseless.

After a moment, he realized he was lying on his side on the ground. He moved his head. He shifted to his feet. Nothing was broken.

Not even the ground. There was a massive dent. His horns had scratched away deep ruts, but there was no gaping crack to offer a peek of bloodstone. He staggered, still dizzy, then reeled about to try again.

The look of shock on a near Green made him pause. He looked from face to face among the dragons surrounding him. They all stared, mouths agape. Were they so surprised to see him? Had they expected him to be gone longer?

Orman wedged through to stand at the front of the circle. "Kallon?"

"Orman, I need the bloodstone. I can save her. Have the others stand back, I'm going to try again."

"Kallon Redheart," said Orman, one hand outstretching. "Have you gone and dipped yourself in sparkles?" Orman's hand gingerly touched Kallon's jaw.

"Have I what?" He looked down at his forelegs, and then his chest. His familiar red scales had taken on an unfamiliar glow, as though he'd been draped with a shimmering, golden net. His palms, knuckles, even his claws, radiated with it.

"You made it, didn't you, my boy?" Orman's wrinkled face opened wide with a smile.

As their eyes met, Kallon returned the smile. "Yes. I made it. I met him."

The staring mass of dragons collectively gasped. They closed in, pressing in suffocating waves.

"Stay back!" Kallon cried. "I need the bloodstone! Everyone stay back!"

"Bloodstone?" came a male dragon voice. "He said stay back, everyone."

"Move aside," came another.

"Get out there and help him, Restas," said a female.

Slowly the throng retreated. Kallon pressed off to fly. He circled around to dive again, but a Blue met him in the sky.

"Let me have a go," said Restas Blueeyes.

"And me," said a Yellow, who swung around to join them.

"Me, too!" A young female Gray dipped low beneath them, and then swerved to be first in line.

Kallon's breath was stolen. "Thank you," he said.

One by one they dropped, shooting for the earth like glistening arrows. Each landing echoed up, followed by a shout of encouragement from the others. Again came Kallon's turn, and he reared back, drew in a breath, and released a war cry as he plummeted, head thrown back.

He would fall again and again, as many times as necessary, until the mountain relented and gave up that crystal. He would find that place between waking and dreaming where she roamed alone. He would die again if needed. And again. And again.

He slammed into the weakened patch of ground, claws tearing. This time, the ear-splitting crack came not from inside his head, but from beneath him. The earth caved in, then ripped open in a jagged fissure. Dragons cheered.

The crack was the length of Kallon, but only wide enough for him to push in his paw to his wrist. He couldn't see anything inside it, but he could feel the bloodstone pulsing as strong as his own heartbeat. "Bring the girl. Quickly."

"You heard him," Orman said.

As a dragon scrambled to obey, Orman knelt beside Kallon. "You're hurt. You're bleeding. Are you sure you know what you're doing?"

Kallon glanced to his paws, and only then noticed the throb of pain from where a claw had snapped at the base of his digit and was oozing blood. "It's nothing." He gripped the wizard's arm, smearing blood on his sleeve. "She's not dead, Orman. She's only sleeping."

Armitage brought Riza. The man's face was stoic, but Kallon could see the grief in his eyes.

He reached for Riza. "Let me take her."

Armitage hesitated, and then offered her out.

Kallon took her into his paws. She weighed little more than a bird, and hung listless and pale. For the first time, he really looked into her face, marred by death, and a ragged jolt of pain sliced his heart. Not death, he reminded himself. She's only asleep.

"Someone get these chains off of her," he snapped, without meaning to.

A ring with a metal key was passed claw to paw, and worked its way to Armitage's hands, his own still bound in front of him. Armitage knelt and twisted the key in Riza's cuffs. When they popped loose, he gently removed them from her wrists, and ran his fingertips over the welts left behind.

Kallon laid her on the ground directly over the split in the earth. His heart surged, suddenly fearful. How could he know he'd found the right crystal? How did he know the crystal would work at all? What if he didn't believe enough?

He looked around at the expectant faces, watching him intently. Breaths were held.

Armitage's hands were clasped together, his jaw tense, eyes filled with warning.

Orman, still kneeling, regarded Kallon with strange sorrow, as though waiting to be disappointed.

Kallon looked down into the face of Riza Diantus. Her eyes were closed to the sun. Her mouth was silenced. Her heart was quietly cold. He clenched the linking stone around his neck, and, sure enough, he felt her there, eyes open and searching, heart racing.

He snapped the crystal from around his neck and laid it on her chest. Then he bent his face low to her ear and whispered with all the conviction that had been released in his soul, "Wake up, Riza. You want to fly."

The linking stone exploded with such white, forceful light, he had to turn his face from the heat.

Orman and the others turned away too, from what he could see, squinting through the rays.

Beneath his paw, he felt a stirring. His eyes darted back, despite the blinding glow, and just before his eyes were forced shut against the white fire, he saw her eyes. They had opened!

"Riza!" His voice was swallowed by a sudden wind that toppled him back against the ground. He squeezed his eyes open once more to find a vortex of air blasting from the fissure beneath Riza, lifting her, her arms outstretched. "Riza!" he shouted again, now worried she'd be snatched away. He reached for her, but was forced back by the wind.

"What are you doing?" Armitage crawled toward Kallon. He'd been knocked back by the wind, as well.

Other dragons were struggling to stay upright.

Orman was clutching the young Gray, though Kallon wasn't sure who was keeping who held to the ground. "What have you done to her now?" Armitage shouted through the wind, his bound hands gripping Kallon's shoulder.

Before Kallon could answer, the wind turned blood red. It folded in on itself, collapsing like a deflated cloud, and immersed Riza in what seemed a bath of blood.

"Get her out of there!" Armitage shouted.

Kallon lunged to grasp her arm. When he made contact, a spark jolted his paw and threw him back into the legs of a nearby dragon, who fell back against another.

Armitage rolled helplessly against Kallon's belly and was plastered there. An explosion erupted. Crimson light discharged and blanketed the entire arena.

Dragons shouted. Some screamed.

Then all was quiet. The crimson wind drained of color and floated above the treetops. In the sky, it twisted once and evaporated. Low thunder rumbled. Rain clouds gathered. The sky heaved a great sigh, and it rained.

"Rain!" cried a dragon voice.

Whoops and hollers broke out, and along the outside fringes of the crowd, wings flapped in celebration. Dragon feet splashed in growing puddles.

"It is raining!"

"No," moaned Armitage. Kallon turned to find the man kneeling beside a crimson dragon who lay on her side in Riza's place over the gap in the earth.

Kallon froze.

The dragon lifted her head and weakly opened her eyes. Eyes as green as the fir trees.

"Riza?" he whispered.

She smiled and laid her head against the ground.

He couldn't move fast enough to her side. Was it really Riza? He knelt and touched his knuckles to her muzzle. A muzzle long and sloped, and covered with scales so soft he had to touch them again. Thorny ridges jutted from the top of her head in a spiral like the vortex of wind, and trailed down her neck and between her shoulder blades. His paw followed the path of rainwater down her spine, then smoothed over the curve of her rump, and the slender coil of her ruby tail. "Riza," he said again, struggling to breathe.

"It was dark there," she said. Her sultry voice sent a tremble down his spine. "There were voices, and spooky shadows, but I wasn't afraid." She reached an elegant paw, watching him. "I was in the dark, but I wasn't afraid."

"No," Armitage said again, and crawled slowly away, his hands and knees splashing mud. "Not this. I'd rather her dead than this."

"Riza, is it really you? How did…? I did not know this would…." Kallon shook his head. He closed his eyes to clear the rain from them, but was afraid to open them again, for fear the spell would be broken.

"Leland is coming into balance," said Orman, water dribbling from his beard. "Could have been your wish. Could have been your love. Something vanquished the dark hold over the land. Goodness rains again."

Kallon opened his eyes. "My wish?" He looked at Riza and was awash again in awe of her form. She'd been a beautiful human, but she was an exquisite dragon. Had he wished it into being?

"The heart makes wishes the head can not always hear, my boy." Orman nudged Kallon with his elbow and winked.

Kallon felt his blush rise up from the tips of his toes to splatter across his face. "But it is not my place to decide for her."

"Kallon," said Riza, and tugged her paw to draw him close. She gazed up at him and breathed a curl of wispy smoke against his mouth. "Your heart isn't the only one that makes secret wishes."

Kallon drew in the sulfur of her breath like perfume.

"Indeed," said Orman. "Powerful magic. Two identical desires of the purest form. That could do it, I think."

Kallon heard him, but was sinking into the depths of Riza's new eyes.

"The others are watching. They're staring at me," said Riza. "I'm afraid to move, or to say something. I feel so…big."

Kallon felt a smile rise up from his throat and burst

into a rich laugh. "Don't worry about speaking to them until you've learned their language," he said. Then he drew her up and held her close against his chest. "Riza. You died for me."

"I would do it again, if it would save you."

"I couldn't bear to lose you again." He drew back to look into her face. "Don't you know what you mean to me?" He stroked his paw across her cheek.

She reached her own velvety paw to his snout and smiled. "I love you, too, Kallon."

CHAPTER TWENTY-TWO

Riza clung to Kallon as sheets of rain drenched them both. He didn't seem to mind, and neither did she. The rain was medicine to a weary, unfamiliar body that still burned from the change.

Anxious shouts worked their way through the group of dragons who gaped at her. Finally, the shouts grew so loud, Kallon released her to turn and find what the noise was about.

The big gray dragon broke through the edge of the circle. "Leader Redheart, Fordon Blackclaw is gone."

When Kallon looked around himself, Riza nudged him. "He means you, Kallon."

"But I am not—"

"Leader Redheart," said Orman, placing his hand on Kallon's shoulder. "It is time for a command decision."

Kallon looked from Orman to Riza.

She smiled and nodded.

He drew himself up, planted his feet against the

muddy ground, and lifted his chin.

Her heart swelled. For the first time, she felt allowed to love him. She watched the rain gather in tiny puddles against his skull and cascade down his neck scales, and she shivered, but not because she was cold.

"Take four volunteers to cover each direction away from the manor," said Kallon. "Two to search the ground and two to search the air. If he is found, I would like to question him, but if a fight is inevitable, tell your volunteers it should be his death before theirs."

The gray dragon looked up at the sky. "The rain will destroy his trail."

"Yes, and when the volunteers grow tired, replace them. We will search through the night."

"Very good, sir." The gray dragon nodded.

"I will be along shortly," Kallon said.

The gray dragon nodded again, but hesitated. He glanced toward Riza, but his eyes didn't linger long, instead fixing on Kallon's face.

"There is no time to lose, Grayfoot," said Kallon.

"The council members are gathering in the Great Hall, and wish your attendance." Grayfoot glanced to Riza again. "About the girl. The, uh, Red."

Kallon stretched his paw to Riza and smiled. "We will be right there."

Grayfoot shuffled his feet, but didn't move.

Kallon turned a scowl to the guard. "Blackclaw is gaining a considerable lead."

Grayfoot cleared his throat. "The female is not… the council members wish *your* attendance." Then

Grayfoot darted another quick look to Riza, spun around, and hurried off.

Riza looked up to Kallon. "I suppose they want to talk about me while I'm not there." She shifted to move, then tried standing for the first time. She reared up to perch on back legs and lost her balance, her forelegs waving about in crazy circles.

Kallon steadied her. "Slowly. Place all four feet down for now."

She'd forgotten she had four feet. She settled them, and felt oddly as though she were crawling on her hands and knees. Her vision was high. She felt tall as a tree. She even looked down onto the top of Orman's gray head. She hadn't realized how thin his hair was. "This will take some getting used to, but I like it."

Orman smiled up at her. "You are a lovely Red, my dear. Quite lovely."

The other dragons nodded and murmured. What she really wanted to know was what Kallon thought. She didn't ask aloud, but searched his face.

He moved close, guiding her head so he could whisper in her ear. "You are the most beautiful creature I've ever laid eyes on." Their eyes met, and she knew he spoke the truth. She blushed a little, and wondered what they were going to do now.

"I'll meet with the council, keep it brief as possible, and then we'll find a quiet place to talk," Kallon said.

She blinked. "Are you reading my mind?"

"Am I?" He looked between her and Orman.

A young, female gray dragon sidled up to Riza,

eyeing her. She poked a claw at her foreleg. "Are you real? My mother says you are a trick."

Riza stretched out her paw for the young gray dragon to inspect. "I am quite real."

"How come you are a dragon now? I thought humans hate dragons."

"Not all humans hate dragons."

"So, how come?" asked the young one. "Does it hurt? Did it hurt when you were in that wind? Were you scared? Are you going to stay a dragon?"

Other females descended and pressed in close. "We saw you die for Kallon Redheart."

"Is Kallon going to be our new leader?" the young gray female asked.

"Did you want to be a Red, or was it luck?" asked another one of the females.

"Are you going to stay? Are you going to be Kallon's mate?" asked another.

Questions came so quickly she didn't know how to answer them. It took several seconds for her to realize she could understand what each of them was saying. She looked through the chattering females to Kallon.

He didn't speak, but she knew he understood. He had to go, but he would be back as soon as possible. He didn't want to leave her. She sensed it. He moved away slowly. "Orman, you will help Riza?" he asked. "She needs rest, and food."

"I'm starving," she agreed. She was sure she could swallow an entire pig.

"We can do that," said a blue dragon. "We will

help."

"Yes," said a yellow one. "Bring her to the Manor. We will have a feast!"

The group of females hurried off to leave her with Orman. They'd been the last of dragons in the arena. It suited her fine. She'd been uncomfortable with all the staring.

Orman planted his fists on his hips and looked up at her through the rain. "Are you going to regret this? You know there is no going back."

"I don't want to go back," she said. "There is no life for me as who I was."

"What if the dragons don't accept you? What if Kallon becomes a leader of a Kind who won't let you in?"

"Then I will be my own Kind, I guess."

"And you are back to where you began, except in a body that you don't recognize."

"Orman, are you upset about this?" She settled onto her haunches and tilted her head at this man whom she thought was her friend.

He softened. "No. No, my dear. But when the heart makes wishes without consulting the head, sometimes…"

Riza smiled. "Don't worry. I left behind a life that didn't fit me. This is what I want. I think this is what I've always wanted."

"Well, then. I won't worry." He returned her smile, though his eyes remained full of doubt. "Let's eat. I could eat a whole pig myself." He turned and led her across the sloshing arena grounds.

She was slow to coordinate all four legs, and concentrated on which two ought to touch the ground at the same time. After several clumsy steps, she realized it was easier if she didn't concentrate, and just let her feet decide. When she looked up again, Orman was gone.

She heard something above the din of the raindrops hitting the ground. At first she thought she was mistaken. The sound was too faint and far away for her to have really heard. It sounded very much like someone crying. She turned to find it.

Several feet into the trees outside the arena, she came across a brown, dragon stretched across a mound of musty pine needles. The female's paws touched either side of her own face, and her great shoulders quaked.

"What has happened?" asked Riza.

The brown dragon jerked upright. When her golden eyes found Riza, she glared. "You."

It was the brown female who had stolen Riza from her bath and had given her over to the dragons. The one who had begun Riza's nightmare in the cell. Acid churned in Riza's belly and surprised her.

"You can not hide your inferior self behind that crimson facade, human. The scent of your fear and weakness oozes through your scales." The female snorted and laid her head against the ground.

"Harsh words for someone who has never wished you a moment's pain," Riza said.

"Wish it or not, you have caused me nothing but."

The female grimaced and clenched her legs to her belly with a moan.

Riza surged forward. "What is wrong? Are you injured?"

"Get away from me!"

Riza paused. She crouched and found herself sniffing the dragon, which unnerved her, but revealed the female's pain to her. She reached out to touch the her distended belly. "Let me help you."

"I said get away from me! I do not want your help!" The female jerked forward and released a sharp cry. "Get out of here!"

"I will not leave you," Riza said. "You are injured. I smell blood."

"I am not injured," she moaned. "Please. I beg you to go." This time, her eyes were dull and frightened. "I can not hold back any longer, it only increases the pain."

"Then do not hold back." Riza grasped the other's front paw.

"You must leave. Leave, like all the others." She whimpered, her eyelids drooping. "Leave without saying goodbye, just as Kallon did. Leave while I beg you take me with you, just as..."

The brown dragon stopped herself from finishing, but Riza somehow knew the female meant to say Fordon.

"It all comes around to the same thing," the brown dragon said.

"What does it come around to?" Riza asked quietly.

"I am still alone."

"You are not alone now. I am right here." Riza tightened her grip around the female's paw.

"I hate you," the female murmured. "I hated you as the human you were, and I hate you for the abomination you have become." She convulsed and twisted to her side, claws digging into the back of Riza's paw. Her eyes churned wild and afraid. "Help me!"

Just under the female's tail, a trail of dark blood seeped onto the ground. Then a rounded bubble of black swelled from her broken skin. She cried out again.

"When I say, bear down hard." Riza had helped birth enough piglets, and her share of babies. She knew what to do. One paw went to brace under the female's tail as the other squeezed her digits. "Now. Push!"

The female dragon grunted.

Riza pressed the skin around the black protrusion and it slid out onto the cold pine needles without a sound. An egg. An egg so black and sleek, it seemed made of polished coal.

"Let me see it," said the female, lying still.

Riza cradled the smooth egg, carefully placing it in its mother's forelegs. She then buried the spilled blood and rearranged the pine needles to cover it. "The two of you should get out of the rain."

"I should crush it. I should leave it to shrivel."

"Riza?" Orman called from a distance. "Riza, child, are you out there?"

The female grasped Riza's paw. "Do not speak of me. Do not speak of any of this. No one can know of what has happened here, especially my father."

"You need to gather your strength and get out of the rain. I know of a cave where you can be safe," Riza said.

"Tell me you will not speak of me to anyone," the female repeated.

Orman shouted again. "Riza! Don't tell me you've gone and got yourself lost!"

"Tell me!" spat the female.

"I will not speak of this," Riza said. She crawled back, and onto her feet. "What will you do?"

The female closed her eyes, cuddling the dark egg to her belly. "I do not know. Now go, and forget what you saw."

"Riza!" Orman's voice was so close, he might find them any moment.

Riza turned to meet him before he had the chance. "I'm here! I'm coming!" She glanced over her shoulder to the brown female, who seemed sleeping so soundly she barely breathed. Rain dropped hard to the earth, splattering mud to her snout and belly, and to the egg. Riza couldn't stand to leave her.

"Go," whispered the female. "I will be fine. Take the wizard far from here."

Riza bolted toward the sound of Orman's noisy steps. "I'm here," she said, and forced a smile when she found him.

"What are you doing, traipsing about in the rain? You'll catch your death." Orman shook his head. "Seeing a Red come trudging through the trees when I call your name will be a sight to get used to."

"I'm getting the hang of four feet already," she said. "Let's go, I'm starving."

"I'm not the one holding up the show!" Orman said.

Riza nudged the old wizard with her snout and smiled. She sent a final, worried glance back through the trees toward the female, then drew in a breath and trudged on. "Orman?"

"Hm?" He was scowling at the mud caking around his ankles.

"What happened to Jastin? I didn't see him when I woke up."

Orman paused. "I don't know, child. He was there at first, and saw you change. Don't recall seeing him after that. It was a bit chaotic." He stepped over a fat tree root and waved her on. "Perhaps the brute got away. Let's go find out."

§

Jastin Armitage crouched on the orange stone in the dank chamber, fists so tight his fingernails cut his palms. His teeth were sore from clenching.

The Red should have left her dead. She would have been better off as a memory than the freakish beast she had become. To Jastin, she would always be that stubborn, innocent girl who'd closed her eyes to the world forever. That stinking, massive thing belched from the earth was not Riza, and never would be. That thing was a monster, and Riza could never be a monster.

"You are puddling on my wistful crystal." Layce Phelcher's soft voice stirred Jastin from his heartache. "Are you going to tell me it's raining in Leland Province?"

Jastin stood, his bones resisting. Rain made his joints creak, and cold rain made them downright crabby. He didn't like to feel his age, but today, he felt older than ever. "It's raining in Leland Province." He stared flatly at Layce. "It's raining buckets. Doesn't look like it'll be stopping anytime soon."

To his surprise, she smiled. "Venur Riddess won't like that news."

"I had nothing to do with it," Jastin said.

Layce opened her palms. "Well, technically you did. We all have our parts to play in order to see the ending as it was meant to be." She reached out and guided Jastin off the stone. "You did go back there with the dragon's pouch. Terribly romantic, the way I see it, but your brother-in-law won't think so."

Jastin pulled his arm from her grasp. "Your job was to get me from here to there and back, not lecture me constantly in-between."

"And your job was to start a war, not a thunderstorm."

"A thunderstorm? In Leland Province?" A new voice rang into the empty room.

Jastin straightened his shoulders as he faced the looming man in the doorway. "I'm flattered your batty wizard thinks I can control the heavens and their rain," said Jastin. "But I'm only a soldier, Vorham."

"Yes. With unfortunate timing." Vorham Riddess moved away into Layce's bedroom and Jastin followed.

Light from a torch chandelier bathed Vorham's dark brown face and glittered his wiry black hair. Again Jastin saw the same deep-set brown eyes of his beloved wife. But in Vorham's broad face, those eyes seemed too small and confined. Vorham's height, which was a full two inches taller than Jastin's, only furthered the man's menacing image. Most of Esra Province was afraid of Jastin's brother-in-law. Not Jastin.

"Well?" Vorham pressed his palms together.

"Things were unsettled when I left. There were a few surprises." Jastin slipped his drenched vest from his bare back and it dropped.

Layce clucked and scooped the thing off her rug.

"Blackclaw was in prison, and the Red was poised to take over," Jastin said.

Vorham's face burned red beneath his brown skin, turning it the color of a ripe beet. "So it's true."

"But it's not the end of it," Jastin said.

Vorham pressed toward him. "Jastin. You've never failed me as a soldier. But." His arm slithered over Jastin's shoulders. "You were surprised, which surprises me. I don't like it."

"The Red is not a threat," said Jastin. "He'll be easy to take down."

"It's not the leader, my brother. Leaders come and go. Black, red, strong, weak, human, dragon." He urged Jastin forward, speaking as he guided him into the hall. "What I've lost is the moment. I'll never get that back." He paused. "My men are waiting for the call to battle. Dragons are supposed to be threatening Leland Province, which is supposed to be weak and starving, and desperate for my help."

He pressed Jastin to the wall. His breath smelled of sour wine. "But Leland has been reprieved! There's a new dragon leader! There's no more drought! No war!"

Jastin stood firm against his brother-in-law's rant, accustomed to it. Bored by it. Powerless men shout to affirm their manhood. Despite being the richest Venur in Esra Province, Vorham Riddess was a weakling, and always would be.

"The Red will fail," said Jastin. "He's feeble and sentimental. You haven't lost your chance." He yanked a swatch of purple silk from Vorham's flamboyant tunic, and dried his face with it. "Rain or no rain, Leland suffers."

Vorham narrowed his eyes. "Rain or no rain, you are slipping. If I can't use you to help me get Leland and its mountains, I'll do it without you."

Jastin snarled. In an instant, he'd wrapped the soft silk around Vorham's throat, squeezing. "Don't insult me, Vorham. I lost more than you did today, and not because I'm slipping, but because you are. You couldn't see past your own greed."

The man clutched at the fabric, his tiny eyes popping.

"I've spent weeks hungry and filthy, doing the work you couldn't do yourself. You sat back and waited for Leland to be delivered to you on a platter. It was your plan that failed. Not mine."

Vorham wheezed.

"Say it," said Jastin. "Your plan failed."

Vorham opened his mouth, but he only rasped.

Jastin loosened the grip of the fabric, just a little. "Say it!"

"My plan failed," Vorham managed to croak.

"You might rethink your decision to strangle Venur Riddess just now." A lilting, familiar sort of voice came over the sound of scraping claws as heavy feet drew near. Jastin turned his head to find the glittering face of Fane Whitetail. The White offered a chilling smile.

Jastin looked back at Vorham.

His eyes were fluttering and he weakly pounded a fist against Jastin's shoulder.

Jastin released the fabric from the man's throat.

Vorham gasped and clutched the wall. "You son of a—"

"What is that thing doing here?" Jastin threw the satin sash at Vorham's feet.

"Are you referring to me?" asked Whitetail, pressing his paw to his chest. "This thing that had the situation neatly under control until you let a woman sidetrack you from the plan?"

Jastin pounded his finger into Vorham's chest. "You think I needed a bodyguard? A backup? When were you going to tell me?"

The White cleared his throat.

Vorham looked at the dragon, then back at Jastin. He straightened his back, tugged his tunic into place, and briefly rubbed his throat where it was beginning to welt. Then he fixed his beady eyes on Jastin's face. "He was no bodyguard. He was a babysitter."

Jastin flared. If he'd had his sword, he might have slashed his brother-in-law then and there. But he could only seethe, fists clenching and unclenching.

"It's no fresh news that you're not the soldier you once were, Jastin," said Whitetail. "Do not take it so personally."

"Don't you tell me how to think," Jastin snarled through clenched teeth.

"Let me remind you that the Red causing this trouble is the very Red you were responsible for all those years ago," said Whitetail. "The Red we thought was dead."

Vorham grunted as he bent to retrieve his sash. His thick belly made his fingers miss the first time, and he struggled to try again. He caught it. "Using Whitetail was a judgment call," Vorham said. He straightened and neatly replaced the sash across his tunic. "My mission was too important to risk. Too important." Vorham's face loomed closer, his chubby mouth curling in anger. 'Timing, do you see? Timing." He turned on his heel and marched away. "I should put him down, as a benevolent master does for an ailing dog."

"A bit extreme," replied the White, who bowed his head so low his muzzle scraped the floor. "If you will allow to me say, honorable Venur."

Vorham paused. He paced around Whitetail. "A woman, of all things. I couldn't have planned for that.

How could I have planned for that?"

"You did more than any other human could have managed. All is not lost. The opportunity will come again." The White strode off toward the feast hall and Vorham followed, stomping and frothing at the mouth.

Jastin watched them go, his anger turning cold and stiff in the pit of his stomach. "This is far from over," he said.

He became aware of Layce standing near his elbow.

"Far from over," she echoed. Then she turned her blue eyes to his face. "You left behind many things. Your weapon. Your horse."

"I'll go back," he said.

"Will you go back for the woman?" she asked.

Something inside him twisted. Grief nearly overpowered him, but he fought. He reached for his anger and held tightly to that, instead. It strengthened him. Fueled him. "No," he said, and walked away. "She's dead."

CHAPTER TWENTY-THREE

Kallon awoke to the dark, unnerving silence of his sleeping chamber. Six nights at Mount Gore Manor, and still he missed the drone of crickets and chitterbugs, the lullaby of wind and whispering tree limbs that had eased him into unbroken sleep most nights he spent alone in his now-distant cave.

Alone. For the sixth night on the mountain, Kallon's heart fluttered. Could this be the moment he'd been dreading to wake up to since Riza's transformation? Was this the night that he'd find her human and untouchable again, the spell broken?

He rolled over and reached a paw in the darkness. There she was beside him, soft and warm and loving him.

"Kallon," came a soft call.

He squinted at Riza. Her ruby lids were closed, her snout contentedly purring. He couldn't resist a gentle stroke against her temple.

She stirred, blinked open one eye, and gave a sleepy

smile. "Still restless?"

He nodded, but it wasn't Riza making him restless, except in that way she'd been doing since the first time he laid eyes on her changed, crimson face. Perhaps even before that.

"Kallon," came the call again. Not an audible voice, but a pull inside him that made him look toward the door. Someone was waving a lantern or a torch in the hallway. Golden light chased shadows past the door and up the stone walls.

"Go back to sleep," he said gently to her, and hefted to his feet.

She rolled her head onto a mound of velvet fabric and closed her eyes.

He eased past her, trying to be as soundless as possible. He lifted his claws so as to not clatter them against the floor. He peered through the door and out into the hall.

There was no lantern after all, just a glittering spray of yellow brightness that drew away, leading him down the corridor. Suddenly he knew that light. He almost didn't follow.

In the time that he'd come to call Mount Gore Manor his home again, he'd struggled to feel as though he belonged here. The vast rooms and carved hallways glittered with artisan scrollwork across ceilings and floors. Fat arteries of marble pulsed through iridescent granite walls, and the entire place, all twenty rooms worth, felt cavernous and regal. His old home should have felt smaller compared to his memories as a fledgling, but it was the opposite. The manor was overwhelming. He would never truly fill it.

Watching the golden radiance bathe the hallway and cast light into even the most remote cracks and corners only emphasized the foreign feel of the place. Still, he couldn't help but step out, chin lifting and snout working. "Where are we going?" he asked.

"Forward," said the voice that belonged to the light.

Kallon followed.

The brightness shifted around a corner, and for a moment, Kallon was swallowed by darkness. He surged forward, fighting a panic that surprised him. Reaching the light again, he stuck his snout into the warmth and settled into a loping rhythm. He glanced over his shoulder and found nothing frightening. His reaction was foolish and embarrassing, but he stuck closer to his guide, anyway.

They finally came to a room that Kallon had never seen the inside of, even as a youth. He paused at the double door. A chain had been looped through the massive iron handles, but dangled without a clasp. "This room is restricted," Kallon said. "Did you unlock it?"

"No," came the voice that was now clearly inside the room, muffled through the bulky doors.

Kallon pulled open the right door, but the left swung open as well. Inside the room three torches lined the wall, all of them burning. Wooden boxes were stacked atop each other and wedged end-to-end, forming low walls that filled the room like a hedge maze. Dust was a gray carpet over everything, the boxes, the torch sconces, the floor. In the center of the room, watching Kallon with a tipped head, lounged the young Gold.

Despite the low torchlight, the Gold's scales managed to sparkle as though in the noonday sun.

"Who let you in here?" Kallon asked.

The Gold pointed his nose toward a corner.

Claws had scuffled through the dust, leaving scratch marks on the floor. A box had been hastily tossed to the top of a stack, knocked sideways and left unlatched. Scrolls were spilled out in a puddle of parchments, some dropped to the floor.

Kallon scowled. He scooped up a parchment. "Whoever is responsible for this will have to be dealt with. This room is locked for a reason. We can't have just anyone..."

Kallon stopped. His eyes fell onto the words of the scroll. "Any citizen of Leland Province who feels the chosen leadership is failing in its responsibilities to the greater whole may challenge any council seat to be replaced," Kallon quietly read aloud. He looked to the Gold. "This is the scroll concerning the Ritual of Challenge."

The Gold nodded. "There has been some confusion in the aftermath."

Kallon narrowed one eye. He replaced the scroll into the wooden container, righting the box and closing the lid. "Understandable. The spellcatch needs to be replaced, though, and the room sealed again."

"Does it?"

"Of course." Kallon gesture his paw around the room. "These scrolls are our laws, our stories. Our heritage."

"These scrolls are forgotten," said the Gold. He crossed one front paw over the other.

Kallon felt a brush against his shoulder and glanced over to find Riza, sleepy-eyed and smiling. He hadn't even heard her approach. He looked at the Gold, looked again at Riza. He opened his mouth to introduce.

"Hello, Riza," said the Gold.

"Hello again," she said, and rested her head against Kallon's neck, still smiling.

The Gold gazed at her, tipping his head. He smiled, and as the corners of his eyes crinkled, even the torches couldn't compete with the shine from his face. Kallon wouldn't have thought the dragon could get any brighter.

"As I was saying," Kallon said, and shifted to move back, "This room is too important to leave unprotected."

"Why?" Riza asked. She crossed over to a stack of boxes and cut a claw through the film of dust.

"You wouldn't understand," Kallon said.

"Why not?" Riza asked.

"You are new to this place," Kallon said.

"So are you," said Riza.

Kallon reached a paw to stop her from trying to open the box's latch. "Riza. All of Leland history from the time we first learned to write is contained in this room."

She paused. "All your history? Everything?"

"As much as our scribes could record over the years. History annals, journals. Letters of transmit between province leaders."

"Love letters?"

Kallon smiled. "I hardly think the scribes would consider something like that important enough to keep for all time."

Now Riza smiled. "Love can direct the decisions of a great leader as much as anything else." She gazed at him through half-lids, a sultry curl of smoke escaping from her nostrils.

Kallon was so overcome with a sudden tremor that he felt it at the base of his tail. How did she manage to make his feelings sneak up on him like that?

She eased past him to take in the full sight of the stacks. "It's so overwhelming. I can hardly think where to begin."

Kallon stared. "Begin what?"

She blew away the dust from a silver placard trying to shine beneath the latch of chest-shaped box. "Ancient Skies. I wonder what that means." She wedged her claw under the edge of the lid. "I don't see a keyhole, how does it open?"

"It's a spellcatch. You need two separate dragons to release it. It prevents just anyone from…"

She carried the chest to the Gold, who obligingly pressed his thumb to the lid. Riza mimicked him, and the lid popped open. "Oh! How clever," she said. She reached inside.

"Riza!" Kallon moved so quickly he rattled a stack

of crates. "That parchment is delicate. You'll be violating bylaws just by touching it."

"I'll be careful," she said.

"I can't let you."

"Yes, you can." She settled to the floor, curled her crimson tail against her haunches, and began to read.

Kallon was helpless. He shook his head. But her touch was gentle as she held the paper, and it didn't seem in any danger of disintegrating. He watched her eyes move across the words. Her mouth curved up into a tiny smile of awe. "Look," she said, and lifted her face toward the Gold. "You're in here."

The Gold bowed his head.

Riza's eyes returned to the scroll. "I'm a part of this now. It's my history, too."

The Gold regarded Kallon. "And you now know more of that history than most dragons. Including Kallon."

"What is that supposed to mean?" asked Kallon.

The Gold slowly stood. He stretched, arching his back and curling his tail in tightly against himself. "You have much reading to do, Kallon Redheart."

"This is amazing," Riza murmured, shaking her head. "I might not even believe it, except I've met him for myself."

"Who?" Kallon leaned forward to look down over her shoulder.

She gazed up at him. "Of course we can't risk the parchments to the general public, that would be foolish."

"Exactly," said Kallon. "So you do understand."

"But I can't be the only dragon to wonder who I really am. Now that I'm a part of your world, I need to know how I fit in. What do I believe? Why do I believe it?"

"I can help you understand that." Kallon moved to her and rested a paw on her shoulder.

"You could try, but even you cannot answer all of my questions." She looked at the Gold for several minutes, who was still silent, and watching their conversation with that small, patient smile. Then she gazed around the room again. "Just think of the stories waiting in all of these boxes. Just think of the answers. The lessons. Who decided it was best to keep them behind locked doors? And why?"

He followed her gaze around the room. In the back of his mind, his own voice echoed with the wisp of a memory.

"Why, Father?" he'd asked, standing outside the bulky doors, his claw poking curiously into a massive lock. "Why are they secret?"

"Not secret, my son," his father had said, "But important. Too important to risk to damage and decay."

"Too important to risk to damage and decay," Kallon heard himself say. "My father told me that."

"So your father decided to keep them locked away?" she asked.

Kallon shook his head. "No, I don't think so. Perhaps his father. I remember being told that 'as our history goes, so go our ideals. If our ideals are lost, then all is lost'."

He felt the glittering eyes of the Gold. "These ideals are forgotten," the dragon said. "As forgotten as the reasons they were even written down."

"You know it's true, Kallon," said Riza. "Blackclaw wouldn't have been able to affect this province as he did if the dragons had remembered what they'd been taught. Why they'd been taught it."

"Yes." Kallon sighed. In his heart, her words rang true. He'd been wrestling with that thought since he first knew Blackclaw was a traitor. He just hadn't realized until she voiced it now.

"I wonder if the scribes stopped writing altogether whenever it was decided to store the parchments," said Riza. "Eventually, we'll have to fill in the gaps."

"How can we do that?"

Riza looked from the Gold, back to Kallon, and smiled. "Surely there are dragons who remember."

"Yes," Kallon said. "The council members would be a good start. But that doesn't help us with the scrolls we have now."

"Why can't we copy them?" asked Riza.

"Copy them?" asked Kallon. "Do you have any idea how long that would take?"

She rolled the parchment she'd been holding. She settled it into the chest. "Orman will help, and our own wizards."

Kallon turned his eyes to column after column of written words, hidden away inside ancient boxes. "I do wish my father were in here somewhere."

"Of course we'll have to organize them, put them

in order." Riza stood. She set the closed chest on a short, carved box. "And we'll make sure that every dragon can read and study them as they desire."

"Listen to what you're saying, Riza," Kallon said. "All of Leland history copied and organized? Available to any dragon who wishes it?"

"Yes, Kallon," she said. "Listen to what I'm saying."

He released a long breath. "It's impossible. Years of work. Overwhelming."

"Years of work, yes. Overwhelming, yes. Which is probably why no one took the trouble to do it already."

"A library," Kallon said, shaking his head, still unable to fully grasp, but knowing she was right. "Here at the manor."

Riza smiled. "You can remind us all why we choose the way we choose, and why we believe the way we believe."

He shook his head again, but he smiled, too. "Not me. The words themselves will do that."

He then realized the room was dimmer, lit only by the feeble torches. He hadn't even seen the Gold leave. There were footprints in the dust, though, and he regarded them for a time, before looking back to Riza. "We'll need the council's approval."

Her smile widened and he saw a glimmer in the emerald of her eyes. "Let's go ask."

CHAPTER TWENTY-FOUR

Kallon rose from bed. He moved slowly, having irresistibly grown accustomed, over time, to the indulgent lifestyle of the manor. He would remedy this after today. Today was his installment ceremony; he would soon begin the process of turning the ancient scrolls into a library. He would allow more access to the manor by other needful dragons. And he would live less like royalty and more like the plain and simple dragon he was.

He emerged from his sleeping chamber to the sound of hammers and chisels filling the hallway. He followed the ruckus to the manor entrance and stepped out into sunshine. There, he found Riza.

She turned her graceful, crimson head over her shoulder and smiled at him.

He'd lost count of the times that smile had sent a tremor down his spine, but he added another as he gazed at her. They shared a home, a name, and a future.

"Come look," she said.

Three artisans hovered at the manor entrance in a multi-colored heavenly host, their wings barely moving. Chisels and claws were put to stone as the three carved finishing touches into the new statue for the arch.

"It's us," Riza said. "See?"

The likeness of Kallon thrust his chest, and his wings, to the sky. Against him, near his belly, a second dragon with Riza's new face emerged from a limp human body as though from a cocoon. "Isn't it marvelous?" Riza stared at the statue and sighed.

"It is." Kallon nuzzled his chin on top of her head. "Quick work. Will it be finished in time for the ceremony?"

"Just!" called the Green who smoothed the tip of Kallon's statue wing. "Unless Eamon insists on dawdling with that foot!"

"I have never carved a human foot! This is not as easy as it looks!" Eamon shook his chisel at the Green.

"Riza Redheart," came a soft voice from the steps behind them. They turned to find a young Blue with a drape of cloth over her forelegs. "My mother wants you to try the size before the service." She smiled.

"Thank you, Amele." Riza took the fabric with a bow of her head. "If it needs adjusting, I will bring it to your mother myself. There is a plate of braised piglets in the kitchen that you can sample for the cooks, if you like."

Amele brightened and hurried into the manor with a giggle. Riza watched her go, and then turned to Kallon. She tilted her head and smiled. "What?"

"I wish my mother and father could have known you," Kallon said. "You have risen to your station with grace."

"I wish I could have known them, too," she said.

Beside them, several statues away, an explosion of stone rocked the air and sent rubble down the steps. Gray stones collided and crashed in an avalanche to the ground. Tips of carved wings, tooth-shaped rocks, and an eye, black as onyx, were among the body parts strewn.

"All that remains of that foul traitor," said Hale Brownwing as he climbed the steps to join them.

Behind him, his daughter, Vaya, followed, her head low.

"As official leader, Kallon, your first act should be to strike him completely from the record. He does not deserve even mention in our history."

"To do that would be to remove the lesson as well. We must always remember him, so we will not repeat the mistake."

"I suppose," said Brownwing. "The worst irony of all is that he may never be punished for what he did."

"There has been no sign of him?" asked Riza. A strange, secret expression came over her eyes, and Kallon followed her gaze to Vaya, who had lifted her head.

"None, nor of that coward, Whitetail, who turned him loose." Brownwing snorted. "All we can do is spit on the corpse of Blackclaw's statue, and be glad that is the last of him."

Kallon watched something pass between the females he couldn't identify. Their eyes spoke something between them, but when he touched Riza's foreleg to draw her gaze, that moment vanished with her smile. He looked back at Vaya, who seemed pale and withdrawn, but expressionless.

"But let us not destroy a festive occasion with talk of the past!" Hale Brownwing clapped Kallon's shoulder. "Your father would be proud, son! This ceremony will mark the beginning of Red leadership again, as Leland has been waiting for. Though it is just a formality. You have already proven to be a leader of vision, with the plans you have for the scroll library." He leaned toward Riza. "I had hoped, of course, that my daughter would be in your place today, but I can think of no other disappointment that has brought me such pleasure."

A flutter of sparkles spat like a fountain into the sky from an empty place on the steps. As the glittering mist filtered to the ground, Orman Thistleby stood within it. "Did you see it?" he asked, waving his hands. "Did I sparkle?"

"You did," said Kallon with a laugh.

Riza giggled.

"By Jove, I like it! Does nothing but add drama, but if an old wizard can't make a proper entrance, what does he have left?" Orman slapped his palms together, and the glitter was gone. "Now. When do we eat?"

"After the ceremony," said Riza. "Then we'll feast."

"Well, let's get a move on! Strike up the band! Hang the flags, carnsarn it, before I get any more feeble!"

"Oh, no. Not yet." Kallon took the fabric from Riza and wrapped it around Orman's shoulders. "You should all be able to manage just fine without us. Riza and I are going to begin our day the way we have begun every new day. You will have to wait."

Orman grunted. "Plenty of time for that later." He elbowed Hale Brownwing and rolled his eyes. "Newlyweds."

Kallon just laughed. Let them think what they like. He offered his paw to Riza.

Her eyes brightened. "I love this part."

Together, they rose up straight into the sunshine. Kallon and Riza flew.

Science Fiction

Living Things

Short Tales of Science Fiction and Dystopia

Living Things is about aching to be, striving to embody our best selves, and remaining optimistic in the face of adversity; success not guaranteed.

- Anthony Taylor
author of *Voyage to the Bottom of the Sea: The Complete Series - Volume 2*

Find *Living Things* in both print or digital versions online, and wherever you buy books!

Explore our Films

Big Imagine doesn't only publish books. We make movies, too! Our film projects are circulating in festivals and are offered on streaming sites. We'd love to have you as a supporter!

bigimagine.com/films

Made in the USA
Columbia, SC
05 March 2022